FLIRTING WITH THE
SINGLE DAD

SINGLE DADS OF SEATTLE, BOOK 9

WHITLEY COX

ISBN: 978-1-989081-31-0

For Crystal Onions who has loved Atlas since book one.
For Nicki Holt who has made my life so much easier by helping with my review team.
For Andi Babcock a fan turned beta-reader turned friend.
Without fans, readers and friends like you I wouldn't be where I am today.
Thank you from the bottom of my heart.

1

THUMP!

"What the fuck?"

Atlas Stark rubbed his forehead and then his hip as he opened his eyes and found himself lying on his daughter's bedroom floor.

He must have fallen asleep again in Aria's tiny twin bed while reading her a bedtime story. He'd been doing that a lot lately. Usually woke up with a horrible crick in his neck, one of his hands asleep and more exhausted than when he nodded off.

He wasn't a young man anymore either. He needed the comfort of his own bed and his therapeutic cool gel pillow. But Aria—like most nights—had complained when he tucked her in, so he gave in to her demands, crawled in next to her and read her the twelfth book of the night. He wasn't sure who fell asleep first.

Rubbing the sleep from his eyes, he stood up to his full height, his back cracking and knees grinding as he hinged over to kiss his daughter on the cheek.

Fuck, he hoped he hadn't slept the entire night away in

her room—wouldn't be the first time. If luck was finally on his side, it'd be like ten or eleven and he could still pass out in his own bed. That was if Cecily down the hall didn't freak the fuck out and require him to hold her while she chugged back a bottle for twenty minutes.

Yawning, he reached for his phone off the dresser. Oh thank God, it was only ten thirty. He brought up his messages as he wandered out of Aria's room, making sure to leave it open just a crack, otherwise his three-and-a-half-year-old would give him shit in the morning.

There were only a handful of messages—most of them work-related—and they could wait until tomorrow. But there was one that had been sent two minutes ago from a number he didn't recognize.

He scratched the back of his neck, wandered into the kitchen and poured himself two fingers of bourbon, a nightly ritual. The bottle nearly slipped through his fingers as he read the slew of messages from this strange number.

Did you know that Carlyle was engaged? Well, you do now. And if you DID know that he was engaged, shame on you for sleeping with an attached man.

Please tell Carlyle when you see him that he can find his belongings on the front lawn of MY apartment, though he might want to get there soon, as the weather report is calling for thunder-showers.

I'm keeping the ring. That asshole took five years of my life.

The text messages began rather polite, almost rational, and slowly meandered into more and more profanity, caps lock and exclamation marks.

And another thing! WHO THE FUCK NAMES THEIR KID CARLYLE? You can have him! WHO GOES BY CARLYLE and not CARL?! Pretentious fuckers, that's who!

Carlyle isn't returning my calls or messages. I'm assuming he's with you, so please relay these messages to my lowlife fucking EX-fiancé.

I want my dog back! Who the hell steals a dog? I want him back or I WILL call the cops, get a lawyer and sue his fucking ass.

The apartment is in MY NAME! So if he tries to get in, I'll call the cops! The two of you can go FUCK YOURSELVES. Have a nice life!

At this point, Atlas was wide awake, sitting on his black leather couch and sipping his bourbon.

Did you text back a wrong number? Particularly one this enraged?

But the person on the other end deserved to know that their message was not received by the intended recipient, right?

Did he want to engage with this person? They sounded kind of psycho.

But whoever they were, they deserved their dog back, didn't they? A dog was a family member. Who the fuck kidnapped a family member?

Pinching the bridge of his nose, he finished his bourbon, then tapped out a quick message to the furious texter.

You have the wrong number. I'm a man.

He squeezed his eyes shut and allowed the silence of the evening to wrap around him. He himself was a quiet person, preferring to have the television down low, the same for the music in the car. He liked things quiet. Or at least he used to.

It had been over a year and half since his wife, his best friend, the other half of his beating heart had died, creating not only a void in his heart but deafening silence in his home. Now, he hated the quiet.

Samantha had been the light of his life. She had been *the* light. Always bubbly and chatty. The house was never truly quiet when she was home—and he'd been completely okay with that. Whether it be her busy baking in the kitchen, playing the piano downstairs or humming softly to their daughter, the sound of his wife filled their home in a way that he knew could never be replicated.

From the moment they met their sophomore year of high school, he had been in love with her. Kind and courageous. Fearless and positive. No matter who or what, his wife was always willing to go out of her way to show somebody, usually a total stranger, just a small act of kindness. She had been the absolute best mother to their daughter, even if it was for only two years.

But the universe and its fucked-up ways robbed Atlas of his wife. Had robbed the world of a light brighter than the sun itself. And now that she was gone and the kids were in bed, he was alone in the unforgiving silence. In the all-consuming dark.

Anger had engulfed him after Samantha passed. He hated himself for not trying hard enough to save her. He hated Samantha for making peace with her death and refusing any more treatment. And he hated the doctor that ignored her symptoms and the nurses and doctors for honoring her wishes to no longer continue with treatment, even after he begged her not to.

He hated a lot.

The only bright spot left in his life was Aria. His sweet, angelic, beautiful little girl. The spitting image of her mother in both looks and feistiness. He'd known within an hour of her birth that he was going to have a wild, fearless princess on his hands. Always ripping off the tiara and glass slippers to go run barefoot in the mud. Her mother had been the exact same.

And now he had Cecily as well. She wasn't his, but she was. She needed someone, and unlike the rest of Atlas and Cecily's family, Atlas was able to provide for her.

It'd been touch and go at first with the baby. Born to two

meth dealer parents—Atlas's cousin, Tamsin, and her skeezy boyfriend, Ty—Cecily had been raised the first three months of her life in a house that also served as a meth lab. And when that meth lab blew up, killing her father and burning eighty percent of her mother's body, Cecily was found under a bed, barely alive.

His mother in Portland had called him the moment they got the call about Tamsin and Cecily. Atlas and Aria were on the next flight out. His parents had raised Tamsin since she was thirteen, after her mother—Atlas's aunt—died in a car accident. Atlas's parents became her guardian, and Atlas became more of a big brother to Tamsin than a cousin she saw twice a year on Christmas.

But Tamsin turned wild after her mother died, and she put Atlas's parents through the wringer. More times than he could count, in his final year of high school and then while attending college in Portland, he got a call late at night to go and pick up his cousin from some filthy party he wouldn't step foot in without a hazmat suit.

His parents did their best, but Tamsin's wild streak was more than they could manage. He knew he had to do better by her daughter though.

And even though it was Cecily who had come from the meth-lab home with the negligent parents, it was Atlas's daughter Aria who was giving him the endless grief these days. Her acting out and constant outbursts for attention were wearing him thin. What was worse, she was starting to take her frustration and aggression out on Cecily. A few times now, Atlas's nanny, the very grandmotherly Jenny, had called him at work because Aria had hit, scratched or screamed in Cecily's face.

He was at his wits' end. He loved his daughter more than life itself and knew she was struggling with not only not having her mother anymore, but also having a new baby in her life and her father constantly working. It was a lot for a three-and-a-half-year-old to absorb and accept. Hell, at thirty-nine, Atlas was still having difficulty absorbing and accepting it all. Was life supposed to be this hard?

Which was why, against his better judgment and his lack of confidence in the artsy-fartsy types, he made an appointment for Aria with an art therapist that his buddy and fellow single dad, Zak, recommended. Aria went for her first session on Monday.

He was so deep in his thoughts, with his eyes closed once again, caught up in the whirlpool of his never-ending problems, that when his phone buzzed in his hand, he actually jumped in his chair.

His eyes opened, and he glanced at the screen. It was that unknown number again.

I'm sorry. You must think I'm crazy. I'm really not. Just hurt. And angry. And I miss my dog.

So much.

A bizarre sensation filled his chest.

His fingers were flying across the touchscreen keyboard before he knew better.

It's okay. I'm really sorry that your fiancé cheated on you and stole your dog. I hope it starts raining before he manages to get his things off your front lawn.

He chuckled to himself at the thought of some philandering asshole scrabbling around the grass in the pouring rain gathering all his worldly possessions. In a weird kind of way, that made him smile, and warmth fill his extremities.

Did that make him a psycho?

Well, even if it doesn't rain, I took the extra bit of care and threw all of his clothes in the shower first. Just in case.

He tossed his head back and laughed, startling himself with how good, but also foreign, it felt to smile that big and laugh.

He could tell by her area code that this person was somewhere in the Seattle area. He texted back. *That was really smart. Incredibly devious, but very clever. Have you heard of the Rage Room? It's a great place to destroy things and let out the anger without becoming a wanted felon.*

He'd been prepared to head to bed after his nightcap, but decided to wander back into the kitchen where he poured himself another drink and then sat back in his chair, waiting —and hoping—for this person to reply.

His phone buzzed.

I have heard of the Rage Room. I haven't gone yet, but I might need to after all of this. I certainly want to smash Carlyle's face in with a baseball bat.

Oh, Luna at the Rage Room could definitely help her with that.

Take a picture of him to the Rage Room and Luna will put it in a tacky frame for you and then you can demolish the frame... and his face. I know people do that and they say it helps a lot.

Then it hit him: He didn't even know if the person he was chatting with was male or female.

Not that it mattered, because they weren't flirting or anything, but he'd just assumed it was a woman. But it could just as easily be a man who had been engaged to another man.

Men exchanged rings sometimes, didn't they?

Love was love and all that rainbow equality stuff. He took Aria to the last Seattle Pride parade with all the other single dads. He just wanted nothing to do with dick personally.

Not that he was interested in women either. That ship had sailed, crashed into the rocks and then spontaneously caught fire when Samantha died. He would never love another—he knew that the moment she took her final breath in his arms.

Could he ask if the person was a man or woman?

Did he care?

And if so, why?

Taking a long, healthy sip of his bourbon, he held the liquor on his tongue as he typed out his message. *What's your favorite brand of aftershave?*

The moment he hit *send,* he smacked himself on the forehead with the heel of his other hand. What the fuck was that?

Did he really just ask a complete stranger what their favorite brand of aftershave was?

He squeezed his eyes shut and counted to ten, hoping to fucking God that when he blinked them open, that lame-ass response would not be staring at him, mocking him.

His phone buzzed in his hand before he got to ten.

I love Old Spice on men.

Shit, that didn't help at all. Was it a man or a woman? He still didn't know.

Another text came in. *Do you want to know if I'm male or female?*

Fuck. Sheepishly, he texted back a *yes, please.*

I'm a woman, but I'm not sending you any pics to prove my sex. And that wasn't an invitation for unsolicited dick pics either. I believed you when you told me that you're a man. Just believe me when I say I'm a woman.

He stared at the message.

Was she teasing him or pissed off?

He needed to test the waters.

No dick pics from me. I promise. I bet you have enough pics of that dick of a fiancé lying around and clogging up your phone that you don't need one more added to the burn pile.

He held his breath.

His phone vibrated seconds later.

That burn pile is MASSIVE! And thank you for respecting my preference to not be sent pictures of random men's junk.

He let out a sigh in his head and took another drink of his bourbon.

I'm nothing if not respectful. And random.

This was fucking weird.

He'd never done anything like this before in his life, and yet, he was actually enjoying himself. Maybe it was the fact that this "woman" knew jack shit about him—unlike everyone else in his life—and he could just relax. Not that they were really diving in deep with the personal information or anything—because that was the last fucking thing he wanted to do—but it was just nice having a "conversation" with someone who didn't know he had a dead wife, a wild three-year-old and a meth dealer's baby. As much as he'd tried to hide it all, his baggage was just too damn big and kept tumbling out of the crawl space he repeatedly shoved it into.

He finished his bourbon and stood up from the couch.

I hope you get your dog back.

He wished he had time for a dog. He loved dogs. But owning a dog with his demanding career and attention-hungry children would feel like neglect from the get-go. That poor pet would never get the love or affection it deserved. Atlas was already being pulled in a million different directions. He'd love nothing more than to have a dog trotting down the hallway after him right now, prepared to leap up on his bed and claim Atlas's pillow as his own. But when morning came and all hell broke loose as he fought to get Aria dressed, Cecily fed and his teeth brushed and tie straight, that poor dog would be forgotten about or possibly even cursed at for being underfoot.

He wanted a dog. Probably needed one. But a dog didn't need him right now, not in his current state anyway.

Me too. Do you think I should get a lawyer?

Well, now that he could answer.

If he legitimately stole the dog from you, then yes. That dog is your property, and he was taken from you.

We rescued the dog together. But ... he feels more like mine.

Ah, now things were tricky. If she'd adopted the dog before she and this Carlyle fuckface got together, then it would be a no-brainer. But since the dog was property and joint property at that, this Carlyle douche had just as much claim on the dog as she did. But theft or not, this wasn't normally what a lawyer was used for. Unfortunately, a dog was considered small potatoes and the custody of one would be handled in small claims court, without attorneys.

However, the thought of her losing her dog because she went into claims court ill-prepared gnawed at his gut like a rusty bread knife.

He texted back *Something like this is normally handled in small claims court, without lawyers. BUT, I would seek legal counsel anyway, just to give yourself an advantage. Better to be over prepared than under prepared.*

Legal counsel, nobody calls it that besides lawyers themselves. Wait... are YOU legal counsel?

Not for a random text message I'm not. I hope the fleas of a thousand camels infest the crotch of your beloved Carlyle.

That had been Samantha's go-to insult. *May the fleas of a thousand camels infest the crotch of the person who ruins your day.* He snorted and smiled as he flicked on the light in his bedroom and her beautiful face and even more bright and beautiful smile met him on his nightstand. She was the most exquisite thing he'd ever laid eyes on. Fair and kind but still so fierce. Aria took after her in every way. Creamy complexion, light blonde hair, unique hazel eyes. And their smile ... When Aria smiled, it really was like Samantha was smiling back at him—through their daughter.

He undressed down to his black boxer briefs and plugged his phone into the charger on the nightstand next to Samantha's picture. It was a photo of her on their wedding day—he'd never seen her look more incredible—until the day she had Aria, that is. Motherhood made her nearly angelic.

After brushing his teeth, splashing some cold water on his face and scrutinizing the ever-darkening circles beneath his eyes, he hit the light and crawled into bed.

Even after a year and a half of his wife being gone, he still couldn't bring himself to take up more space in their king-size bed. Only when Aria came in to cuddle did he move from his side at all. Otherwise, Samantha's place on the left remained untouched.

He rolled over to his side, facing the nightstand, facing Samantha and said goodnight to her like he always did. Never out loud, but in his head. He said their vows; he asked her to be his forever.

Once she said "I do" just like she always did, he closed his eyes and willed the sleep to take him. Only God knew how long he had before one of the girls woke up with one demand or another. He really wished the nanny, Jenny, was able to be a live-in nanny. But she had her husband to get home to, and as she put it, she loved kids, but she did the late nights and early mornings with her own children, who were now all grown up. Now, she wanted sleep.

He thought about finding someone else other than Jenny, someone who could live in. But Jenny was just so damn good at her job. Aria loved her. Cecily calmed right down in Jenny's arms, and she cooked—and cleaned. So he took the pros with the cons and kept her on even though he wished like hell the woman was willing to do even a bit of overtime —which she wasn't. Thankfully, the single dads and their women stepped up to help Atlas a lot when Jenny couldn't. His job as a senior partner at Wallace, Dixon and Travers was demanding, and he was up for name partner soon, so his hours were insane. He didn't know what he would do without

Jenny or the single dads. They all seriously saved his life, his job and his sanity.

He was halfway asleep when his phone on the nightstand vibrated.

Oh God, please don't be Jenny calling in sick or something. I have a deposition in the morning and then I have to be in court at one o'clock.

He grabbed it and checked the messages.

It was from the unfortunate stranger.

The fleas of a thousand camels, huh? That's gotta itch. I just hoped his dick fell off altogether, but I like your wish too.

He chuckled to himself, rolled over to his back and typed.

It's too cloudy to find a shooting star tonight. But if I see any double digits on the clock in my car or an eyelash somewhere, I'll be sure to wish for Carlyle's dick to spontaneously remove itself from his body AND the fleas of a thousand camels to infest his stump.

An ache pulsed in his jaw, and with his free hand he reached up to massage it. That's when he realized his cheeks and jaw hurt because he was smiling.

Fuck, had it really been that long since he'd done it that his muscles cramped after only a couple of seconds?

She texted back.

Thank you for this. I was on the warpath and you brought me back to reality. I really needed this. You're a kind stranger. Good night.

She finished the message with a smiley-face emoji, which made him smile even more. Prickles raced down his arms and across his bare chest. He had no idea what this woman looked like, no idea how old she was or what she did for a living, but knowing that he'd helped her made an unusual sensation take over his body.

Smiling wider and about to text back *Good night,* he rolled to the side to set his phone down again, but when Samantha's hazel eyes hit his, his smile dropped like a stone in a pond.

He put his phone down without replying to *her* and rolled over to his back again.

Damn it. He was enjoying the witty banter with another woman. He was flirting ... kind of. And that—his throat grew painfully tight as he stared up blankly at the ceiling—was a betrayal of the love of his life.

2

TESSA COPELAND GATHERED HER LONG, curly blonde hair at the nape of her neck and flipped it off her shoulders. Tucking the loose strands behind her ears, she tidied up her paints and turned the canvas she'd been working on toward the window and away from the doorway. She had a new client coming in at four, and even though she wasn't ashamed of her art, it wasn't finished, and she didn't need to deal with curious eyes on her unfinished piece.

She'd filled her essential oil diffuser with a stress-relieving and calming blend of cedarwood, ylang-ylang, patchouli, lavender and bergamot, and even though it made the studio smell lovely, it was doing very little to take the tension from her shoulders or jaw.

Washing her hands in the sink, she ran the thumb of her right hand over the ring finger of her left. The moment she found the photos, she'd ripped that ring clean off and tossed it against the wall. Now, it was tucked in a small box in her underwear drawer for safekeeping, and her hand felt significantly lighter and certainly looked duller. A faint tan line ringed the base of her finger, a painful reminder of what had been.

Not two days ago, she thought she was going to spend the rest of her life with Carlyle Rickson. Until death do they part. Three years ago, he'd gotten down on bended knee at the top of the Space Needle on New Year's Eve and professed to not only love her forever, but to spend the rest of his life working to make her as happy as she made him.

Then yesterday she found Carlyle's ancient iPad sitting around—which was odd on its own. She plugged it in, and because it was so old, she didn't even have to enter a password. But what should pop up? Pictures of him and some other woman ... in bed. And then the messages between him and this other woman, Blaire, and all the back-and-forth sexy pictures and suggestive sexting.

Every cell in her body had instantly turned ice cold, her hands began to shake, and her teeth chattered like she'd been caught outside in the freezing rain. But there was no freezing rain outside. It was a gorgeous and warm May in Seattle, with flowers, birds, butterflies and an unusually minimal amount of rain.

Too bad she was unable to enjoy that weather or the flowers on her windowsill after finding out her boyfriend of five years and fiancé of three of those was cheating on her. And it wasn't like his relationship with Blaire had just started either. His text messages with the woman went back for almost a year.

For a year, he'd been leading a double life. Cheating on Tessa with another woman while pretending he still loved her, that he still wanted to have a future and a family with her.

Well, no more.

She'd tossed all of his belongings into the bathtub, soaked them and then chucked them out onto the front lawn of her apartment complex. So whether it rained or not, his shit would be drenched.

A tear slipped down her cheek as she shut off the water and dried her hands on a towel. As much as it hurt to lose Carlyle and the future she thought she had with him, he'd stolen her dog, Forest, as well.

Who stole a dog?

She didn't even think Carlyle really liked Forest that much.

Forest had never been too fond of Carlyle either—probably because he usurped Forest's position on Tessa's bed. Maybe she should have listened to her dog's protestations. After all, didn't animals have a sixth sense about humans?

But now, she had no Carlyle and, what was more devastating, no Forest.

Her two-timing ex had been raised by country-club elitist parents down in Georgia who were more concerned with the latest gossip and their upcoming tennis tournaments than giving two figs about their only child. They would be of no help. He wasn't returning her calls or messages, and his voicemail was now full. She had no idea where he was staying. She'd called the few friends of his that she knew of, but either they had their *bro's* back or they had no idea where he was.

Should she text Blaire? After drinking three glasses of wine in under thirty minutes last night, she'd gone and accidentally mis-texted a complete stranger her insane rant. She wasn't so sure texting Blaire was even a good idea, sober or drunk.

She'd felt a whole lot better after texting back and forth with that random mis-texted number, though. Whoever he was, wherever he was, he had made her smile. And that was saying a lot.

Who knew that her dyslexia and typing 6789 rather than

7689 would have proved to be a blessing rather than a curse? Reading back through her barrage of texts, she realized how totally nuts she must have sounded. Thankfully, the stranger had been understanding and cool about it.

That could have gone a whole lot worse, and if the wrong person was on the receiving end, she could have been charged with harassment or something.

Her eyes fell to the dog bed in the corner of her art and therapy studio, and her throat grew tight and more tears welled up in her eyes.

Forest.

God, how she missed him.

She hoped he was okay. That Carlyle was taking care of him. Normally, Forest accompanied her to work every day, but yesterday Carlyle had asked for Forest to stay home with him. At the time, she'd thought nothing of it. Figured her fiancé had the day off, he'd take the dog for a run in the park. She never dreamed she'd return home to no Forest, no Carlyle and a weird vibe. A few shirts and pants of his were missing, but for the most part, all his stuff was still in the apartment. When dinnertime rolled around and they still weren't home, she started to get worried. She called and texted, but there was no answer. Were they okay?

It wasn't until she found the iPad and the evidence of his cheating that she realized where he must have gone.

Had that been Carlyle's plan all along? Did he leave the iPad out on purpose so that she found it? Was that how he planned to end things with her? Why didn't he move out entirely while she was at work? Why did he take the dog? None of it made any sense.

What a coward.

She crouched down next to Forest's bed and ran her hand over the worn but clean and soft cushion. The teak bangles around her wrist jangled. He loved this bed.

There wasn't much her rescue mutt didn't love—besides Carlyle. Even though they'd adopted him together, Forest had always preferred Tessa.

A lab, collie, shepherd, malamute mix, he was a gorgeous creature with soulful light brown eyes, big paws, thick, long, dark chestnut fur and the most enormous heart she'd ever met.

Her own heart throbbed painfully at the thought of never seeing him again, more so than never seeing Carlyle again. Because unlike Carlyle, Forest hadn't hurt her. He'd done nothing but love her, even with all her faults and idiosyncrasies. A piece of her soul had been taken from her, a hole the size of her fifty-five-pound best friend permanently carved into her heart, never to be patched, never to be healed.

She crumpled to the ground in a heap and a sob clutched at her throat. Her turquoise and paisley flowy boho skirt pooled around her like a mermaid's tail. Sadness and pain, anger and fear burned in her chest like a fire she had no way of containing. Searing her from the inside out, until her body burned with an agony, a loss so severe she wasn't sure she'd ever recover.

She was thirty-five years old. She'd wasted five years of her life with Carlyle, and now she had to start over. And she didn't even have her beloved dog to help her get through it all. Carlyle had taken everything from her. Everything that mattered. Her dog, her future, her trust.

Using the hem of her white cardigan to blot at her eyes, she rose from where she stood and went to check herself out in the mirror.

It wouldn't do for the new client and her father to wander in and see Tessa looking like a mess. A therapist unable to get her shit together didn't really evoke much confidence, did she?

Her gold gladiator-style sandals slapped lightly across the

white tile floor of her bright and open studio as she headed to the mirror.

What stared back at her was a sad, lonely, broken woman. Red-rimmed blue eyes, puffy and tired. Her cheeks were blotchy and her nose was running. She grabbed a tissue and blew her nose.

Using another tissue, she blotted at her eyes and slathered on some lip gloss, hoping that it simply looked like she'd been outside for a brisk walk and not tearfully mourning the loss of her best friend and the future she'd planned down to the names and middle names of her three children. Two girls and boy.

Crazy that the little girl coming in a few minutes was named her top choice for girl's names, Aria.

And Aria Stark at that.

Her parents had to be *Game of Thrones* fans. Though they spelled her name different. Aria. Not Arya.

Tessa would have spelled her daughter's name with an *I* rather than a *Y* as well.

Aria Jocelyn. Aria because an aria was a beautiful piece of music that often moved her to tears, and Jocelyn after her grandmother.

She also liked the name Zoe. Zoe Rosalie. But Carlyle had thought that name to be dumb.

Carlyle was dumb.

The name Carlyle was dumb.

So was the name Blaire.

For a boy, she'd always been partial to Magnus. Magnus Bruno. Bruno after her father, of course, and Magnus because it was strong and uncommon

But now that she was thirty-five and having to start over finding a man to share her life with, she could probably kiss Aria, Zoe and Magnus goodbye. She'd be lucky to have one child before her eggs ran out or ... she met the same fate as her mother.

Maybe she was better off not having children. Maybe this was a sign. She wasn't meant to be a mother. She knew first-hand how hard it was dealing with a mother's illnesses. She couldn't imagine putting her own children through that. Never in a million years.

She already spent most of her days wondering whether there was more to an unhappy moment or a sudden mood shift. When her low moments got really low, whether that was her first slip into manic depression and if it was just a slippery slope after that, one she wouldn't be able to climb back up. And then every time she forgot something, whether it be her keys or what she was supposed to grab at the grocery store—even though it was right there on the list—she could not stop the plaguing thought that it was the big *A* finally coming to claim her, just like it had her mother.

Alzheimer's.

It had attacked her mother at the age of forty-five. Though she and her father were so consumed with handling her mother's bouts of extreme depression, she'd bet the Alzheimer's had come on sooner, they just hadn't recognized it as such.

Now in a home, her mother was rarely lucid and had no idea who Tessa was most days. Lily spent nearly every moment she had standing at the window in her room painting canvas after canvas of the same thing—a baby being held by its mother.

Taking a deep, fortifying breath, she shook herself free of her grief as best she could.

She needed to get into therapist mode.

She was there to help people.

And today, now, she was there to help a little three-year-old girl harness her frustrations and channel them into a positive and non-harmful direction.

She straightened her pale pink tank top across her chest, made sure her cleavage wasn't exposed, fixed the clasp on her long crystal pendant—it was supposed to be a healing crystal, but she didn't feel the least bit healed—and smiled at herself in the mirror.

She could do this.

It was only an hour.

An hour to smile, help someone else, allow her career and a sweet little girl to distract her. Then she could go back to her empty apartment, change into her pajamas and cry until she was empty. Well, emptier than she already felt.

But for now, she needed to stow all that and help little Aria.

A knock at the open door had her inhaling deep, throwing on an even bigger smile and turning to face her new client.

"Hi, I'm Tessa."

3

ARIA HID behind Atlas's legs. She reached up and clutched at his belt, practically pulling down his pants as she resisted going inside the therapist's office.

Though he wouldn't call it an *office* at all. It was more like an art studio slash theater dressing room on steroids.

There was a pottery wheel in one corner, several easels along the window, paint bottles housed neatly on a four-foot shelf next to several coffee cans of paintbrushes. Then along the other wall there was what looked like a puppet theater, a rack of dress-up clothes and even a small stage.

Paper of all shade and manner took up a high shelf close to a desk, and there were probably close to a million colored pencils, felt pens, crayons and pastels all tidily organized and labeled in various clear plastic drawers.

"Come on, honey," Atlas urged, grabbing a whimpering Aria by the wrist and dragging her out from behind him. Cecily was in the bucket car seat in his other arm, thankfully fast asleep. Though it'd been a fucking scream-a-thon in the car on their twenty-minute drive here until she finally passed out.

All of a sudden, the kid hated her car seat.

Fuck his life.

No break could be caught.

Seriously, none.

"No!" Aria protested, managing to both yell and growl at the same time. She scrambled back behind him and tugged harder on his belt, attempting to pull him back out into the hallway. "I don't wanna!"

He hadn't even had a chance to look at the therapist, he'd been so consumed with his child and hoping to God she didn't wake up the finally sleeping baby.

Jenny guessed Cecily was teething, which meant she would be miserable for the foreseeable future.

Fucking great.

"Come on, sweetie," he cooed gently. "The nice lady has felt pens and lots of paper. You love art." If he let go of her, she'd probably take off down the hallway, so he set the car seat down on the ground and whipped around, grabbing Aria's other wrist and hauling her into the office.

She started to scream.

And it was a fucking ear-piercing, glass-shattering shriek. Dogs within a five-mile radius were probably running for cover, burying their heads beneath a pillow or whimpering because they thought their brains were going to explode.

Then the crying started.

Not Aria's, because she was still screaming.

Cecily.

Of course. Because Aria had woken her up with her banshee wail.

Atlas's blood began to bubble, and heat flooded his limbs and face.

A flurry of light blue or whatever the fuck color it was swooshed past the corner of his eye as he hunkered down to a squat and grabbed his frustrated daughter by the shoulders.

"Hi," came a soft, melodic female voice beside him. "I'm Tessa." He barely heard her, even though she was right next to him, what for the screaming and crying that was louder than the Foo Fighters concert Samantha had dragged him to six years ago. "I can tell you're really frustrated. You probably have a lot of feelings going on inside your body right now, and that is completely okay. You are allowed to be angry. You are allowed to be scared and nervous and sad. You can have as many and whatever feelings you want."

Aria blinked a few times, and her screams ebbed into a whine.

Cecily was in full-on freak-out mode though.

Aria's hazel eyes focused on Tessa. Atlas hadn't even looked at the woman yet. But he did know she smelled really good. Like vanilla and something else.

"You know what?" Tessa continued, her voice low and calm. "You don't have to do anything you don't want to do. If you don't want to draw or paint or even move from where you're standing now, you don't have to. You don't have to talk to me if you don't want to. It's up to you. You have all those choices."

Aria's blonde brows knitted together.

"I'm going to go over to that cool-looking triangle table over there and do some coloring. I have paper and felts and crayons all set up if you'd like to join me. You don't have to. And if felts aren't your thing, I also have paints. We can even finger-paint if you want."

Light and interest flashed behind Aria's eyes. Her breathing slowed down, and the mottled red of her complexion began to fade.

Tessa leaned forward a bit more and cupped her mouth with one hand, pretending to exclude Atlas from the conversation. "We can even take your socks off and you can paint with your toes if you want."

Aria giggled. Her gaze flicked back up to Atlas, and her eyes turned wary again. "Daddy, where you going?"

Cecily's screams had quieted down a bit, but the baby was still upset. He needed to get to her, but he also couldn't abandon his daughter for the baby. That was the root of the problem right there. That was why they were at this "therapist" to begin with, because Aria felt abandoned by her father.

"I'll be right outside, sweetheart. I'm just going to plop Cecily in the stroller and go for a walk around the block with her. She needs to nap."

His daughter's lip wobbled, and her eyes flicked back and forth between him, Tessa and the triangle table. She wasn't sure what to do. She wanted to do all the fun things the therapist had mentioned, but she also didn't want him to leave.

"I have an idea," Tessa said, standing back up from where she was crouched next to him. He rose as well, and his eyes followed her across the room.

Of course she was dressed like a freaking hippie.

Long flowy skirt to the floor, bangles up both wrists that clacked together as she walked, and long golden mermaid hair down between her shoulder blades. That explained why the whole hallway and even more so the "office" smelled like a hippie commune. What was that? Patchouli?

His inner cynic rolled his eyes.

What next? When he came to pick his kid up, were they going to be in their own little drum circle? Tapping away on the bongos or some shit.

Despite the fact that Aria had calmed down, he was beginning to think this art therapist thing wasn't such a good idea. He could give his kid crayons and paper at home for her to "channel" her frustrations, rather than indulge in the notion that "art" was therapy. Not that he didn't have medical coverage through work; that wasn't the issue. It was that he didn't necessarily believe in this crap.

He'd gone to mandatory grief counseling after Samantha died—as was necessary before he could return to work—and it had done jack shit for him.

Maybe his therapist had been a hack or whatever, but either way, he'd only gone because he had to, only spoke when he had to, and as soon as his five sessions were up, he was out of there and back behind his desk at the office.

Work was his therapy. He was good at his job, and it was how he escaped the memories of Samantha. Home and Aria flooded him with nothing but reminders of his wife, but work —even though Samantha had been a lawyer too—she voluntarily gave up her career as a public defender to become a mother, so there were no memories of her at Atlas's office. It made working easier. It made each day easier.

Aria was now quiet, and Cecily, by grace and by God, had quieted down too. Poor soul, she probably thought she was right back to being neglected. His gut twisted at the thought of Cecily quieting down because she just didn't believe anybody cared.

He cared. He did. He just couldn't let his daughter think he didn't care about her either. He was being pulled in too many directions. He was only one man, one person, but two very demanding little girls needed him, and there just wasn't enough of him to go around.

Would there ever be?

The therapist turned around, and he nearly swallowed his fucking tongue.

She was gorgeous.

The intensity of her blue eyes smacked him hard in the solar plexus, the way her cheeks held just a touch of pink, and when her smile widened, it was like the roof had suddenly blown clear off the building and the sun was shining right in on all of them.

He cleared his throat and looked away for a moment.

He needed to get a grip.

What the fuck was going on? He should not be having these thoughts right now. He should not even be noticing attractive women, let alone his child's "therapist."

Slowly, he slid his gaze back to her and watched as she approached them again, a bunch of big wooden beads in a hippie craft-fair-looking woven basket, along with various colors of thin leather rope.

"Why don't you make a couple of quick bracelets," she suggested, motioning for Aria to follow her over to another table, this one a red circle with a bunch of child-size chairs around it. "Make one for you and one for Dad, and then while he's gone, you both wear them. They are your *connection* bracelets. That way, even when you're apart, you're still connected. You can look at the bracelet and think of him, and he can look at the bracelet and think of you."

Aria nodded and sat down at the table, diving into the assortment of rainbow-colored wooden beads.

This wasn't going to really work, was it?

Connection bracelets?

He snatched the bottle of formula out of the diaper bag on his hip and handed it to a now quiet but fiercely fist-munching Cecily. The baby grabbed it with enthusiasm and began to guzzle in earnest. Hopefully that would knock her out and she'd be able to sleep for an hour on their walk. Maybe he could just push her for fifteen minutes, then sit on a park bench and get through some emails while she slept. Wouldn't that be a novel idea? Rather than having to stay up until fucking midnight or later working because he'd been forced to leave work early to get Aria to this therapist.

"Okay, I'm done," Aria announced, handing the first bracelet to Tessa. "Can you tie this around my wrist, please?"

"I'd be happy to," Tessa replied.

"Thanks."

Tessa went to task, tying the colorful bracelet around Atlas's daughter's tiny wrist. "You're sure polite. Please *and* thank you." She glanced up at Atlas. "Good job, Dad."

He rolled his eyes, and his cheeks grew hot.

Yeah, he'd managed to drill *please* and *thank you* into his kid, but she was still a wailing siren when she didn't get her way. He wasn't sure one made up for the other.

"Okay, I'm done this bracelet, too," Aria said, handing the bigger one to Tessa. "Can you tie it around my dad's wrist, please?" Her hazel eyes grew eager and gleeful as she waited for Tessa to stand.

Rolling his eyes again, he held out his right hand, as his left sported his watch.

Her long fingers, with nicely trimmed nails, gently wrapped the purple, pink and yellow wooden beads around his wrist. Her movements were precise, but that didn't stop her from brushing her fingers across his skin a couple of times as she secured the knot. Each touch sent a jolt through him. It was if he just kept sticking that fork in the electrical socket. Hadn't learned his lesson the first time.

But he didn't want to learn. Her touch was soft, gentle, and it made his gut flip and his chest tighten. That's when he noticed the faint white tan line on her ring finger.

Hmmm.

He was mesmerized by her movements, by her fingers. What was probably close to twenty bangles between her two forearms jostled and clacked together as she moved. Wind chimes indoors. He noticed a small tattoo along the back of her wrist below her right pinky finger, but he couldn't see it enough through the teak forest on her arms to make out what it was.

"Okay, all good," she said, lifting her gaze to his and smiling infectiously before glancing down at Aria and grinning even wider. "Now you have your connection bracelets. So even though you'll be apart, you'll still be together. Connected."

Aria beamed and stood up from the table. "Okay, bye, Dad. See you in a bit." She ran over to where a row of smocks on hooks lined the walls. "Can I take my socks off and paint with my toes?" she hollered across the space.

Tessa returned her gaze to Atlas, her smile smaller now but no less beautiful. "You filled out the intake form online, so we're good to go. The first few sessions or so are more just get-to-know-each-other sessions."

Great, so his insurance was paying for his kid to have a glorified playdate with an adult. He fought another eye roll, grunted and nodded.

Tessa's eyes shifted to the painted plate turned into a clock on the wall near her desk. "An hour work for you?"

An hour? Didn't they have like thirty-five minutes left after that performance at the door and the snail's-pace beading of his child?

"She's my last client for the day," she went on. "I usually reserve ninety minutes for the first couple of sessions with a new client, in case it's a bit of a battle to get the kids inside. By the third or fourth session, they're usually sprinting down the hallway to get here and telling their parents to scram." She glanced over to where Aria was sitting on the floor, peeling off her socks. "She may not need a ninety-minute session next time."

Atlas grunted again, grabbed Cecily's car seat and murmured a thanks before he turned to go.

"Don't forget to look at your connection bracelet," Tessa called behind him, a chuckle to her tone.

He turned the corner and rolled his eyes again, but then they landed on the bracelet on his wrist, and warmth filled his chest as he thought of his daughter.

Ah, fuck. The hippie was right.

EXACTLY AN HOUR LATER, there was another knock at the door, and in walked Aria's father, Mr. Stark, with the baby now strapped to his chest in one of those adorable baby carriers.

Even though she was pretty sure she was swearing off men for the rest of her life, destined to be childless, dog-less and with no memory of anybody by the time she was fifty, her ovaries damn near exploded. Was there anything sexier than a man wearing a baby in one of those carrier things?

No.

She could confidently say there was not.

At least not to her.

A man who loved children, who was a doting and devoted father, was one of the most attractive guys out there. Which was weird in itself because that generally meant that that man was already taken.

She knew, though, from the intake form Aria's father had filled out, that Aria's mother had passed away recently, so chances are he was not taken.

But he probably wasn't looking either.

Without saying anything, the father, Atlas, wandered up to where Tessa and Aria sat at the green triangle table gluing various dried pastas to a piece of orange construction paper. Aria was deep in concentration mode, her tongue sticking out and pinched between her teeth as she carefully placed the penne in a neat row.

"That's the fence," she said, straightening up, her smile full of pride. Her eyes shifted to where he stood behind them, and her face paled, her brows scrunched and her lips fell into a deep frown. "Noooo, Daddy. I'm not done yet. Nooooo. Go for another walk."

Tessa smiled inwardly. That was an awesome sign. She'd already made great progress with Aria in their first hour, and the fact that the little girl was eager to stay longer meant it wouldn't take long to dig deep and help her channel her frustrations. Help her manage and redirect her impulses to lash out at her father and the baby.

"It's time to go," Atlas said softly. "We need to get home for dinner. Jenny said she made us chicken parmigiana, your favorite."

Jenny?

Aria stuck her tongue out and made a disgusted face. "I don't like chicken parmi-gong-gah."

Atlas rolled his eyes. He did that a lot. "Yes, you do. Now let's get going."

Aria stood up and stomped her foot. "No!" Her fists bunched at her sides, and she glared up at her father, their difference in height not appearing to bother her at all. "I am staying!" She crossed her arms in front of her, and her frown turned into the mother of all scowls.

Tessa was forced to turn away and smile into her shoulder. She knew that this was a serious moment for Aria and her father, but that didn't mean the little girl's ire wasn't also adorable.

Atlas's nostrils flared, and the muscle in his jaw flexed. "Sweetheart," he said through gritted teeth, "we need to get going."

She could tell he was trying his damnedest to keep his emotions in check. It did nobody any good if, when the kid was losing their cool, the parent did too. Chaos greeted by more chaos did not beget calm.

He was a good dad, though. And the fact that he cared enough to see that his daughter needed help and sought out art therapy for her said a lot about what kind of a dad and man he was.

Her heart went out to Mr. Stark and his obvious struggles. He had a lot on his plate. It made her troubles with Carlyle, Forest and her mother seem small in comparison.

Aria uncrossed her arm and stomped her foot again, continuing to have a stare-down—or more like a glare-down—with her father. There was a lot of fearlessness in this little girl. He was raising a warrior. It would be tough in the beginning, having such a headstrong daughter to contend with, but she would grow up to be an incredible adult. He didn't have to worry about Aria taking shit from anybody.

The only thing he needed to worry about was finding that balance of allowing her to be her fierce and headstrong self while still remaining the boss himself. He didn't want to break her spirit. It was a delicate balance and one she saw so many parents struggle with.

She knew she should probably intervene, but this was also part of the therapy process. Observing how dad and daughter interacted, how he handled her obstinate behavior and how she reacted to his authority.

So far, Aria was a typical three-and-a-half-year-old girl. Stubborn, emotional and demanding.

"Aria Elaina Stark," Atlas said through clenched teeth, "we need to go. You will be back next week."

"No!" Aria snapped back.

Okay, they'd had enough of this back and forth. He was obviously either without the proper tools in his belt to shift past this and get his kid moving, or he didn't want to haul her ass out of there and cause her to start screaming. Tessa had seen it all, so she wouldn't have been fazed in the least, but a part of her job as a therapist—and one of the topics in her PhD dissertation—was helping parents communicate with children after their child has experienced some form of trauma. Yes, art was a big component of her work, but it was just one component. Her master's thesis had been on the benefits of art therapy for people who had experienced trauma, but children had always been her passion. She wanted to dig deeper for her PhD. She wanted to help parents and caregivers find the tools and resources required to help their struggling children after a traumatic experience.

And given how young the baby in Mr. Stark's carrier was, she would say Aria's mother died quite recently. Even at thirty-five, she knew how traumatic the death of a parent could be. She couldn't imagine how much a three-and-a-half-year-old was struggling with it.

Remaining in her seat, she gently put her hand on Aria's shoulder, applied a bit of pressure and encouraged the little girl to turn and face her. Aria obliged, her shoulders lifting and falling exaggeratedly at the same time the headstrong child sighed. Tears brimmed her eyes, and her lip and chin trembled.

"I don't want to go yet," she said. "I'm not done."

So many emotions in such a small package. How did children do it? As an adult, she still struggled to manage her emotions, and she had impulse control (most of the time) and was self-aware. How did these little beings handle their feelings without exploding?

That's why children fascinated her. Always had.

She slid her hands down from Aria's shoulders to her hands and held them, squeezing gently. "I know you don't, Aria. I have had *so* much fun with you. But you know what? I have to get home too. I can't stay here forever either." She cupped her ear. "You hear that?"

Aria shook her head.

"That was my tummy rumbling. I'm hungry. Are you hungry?"

Aria nodded.

"So you know what? I bet that part of the reason you're so upset right now is because your tummy wants to go home, but your heart and your coloring fingers want to stay here. There's a bit of a tussle going on inside you right now, isn't there?"

"What's a tussle?"

"A bit of a fight."

Aria nodded. "I am hungry."

"Me too. And you know what?" Keeping one of the little girl's hands in hers, Tessa rose and led Aria over to where a bunch of IKEA bins lined one wall. She pulled out a shallow green drawer. "This is now your drawer. Anything you don't finish will go in here for next time, okay? You can take it home if you'd like, work on it at home, or you can leave it here for next week. Totally up to you. It's your choice."

Aria nodded. Then her tummy grumbled. Even Tessa heard it. She lifted unique hazel eyes up to Tessa's face, and her mouth formed a cute little *O* in surprise. "That was my tummy. It's really hungry."

Tessa nodded. "I heard that. It's like a little monster growling."

Aria nodded again, then took off back to the green triangle table, grabbed her pasta art, and with determined strides and an intensity in her gaze far too serious for somebody so young, she marched back toward Tessa. "Put my name on the drawer, please? So no other kids put their stuff in there."

Tessa nodded. "I absolutely will."

"A-R-I-A is how to spells it."

"Thank you. That's really amazing that you can already

spell your name." She glanced back up at Atlas, who had remained quiet, his facial expression tight, his dark gray eyes holding a melee of emotions she couldn't quite put a pin on. "You have a very bright little girl," she said, hoping to get the man to relax a bit. "She can already spell her name? That's incredible."

A flush formed in his cheeks beneath the short, wiry dark blond scruff. The man was handsome, she wouldn't deny that. Tall, lean and fit, with short, dark blond hair and an intensity about him that was as intriguing as it was a touch frightening. She also couldn't ignore the air of sadness that seemed to follow him around like an invisible cloud. Not to mention the stress he carried in his jaw and shoulders. The two practically met, he was so tightly wound.

"I can spell our last name too," Aria said with pride. She was now skipping, after having tidied up the art supplies without even being asked. "S-T-R ... " Her brows pinched. "That's as much as I know."

"That's a great start," Tessa encouraged. "Spelling is really hard."

She knew that firsthand. Spelling was her nemesis. It took until the sixth grade for her teacher and parents to figure out she was dyslexic. Up until then, they all just thought she didn't know how to read. Math had been a problem too. One teacher had actually called her hopeless and suggested holding her back. It wasn't until her sixth-grade teacher, Mrs. White, a dyslexic herself, that Tessa got the help, support and compassion she needed to thrive.

"Ready to go?" Mr. Stark asked, bouncing slightly and patting the baby's butt in the carrier when she started to stir.

Aria nodded. "Yeah, my tummy monster is growling. There is a bear *and* a monster in there seeing who can growl the loudest."

Tessa chuckled. Kids had the best imaginations.

Aria's father's lip twitched. "Well, let's go feed the monster and bear then."

Aria's head bobbed. She reached for her father's hand and waved at Tessa with the other one as they turned to go. "Bye, Tessa. See you next week."

Tessa's heart constricted at the sweetness of this little girl, and she waved back as she saw them to the door. "Bye, Aria. I can't wait until we meet again." She glanced up at Mr. Stark, and another look passed behind his eyes, but this time it not only confused her, it also alarmed her. Was that anger? At her?

"Goodbye, Mr. Stark," she said, hoping to disarm the man a bit and get him to at least acknowledge her.

All he did was grunt, nod and lead his kid out into the hallway. Aria was once again skipping as she held her father's hand, nattering his ear off, her blonde curls bouncing.

Oh well, she couldn't win them all. Mr. Stark or Atlas or whatever was not her client. Aria was. And as long as Aria liked her, as long as Aria was willing to open up to her and could be helped, that's all that mattered. Besides, she was done with trying to impress, win over or please men.

The only person's happiness that mattered now was her own, and today was the first day she intended to make that priority one.

4

_____

"THERE ISN'T a lot we can do, ma'am," the police officer said on the phone that night. After work, Tessa had called in and reported Forest being stolen.

In the eyes of the law, Forest was half Carlyle's. Tessa and Carlyle had adopted him together, and lived together for a number of years, so according to the state of Washington, her jerk of an ex had as much of a claim on the dog as Tessa did.

"But then, if he's half mine, shouldn't I at least get shared custody?" she pleaded. "If he's half mine, shouldn't I get him _half_ the time?"

"That's not a police matter, ma'am," the officer said, regret in her tone. "This a civil matter. To be handled in small claims court. I mean, you could get a lawyer ... "

"But I don't even know where he is to send any papers. I have no clue where to even start." She was on the verge of tears again for the millionth time that day. The only bright bit of sunshine in her whole day had been little Aria, and even that was fleeting and shadowed over by her cold and surly father, whose gray eyes reminded her of a Pacific storm ready to ransack the coast.

"I suggest you speak to a lawyer, perhaps hire a private investigator," the officer offered.

A hot tear slid down her cheek, and she nodded. "Okay, thank you."

She couldn't afford a private investigator. Not with the rent she paid for not only her apartment but the studio, along with her mother's nursing home fees. She was stretched thin already.

Was this it then? Was Forest just ... gone?

"What about a chip? Did your dog have a microchip or a tattoo?" the cop offered.

"That only works if someone takes him in to the vet or police and has the chip or tattoo read. They're not homing devices." Clearly this woman didn't have any pets, because she had no clue how it worked.

"Right, sorry."

"Thanks for your help."

Or lack thereof.

"You're welcome, ma'am, and good luck." She disconnected the call, leaving Tessa more crestfallen and broken than before. It was hopeless. She would never see Forest again.

Unable to pull herself out of her funk enough to make dinner, she ordered a heart- *and* brain-healthy meal for delivery. Poached salmon and a delicious-sounding salad with nuts and berries and an olive oil and raspberry vinaigrette. After her mother's diagnosis and the realization that she could very well be a carrier of the early onset Alzheimer's gene as well, Tessa had changed her diet completely. She researched until she nearly went cross-eyed the best foods for preventing Alzheimer's. Not that she'd been a big meat eater to begin with, but she cut out all meat besides fish, went clean eating with no processed foods, very few sweets, no butter or margarine, and lots of nuts and beans, leafy veg and plenty of good healthy fats. Good fats like fish oil and avocado were brain food. At least according to the Mayo Clinic.

It'd been damn near torture cutting dairy out of her diet. She loved cheese, but the silver lining in all of it was how beneficial wine was to the aging brain.

A glass a day was exactly what the doctors at the Mayo Clinic ordered. And who was she to argue with a bunch of doctors? Particularly those at one of the country's most esteemed hospitals?

After finishing her online order, she grabbed the three-quarter-full wine bottle off the counter, unscrewed the cap and upended the rest of the contents into her stemless glass.

Nowhere on the Mayo Clinic website did it say how *full* that one glass was allowed to be. Or if it did, she'd "missed" it.

In penguin flannel pajama pants, no bra and a tight black tank top, she wandered into the living room of her apartment. Not that Carlyle had moved into her place with a ton of stuff, but the few things he had brought, which were now on the front lawn of her apartment, left gaping holes in the place. She'd tucked away a few photo frames of the two them for the Rage Room on her next day off. She planned to hawk his record collection and comic book collection if he didn't return Forest. She wasn't stupid enough to drown those and chuck them on the lawn. Technically *in the eyes of the law,* because he'd acquired all that memorabilia while they were together, it was all half hers. Perhaps she should sell half of it. Break up a few collections just to spite him.

Everything else he'd brought with him when they moved in together, like his clothes, a few personal effects, his video game console and games were all out on the grass. She was sure by now some of it was gone. As was the way in Seattle— and most places at that—if you wanted to get rid of something, you put it on the curb and waited. Either some deal-hungry citizen grabbed it up or the city disposed of it.

She kind of hoped somebody else was playing Carlyle's beloved Halo and Final Fantasy right now rather than it ending up in the city landfill.

With her phone in one hand and her wine in the other, she sat down on her couch and stared at her black television screen.

"*That shit will rot your brain,*" her father used to always say.

Yeah, well, that was the least of her concerns for her brain right now. It was probably rotting from the inside out already, television-watching or not.

Carlyle hadn't even bothered to call her. Or return any of her emails. Which of course, had been similar to the texts she *thought* she'd been sending Blaire. Only to find out they'd gone to another number instead. She still hadn't texted Blaire. If Carlyle wasn't replying to her, why would his home-wrecking sidepiece?

Unless she still doesn't know she's a home-wrecking sidepiece.

Right.

She brought up her text messages and hit *compose*.

This time she was going to punch in the correct numbers in the correct order. She just had to slow her brain down and double-check before she hit *send*.

Hello, I am Tessa Copeland. I am not sure if you are aware, but I'm actually Carlyle Rickson's fiancée. Or I guess I should say, EX-fiancée. I hope that you are as ignorant to my existence as I was of yours. I found photos of the two of you and text messages on his tablet. Needless to say, it was pretty upsetting. I have not seen Carlyle for two days. I emailed him asking for an explanation. Carlyle and I had been together for five years. We were engaged. If you know where he is, could you please have him call me. I would like to discuss Forest. I miss my dog greatly, and having him back would make going through this breakup a whole lot easier.

She read and re-read her message. Made a few grammatical and spelling changes, in case Blaire was a grammar Nazi. She could just imagine Carlyle and Blaire sitting together laughing hysterically over Tessa's spelling or grammar blunder. Carlyle had always teased her about her poor spelling.

Once she made sure her message was being sent to the right number, as polite, calm and non-aggressive as possible, as well as grammar- and spelling-error free, she took a big sip of wine, shut her eyes and hit *send.*

Then she waited.

And waited.

And waited.

It was seven thirty on a Monday night. Maybe Blaire was at a Zumba class or something.

She shouldn't let her mind race too much and think that Blaire and Carlyle were busy laughing at her desperation and sorrow. People weren't that cruel, were they?

With her wine gone and her dinner app saying that her food was three minutes away, she flicked on the television and cast Netflix from her phone to the screen. Why did serial-killer documentaries intrigue her so? What was wrong with her?

But, like any addiction of the most bizarre kind, she loved them. Carlyle hated them, said she was weird for getting so invested in the stories.

She didn't understand the fascination herself, but she did know she wasn't the only person out there with such a penchant.

Deeply engrossed in the story of a man who liked to kidnap, torture and taxidermy child molesters he catfished on the internet—yeah, talk about sympathizing with the killer—she nearly jumped out of her skin when her phone started to ring to indicate the delivery driver was there.

With food in her belly, more wine in her glass and a hell of a lot of lavender essential oil diffusing in the corner, she finally felt herself relax.

It was about damn time.

She was still incredibly sad and wished like hell Forest was snoring on her feet as she curled up on the couch, but her feet were cold and the house too damn quiet for her liking. She turned up the volume on the television.

She didn't want to have to resort to filing a civil claim or get the lawyers involved, if it came to that. But she'd do it all, hire a PI, hire a lawyer, heck, she'd hire a muscled-up thug who swung punches for cash if it meant she could get her dog back.

She'd deal with the financial repercussions later. Get a job moonlighting as a delivery driver for her favorite vegan restaurant or something. Perhaps she'd get a discount on the food? Win-win?

When the episode of the serial-killer documentary ended, she stared at her phone and scrolled through Netflix for something else to watch.

Romantic comedies?

Uh, hell no.

She was in no mood to watch *Ethan and Isla* have a dating montage set to Wham's "Wake Me Up Before You Go-Go" or whatever the hell upbeat song they chose. She needed something like Linkin Park's "Numb" to play while the "happy" couple slowly realized that one or the other was a selfish, dog-stealing prick.

Still scrolling through her phone, with a slight buzz from her fruity merlot, she tensed when her phone vibrated in her palm and a text message popped up.

Was this Blaire?

Was she as ignorant to Tessa's existence as Tessa had been to hers?

Taking a deep breath that did nothing to calm her jittery nerves, she opened up the message.

I knew about you. Carlyle is not ready to see you. He will be in touch. Forest is fine.

And that was it.

That. Was. It.

The bitch.

It took every ounce of self-control she had not to hurl her phone and wineglass at the wall. That would only cause her more grief. And the wine was too good to waste.

"That fucking BITCH!" she screamed out to nobody in particular.

Because she had nobody.

She was alone.

Carlyle, Blaire and Forest were all together. Probably cuddled up on Blaire's couch while Tessa was all alone in her apartment. Just her, her wine, her serial killers and her rotting brain.

She stared at her phone and re-read the message over and over again, willing the woman on the other end to at least have the human decency to send her a picture of Forest so she knew he was okay. But nothing.

With trembling fingers and molten hot rage pumping through her veins like an angry volcano, she typed slow.

Could I at least have a photo of Forest, please. I need to know he's okay.

She held her breath again and hit send.

Nothing.

More nothing.

She was helpless. So entirely helpless.

Despite how much she'd cried already, she still had more

in the well, and another tear sprinted down the crease of her nose.

Her phone vibrated in her palm, but her eyes were too blurry to see the number.

Please let this be a photo of Forest. Please.

It wasn't.

Did you get your dog back? How was day two?

It was her misdial.

Sniffling, she texted him back.

No. But I texted the home-wrecker, and she wasn't ignorant to my existence. She also said Carlyle isn't ready to talk to me but that my dog is fine. I asked her for a photo of him.

Was this what her life had come to? Texting with a total stranger while buzzed on wine because she had nobody left in her life who loved her? Nobody lucid, anyway, because as much as her mother was still alive, she had no idea who Tessa was anymore. So that was pretty much the same as having nobody. She used to at least have her father until he died in a helicopter crash two years ago.

Her poor mother had absolutely no idea he was gone, no idea that the man who loved her implicitly, even through her deep, dark depression and her worsening Alzheimer's, who looked at her every day like she was the light at the end of the tunnel, had died.

He texted again. *I'm really sorry. That sucks. Have you filed a claim? Spoken with a lawyer?*

She didn't know the first thing about finding a decent lawyer. The only thing she did know was that some were as crooked as the Norwegian coastline and willing to screw over even their own clients for the bottom dollar. Could she ask him for a recommendation? If he knew a lawyer who had integrity but also didn't break the bank.

I haven't yet. I was waiting to see if Blaire (the home-wrecker) was going to be reasonable. Or if Carlyle was going to finally get in touch. But I think I have to go the lawyer route. Or hire a PI to find out where he's living and then go and take my dog back myself. Small claims court will take too long.

She drew a blanket over her cold feet and legs. Even though it was a warm May evening and she was in flannel pajama bottoms, she couldn't chase away the chill that seemed to have buried itself deep in her bones. The chill that came when someone was as alone as she was.

Do you have any lawyer recommendations? Or a PI you trust? I can't live without Forest. Carlyle, yes. But not my dog.

She felt better texting with this misdial stranger. That didn't stop the half dozen tears from dropping down her cheeks and chin into her wineglass as she stared at her phone, waiting for his reply.

I could recommend a few of both, yes.

She swallowed the harsh, jagged lump in her throat.

Thank you. Do you think I should go with a PI or lawyer?

His texts were coming in quicker.

I think you should obtain legal counsel first and then go on the advice of that council how to proceed next.

Her breath shuddered, and she used the edge of the blanket to wipe up her damp chin and cheeks.

Thank you.

I will text you the names and numbers of a few good lawyers tomorrow when I get to work.

Thank you.

Now what could she say? What *did* you say to a total stranger? She'd dabbled in chat rooms and messenger-type things when she was younger, but she'd never been big on holding long conversations with total strangers. Particularly when those strangers usually only had one thing in mind.

But she wanted to keep talking to this guy. Even though she didn't know his name, his age or what he looked like, speaking with him and knowing he was on her side, she felt less alone.

And then it hit her.

What if he was married? Was this considered flirting? Or cheating in some way? Oh God. Was she the *other* woman? Was she no better than Blaire?

Of course, you're better than Blaire. You're having a conversation with the man, not sleeping with him or sending him nude photos of yourself.

Either way, she needed to find out if he was married. She wouldn't have been too happy if she'd found out Carlyle had been texting some strange woman who had misdialed him, even if it was totally innocent.

Or maybe he and his wife were both sitting there together texting her because they had an open, honest marriage where they didn't keep any secrets from each other.

What a novel concept.

If it wasn't for the deep, unrelenting love she saw between her parents, she may have lost hope in a relationship like that. One where the couple was honest and true to each other. But her parent's marriage had been like that, and she hoped to God those relationships weren't going the way of the Dodo, that they still existed, still happened, were still possible—even for her.

Biting down hard on her lip, she asked the question she needed to ask before she spoke another word to him.

You're sure your wife doesn't mind you texting some crazy woman who misdialed and dumped her relationship baggage on you?

Her lips rolled inward as she waited.

He texted back right away.

No wife.

She swallowed and texted back.

Divorced?

No.

How old are you?

39. You?

35. Children?

Yes.

But no wife?

No.

Did that mean ... ?

Yes, it probably did mean that he was a widower.

How tragic.

How long have you ...

She wasn't sure if this question was appropriate, but she knew she needed to know the answer.

1 year, 5 months, 3 weeks, 4 days, 6 hours and 37 minutes.

Oh God. Fresh, hot tears stung the back of her eyes. Now this was a man who had been madly in love with his woman. This was not the type of man who would steal her dog and abandon her, even if she developed some horrible brain-rotting disease. This was a man who had loved his wife with the same intensity Tessa's father had loved her mother. Fully, unabashedly and until his final breath.

Unless he's a serial killer and killed his wife and he knows the exact moment he killed her.

She needed to tell her imagination to shut the hell up. All those Netflix documentaries were beginning to make her suspicious of everyone. Though to be fair, given the way the world was going, she often wondered if the real question wasn't *are you paranoid?* But in fact, *are you paranoid enough?*

I'm sorry, she texted back, determined to not assume this guy was a cold-blooded wife killer. Then she cringed at her message. She knew firsthand how telling someone grieving that "I'm sorry" just wasn't enough. So many people had said that to her when her father died that eventually the words became hollow and meaningless.

But what else could you say?

She texted him again. *How many children do you have? How old?*

How many children had been left motherless? How many children was he forced to become mother and father to in most likely the blink of an eye? Even though her mother had been alive, there were a lot of days, sometimes weeks where her father had been forced to step up and be both parents. When her mother had retreated into her bedroom, into the dark, unwilling to come out—not even to eat. She knew the toll that had taken on her dad, and she could only imagine it was compounded significantly for a widower.

Her phone buzzed with his reply.

What's your favorite flavor of ice cream?

Well, that question came out of nowhere.

Did it, though?

No. It didn't. She was a therapist and knew redirection and deflection when it clobbered her upside the head. He was done talking about his life, about his wife.

She was just grateful he wasn't done talking to her.

Smiling, she texted back *Pistachio.*

God, how long had it been since she'd had ice cream? Years? Yeah, probably. She'd gone clean and dairy-free after reading up on Alzheimer's prevention, and although it was hard, the alternative scared her straight.

She would really like a bowl of pistachio ice cream right about now, though. Wasn't that what you were supposed to do during a breakup? Eat ice cream and dish with your girl-friends?

Only she didn't really have very many girlfriends. A lot of her high school friends had moved away, the same with her college friends. And the ones that were still in town had demanding lives with work, husbands and children. They had no time to come over to Tessa's place and listen to her lament about her pathetic love life. A few of them (only her three besties) had actually snubbed her because she didn't have kids. They said she just didn't understand the demands and challenges of their lives, and that sure, she worked with kids, but when she went home the kids didn't follow her. Those words had stung her worse than when she stepped on that wasps' nest on her ninth birthday. Never once did she ever judge or criticize her friends and their busy child-filled lives. All she'd ever been was understanding, envious and willing to bend over backward to make a drink night or coffee meet up work. Whether her friend Jill packed her four-year-old twins along while they had coffee in a park and watched the boys play, Tessa didn't care. She just wanted the friendships, no matter how they came packaged. But her friends didn't feel the same way, told her as much, and then stopped calling. She hadn't heard from Jill, Kailey or Addison in over three years, but she was either an idiot, a stalker or a glutton for punishment, because she refused to unfriend them on social media. So every now and then something about one—or all three of them together with their husbands and kids—would pop up on her feed and the scab would just rip open all over again.

Pistachio is a good pick.

She smiled at his response and asked him his preference.

What's yours?

Citrus cooler. They don't make it anymore, but as a kid I couldn't get enough of the stuff in the summer from the ice cream man who set up his cart along the river in Portland.

Oh, so he was from Portland.

But he must live in Seattle now if he mentioned the Rage Room.

Interesting.

I've never heard of that flavor, but it sounds delicious. How long have you lived in Seattle if you're originally from Portland?

Even though she wanted more wine, she was out of wine, and it was only Monday after all. She did have work in the morning, and as much as she would love to drown her sorrows in vino until she was numb, buzzed, and giggling instead of crying, she had to remind herself that she wasn't twenty-one anymore and she would be paying for it in the morning.

So, like a responsible adult, she brewed herself a cup of apple cinnamon herbal tea as she and this mystery person on the other side of her phone slowly got to know each other.

Despite the fact that she was sad, alone and without her best friend in the entire world, by the time Tessa pulled the covers over herself, flicked off the light and said good night to the misdial lawyer originally from Portland, she didn't feel like the entire world was against her.

Because at least she had one friend ... sort of.

5

ON FRIDAY, Tessa rode her bike to work. And not like a Schwinn or a mountain bike with gears. She rode her 2017 Ducati Pengale. The only thing in the world she loved nearly as much as she loved her mother, father and dog was her Ducati.

Her father had been a big bike nut for as long as she could remember. When her mother would retreat into her bedroom for days on end, Tessa and her dad would head out to the garage and tinker on bikes. He liked Harleys, but she had a need for speed and was always drawn to the crotch rockets. For her seventeenth birthday, he bought her a beat-up old Yamaha, and the two of them fixed it up together until it was shiny and new-*ish,* well, new to her, anyway. She turned quite a few heads the first day she rode that beauty to high school. Too bad they didn't have GoPros back in the day.

For longer than she could even remember, as she and her dad worked in the garage, they would argue over the superiority of one make over the other. She liked Harleys, but nothing beat the beauty and speed of a Ducati. They'd always end their evening together with a Dr. Pepper and a bag of salt and vinegar chips shared between them to call it a draw.

She missed those nights and weekends more than anything. So when she was on her bike with the wind hitting her helmet and the power beneath her, she felt just a little closer to her father.

She couldn't very well wear her flowy skirts when she rode her bike—as much as she loved them—so she was in a pair of dark wash jeans and a sleeveless black and white checked cotton blouse. Though she always wore her leather jacket when she rode—a gift from her father for the last birthday he was alive to help her celebrate. When she wore it, she liked to think he was hugging her, keeping her safe as she zigged and zagged her way through traffic.

Her small tattoo peeked out from beneath the cuff of her jacket as she pulled her bike into her usual spot out in front of her office building and lifted her helmet off her head, releasing her hair loosely behind her.

When her dad gave her the leather jacket, he'd included a small, hand-scrawled card with it.

I love you, kiddo.

~Dad

After he died, she had that little note, in his writing, tattooed on her wrist as just another way to always keep him with her, always keep him close.

She wasn't sure if it was a weird sound in the traffic behind her or a gasp, but either way, she turned her head to see what made that sound.

It was Aria's dad, Mr. Stark, holding Aria by the hand and the baby in the carrier.

She squinted at them, then lifted her hand to block out the morning sun. She'd received an email Thursday after-noon from Mr. Stark asking if she had any openings on Friday, that Aria had been acting out again at home, had hit the baby with a toy, and that he thought maybe two sessions a week to start would be better. Normally, she was fully booked weeks in advance, but she miraculously had a nine o'clock opening the very next day. Hence why the little firecracker with the exhausted-looking father and the rosy-cheeked baby were headed toward her.

Aria released her father's hand and ran up. "Hi, Tessa!"

"Hi, Aria, how are you?"

The little girl pouted. "I hit Cecily with a toy."

Tessa pressed her lips into a thin line and hummed as she crouched down to Aria's level. "And do you think that was a good idea?"

Aria shook her head. "No. I know it was wrong, but she ... " Her lip wobbled, and she glanced back at her father. "*I* was talking to Daddy about school, and Cecily wouldn't stop crying."

"Hmm, yes, I can see how that would be very frustrating for you. I bet you were probably feeling a lot of different feelings, weren't you?"

Aria nodded. "I was mad. And sad. And ... not happy."

Tessa reached for Aria's hand. "Well, let's head into my studio, and we can maybe talk about our feelings a bit more. I'll tell you right now how I'm feeling. Do you want to know?"

Aria's hand was small and satin-soft in her palm. "How are you feeling?"

"I'm feeling really happy that you're here today. I've been looking forward to seeing you again. My day yesterday wasn't very good, but now that you're here I'm happy again."

When Aria smiled, she beamed. It was like the world instantly became ten times brighter.

They headed off toward the front lobby door of the office building. She didn't have to turn around to know Mr. Stark was following them.

Up the elevator they rode to the fourth floor, the only

sound in the small space being Aria showing Tessa how she could now "wink" even though she couldn't. She kept asking, "Am I doing it? Am I doing it now?" and Cecily slurped away on her fist like it was a lollipop made of Pablum.

Did babies still eat Pablum? She had no clue.

They were nearly to the top floor when Mr. Stark's deep voice made goosebumps prickle up along her arms—even beneath her leather jacket. "You ride a bike?" Even with the rough and quiet timber of his voice, she couldn't mistake the surprise in his tone.

She glanced over her shoulder at him. "I do."

He grunted. "Didn't expect that given the patchouli and skirt on Monday."

What the heck?

She rounded on him. Despite her fun and almost flirty conversation with her mystery texter last night, she'd had a terrible sleep and woke up in a funk. She was in no mood to be dealing with a man who had obviously taken one look at her and thought *hack*. "What is that supposed to mean?" she asked, squinting at him.

He took a visible breath, and she watched as every muscle in his tall, fit body went rock-solid. It was as if he'd just stepped into full body armor and was preparing to protect himself. But then something else flashed behind his eyes. He shrugged off the steel and blinked before he shook his head and broke their gaze. "Never mind."

What the actual hell?

But she wasn't ready to let that comment go. "No, tell me what you meant, Mr. Stark. Please? Did you think because I wore a comfortable, pretty, flowy skirt, a few bracelets and my hair down that I also like to dance naked in a field, praying to the sun gods while high on peyote?"

It was obvious now he was fighting a grin at that response

and trying desperately to keep his expression serious. He still hadn't pivoted his gaze back to her though.

"And that patchouli comment? There's a meat smoke-house next door, and I like to open the window on nice days and *not* constantly smell jerky. I also happen to believe that essential oils *do* have the ability to alter our moods. When I smell something gross, I'm certainly in a less happy mood. Wouldn't you agree?"

Slowly, as if it pained him to do it, he swung his head back to face her, and his dark gray eyes zeroed in on her like laser beams, then drifted down to her chest. At first, she thought he was staring at her breasts, but then she realized it was the healing crystal that she wore that had drawn his attention.

One of his dark blond brows rose just slightly at the same time the elevator dinged and the doors slid open.

What. An. Asshole.

She turned herself back around and, still holding Aria's hand, she led the little girl down the hallway toward her studio. "We can take it from here, Mr. Stark. You go ... do what you need to do. See you in an hour." She hadn't both-ered to glance back at him, but she could certainly feel his eyes on her.

Thankfully, Aria seemed none the wiser and was happily skipping beside her, talking about how she planned to finish her pasta art this session.

She'd dealt with jerk parents before who thought art therapy was a joke, but none that made her skin tingle or her heart thump the way Aria's father did.

He's a widower. He's a jerk. You've sworn off men.

She needed to repeat that to herself until it sunk in, because she was tired of falling for the jerks. She was tired of falling, period. Because no matter how hard she thought she'd fallen for someone, thinking they would be there to catch her and hold her for the rest of her life, she always seemed to wind up face-first in the dirt.

No, she was going to have to find a way to be happy on her own. Her late-night text messages with the stranger were enough. He was kind. He was supportive. He was interesting. They never got *too* personal, but that was okay. They'd spoken every night that week, sometimes for a few hours as she went about her evening routine. But what made her go to sleep with a smile on was that they always said *Good night* to each other. He never left her hanging, and she never left him.

She doubted Mr. Stark even said *thank you.*

She unlocked the door to her studio, and Aria took off toward her now-labeled drawer. Tessa stepped inside, but then for some stupid reason, she peeked her head back around the corner.

He was there. Standing at the end of the hallway, staring at her. Even from that great a distance, she could see the fire in his eyes, and it was hot enough to torch the entire building.

Damn it. She'd always had a weakness for a good smolder.

ATLAS STARED down the hallway until he saw her head disappear back into the studio. His brain was running a million miles a minute, and his heart thumped wildly in his chest.

He didn't know what the fuck was going on, but whatever it was, he fucking hated it.

She'd put him in his place, and it had been hot as fuck.

He hated that he thought that.

He hated that another woman had made him feel something he never, ever thought he'd feel again. Never wanted to feel again.

That ship was supposed to have sailed, crashed into the

rocks and caught fire. How was it still afloat? How was it still seaworthy?

And what was even more fucked up was this was not the first time he'd had these stirrings in the last twenty-four hours. He'd had them last night too, and they were over someone he had never even fucking met. For all he knew, the person he thought was a thirty-five-year-old woman who'd just had her life come crashing down around her was actually a fifty-year-old guy who still lived with his parents and had a collection of human teeth—that weren't his. He could be catfishing Atlas, trying to get them to meet, only to skin him alive and harvest his teeth to make a new necklace.

He really needed to stop watching those serial-killer documentaries before bed. That was one of the few things he and Samantha had disagreed on. She hated them, thought they were freaky as hell, and would leave the room when he put them on. He couldn't get enough of them, even listened to serial-killer podcasts when he was alone in his car.

It was his obsession with serial killers that dissuaded him from going into prosecution or defense. He didn't want his work to interfere with his fucked-up obsession. Because yes, he knew it was fucked up. Oh well, *he* wasn't the one doing the killing; he was just interested in the stories.

He was back in the lobby in less than a minute, a snoozing Cecily on his chest. The kid had been up all fucking night again screaming about her teeth. Tylenol didn't work, a frozen washcloth didn't work, nothing. Nothing besides being held by Atlas, that is. All. Fucking. Night.

He was goddamn exhausted.

Normally, Jenny would have had the girls this time of day, but she needed to go and get emergency dental work. Apparently, a crown had broken at dinner last night. So there he was, at ten past nine on a Friday, wandering down the sidewalk in his suit, wearing a sleeping baby.

It was hot and sunny out, so he threw on his shades and set his jaw tight. He needed to head into the office and see if his secretary could move a few of his meetings until Monday. He should probably just take off the whole day. He was too tired to fucking function as a human being, let alone a family lawyer.

Luckily, his office was not more than four blocks from the therapy office, and he was there in ten minutes, sweat on his brow and a tension headache growing in his temples from having clenched his jaw the entire way there.

His dentist and doctor told him to cut that shit out, but it was better than the alternative—losing his shit entirely.

That Tessa chick rounding on him in the elevator had set his nerves right off—and it made him think and feel things he fucking hated.

Clenching his jaw until the ache pulsed and blurred his vision was one of the only things left that he had any control over in his life. The headache was painful, but he took it as punishment for how he felt about the therapist—and the *woman* he was texting with.

After speaking with his secretary and having her move his meetings, he headed down the hallway toward Liam's office.

Liam Dixon, name partner at Wallace Dixon and Travers, was not only a fucking incredible lawyer but also one of Atlas's best and closest friends. For all the man's faults—because he had a fuck-ton of them—he was loyal to the end and had seriously saved Atlas's ass and sanity, bringing him into Liam's single-dad fold.

He'd been reluctant at first and rebuffed Liam's offers for months after Samantha had died. He just hadn't been ready to face the fact that he was a single dad. That he was part of a new *club*. But eventually Liam's "nagging" wore him down, and he started attending the weekly poker games on Saturday nights.

It was a small blip in time where he felt remotely normal. Where he felt sort of human. There was no judgment among the guys, just ribbing and support. Those nine other men got what it was like to be a single father. They were all just trying their damnedest to not create sociopaths that in fifteen or so years they would have to release into society with nothing more than their fingers crossed the kids didn't end up with their own Netflix documentary. And the guys had covered his ass more than once, taking Aria for a few hours so he could take a deep breath and not lose his shit.

Cecily was still asleep on his chest in the carrier when he rounded the corner into Liam's fancy corner office, with its abundance of windows overlooking the water and the shipping yard to the southwest. A bunch of fancy diplomas lined one of his two walls, along with a few pictures of Liam and his son Jordie.

"Well, you look like shit," Liam said before Atlas was even completely in the room.

"And you're a dick," he replied, rolling his eyes. He went to take a seat across from Liam's desk, but Cecily protested, so he remained standing. He also began to sway.

Liam's rebuttal normally would have been witty and sarcastic, accompanied by a cheesy grin, but it wasn't. His face sobered. "Dude, you seriously look like shit. When was the last time you slept for more than two hours in a row?"

Atlas's brain was so fucking foggy, he had no freaking clue. He shrugged.

Liam pursed his lips together, his expression turning grim. "Yeah, that's what I thought."

"I just came in to take the rest of the day off and have Donna move my meetings to Monday. Cecily was up all fucking night teething." He yawned and blinked, his eyes protesting the need to be open and stinging with each blink.

Dark brown eyes focused on him, and Liam narrowed his

brows. "I was going to come talk to you later. In fact, the partners and I were. But since you're here ... " Exhaling, he grabbed his phone. "Judy, could you see if Jerrika and Rocky are free for a quick meeting? Atlas is here ... Thanks."

What the fuck? They weren't going to make him name partner *now,* were they? He knew they needed the buy-in money for that and that his workload would double if not triple once he became name partner. It was something he wanted more than anything in the world, but he just wasn't sure he could take it on right now.

Possibly ever.

And that thought gnawed at his insides more than the ulcer he was sure he was developing because of all the stress.

"How's Aria?" Liam asked, sitting forward in his seat, resting his elbows on his desk and pressing his hands together like he was praying.

What the fuck was going on? Liam was acting really fucking strange. Any other time Atlas had wandered into Liam's office his friend would have poured him a drink and then kicked back in his chair with his feet on his desk. Liam was a shark of a lawyer, but he was also laid back as fuck.

"She's fine," he said with a grunt. Something was up, and it wasn't the good news that he was finally being made name partner. He cracked his neck side to side when the sensation of what he could only describe as a spider crawling across his skin made his whole body go ramrod-straight.

Liam eyed him warily. "Didn't you have her starting with an art therapist this week? The one Zak recommended. How's that going?"

"She's there now."

Liam's brows rose. "And she's enjoying it."

"So far. This is only the second session. Too soon to tell."

"Well, Zak said the therapist did a great job with Aiden, so I'm sure she's going to work wonders with Aria, too." His lips flattened out again, and he pinned his gaze on Cecily. "Baby sleeping?"

Atlas grunted and nodded.

A light knock at the door behind him announced Jerrika Wallace and Rockwell Travers. The other name partners at the firm Wallace Dixon and Travers.

Atlas made room for the two of them to enter.

"Atlas," Jerrika cooed, resting her cool, dark hand on Atlas's arm. "How are things?" She leaned in to take a better peek at Cecily, then pulled back and made that face that everyone makes after they've seen a cute baby. Her hand went to her chest. "Such a sweetheart. How's she sleeping?"

She wasn't. That was the fucking problem.

"Not great," he muttered.

Rockwell Travers gave Atlas a handshake but gripped his elbow with his other hand. "Good to see you, Atlas."

Atlas murmured something similar and forced the corners of his mouth to lift a touch.

"Shall we sit?" Jerrika asked, taking a seat across from Liam. She was a pretty woman. Mid-forties with curly dark hair to her shoulders, dark brown eyes and the whitest teeth and most genuine and friendly smile Atlas had ever seen—until Aria's therapist anyway. It was one of her biggest tools in the courtroom. She flashed her smile, batted her lashes and won the jury over with her can-do, anything is possible, unicorns *do* exist if you just believe attitude.

Atlas liked her, but he could only handle being around that much optimism for about sixty minutes, tops. After that, his skin began to crawl as if rainbows and sunshine were trying to burrow into him. Nobody was really that happy and positive, were they?

"Yes, let's sit," said Rockwell, or "Rocky," as he preferred to be called. He sat next to Jerrika, and then both their eyes, and

Liam's, drifted to Atlas as they waited for him to take the third and last chair.

"I'll stand," he said. "She doesn't like it when I sit."

"Very well," Rocky said, propping one ankle on his knee and leaning back. Even though he was probably only a year or two older than Atlas, the man had gone gray early. He'd also grown a bunch of facial hair recently and lost probably thirty pounds. Atlas heard murmurs around the office that Rocky had turned into a "silver fox" almost overnight. Atlas chalked it up to Rocky's recent divorce and the fact that he was now on the prowl. To each their own.

Liam cleared his throat, tapped his pen on his desk, clicked it a few times and then finally lifted his gaze to Atlas. The man looked tortured.

What. The. Fuck. Was. Going. On?

"We understand that you're under a lot of pressure right now," Liam started. "What with Aria and now baby Cecily, and work—"

"I can handle it," Atlas said, cutting him off. Fuck, were they firing him? Was this what the impromptu meeting was about? Were they fucking firing him?

Oh, he was going to fucking sue all their asses if that was the case. Yes, his life was chaos right now, but that didn't mean he wasn't a damn good lawyer. The best senior partner at that fucking firm despite the pandemonium he had going on at home.

Liam shut his eyes.

"We know you can handle it," Jerrika said smoothly, her voice calm and deep, like a well-aged port. "What we're trying to tell you is that you don't have to."

"What?" His eyes darted back and forth between the three name partners so fast, he was starting to get dizzy. "Is this your fucked-up way of telling me I'm fired?"

"No!" all three of them practically shouted. Cecily stirred

in the carrier from the noise, but thankfully her eyes remained glued shut.

"We're not firing you," Rocky said, shaking his head. "Not at all." He stood up and stepped in front of Atlas. "Atlas, you are one of the best lawyers at this firm. We don't want to lose you. But we also see that you are struggling."

"We want to suggest you take a short leave of absence," Jerrika said from her seat, careening her head around Rocky's body. "A month, just to decompress and get some rest."

"Maybe hire another nanny, a live-in one. Just temporarily," Liam chimed in.

"You want me to go on fucking stress leave, is that it?" Atlas asked, heat infusing not only his words but his limbs and gut. He blinked a bunch of times when spots began to cloud his vision.

"A sabbatical," Jerrika corrected. "There's no shame in taking some time for yourself. For your family."

Atlas clenched his molars and glared at the three of them. They didn't meet his glare though and looked back at him with nothing but compassion. It deflated a bit of his ire.

"What if I refuse?" he asked, determined to not go down without a fight.

Rocky stepped to the side so Jerrika could be in full view. She was managing partner and had the lion's share of the power. "It's not a request," she said softly. "As of today, you are on a thirty-day sabbatical. After thirty days, we will have this meeting and conversation again and see where things stand." She stood up and smoothed her hands down her white and gray pinstripe pencil skirt.

"This doesn't mean name partner is off the table," Liam said, looking like he was ready to puke. "It's just postponed until things settle down a bit. The associates will take care of your cases, and anything they can't handle, we will."

He was going to chip a fucking tooth if he gnashed his

molars together any harder. Taking a deep breath through his nose, he fought his shoulders down from his ears. "You making me see a shrink again?" he ground out.

"Not unless you give us reason to," Jerrika said, heading for the door. "Though it might not be a bad idea if you saw one of your own accord."

"We all love you, Atlas," Rocky said, right behind Jerrika. "We want you back, one hundred percent, and right now, you're just not. Take some time, buddy." He slapped Atlas on the shoulder, then he and Jerrika left.

Atlas lifted his gaze back up to Liam. He wanted to punch his "friend" in his fucking face.

"I'm sorry," Liam said, his complexion pale and his eyes sad. "I do think it's for the best though."

He was too furious to say anything and just stood there, his head shaking, his body a Coke bottle ready to explode. "I'm fine," he gritted out.

Liam rose from his chair and came to stand in front of Atlas. "Dude, you're not fine. Your kids aren't fine. After Samantha died, you took two weeks off work and then were back in the office. Everyone thought you were fucking crazy."

That was because not everything at the office reminded him of his dead wife like it did at home. At work he could lock himself in his office and smother his grief with other people's problems. At work he didn't have to stare into the sad, confused hazel eyes of his daughter—the same eyes as Samantha—and come up with yet another tortuous way to explain where her mama was and why she wasn't coming back.

"You need to take care of yourself, and in turn that will take care of your kids," Liam continued, stepping forward and resting a hand on Atlas's shoulder.

Atlas jerked him away and snarled. "Did your wife die?"

Liam didn't respond.

"Did. Your. Wife. Die?" he repeated.

Liam released Atlas's shoulder and cast his eyes to the floor. "No, she didn't."

"Then you have no FUCKING clue what I need. No FUCKING clue what I'm going through." He tried his damnedest to keep his voice low so as to not wake Cecily, but she must have felt his rage because she began to stir and whimper.

Liam's head lifted, his gaze probing. "I didn't lose my wife, no. But that doesn't mean I can't see when a friend, when a *brother*, needs help. And you, Atlas, need some fucking help."

Fucking fuck.

Of course he was fucking right.

Atlas just hated to admit that he needed this time off work. He needed to get his head on straight, get his family sorted and organized. Maybe hire another nanny so he could sleep more than two fucking hours in a row. Because between working late and getting up with the kids, he was well past running on fumes. He'd damn near worn a hole through the gas tank.

"Does McGregor owe you any favors?" Atlas asked, the tension in his jaw subsiding a little.

Liam's eyes softened, and his interest piqued at Atlas's sudden change of subject. "He does, in fact. Why?"

"That favor is mine now. Let him know." He turned to leave.

"What do you need a PI for?"

Atlas didn't answer.

"You still coming to poker tomorrow night?" Liam called back, humor back in his voice.

All Atlas could do in return was grunt.

Of course, he was going to be there.

He wouldn't miss it for the world.

6

"DADDY HAS TO GO NOW, ARIA," Atlas said Saturday night, peeling his whining three-and-a-half-year-old off his leg as he fought his left foot into his shoe near the front door. "You know the drill, kiddo. Kimmy comes over on Saturdays, and you get to stay up a little bit later, watch a movie and have popcorn while Daddy goes out."

Since Jenny only worked weekdays—ten-hour days, but still only Monday to Friday—one of the other senior partners at the firm's teenage daughter came over every Saturday to babysit the girls so Atlas could go to poker night.

Kimmy seemed like a responsible enough sixteen-year-old. Captain of the debate team, mathlete, honor roll student. She seemed trustworthy enough—though that didn't mean Atlas didn't have a nanny cam anyway, one he made sure Kimmy was well aware of—because, you know, lawsuits and crap.

Aria usually loved it when Kimmy showed up and some nights was even kicking Atlas out the door.

Not tonight, though.

Tonight, Aria had done nothing but glare at Kimmy the

moment the girl showed up. His daughter then proceeded to throw a steamed broccoli floret at Cecily across the dinner table, beaning the poor child between the eyes, and then run screaming to her room, where she slammed the door.

All this took place as Kimmy fed the children dinner and Atlas showered and got ready for poker. Though the screaming and door-slamming could be heard even through the walls and the pummeling water. His kid had a set of lungs on her.

"You can't leave, Daddy!" Aria protested, gripping him by the back pockets of his jeans and letting her feet slip out from under her. He heard a rip. Fuck, had she wrecked another pair of his pants? "I hate Kimmy!"

He resisted the urge to roll his eyes. She'd come home with that word, *hate*, from preschool last week and now proceeded to use it to describe a fair number of things.

I hate bedtime.

I hate Cecily.

I hate broccoli.

I hate bath time.

I hate yellow.

"Yellow what?" he asked.

"Yellow *everything*," she replied.

According to some of the single dads who also had children either older than Aria or around her age, this behavior was totally normal.

Didn't make it any less freaking frustrating though.

Once he pried her off his jeans pockets, he flipped her around and plopped her boney butt on his hip. She grabbed his face between her tiny human hands and smooshed his lips together so he would be forced to speak like a duck. "Aria Elaina Stark, you know the drill."

She scowled, reminding him so much of her mother. His

heart tightened inside his chest. "What *drill?*" she asked, playing coy. "I don't want you to go."

"This is my one night a week where I get do something for myself, honey." Why was he reasoning with a three-and-a-half-year-old? He rolled his eyes inwardly at himself. He knew better. Before he became a father, he'd been a hard-ass. Took no shit from anybody.

Having a child—a daughter—had turned him soft.

And now he had two little girls.

He'd be a fucking marshmallow by the time they were off to college. God forbid they give him granddaughters. He'd have no spine left by the time he died.

"But you can hang out with me and have some time to yourself," she said, full of confidence. As if she'd just solved all his problems. Her shoulders bounced on a shrug. "See, easy solve."

"No, sweetie." He pecked her on the nose, forehead and cheek. "You go upstairs and see Kimmy. And no throwing food—or anything else for that matter—at Cecily." He plunked Aria down on one of the steps leading up to the living room, her pout out and her hands on her hips.

"I hate you!" she declared. Then she spun around and stomped like a sumo wrestler up the stairs, her feet equally thunderous as she sprinted down the hall.

"Don't you dare slam that door, young lady!" he called after her, hating that this was how he was leaving things with his daughter but also knowing he couldn't let her get away with her behavior.

Wasn't the art therapy supposed to be helping with these outbursts? She'd colored nearly all day. Why hadn't she channeled her frustrations? Wasn't that how it worked?

He stepped up the stairs a few steps and craned his neck around the corner to look down the hallway toward Aria's room. She was standing in her doorway, arms crossed, glaring at him.

Within five strides, he was crouching down in front of her. "I'll be home before you know it, okay?"

Her chin jiggled, and her lips twitched. She was trying so hard to be strong and not break down. God, it still floored him how much she was like her mother. Samantha had been stubborn as hell too.

"I don't want you to go," she managed through clenched teeth. The tears began to well up in her eyes, then she lost her battle and flung her arms around his neck, burying her face in the collar of his light blue polo shirt. "Please don't go, Daddy," she muffled against him. "I don't hate you. I'm sorry I said I did."

He stroked her back and let her get her tears out, her sobs causing her entire body to quiver. Eventually, she calmed down and loosened her vice grip on him. With his hands on her waist, he helped her stand up tall. "Feel better?" he asked, using his thumbs to wipe the tears from her blotchy cheeks.

She nodded. "Will you wake me up when you get home and let me know you're back?" she asked, sniffling and wiping the back of her wrist beneath her nose. Her hazel eyes shone bright from all the tears, and her lips and nose were puffy.

He nodded. "I will, sweetie. I will come and give you a super-big hug and a kiss when I get home and wake you up and tell you how much I love you."

He watched as she visibly relaxed, and the frustration that had consumed her dissolved into the air around them. It was almost like a mini-exorcism really, the way his child flipped her switch so quickly. Her radiant smile illuminated the dimly lit hallway. Every muscle in his body relaxed too, and at the same time, they both took slow, deep breaths.

"I'm going to go find Kimmy," she said as he stood up from his crouched position, groaning from how it made his knees pop and grind. He'd feel that twinge in his back tomorrow for sure.

She skipped off down the hallway calling Kimmy's name.

Phew.

Crisis averted.

Or was that crisis handled?

Either way, he waved at Kimmy, who was wiping up a filthy-faced Cecily, and headed down the stairs. He needed to make a quick and clean getaway before Aria decided to rip his other back pocket and start the histrionics all over again.

Her mother had always had a penchant for the dramatic as well.

It was one of the things he loved most about Samantha. Her zest for life and fun. And even though right now, Aria's emotions and dramatic behavior were taxing on him, he knew beyond a shadow of a doubt she was going to grow up to be one incredible, passionate human being.

He swung his long legs behind the steering wheel of his Land Cruiser, turned on the ignition, rolled down the windows and let the sunroof slide open all the way. It was a hot May evening, and he needed the breeze around him to blow away all the thoughts that seemed trapped inside his brain.

As he was about to pull out onto the road, his phone began to ring in his pocket.

Please don't let this be Kimmy saying that Aria is losing her shit again and just coldcocked Cecily over the head with a frying pan.

Thankfully, it was not Kimmy.

"Hey, McGregor, what do you have for me?"

"Atlas." The way McGregor said his name with his deep Southern drawl made it sound like Atlas's name was five syllables rather than two. "Found the guy and girl you're looking for. Holed up in an apartment in Greenwood."

His heart hammered in his chest. "And the dog?"

"There too."

"Is the dog okay? Are they taking care of him?"

"Seem to be. You only called me yesterday, so I've only been watching them since this morning. Took me a few hours to track 'em down."

A few hours. McGregor was one of the best PIs in the freaking city. He did in a few hours what took other PIs days if not weeks. The man could find a needle in a haystack and not even break a sweat.

"I'll send you their address and info via text," McGregor said, the sound of seagulls and waves crashing in the background competing with his words. The guy was probably somewhere down by the water enjoying a cool beer after a hard day of spying on people.

"Thanks, McGregor," he said, surprising himself with his chipper tone. He finally got a win, and it felt damn good.

The line went dead, because McGregor never said goodbye, and Atlas pulled out of his driveway. He needed to hit the liquor store before he headed to Liam's. Even though their host was flush with cash and kept his bar stocked, not one of the guys showed up empty-handed.

He shifted into third gear and headed off down the road only to nearly drive clear off the road when he caught a glimpse of himself in his side mirror. He was fucking smiling.

Holy shit.

He hadn't smiled in a while, and yet the thought of bringing somebody he didn't even really know good news had him smiling like an idiot.

He'd wait to text her until later tonight though. He didn't want to be distracted at poker, and he certainly didn't want the guys asking questions about who he was messaging.

Yes, tonight, he was going to take his win all the way to

the bank. He was going to help his new friend get her dog back. And he couldn't believe how good that made him feel.

"HI, MOM," Tessa whispered, stepping into her mother's bedroom at the nursing home for seniors with Alzheimer's and dementia. "How are you doing today?"

"Gotta finish this," her mother muttered, most likely to herself and not Tessa. As always, Lily Copeland had paint all over her fingers, a couple of smudges on her cheeks and neck and all over her painting smock. At least she wore her smock now. It had taken months for Tessa and the staff at the home to convince her mother to wear the smock. Otherwise, she got acrylic paint all over her clothes, and it didn't always wash out.

Tessa tucked her motorcycle helmet under her arm and wandered deeper into the bedroom to where her mother stood in front of the window with her canvas. Tessa had pulled a lot of strings and greased a lot of palms to get her mother that room with all the natural daylight coming in. It had more windows than other rooms and faced southwest, so her mother got all the natural light she needed to paint from ten thirty in the morning until sunset.

She no longer needed to brace herself for what was undoubtably going to be on the canvas. A baby in its mother's arms. Sometimes the painting was sweet and serene; other times it made Tessa want to curl up in the corner and cry. Sometimes her mother painted a dead baby.

How did she know the baby was dead?

She just did.

And then the mother would be full of sorrow, crying or sometimes even wailing.

It took her a while to not let those paintings affect her.

It was times like those that she really wished her father was still alive to shed some light on why her mother was so obsessed with painting babies—dead and alive. Had her mother had miscarriages? A stillborn? Did they occur before or after Tessa was born? Was that what had triggered the depression?

These were questions that plagued her thoughts morning, noon and night. Questions she knew she'd probably never get the answers to.

She made sure her mother saw her before she leaned in and pecked her on her cool, papery cheek. "Hi, Momma. I've missed you."

"Needs more blue," her mother murmured, dipping her paintbrush into the indigo and swirling it around the background behind the mother's head.

She let out a small sigh of relief. At least today's painting had both mother and child alive and seemingly happy. That must mean her mother was having a good day.

"I'm sorry I haven't been by all week. It's been ..." She swallowed. "It's been a really awful week, Mom. I wish I could talk to you about it."

Her mother's gaze pivoted to her, and for the first time in a while, it didn't appear as though she were looking through Tessa but actually at her. "You need to talk?"

Was she having a lucid moment?

Eagerly, she nodded and reached for her mother's hand. "I do, Mom. So badly. My life just feels like it's falling apart. Carlyle left me, and he stole Forest. I have no idea how to find either of them. I mean, truth be told, I miss Forest more than I miss Carlyle, because how can I miss a man who would steal somebody's dog?" Her throat grew painfully tight, and the back of her eyes stung with unshed tears.

Her mother's light blue eyes squinted, and her nose wrinkled, which only accentuated the already deepening lines at the corners of her eyes and on her forehead. "Forest ... " she whispered. "Forest ... "

"My dog, Mom. Remember Forest? You used to love him."

"Forest ... " She blinked a few times, then turned back to her painting. "I knew a Forest once. Dreadful boy, always pulled my ponytail in algebra class. My mother said it was because he liked me. I think it's because he was an unmannered fool. If I ever have children—girls in particular—I will teach them that the pulling of ponytails and shoving in line is no way to show affection. That's just perpetuating the ideology that violence is akin to love. And if I have sons, you bet your booty I'll teach them not to pull girls' ponytails."

She swirled the blue-tipped paintbrush into some white and then added highlighting around the baby's head.

Tessa chuckled and wrapped her arm around her mother's shoulder. "You will raise a strong daughter, Mom. Believe me. I love your feminist ways. They certainly rubbed off on Dad."

"Dad?" Her mother's eyes shifted to the side. "Whose Dad?"

"My dad, Mom."

Her mother shook her head and continued painting. "Well, I'm sorry, but I've never met your father before. I'm not married yet, but I will say that there is a very charming man who saved me the last chocolate croissant at the bakery the other day—even though somebody else ordered it before me. I think he works there. Looker. Blond hair, blue eyes, dimples. And boy, is he tall." Her cheeks pinked up, and she got a glassy look in her eyes. "I wonder if he's seeing anybody?"

Tessa smiled. That was her father. He'd worked at his family's bakery on the weekend while going to flight school during the week. It wasn't long after that first meeting that her parents started dating. Her mother was an art teacher at one of the middle schools, her father in flight school training to be a helicopter pilot.

She loved hearing about their courtship. Fairy tales and romance novels could learn a few things from the budding love of Lily Pendergast and Bruno Copeland.

"If you'll excuse me," her mother said, shooting Tessa an almost irritated look, "I really need to finish this before I lose my light."

Right. Because her mother had a million other things to do tomorrow and couldn't finish the painting in the new light of the new day.

Exhaling in defeat, Tessa nodded. "Okay, Mom. It was good to see you." She ran her fingers over the stack of blank canvases leaning against the wall. She counted fifteen. Enough to get her mother through at least a couple of weeks. Lily usually only painted one a day. Leaning in, she kissed her mother on the temple. "Could I have a hug, Mom?"

Her mother was engrossed in her painting and didn't even lift a brow or twitch a lip to acknowledge.

"Mom? Could I have a hug goodbye, please? I promise to come back in a few days." She rested her hand on her mother's shoulder and felt it tense beneath her fingers.

"I don't have any idea who you are. Why would I hug you?" She flinched until Tessa removed her hand from her mother's shoulder. Her mother's body began to tremble, her head to shake, and the paintbrush fell out from between her fingers. "Why are you here? Why are you here? Who are you?" Her voice rose.

"Everything okay in here?" A nurse popped her head around the corner. "Hi, Tessa."

Tessa's bottom lip jiggled, and she crushed her bottom lip between her teeth to keep herself from breaking down. She swallowed and bobbed her head vigorously. "Everything's fine. I just ... overstayed my welcome is all."

"I don't know who this woman is," her mother said, becoming even more distraught. "But she interrupted my painting and now ... " She looked frantically around for her paintbrush, then her eyes pivoted out the window. "And now I've lost my good lighting."

"I'm sorry, Mom. I just ... "

I just wanted to hug you.

It's not your mom, it's the disease talking. It's not your mom, it's the disease talking.

She repeated her mantra over and over again in her head. It was the only way she was able to leave her mother without letting the anger take over.

Red filled her mother's cheeks, and she bunched her fists. "I've lost my light all thanks to this ... woman! This intruder." Then she drew her hands down the canvas and over the wet paint. Scraping her fingers through the image until it was indiscernible and Lily's nails were caked in paint. "It might as well be ruined. You ruined my work. You ruined my painting." Her fiery rage lasered in on Tessa, who had already taken several steps toward the door and the safety of the nurse. "You ruined *me*." She lunged at Tessa, running for her, her arms out, paint-covered fingers looking like they were ready to choke.

Thankfully, Tessa was trained in nonviolent crisis intervention and deflected the attack with her forearm and a quick pivot. The nurse behind her was also quick on her feet and stepped inside, catching Lily before she ran headfirst into the wall.

"Get her out of here!" Tessa's mother screamed. "Get her out!"

Unable to keep the tears from spilling over, Tessa gave the nurse and a screaming Lily a wide berth as she skirted around them and found her exit. She wanted to sprint down the hallway to the parking lot but didn't. She must have looked like one of those ridiculous competitive speed walkers, hips a-swaying, arms swinging.

The whole world seemed to be moving in slow motion. She felt like she was walking in a dream world; a horrific, nightmarish dream world. When she finally reached the front doors, she burst through them and gulped the fresh air like she'd been holding her breath on the entire walk. Her lungs ached, her heart constricted and a pain so intense filled her chest and gut, she wasn't sure she would live through it. Her hands fell to her knees and she hunched over. The need to puke was way too real.

Not every visit with her mother was like this, but when they were, it took a lot out of her. She needed a drink. She needed several drinks.

Have you been to the Rage Room?

Her mystery texter's question came back to her. No, she hadn't been to the Rage Room. But after that fiasco inside with her mother and the terrible week she'd had with Carlyle, Blaire, Forest and that jackass father of Aria's, she needed to smash, destroy and demolish like her life depended on it.

With her chest still heaving, she brought up the directions to the Rage Room on her phone. Only nine minutes by bike. Perfect. And there was a liquor store in that same strip mall. Even better. She'd bash some stuff, grab a bottle—or two—of wine, and then go home to her flannel pajama pants, her empty fridge and her empty apartment and watch how serial killers operated.

Maybe her new friend would be holed up at home on a Saturday night, too. Could she ask him if he liked serial killer documentaries? Was that saying too much about her? Maybe they could watch one "together."

She swung her leg over her bike, kicked up the stand and plopped her helmet on her head, tucking her hair beneath her leather jacket before she zipped it up. Pulling the visor down so she didn't get bugs in her face, she turned the key and let her baby purr for a moment.

If the Rage Room was closed or full, she'd go for a ride into the mountains for a bit, let the throttle out and feel the speed and power beneath her. She needed some kind of outlet. Painting was usually one way of channeling her emotions, but after tonight with her mother, she couldn't bear to even look at a paintbrush.

She taught her clients how to channel their emotions in positive, constructive ways. Using art to convey their feelings, to let out the demons and the pain that they kept bottled up, that ate away at them morning, noon and night.

But tonight, art just wasn't going to cut it for her. She believed in her practice, whole-heartedly. Believed that art could and did change the way our brains processed grief and anger, sadness and confusion. But sometimes a canvas and paintbrush just weren't enough. Sometimes the emotions were too intense; the pain too unbearable. The anger too scalding that if she didn't let it out, didn't embrace it, it would burn her from the inside out.

Tonight, she needed to maim and decimate. She needed to demolish things into tiny pieces until they resembled the last remaining fragments of her heart. Because after this week and seeing her mother just now, she wasn't sure the pieces left were even salvageable.

7

"ANTE UP, boys, I'm dealing tonight," Scott said, grabbing the deck of cards from in front of Atlas with a sly but cheesy grin. "You hog the cards, Atlas. Give someone else a turn." He began to shuffle, his slightly crooked nose looking even more crooked in profile.

Atlas grunted and sipped his bourbon. He liked dealing, and the job usually fell to him. It was just another way of maintaining control. He wasn't much of a gambler—never had been—but poker night at Liam's was more than just ten guys playing cards and taking each other's money. So much more. So that's why he went. For the camaraderie, the support and the break from his children—as much as he loved them.

"How's the therapist working out for Aria?" Zak asked, scrubbing a hand down his rusty beard and pulling on his chin. "You fall in love with Tessa yet?"

What the fuck?

Atlas's head shot up from where he'd been staring at the ice in his glass.

Zak's blue eyes sparkled. "She's pretty, isn't she?"

Atlas grunted and shrugged. "Haven't really looked at her."

It was Zak's turn to snort, and he shook his head as he took a pull off his San Camanez summer wheat ale. "Is that the lie you're telling yourself, then?"

"That's the truth. I'm focused on my kid, dipshit. Now are we going to play fucking cards?" He glanced at the rest of the guys around the table, who were all watching the interaction between him and Zak with keen interest.

"We're all focused on our kids," Aaron said with a touch of snark. "Doesn't mean we can't *also* be focused on our women." Aaron was another redhead, like Zak, and equally beefy and tattooed. Though unlike Zak, who owned a gym and worked out nearly as much as he breathed, Aaron was a former Navy SEAL turned contractor.

"I don't have a *woman*," Atlas retorted. "I'm focused on my kids."

"And how is therapy helping Aria?" Mark asked, defusing the tension around them. "Gabe's been doing therapy since his diagnosis, and then ever since Tori took over his intervention, he's come leaps and bounds. If the kid and therapist are a good fit, it really can work wonders for them."

Scott began to deal out the cards. "Yeah, we thought about sending Freddie to therapy after the divorce, but he adjusted pretty well, all things considered. That's not to say I didn't spend a shit-ton of time in a therapy office myself."

Several of the other men around the table nodded to agree that they too had been in therapy and found it helpful.

Atlas merely grunted.

He'd been forced into therapy and hadn't found it helpful in the least.

"How many sessions has she had?" Mark asked.

"Two." He was still hung up on Zak's question about whether he was in love with Tessa already. What the fuck kind of question was that? Had Zak *fallen in love with her?* Was that why he was asking?

"So not enough to really tell if it's working yet, then," Adam chimed in. "It will though. Aria's a good kid. She's just going through some shit, which is totally understandable." His smile was supportive as he fixed his gaze on Atlas. Mitch, who was sitting next to Adam, made the same face. Mitch was the only other widower in the group. His daughter Jayda was a sweetheart and seemed to have adjusted well to the new woman in her father's life. Who just so happened to be Adam's ex-wife.

Yeah, crazy.

Adam's new partner, Violet (Mitch's sister), was a widow, so once in a while she, Atlas and Mitch would go for coffee. It was usually prompted by one of them who was feeling a little dark—after a memory triggered a new wave of grief, or an anniversary of some kind with their deceased partner was coming up. Having other people in his life who understood his loss and daily struggle was a huge comfort. He needed Violet and Mitch almost as much as he needed the rest of the single dads.

"JoJo has been asking about Aria," Emmett piped up. "Wants to know if they can get together for a playdate."

Emmett's daughter Josie, or "JoJo," was six, but she and Aria got along like a house on fire. All the kids in their little makeshift family got along really well, thankfully. Tia, Mira, Jayda and JoJo—although all older than Aria by at least a few years—didn't treat her like a baby and instead drew her under their protective wings and clucked around her like little mother hens. They had no problem letting her hang out with the "big girls."

Atlas grunted as he nodded. "Maybe Sunday next weekend."

Emmett grinned. "JoJo would love that."

Atlas sniffed, though he didn't actually have to. "I mean, I guess we could do it *any* time, seeing as I've been forced to take a mandatory leave of absence from work." He lifted his head and hit Liam with a gaze he hoped made the man's asshole pucker.

Judging by the look on Liam's face, it had.

Now he had to stop thinking about another man's asshole.

The table was suddenly dead quiet, and wary eyes shifted back and forth between Atlas and Liam.

Liam cleared his throat and chuckled, though it was clearly forced, and the unease on his face made Atlas smile inwardly. "It wasn't mandatory. It was strongly *encouraged.*"

"You said I didn't have a choice," Atlas ground out, collecting all his cards after Scott had dealt everybody in. He fanned them out in his hand. "Sounds pretty *mandatory* to me."

Liam fanned his own cards out in his hand. "And name partner will be there waiting for you when you get back. Look, Jerrika, Rocky and myself are all parents, too. We understand that sometimes you have to take a step back and focus on family; otherwise everything else begins to suffer. We're a *family* law practice. If we didn't put family first, we may as well go into corporate litigation." He snorted a laugh, but the joke was lost on everyone but Atlas, and even he didn't think it was *that* funny.

"How long is this *mandatory leave of absence?*" Mitch asked, scratching the back of his neck, his green eyes probing. "Not indefinitely, if they're holding name partner for you."

"A month or so," Liam said, shrugging. "Just until he gets some rest, gets Aria on track and maybe hires a part-time live-in nanny or something to help with nights if Cecily still won't sleep. It's not forever. And it's not a leave of absence, it's a sabbatical. People take them all the time."

"It's mandatory stress leave," Atlas countered, not bothering to look at Liam.

Liam's face turned incredulous before he polished off his short, stocky tumbler of scotch. "And I thought we were cool because I gave you my McGregor favor. Which, by the way, you never told me what it was for. Those favors are worth more than gold, so I hope you used it wisely."

"None of your goddamn business," Atlas replied.

Liam rolled his eyes and stood up. "God, you're a snarky fuck. I'm getting another drink. Anybody else want one?"

A few heads bobbed, and others shook in dismissal.

"Are we going to play fucking cards or what?" Atlas barked, irritated that he had been the topic of conversation since they all sat down at the table.

"Untwist your G-string," Liam said from behind his leather-top bar. "Just gimme a fucking minute. You guys place your bets."

Fuck, he was in a bad mood now. He'd hoped to keep his stress leave under wraps, at least until he wrapped his own head around not working. And here he'd been the one to go and blurt it out. He thought for sure it would have been Liam and his big mouth. But nope.

Fuck.

"I gotta piss," he murmured, getting up from the table just as Liam came to sit back down. He tossed his chips in the center, grabbed his cell phone that sat next to his bourbon and headed down the concrete-floored hallway toward Liam's bathroom.

He didn't actually have to piss, he just needed something to lift his mood. He brought up his phone, the mystery number and punched in a message.

Apt 204-7890 Ladybird Way. That's where Forest is.

He pissed anyway because he was there and hoped that she was close enough to her phone he wouldn't have to wait long for her response.

Thankfully, he didn't.

OH MY GOD! How did you find this? Thank you! Thank you! I'm literally bawling right now I'm so happy.

His face split into a huge grin, and he opened the bathroom door, texting with his other hand. *PI friend owed me a favor. Use that information wisely. I really hope you're who you say you are and I'm not sending a serial killer to go and finish off his/her last two targets. And if I am, please spare the dog.*

He snickered as he rounded the corner.

Did you see that serial killer documentary too? Spared the pets, even gave them treats and toys but offed the owners.

He had watched that documentary. He'd stayed up way too fucking late finishing it. He texted back. *Made me kind of like the guy, to be honest. I'm a huge dog person, and he was just so kind to all the animals. Didn't like him so much when he beheaded the owners with a chainsaw while they slept though.*

He'd paused in the kitchen and was typing away, his cheeks hurting from smiling. Who'd have thought he would have found another serial killer documentary lover by way of random texting error?

"What the fuck's got you so happy all of a sudden?" Aaron asked, wandering in the kitchen, opening the fridge and grabbing a beer. "Don't think I've ever seen you smile like that before." He popped the cap and tossed it into the trash beneath the sink, taking a long pull on his lager. "Come to think of it, I'm not sure I've ever seen you smile, period."

"Nothing." Atlas grunted as he waited for her to reply.

Aaron shook his head and wiped the back of his wrist over his mouth. "Sure doesn't look like nothing. Iz makes me smile like that too when she messages me." He lumbered back into the dining room, his T-shirt looking like it was about ready to snap off him, it was so fucking tight.

I completely agree about sympathizing with the killer. Honestly, though, I don't know how to thank you for finding their address. I wish I could repay you somehow. But then that would break our code of ... whatever this is. I went to the Rage Room tonight and it helped so much, thank you for the recommendation.

"You coming?" Liam called from the dining room.

Atlas grunted and shot a quick text back to her. *Gotta run. Wanna watch a documentary tonight? We can text about it.*

Then he stowed his phone in his pocket and joined the guys, hoping that when he finally got a chance to check his phone again, she had messaged him back and her answer was a resounding *yes.*

BETWEEN A SUCCESSFUL DEMOLITION session at the Rage Room, taking the long way home on her bike, and the good news from her mystery friend, Tessa was practically floating around her apartment as she poured herself some wine and hunkered down on the couch in her pajamas.

Her new friend had texted her about half an hour ago saying he was just leaving his poker game and was heading home. They planned to start the same documentary at eleven and then text back and forth through it.

Was this a date?

She had no idea.

He was a widower, after all, and she was on the rebound.

Was she on the rebound?

Could you simply decide that you weren't going to *be* "on the rebound"?

Either way, even if she was "on the rebound," it wasn't like she was jumping into bed with this guy. They were going to watch the same serial killer documentary at the same time in their respective living rooms while texting back and forth.

That was her kind of date. Pajamas, wine and a man who liked her taste in television. There was no need to get all gussied up, sit in a restaurant with a bunch of strangers and whisper as they ate overpriced food and egregiously over-priced wine.

Nope. Her ten-dollar special from the liquor store was doing her just fine.

Her phone said it was five minutes to eleven. She bounced on her toes as she cut up cucumbers and bell peppers to munch on. She hadn't been this happy or this excited in far too long. And after the week she'd had—losing Forest, being dumped by Carlyle, being treated like an intruder by her mother, and enduring Aria's jerk of a father—she needed this win more than ever.

Taking her container of veggies and her wine into the living room, she giggled as her phone in her pajama pants pocket buzzed.

Ready? was all it said.

She grinned like an idiot at the screen.

So ready! she texted back, bringing up the documentary on Netflix.

I'm hitting play. Are you hitting play?

She laughed again. This was so stupidly fun. Two grown-ass adults timing things like they were children trying to tape their favorite song off the radio. Kids today would not even know what that meant. *I'm hitting play ... now!*

She hit play and sat back on her couch, munching on a cucumber slice.

They began to text back and forth over the course of the next thirty minutes. Mostly about the show and the serial killer but a bit about their lives as well. They seemed to have an unspoken understanding, though, to not dig too deep or ask questions that were too revealing. Everything remained rather vague. Like she knew he had two kids under four, but she didn't know if they were boys or girls or one of each. And it felt too nosy and prying to ask. He also didn't volunteer.

He also never asked her what she did for a living, and even though she was damn proud of all she'd accomplished career- and education-wise in her thirty-five years, she wasn't ready to play her shrink card. Whether that was an ace in her back pocket or a joker, she didn't know.

Some people got all weird when they found she was a therapist. Or others, like Aria's dad, Mr. Stark, thought she was some hack—at least that's the vibe he was throwing her way. The guy was such a jerk. Too bad he was a hot jerk she'd found herself thinking about more than once over the weekend. Those gray eyes, that smoldering, broody demeanor. Why was she attracted to men who were clearly bad for her? Either enormous jerks like Carlyle, though she didn't know he was a jerk until it was too late, or a grumpy widower like Mr. Stark.

Another text message buzzed on her phone, pulling her from her oh-so-confusing thoughts. *So are you going to go to Carlyle and Blaire's apartment and confront them?*

She'd been thinking hard about that for the last few hours. What was she going to do? She couldn't very well go knock on their door, walk in and just take back her dog. This wasn't *Legally Blonde.*

She didn't want to ask her mystery friend for more legal advice because, clearly, he wasn't keen on giving it to her, but she wished she had somebody to talk this stuff through with.

To be honest, she really wished she could speak with her mystery friend. Hear his voice. He was the only person who knew what she was going through, and he'd been an incredibly big help. Not only uncovering Carlyle's whereabouts, but also just being somebody she could vent to and use as a bit of a sounding board. He didn't know her, know her family or her past, so like a therapist, she was going into this "relationship" with him with a blank slate.

Another text message buzzed. *You still there?*

Oh, right. She sipped her wine and tapped in a response. *Yeah, sorry. I don't know what I'm going to do about Carlyle. Can I just go up to his apartment and demand my dog back?*

The cop on the phone had said that this was matter for family law, and as promised, her mystery texter had sent her a list of five lawyers he highly recommended. She'd called three of them and only came up discouraged, as their fees were financially debilitating. They also said—when she got her free thirty-minute discovery call—that because Forest was considered property in a "committed intimate relationship" that Carlyle had just as much legal right to him as she did. She could end up losing full custody of him if she pursued this and lost.

The thought of losing her dog made every inch of her turn ice cold. But did she have any other option than to fight? No. She didn't have her dog now, but at least she had a shot at getting him back. Not fighting for him would mean she gave up before she even tried. Not fight for him would mean Carlyle and Blaire won without there even being a battle.

And her parents had not raised a quitter. They had not raised a woman who ran in the other direction with her tail between her legs, only to curl up in the nearest corner afraid to stand up for herself and those she loved.

The serial killer documentary wasn't a very good one, and soon her yawns were becoming more frequent. With heavy eyelids, she stared at her phone, waiting for his response, wishing that even just for a moment she could hear his voice and not feel so utterly alone in all of this.

Just a quick thirty-second power nap.

Her eyelids drooped, and the room went dark.

Not even thirty seconds, and she was jolting upright on the couch as her phone began to ring in her hand.

Wide-awake now, she glanced at the number.

Oh my God.

It was him.

Had she sleep-texted him and asked him to call her?

She glanced at their text messages. No, no sleep text of desperation.

The phone was still ringing.

Shit.

She hit the *call* button.

"Hello?"

"Hey."

A tingle raced through her body from her ear to her toes. His voice was deep. Like sexy deep and kind of raspy. Was he a smoker? Or just blessed with the gritty bass of a Hollywood A-lister?

"You there?" Damn, that voice. It also sounded oddly familiar, and yet she couldn't place how it sounded familiar. A throat cleared in her ear. "Hello?"

Crap! She'd been so busy swooning and trying to place her mystery man, she forgot how to have a proper conversation with someone. "Yes, sorry. I'm here. Hi."

"Hi. I hope it's okay that I called you."

"I-it's fine."

It's better than fine.

"This isn't a very good documentary."

"I agree."

"Do you have a picture of Forest?"

All over her house.

But he meant on her phone.

"Hold on," she murmured, pulling her phone away and putting it on speakerphone before she began sifting through her photos. She found a sweet one of her beloved Forest lying on his bed at home, his head cocked to the side, eyes wide. She'd been talking to him and he'd been listening to her intently, adorably tilting his head side to side. She'd snapped a few photos of him acting all cute like that.

Her chest tightened to the point of pain and her heart stuttered. For a brief moment there was this falling, spinning-down feeling as she stared at Forest. Would she ever get him back? She sent the photo to ...

Hmm, could she ask him his name now that they were speaking on the phone and not just texting?

"He's a nice-looking dog," he said.

The lump in her throat swelled. He was a beautiful dog. Unique and wonderful in every way. "Do you have a dog?" Her voice was hoarse from restraining her emotions.

"I don't. I don't have time for a dog what with the kids and work. It would not be fair to the dog. I would love one though." The longing for a furry companion came through in his voice, along with regret at how demanding his life was to not be able to accommodate a pet.

"Um ... What's your name?"

There was silence on the other end.

Oh no! Had she overstepped? Was that going against the rules of ... whatever this was?

No, it couldn't be. There were no "rules" for whatever it was they were doing because they were making up the rules as they went. There was no instruction manual for this bizarre meeting and pseudo friendship they'd started.

"You really want to exchange names?" he asked, his voice sounding even deeper than before.

"Only if you want to. I mean ... Are we friends or ... ?"

"Or?"

"I don't know ... Jeez, if you don't want to tell me your name, then don't." His evasiveness was beginning to piss her off. What was so wrong about telling her his name? She just wanted a name, not his first, middle, last and social security number.

"My name is unique and easily recognizable," he

breathed out. "I'd rather keep that under wraps for a bit longer, if you don't mind?"

She rolled her eyes. But she also understood. They didn't know each other from Adam, and even though she was who she said she was, he might not be who he said he was. Maybe he was a celebrity or a politician and revealing his name could prove detrimental to his career and those around him.

Then why not give a fake name?

"I take it by your quiet that you *do* mind," he said. "Maybe this phone call was a bad idea. We can go back to texting if you'd prefer, or I can leave you alone altogether."

"No!" Damn it. She blurted that out far too loudly. What must he think of her now?

His chuckle rumbled in her ear; her panties were noticeably damp. "Well, I'm glad you want to keep talking to me, because I want to keep talking to you. How about we make a compromise? I'll tell you my middle name, and you tell me yours. We'll go by those names instead? At least for now."

At least for now. What did that mean? Did he want this to turn into something bigger than what it was? Whatever it was.

But the longer she thought about it, the more she didn't mind that idea. It was better than nothing, and after all, would this *thing* ever even amount to *something*? Probably not. Did it matter that she knew his real name? As long as she had something to call him, that's all that mattered.

"You can call me Marie," she said.

"Marie." The way he purred her name made her toes curl in her slippers and heat bloom in her chest. Not too many men had a deep, raspy purr like that. She sipped her wine to soften her suddenly parched tongue. "You can call me David."

"All right ... David. It's nice to finally *meet* you ... kind of."

"Nice to meet you, Marie."

8

Monday morning brought forth a war like Atlas had never seen before. Aria woke up on the most obvious wrong side of the bed, despite the two of them having had a very pleasant Sunday, complete with Mickey Mouse blueberry pancakes for breakfast and several hours at the park.

Maybe she woke up on the wrong side of the bed because she hadn't spent enough time sleeping in that bed and was still tired from their busy Sunday. Or maybe a demon had broken into the house and possessed his child. His money was on the latter, because whatever it was, he did not recognize the little blonde tornado that was screaming and ripping around his house in need of an exorcism. He could not say or do anything right. Everything set her off.

"Good morning, sweetie" was apparently the worst way to greet someone when they awake and trudge sleepy-eyed and pillow-creased out of bed. And never ever should one ask their child if they would like whipped cream on their pancakes because you might as well just tell them there was no Santa Claus. Same freaking thing.

Who was this small human, and where did the angelic,

curly-haired little darling he brought home from the hospital in a butterfly-covered sleeper go?

By the time he pulled up to the office building where Aria's art therapy was held, he could not wait to toss his child at the hippie teacher and her finger paints and scram for an hour. Jenny had Cecily at home, so he planned to go for a run around the park. He hadn't worked out in ages, so he'd probably die two miles in, but he needed the fucking stress release if he had any intention of ever going back to work.

"Daddy?" Aria started after he helped her hop out of her car seat and down onto the road.

"Yes, sweetie?" He took her hand and led her up to the sidewalk, locking his vehicle with his fob in the pocket of his black Sugoi running shorts.

"I don't like Cecily."

He sucked in a big breath through his nose. "Well, sweetie, I hope that changes. She is your cousin, and she's here to stay with us. Maybe you can talk to Tessa about your feelings. Tell her why you don't like Cecily."

"I'm telling you."

Damn, she was smart. "Yes, you are, and you can. You can tell me anything, but you're going to Tessa so that she can help you show your feelings in new ways. Through drawings and painting and things. I wish you did like Cecily, but it's okay if you don't. However, the way you treat her is not kind, and like her or not, we need to show each other kindness."

His child growled as he held the door open for her and she walked beneath his arm into the lobby and toward the elevator. "But she is so loud and she doesn't listen and she always takes you away from me." She stomped her foot before reaching out and pressing the button for the elevator. "I want a whale to come up out from the ocean and carry her away."

Well, at least she didn't wish for the whale to eat Cecily.

At least he could take solace in his daughter not being a sadist and simply a little girl going through typical sibling rivalry and what Adam and Mitch had aptly called "a threenager."

"Where would you like this whale to take Cecily?" he asked, hiding his smirk of mirth as they stepped onto the elevator.

Aria shrugged. "I don't know. Don't care. Maybe ... " She toed at a scuff on the floor. "Hawaii? Jayda and Mira brought me back a shell from Hawaii. Cecily can play with shells there."

Damn, he loved the way kids' brains worked. In no time, they were up and off the elevator and walking down the hallway toward Tessa's studio. It was nearly one o'clock, and he hoped that since he'd just fed Aria a big lunch of PB and J, apple slices, cheese cubes and yogurt, that her full belly would mean a pleasant demeanor. The last thing he needed was to come back after an hour to his daughter either losing her shit again and screaming or, worse, giving Tessa her threenager attitude and sass.

They reached the door and it was open, so Aria released his hand and headed inside, beelining for her drawer of unfinished art.

At first, he didn't see Tessa anywhere in the room and thought maybe she'd stepped out for lunch, but then it was difficult to not see her.

A blonde vision stood in front of the window with the light of the afternoon behind her, illuminating her hair like spun gold. She was standing off in the corner behind an easel, humming softly to herself, eyes focused on what was in front of her.

He was mesmerized. Transfixed.

"Tessa?" Aria called out, having not noticed her therapist when she entered the room. "Where are you?"

Tessa's blue eyes unfocused from the canvas in front of her, and she shook her head, blinking a few times before she peered around the easel at Aria. "Hey, Aria. I'm right here. How's it going?"

Aria nodded without answering, taking her unfinished artwork to the green triangle table.

Atlas wandered into the studio toward the easel, his curiosity drawing him forward before he knew what he was doing. Tessa was rinsing brushes in the sink, and Aria was already fast at work with felts and paper.

The easel was set up right in front of the window along with many others, and although he knew nothing of art or lighting, he could tell that where she was painting probably allowed her the best natural light in the entire room.

Making sure her back was to him, he turned to glance at the canvas.

"Oh my God." Much like his feet had moved him forward involuntarily, the words fled from his mouth before he could stop them. It was ... intriguing and complex. Evocative and thought-provoking. But above all else, it was beautiful.

A brain painted in a melee of colors, more colors than he dared to count, more colors than he knew the names of. There were layers of paint too and then scraped away, along with geometric shapes and color blocks in the background behind the brain. Gold leaf was placed thoughtfully throughout, and straight lines both vertical and horizontal were drawn in the background over everything.

He really had no eye for art—it had never interested him —but this ... this painting did. He wasn't sure he'd go so far as to say it "spoke" to him, but it did evoke thoughts, feelings and emotions from him unlike any other piece of art ever had.

"It's not finished," Tessa said, rushing over to him and the easel. She attempted to turn it away from him, but he reached for her hand and stopped her.

"Don't."

"It's not done," she said insistently, wrenching her hand free of his. She turned the painting away from him. "I don't show anybody my work before it's done. And sometimes not even then. It's private." She turned the easel away from him, a glare in her pretty blue eyes.

"I apologize," he said, stepping back. "It's very nice, though. I've never seen anything like it."

Her eyes thinned into slits, and she slid a side-eye his way. "Thank you?"

He grunted and retreated toward his daughter. "I'm going to go, sweetie, okay? See you in an hour."

Aria barely acknowledged him, only replying with a grunt of her own.

He pecked her on the top of the head and then left the studio, the image of Tessa's eyes and the fire in her glare making him feel all kinds of weird things. He needed to put some space between himself and the attractive therapist.

His nose wrinkled as he paused on the threshold of the office. "What's that smell?" he called back into the room. Tessa was now sitting with Aria, and they were chatting, both of them coloring with smiles on their faces.

"Lemongrass," she said, not lifting her head to look at him. "Too bohemian for you?" Finally, she lifted her gaze to his, the challenge in her eyes visible from across the room.

He shook his head and grunted. "No." Then he left.

The woman rattled him, frustrated him and intrigued him to no end.

When he hit the pavement outside the office, he grabbed his earbuds from his pocket, shoved them in his ears and tuned his phone to a radio station that played good running music. Then he set off at a steady lope toward the park half a mile away. If he ran hard enough, fast enough, maybe, just maybe he could shake the pull that Tessa had on him. Not to mention the pull of *Marie*.

What the hell had possessed him to call her?

Because you wanted to hear her voice.

He had. He'd wanted to hear her voice terribly and was calling her before he could think twice, think smart and stop himself. Though he was awfully glad he had called her. They'd ended up talking for nearly an hour. About this, that and everything, but always keeping the topics fairly superficial and innocuous, like books, movies, food and other harmless things. She hadn't probed him about himself at all, and he hadn't asked anything about her either. Not that he wasn't dead curious, but if he asked, then that gave her the right to ask him, and he just wasn't ready for that.

He wasn't ready for what he was doing or what he was feeling for either woman, and yet there he was, having the feelings. And not just about one woman, but *two*. What the hell had he gotten himself into?

He entered the park and ran hard along the woodchip trail, the music thumping in his ears and the thoughts rattling around his brain like marbles in a jar. Thoughts about Tessa, thoughts about Marie. Though the fact that he was lusting after two different women meant his jar was obviously short a few marbles. He had no time to date. He had no time for a relationship. He shouldn't be having these feeling about anybody, let alone one woman he'd never met and the other his daughter's therapist. His days of loving someone besides his children were over. Samantha had been the one. The only. Never could he love another the way he loved her. Never could he feel for another woman the things he felt for her.

And yet, for the past week, he'd been unable to get either

woman off of his mind. They were both so different and yet equally intriguing, equally beguiling.

For a while he was able to push the thoughts of both women out of his head and just focus on his running. It felt good to exhaust his muscles again. It'd been far too long since he'd gone for a good jog, and the sweat was pouring off his forehead by the time he turned around and headed back toward the professional building. His light gray shirt would undoubtedly be dark gray by the time he picked up Aria, but he'd damn near bathed in deodorant before he left, so hopefully he didn't Pepé le Pew his way down the hall.

Maybe he needed to just cold-turkey stop talking to Marie? He'd given her some lawyer recommendations, and she said that if Carlyle wasn't agreeable when she went to see him Monday, then she'd call back one of the lawyers she received a free discovery call from.

That left Tessa.

Beautiful, sweet, motorcycle-riding Tessa. He hardly knew her, but she'd already burrowed beneath his skin and occupied far too many of his thoughts. The way she'd stood up to him when he was an assuming jackass and made it sound like she was a hippie who shouldn't be riding a motorcycle was surprising. She was totally right, and although he hadn't had the balls to admit it or say more than his token grunt and few words, he was impressed with her confidence. And totally impressed—and turned on—that she rode a crotch rocket.

He *had* judged her as some hippie-dippie whacko hack who wore bangles and skirts, burned patchouli and probably danced under the full moon in neon body paint to appease the sun gods. But even if she did do all those things, she was no hippie-dippie whacko hack. He'd been wrong to judge her so quickly.

With his chest heaving and music blaring in his ears, he yanked open the office building door and headed for the stairs. No sense stinking up the elevator if he was gross. He was at the studio door in no time. He turned the music off on his phone and removed his earbuds, only to hear a different kind of music playing from a small but powerful speaker box on the table. Aria was standing on the short stage, wearing a tie around her neck, an oversize suit blazer, and she was carrying a briefcase.

"I'm Daddy, and I have to go to work. Not now, Aria. I don't have time. Be good to Cecily and Jenny. I love you." Then she pretended to walk away, stomping loudly.

His heart stopped along with his feet, and he stepped back toward the door to hide from view but continue to watch.

Tessa was sitting on the stage "playing" with dolls.

"I'm home!" Aria announced.

"Hi, Daddy," Tessa said. "Come play with me."

"Not now, Aria. I no have time for you. I never have time for you. Work and Cecily are all I have time for." Aria frowned, pulled off the tie, tossed it to the floor, followed by the blazer and briefcase. "I have work. Lots of work. I'm so tired. Aria, don't throw broccoli at Cecily. Go to your room." She stomped her foot and pointed her finger in a random direction, glaring at Tessa, who hadn't actually said much and just continued to pretend-play with the dolls. He could tell from her posture, though, that she wasn't the least bit relaxed. This was a job to her, and Atlas's daughter was revealing a whole hell of a lot at the moment.

"But Daddy, I miss you," Tessa said in a soft voice, nothing like Aria's whiny voice, which is what he would have heard if Aria had actually said it.

"No time," Aria barked. "Go see Jenny. Go see Kimmy. You have no Mommy. Your mommy died, and I have no time for you."

It was as if his daughter herself had stabbed him in the

heart with a steak knife. He stumbled back against the door-jamb, his gut churning, his chest once again heaving.

Aria was hurting more than he even knew. More than he could heal on his own. He felt helpless and like a complete fucking failure.

Rather than stepping up and becoming mother and father after Samantha had died, he was barely being her father. Hardly present, never there when she needed him.

"Daddy?"

The gentle music in the room died, and the sound of footsteps filled his ears. But his vision was blurry, and he took a moment to shake his head and clear his thoughts, though it did nothing for the gut-wrenching feeling inside of him that he had failed his daughter and disappointed his dead wife.

"I'm sorry," Tessa said, approaching him. She wasn't wearing any shoes and had cute little rings on a toe of each foot. "You weren't supposed to see that."

Then why had he? The door was open, and they were already five minutes over time. Had she meant for him to see that? Or was it the universe giving him a dose of reality by slapping him in the face with a wet washcloth?

"We were just role-playing. It's a great way to get the children to open up and explore their feelings. Aria grew tired of coloring and wasn't interested in painting, sculpting or mixed media. She saw the dress-up clothes and asked if we could play house."

His house, obviously.

"Hi, Daddy," Aria said, sidling up next to him and wrapping her arm around his leg, but she pulled away almost instantly. "You're all wet. Gross."

His smile was thin and forced. "Sorry, sweetie. I just went for a run, and I'm all sweaty. It's a warm one out there."

He glanced up at Tessa, and what met him was a heated stare that made part of his body jump and tingle. Her nostrils flared and ... oh damn, that pink tongue slid out just barely and ran the seam of her plump, red lips. Jesus fucking Christ.

"Ready?" he asked, running his hand down the back of Aria's head.

She nodded.

"I was thinking we could go and grab ice cream, just you and me. Cecily is at home with Jenny, so we have some time before dinner. What do you think?"

His daughter's beautiful hazel eyes opened wide. "But I never have dessert before dinner. Jenny says it ruins my tummy for good food."

"Just this once as a treat will be okay." He tried to smile wider, but he was still processing all that he'd walked in on and was having a hard time not beating his failing ass to a pulp. "Besides, I'm the Dad, remember?"

"And you're the boss," she said, adding a big, fat eye roll. "I remember."

Tessa's throaty chuckle drew his attention away from Aria. He felt like he'd heard that laugh before. But where? "We had a good session. As always, I typically try to summarize my sessions in threes and then send a report to the parents via email. So I will compile my notes from the last three sessions and send you a copy tonight."

He nodded. "She still have to come?"

Her cornflower-blue eyes held a glimmer of impatience, but she stowed it, letting her smile take over her face. "I would recommend it, Mr. Stark. Particularly after today's little breakthrough."

"Atlas," he grunted. "You can call me Atlas."

"Atlas."

He nodded. They needed to leave. The woman in front of him and all that he'd watched on that stage were seriously fucking with his head. He needed to process. He also needed to fix his relationship with his daughter. Maybe this mandatory sabbatical was a good thing. He had time to repair what he'd inadvertently broken with Aria before it was too late.

"We need to go," he said, turning back to Aria. "Ready?"

His daughter nodded. "I want two flavors. Can I, Daddy?"

"Bye, Aria," Tessa said, turning to head back toward her canvas, undoubtably to make the most of the remaining natural light coming in from the windows.

"Bye, Tessa!" Aria called back.

Atlas nodded in Tessa's direction, then led his daughter down the hallway. "Do you think they'll have your favorite flavor?" she asked. "Citrus cooler."

He shrugged, letting her press the button for the elevator. "Hard to say, but probably not. Haven't been able to find it in years."

"Well, if they have it, I want one scoop of that and one scoop of cookies and cream."

He smiled as they stepped into the elevator. "That was your mom's favorite flavor."

9

ATLAS in a wet gray T-shirt and running shorts. Yes, please.

Tessa fanned herself with a magazine as she stood at the window of her studio and watched Atlas and Aria on the sidewalk below. The ice cream shop was only a few doors down from the office building, and although she never ate ice cream anymore, she did enjoy reading and fantasizing about their monthly flavor specials, which they advertised on a sandwich board outside.

This month: salted caramel pretzel ice cream. Yum.

Could she go in there and ask if they could specially make an ice cream flavor? If she found the ingredients and flavor profile of citrus cooler online, maybe she could custom order a flavor as a thank you for *David*.

They'd spoken for nearly an hour last night, and she'd gone to bed with a big smile on her face and dreamt nothing but good dreams. A first for her in quite a while.

Her session with Aria had been incredible, but she felt bad that Atlas had walked in when he did. Though, in the end, it probably benefited him seeing his daughter act out how she sees him on a daily basis. Too busy for her.

And, of course, he had to come in looking like a sweaty popsicle, and she wanted to lick every drip. He hadn't even smelled bad. Maybe it was a mix of his natural manly smell, sweat and his deodorant, but she'd found it more appealing than anything. Not to mention the way his damp T-shirt clung to his frame, defining every ridge of muscle, particularly around his arms and the planes of his stomach.

She'd been unable to stop herself and licked her lips at the thought of taking care of that delicious-looking bead of sweat on his upper lip. She bet it tasted delicious.

"Down, girl," she murmured to herself when Aria and Atlas were no longer in view. She turned back to her painting, the one he had admired, even though it wasn't finished. She had another hour before she knew that Carlyle and Blaire would be home, then she was going to their apartment to confront them and, hopefully, oh God, hopefully, finally get her beloved Forest back.

In the meantime, she had an hour to work on her painting. It was almost done anyway. In addition to being one of her passions, art helped her clear her mind and focus on what she needed to do. And right now, she needed to figure out exactly how she was going to handle seeing Carlyle and *Blaire* the witch. She couldn't expect them to just hand Forest over, otherwise they wouldn't have taken him so deviously in the first place. But she had to try. She had to let them know that she'd found them and she wouldn't leave them alone until she got Forest back.

Grabbing her paint palette and a fresh bouquet of brushes, she angled the easel toward the beam of late-afternoon sunlight coming in through the window and started to paint.

Her PhD defense was scheduled for exactly five weeks from today, and although she felt adequately prepared, she knew that as the days and weeks drew closer to D-Day, as she called it, her stress level would begin to rise. The same way it had when she defended for her master's degree. She'd been a total ball of nerves, with sweaty-pit stains, a roiling gut and a fat tongue that refused to cooperate. Or at least, that's how she felt.

Her supervisor said she made it through her defense with flying colors and he couldn't have been prouder. Here's hoping she had Forest back by then and Carlyle was out of her life for good, otherwise she'd have more than just nerves to contend with when she defended her dissertation.

She was just finishing up on the highlights around the frontal lobe when her phone vibrated and dinged on the window ledge.

You going to confront Carlyle today? It was David.

She grinned at his message as she typed back her own reply. *That's the plan. Just finishing up at work, then I'm going to head over. How was your day?*

They hadn't asked each other how their days had been before, and she hoped she wasn't breaking any unforged rule.

Day was good. Just hanging out with my kid after a workout. How was your day?

Swoon. A devoted father and a man who took care of his body. Was there anything sexier? Maybe that devoted father working out while wearing his child in one of those carrier things. Yeah, that might be sexier.

She texted back, leaving a paint smudge on her screen. *Day was good. Had my last client and she did great. Mentally preparing to face the Blaire witch and her project though. Need to psych myself up like an MMA fighter heading into a title match.*

She finished her painting, then headed over to the sink to wash her brushes, her phone now in the back pocket of her red denim capris. He still hadn't asked what she did for work. Maybe he didn't want to know, maybe he didn't care.

Or maybe he's actually a serial killer and thinks you might be a cop, so by not finding out you're a cop, he's slowly gaining your trust only to inevitably peel off your face and wear it as a mask.

Wow, that went dark fast. No more serial killer documentaries right before bed. They made her hypotheticals get creepy and morbid.

Her phone chirped in her back pocket as she dried her hands and set her paint brushes in an old pickle jar on the windowsill to dry. *This is the fight for the championship belt. But I have faith that you will kick some serious ass. If not, call one of the lawyers I recommended. They'll help you get your Forest back.*

The time on her phone said it was nearly six. She felt like she was going to be sick.

You got this, his subsequent text message said. *Let me know how it goes.*

She replied with a simple *Thanks. Will do.* then grabbed her keys, her cardigan and her purse and headed for the door. She would have loved to ride her bike to work. It was a hot, beautiful day, but she had to err on the side of hopefulness and have room for Forest to accompany her home. She'd thought about getting her buddy a sidecar for her bike, but he was a bit of a chicken and didn't even like sitting in the front seat of her car, let alone a little metal pod on the side of a crotch rocket with the wind in his face.

She was on the road in no time, weaving through downtown Seattle rush-hour traffic. It would take at least thirty minutes to get to Greenwood and through all the lights. That gave her time to gather her wits, her cojones and her courage, because she would need every single ounce of it all if she was going to get her dog back.

"CARLYLE!" Tessa hammered on the door to his apartment unit again. She saw his car in the parking lot out front, and the hood was still warm, so he'd only just arrived home. She pressed her ear to the door, and the sound of muffled voices and shuffling told her the place was not empty. "Carlyle! I know you're in there. I can hear you. Open up. Give me back my dog!"

A dog's whimper and four paws struggling to gain traction on a hardwood floor drowned out the murmurs of conversation. Then she heard his nose sniffling at the door and his whines of desperation.

The strings of her heart tightened to the point of agony. Her baby was just on the other side of that door.

"Carlyle!" She was now pounding continuously on the door with both fists. "I know you're in there. I can hear Forest. Forest, buddy. Are you in there? It's Momma."

Like she knew it would, that caused Forest to go berserk on the other side. He was now jumping up and dragging his nails down the door, barking. His tail thwacked the wall with a heavy *thump thump,* and his whimpers of need to see her picked up fervor.

Footsteps and grumblings competed with Forest's excitement. "Don't scratch the door," came a woman's voice. "Get back. Get back." Her voice was mean and scolding. If Tessa didn't already hate this woman, she now certainly did for how she was speaking to her perfect Forest.

The door handle jiggled, and the sound of a deadbolt being flicked was like a gong going off in the quiet, empty hallway. The door opened just a crack, and brown eyes peered out. "What do you want?"

Well that was the dumbest question ever. She'd announced it to the entire apartment building at least twice. "I want my dog back," Tessa said plainly.

The woman yawned an obvious fake yawn. "I was sleeping. I have no idea what you're talking about. This is my dog." She made to close the door again, but Forest was no shih tzu, and he managed to wedge his big body between Blaire and door, shoving the door open and launching his fury, wiggling frame at Tessa. She was unable to keep her balance and, laughing, found herself on the floor with Forest's nose all over her face, following by rough licks to her hands and cheeks. He was stepping all over her, his entire body jostling as his tail wagged with intensity.

"Your dog, huh?" she said, scratching behind Forest's ears and taking him under her arm to calm him a bit. Like the good boy that he was, he settled right down on his bottom beside her, his tongue lolling out of his mouth, a big smile on his black lips.

Blaire sniffed. "He's like that with everyone." Wow, she really wasn't going to give up this pathetic ruse, was she? Ridiculous.

"Where's Carlyle?" She had no time for this bullshit or this home-wrecker. As far as she was concerned, Blaire was a nobody and Tessa wanted nothing to do with her. She just needed to deal with her asshole ex and get her dog back.

"He's ... out." Her eyes shifted sideways back into the apartment at the same time a toilet inside flushed.

"Out, huh? Out of the bathroom, I'm assuming you meant. Carlyle? Get your ass out here. I've come for my dog." She stood up, and Forest stood with her, remaining at her side and heeling like the four-legged angel that he was. He'd come to her a timid rescue, and with patience and love, she'd molded him into her ideal, obedient companion. There wasn't anything Forest wouldn't do for her or her for him. She would fight Blaire and Carlyle to the death if she had to.

As if he had all the time in the world, Carlyle sauntered around the corner, looking every bit the blond, blue-eyed frat boy he'd always been. How had she not seen him for the douchebag he was before now? He was beyond a pretty boy; he was a conceited, plastic, vacuous excuse for a human being. "Tessa," he said smoothly, his lips far too red to be natural. "Didn't Blaire tell you that I would be in touch when I was ready?"

"And didn't you know that the world doesn't revolve around you, *Carl?*" She tossed her shoulders back and her breasts out, squaring off with both of them.

Carlyle's eye twitched. He absolutely hated it when anybody called him *Carl*. Which was precisely why she did it.

His lips curled into a sneer. "You always were a bitch."

"Was I?" She wasn't playing into his insults. She didn't care about him or his witch with obvious implants, lip injections and gray-blonde-platinum-dyed hair. She just wanted her dog back. "Whether you think I was a bitch or not is irrelevant at this point. You proved who the true monster was in the relationship when you left me the way you did. Taking my dog. Not even having the decency to end our engagement, our *five*-year relationship to my face." She shrugged, hoping her body language told them she already knew she was so much better off without him. "I am here to make an exchange. Your comic books and records for Forest. I want my dog."

Blaire's dark eyeliner covered eyes slid sideways toward Carlyle and his toward hers. They both smiled slyly.

"He's actually *not* just your dog. He's considered joint property because in the eyes of the law we were married, given how long we lived together. My name is on his registration too. I am just as much his owner as you are. He's like a couch, not a child."

Heat flooded every cell in her body, and she speared him with a glare she hoped punctured that shriveled organ he called a heart. "He doesn't even like you."

Carlyle's eyes rolled, and she wanted to smack the smirk off his face. "Blaire here is a first-year law student. She knows things."

Oh, she bet Blaire knew things, like how to suck the chrome off a bumper.

With gritted teeth, she exhaled through her nose and swallowed down the lump of ire building in her throat. "Even so, he's *half* mine. I want him back."

Carlyle rolled his eyes again and leaned against the door, crossing his ankles, appearing bored. He glanced at Blaire and she nodded, leaving them and wandering back into the apartment.

"Look, Tess," Carlyle started. "You're too busy with work and school to take care of a dog anyway. Blaire is a student, and yeah, she works a lot and is studying a lot, but she's also here studying. And I've been working from home a bit as I wait to hear back about that new job. He's just happier here. Don't be selfish."

Selfish?

Selfish!

Sputtering, she took a step back. Forest went with her. "Selfish?" Her voice was squeaky high. "He's *my* dog. I take him to work with me every single day. I walk him on my lunch breaks. I walk him after work. I gave that dog more of my precious free time than you ever did, and he loved me a million times more than you for it. He is never not by my side. How is that *too* busy?"

"I've called the police," Blaire said blandly, coming back around the corner, her phone in her hand. "You're harassing us. You also let yourself into our building without an invitation, so technically you're trespassing on private property. If you want the dog back, file a claim or obtain a lawyer. But you're not leaving here with him today. You do, and I'll have you arrested for theft, trespassing and harassment."

Holy shit. This was not how she saw this going at all. Yes, she had let herself into their building unannounced and without invitation, but with good reason. And it wasn't like she broke in. She'd followed somebody else—likely a resident—because she figured if she buzzed Carlyle and Blaire, they wouldn't let her up. But she honestly didn't see them calling the cops on her.

Boiling with a fury she couldn't unleash, she ground her teeth and clenched her jaw so tightly it hurt. "I'm taking my dog." She would not cry. She would not cry. Emotion clawed at her throat, and her eyes burned with tears demanding to be shed. She couldn't let them see her break. It was two against one. She had to hold her own, stand her ground. She was fighting for Forest, fighting for the last soul alive that remembered her and loved her.

Her fingers tightened around his collar.

Carlyle made a noise in his throat, and Blaire stepped forward, gripping Forest's collar and tugging. "Let go."

Tessa jerked Forest toward her. "He's mine."

Forest began growl, and he snarled at Blaire. She released his collar, and he snapped at her. The hair on his back had lifted, his posture changed and he bared his teeth. "If he bites me, I'll have him put down," she said, triumph filling her eyes. "Let go of him."

Forest's growl was deep in his chest. His head dipped low, his body in the pouncing stance. Realizing that she'd been defeated by Blaire witch and her empathy-free frat boy project, she sank back to her knees and shifted her body in front of Forest. His transformation was instant. His tongued lolled back out of his mouth, and his soulful, light-brown eyes turned soft. She pressed her forehead to his. "I'll get you back, buddy. I promise. Just hang tight and don't bite anybody, okay? Be a good boy. Play nice, and we'll be together again soon."

A hot tear sprinted down her cheek, but before she could wipe it up, Forest licked it off for her, his front paw tapping her thigh repeatedly. He knew she was upset. He'd always been so in tune with her emotions. He began to whimper.

"It's okay, Forest. You be a good boy." She stood up and ruffled the fur on the top of his head before turning back to face Blaire and Carlyle. "You two make me sick, you know that?"

Blaire glanced behind them into the apartment. "Cop car just pulled up outside."

Holy crap, the bitch hadn't been bluffing.

Blaire's phone began to ring in her hand. She answered it. "Hello?"

She put it on speaker.

"Seattle PD. We had a call about a domestic disturbance in your unit?"

"Yes, officer. Come right up. She's right here." Blaire looked like a cat who'd just finished another cat's entire bowl of cream, and she didn't give a flying fuck about it.

Tessa's free hand fell to her chest. The rage and pain inside her was nearly too much to bear. She didn't want to leave Forest, not now. Not after finally seeing him again. But she also didn't want to make her chances of getting him back any worse.

Heavy footsteps on the stairs to the right of her echoed through the building. Seconds later, the door swung open, and two tall, handsome, wide-shouldered policemen stepped into the hall.

They both glanced at all of them, and a single eyebrow on each of their foreheads lifted.

"What seems to be the problem?" the redheaded one asked.

Tessa swallowed. "I'm going." Her chin trembled, and she rolled her lips inward to keep them herself from tearing up. She would not let them see her cry.

"Please escort her outside," Blaire said. "She entered the

property uninvited." She stepped forward and reached for Forest's collar again, wrapping pointy, black fake nails around it and tugging his reluctant bulk forward.

Her dog knew how to throw on the brakes when he wanted do, and he was pulling the E-brake this time.

"Looks like he doesn't want to go inside," the bald officer commented. "Whose dog is he?"

"Mine!" Tessa practically yelled. "He's mine."

"He's *ours*," Carlyle said, his tone that of a parent correcting the pronunciation of their child. "We've recently split, and I have the dog, and she refuses to accept that. Her text messages, emails and voicemails have been harassment enough, and now she shows up at my home and harasses me and my girlfriend here." He shook his head. "Really, officers, it's getting to be too much. I just want to live in peace with my dog, start my life over with someone new, without having my past constantly harassing me."

Tessa thought she might puke.

The cops eyed her warily.

"Is that true, ma'am?" the redhead asked. His badge said I. Fox.

"I—I ...I'm going." She hung her head and turned her face to hide the flood of tears. She was down the stairs and out of the lobby as fast as her legs could carry her. She knew at least one of the cops was behind her, but she didn't care. She'd never been so humiliated or felt so defeated and powerless in all her life.

The heat of the sun on her back disappeared, and a big shadow appeared on the concrete in front of her. "How much of that was true?"

She turned around to find the redheaded cop standing behind her. The other one must still be in the apartment getting Blaire and Carlyle's outrageously inaccurate take on the whole situation. His hands rested on his hips, his eyes curious but not harsh. He was probably her age or a bit older, fit, tanned and handsome as hell.

"Want to tell us what really happened?" he asked, his tone encouraging and friendly.

She nodded and sniffled, wiping the back of her wrist beneath her nose. "How much time do you have?"

"WELL, THAT FUCKING SUCKS," Officer Fox said, shaking his head and letting out a breath between his nice lips. "Couple of real pieces of work up there." His blue eyes shifted toward the sundeck of Blaire and Carlyle's apartment. All the blinds were drawn, but she suspected somewhere at least one of them was spying on her and the cops.

"And you've filed a claim or obtained a lawyer?" the bald officer asked, having joined them halfway through her explanation. His name badge said F. Webster.

She shook her head. "Not yet. But I've been given a few recommendations and done a few discovery calls. They're a bit out of my price range though."

Both officers pursed their lips and hummed.

"There isn't really anything we can do," Officer Fox said grimly. "It is a civil issue to be dealt with by the court. Unfortunately, Forest is property. Though, I'm like you, my dog is more like a kid, more like family than a couch."

"I wasn't harassing them," she said, feeling the need to reexplain herself and her case again.

"We know," Officer Fox said, resting a big, meaty palm on her shoulder for a second. "We see that now. But we were called out and had to investigate. I wish now we could have grabbed the dog for you, strong-armed them a bit." He shook his head. "Not that we do that or anything." The corner of his mouth lifted into a crooked smile.

"I appreciate that. But Blaire is a first-year law student, so you know, she obviously knows *everything* about the law. Probably more than you guys and every judge on the Supreme Court." She rolled her eyes.

"Yeah, I definitely got a brainiac vibe from that one," Officer Webster said, chuckling. "You going to be okay?"

Tessa breathed out a long sigh. "No, but I'll muddle through. Might need to hit the Rage Room on my way home."

Both cops laughed.

"We love that place. Luna and Sarah are the best. The last Wednesday night of the month, they give all first responders a fifty-percent discount." Officer Fox's smile was big and toothy.

"I've already used up like four of her ten punch passes," Officer Webster said the evening sun glinting off his shiny hairless head. "And I don't even consider myself that angry of a guy. I really just love smashing shit."

Tessa laughed. She was glad the cops were on her side now. Even though they couldn't do anything to help her get Forest back, it was nice to talk it all out with somebody and know that they had her back—as long as she stayed within the confines of the law.

"Tell Luna Isaac and Finn say *hi* if you see her," Officer Fox said, the two of them heading back toward their patrol car. "And Tessa ... "

"Yeah?"

"We really hope you get Forest back and those two assholes upstairs get like crabs or something."

"May the fleas of a thousand camels infest the crotches of the persons who steal your dog," she said, heading down the sidewalk toward her car.

Both cops chuckled.

"I like that," Officer Webster said before he opened his car door. "Take care, Tessa."

She thanked them both and then swung behind the wheel of her car.

Now what?

Now? Now you need to head to the Rage Room, kick the shit out of a bunch of stuff and figure out how you're going to get Forest back. Starting with calling one of those lawyers David recommended.

The lump in her throat felt more like a sticky wad of peanut butter. But she did her best to swallow it down, turned the ignition and pulled out into traffic. There was no use wallowing in her grief or self-pity. That didn't do anybody any good. Forest needed her, and she needed him. Now all she had to do was come up with a way to get him back.

She'd call David tonight. Maybe between the two of them, they could figure something out. Two heads were better than one, even if she'd never met David or seen his head.

10

ATLAS'S HAND SHOT OUT, and he grabbed Cecily's foot as she tried to crawl away from him, still naked and damp from her bath. "Get back here, you little beast," he said, dragging a giggling baby across the soft carpet in her room. Her arms and legs flew out from under her, and he hauled her back in front of him and spun her to her back. "You need a diaper before you start wandering around. We can't have another carpet puddle like last week."

It was Tuesday evening, and he'd just finished bathing the girls. Separately, of course, because Aria still wanted nothing to do with Cecily, and God forbid he bathe the girls together. His daughter might drown her cousin. He'd asked Aria to go and pick out her pajamas in her room while he dressed Cecily in hers, but his daughter had been gone an inordinate amount of time and been awfully quiet while gone.

Securing Cecily's diaper, then tucking her into a light cotton, footless sleeper with little pink and green turtles on it, he scooped the smiling baby up into his arms and went off in search of his mischievous threenager.

"Aria?" he called, heading down the hallway from Cecily's room toward Aria's. "Aria, honey, I thought you were going to grab your pajamas and then come back so I could help you get them on. Where are you?" He poked his head into her room, but she was nowhere to be found. A tickle of dread began to itch behind his ears and at the base of his skull.

They didn't say a quiet toddler was a dangerous toddler for no reason.

"Aria! Where are you?" He and Cecily continued on into the kitchen. He swatted Cecily's hand away gently as she tried to shove a little finger up his nose. "No, baby. No. Aria?" Rounding the corner, he had to tighten his grip on Cecily. Otherwise, he would have dropped her.

Holy mother of fucking hell.

There stood his three-and-a-half-year-old on a kitchen chair, naked and covered in black, blue and red Sharpie marker. Arms, legs, chest, belly, face. Covered.

"Aria!" He had to set Cecily down on the floor, otherwise he might keel over and take the baby with him. "What are you doing?"

"What Tessa told me to do. Using art to show my feelings. And I do *not* feel like wearing pajamas. I'm too hot. So I drew them on." Her hazel eyes shone proudly, and her smile—through the Sharpie on her face—was big and triumphant.

What Tessa told me to do.

Shaking his head and bunching his fists, he approached his toddler slowly. He needed to remain calm. He didn't want to lose his child, didn't want her to think he had no time for her, but holy fucking fuck.

Sharpie.

Goddamn permanent fucking marker.

She knew better. She damn well knew better. There was a reason he kept the fucking permanent markers way up on the kitchen counter in a mason jar with the rest of the pens and pencils. So short-ass people with not fully developed frontal lobes and cognitive reasoning couldn't get their jammy hands on them. Fuck. Now what was he supposed to do? Scrub his child raw until the layer of skin coated in permanent ink sloughed off?

He felt like screaming. Yelling and hammering his fists into something. But he couldn't, not in front of the kids. Not in front of his already emotionally damaged Aria, who didn't think he had any time for her anymore.

Fuck.

Fuck.

FUCK!

"Aria ... " he started softly, taking the black pen away from her. "You know better than to touch these markers. These markers don't come off with soap and water. You know that. We've had this talk before." With his hands under her arms, he helped her off the chair. She looked like a mess.

"I know. But now I'll always have pajamas on. Even under my clothes." Her eyes lasered in on Cecily, who was sitting contently on the kitchen floor, gnawing on ... oh fuck. But Aria got there before he did, and she snatched the small plastic toy out of Cecily's hand and then whacked her over the head with it.

"No, baby. My train."

It was a little magnetised train piece, meant for a wooden train track, and no bigger than a harmonica, but it could have been a bag of feathers his child wielded and it wouldn't have mattered. Aria had once again, gone after Cecily with the intention of hurting her.

And of course, because she was still a baby, Cecily started to cry.

"My toy, baby. You know that. My toy!" Aria screamed, stomping her foot.

"Aria Elaina, get to your room," Atlas demanded, raising

his voice to authoritative father level. "We do not hit in this house."

Aria let out a wail and stomped her foot again. "I hate her!" She took off down the hallway and slammed her bedroom door, continuing to scream on the other side.

Atlas scooped up a bawling Cecily into his arms and kissed her forehead, cradling her against his chest. "It's okay, sweetheart. You did nothing wrong. It's okay. You're a good baby. You're a good girl." He kissed her again, rubbing her back and whispering shushing sounds to calm her. Luckily, unlike his volatile threenager, Cecily was easy to settle and calmed down within a minute. Big, fat tears rolled down her round rosy cheeks, and her long lashes were spiked as she blinked curiously at him. He checked out where Aria had hit her, and sure enough there was a small bump. Poor kid didn't have a ton of hair to begin with. That lump was going to show.

Shit. When it rained, it fucking poured.

Aria was now crying in her room, but he was too upset with her to go and even look at her, let alone try and reason with her to scrub off the Sharpie. He grabbed his phone from his back pocket and brought up Kimmy's number. Maybe the babysitter knew how to get Sharpie off a toddler? At least he fucking hoped she did.

STILL FUMING MAD, with nowhere else to think of to go, Atlas climbed out of his Land Cruiser and hit the fob to lock it. Her website said she worked late on Tuesdays, until nine. It was eight-fifty, so unless she'd gone home early, she should be there. Walking toward the front door, he spotted her Ducati in the motorcycle parking spot. She was still there.

He didn't know why the hell he'd driven all the way downtown, but he just knew this was where he had to be. She was the reason his child was acting this way. She was the reason his daughter had taken a fucking Sharpie to her skin and drawn on a pair of goddamn long-sleeved pajamas. Her and her *art therapy*. Showing her feelings through art. Fucking bullshit. Fuck-ing BULLSHIT!

He took the stairs two at a time and was down the hallway, heading toward her studio in record time, his anger fueling him. His heart hammered in his chest when he reached her door. It was closed, but he heard music playing softly on the other side. There were no voices, only a gentle humming.

He knocked—well, more like *pounded* vigorously on the door, his leg jiggling and his foot tapping as he waited for her to open it.

Footsteps approached on the other side, and the door swung open. Her blue eyes flashed open in surprise. "Atlas!"

He pushed inside. "You!"

She took a step back, worry and perhaps even a touch of fear on her face. "Me? Me what?" She was wearing one of those long, flowy skirt things again that made her look like some leader of a commune. She said she didn't wear those when she rode her bike. What the fuck? "What are you doing here, Atlas?" The fear in her eyes was already gone, replaced with an irritation he felt tenfold in his own heart.

"My kid covered herself head to fucking toe in Sharpie tonight because you told her to." He pointed his finger in her direction. "Fucking Sharpie."

"I most certainly did *not* tell Aria to cover herself in Sharpie." She tilted her head like she was studying him, her nose wrinkling when she squinted, continuing to watch him like he was some caged animal at the zoo. He refused to look away and threw a glare right back at her. She didn't avert her gaze either. In fact, she stared back at him for so long, it almost felt like a challenge.

Fuck this shit. He wasn't done letting this whack job have a piece of his mind.

"You told her to show her feelings through art. And she wasn't feeling like wearing pajamas. So she fucking drew them on. Because *you* told her to." He stepped forward, but she didn't retreat even one pace. She held her ground, and damn if that didn't make him admire her more. She was fucking beautiful, strong, and even though he wasn't convinced what she did for a living actually worked, he knew beyond a shadow of a doubt she was smart as fuck.

"You're misdirecting your anger at me, Mr. Stark, when you know deep down I'm not the one at fault here." Her lips pressed into a thin line, and she held his gaze, the dark streaks of blue in her irises deepening in color the longer he studied her.

"The fuck I am," he ground out, though he could already feel himself losing steam. The realization of how irrational he was behaving hit him like a fucking runaway train. What had he been thinking coming here?

"You're angry at yourself for what you saw on Monday with Aria. You're angry at the fact that you weren't there for her, you weren't there to stop her from coloring all over herself. Because just like she said on Monday, you don't have time for her. Now, whether your reason for not catching her was a valid one or not—you were probably tending to the baby—but either way, you were not there for her when she needed you to stop her from making a bad decision. And you're taking this out on me because, I'm guessing, you've already beaten yourself to a pulp over Monday's therapy revelation."

He snorted. "Revelation ... sure. If that's what you want to call it."

Heat flashed in her eyes, and her nostrils flared. "You may not think what I do actually works, Mr. Stark, but I have it on good authority that it does. I wouldn't be doing what I do, or writing my PhD dissertation on art therapy and childhood trauma, if I didn't think it worked."

He snorted again and glanced away. Her gaze was hitting him harder than he realized. It was unnerving how unwilling she was to concede to his ire. She was not backing down, and he didn't like how that made him feel about her. Glancing back her way, he shook his head and rolled his eyes. "You're a hack, and I think Aria's sessions here are done."

What the fuck are you saying? You're a fucking fool and you need to rein in that anger.

The noise in her throat made his body go rigid, and the words that followed set every cell inside of him on fire. "You're an asshole, and maybe that's best. Put your own needs and uneducated opinions before the health and well-being of your child. Father of the year, right there."

He was toe-to-toe with her in two and half strides. "Don't you fucking dare speak to me like that. You have no idea—"

"No, *Atlas*, you have no idea. You have no idea what your daughter is going through, and you continue to remain oblivious. You refuse to open your eyes and see that your daughter has indeed been through a traumatic experience and she needs help. Help I can give her. Help I can help *you* give her."

Atlas growled and stared down his nose at the gorgeous, infuriating woman in front of him.

She plopped her hands on her hips and lifted her head to glare right back at him. "You don't scare me."

"And you don't impress me."

A muscle ticked along the smooth line of her jaw. "I don't care. You're an asshole, and you know it."

"Maybe."

"Maybe?" she scoffed. "Definitely."

Her glower intensified. So did his.

But then, like a light switch, something changed between them. The heat between their bodies was still there, but it was a new kind of heat, one he didn't recognize, but it warmed him in a much different way. A pleasant way. A way he wanted a hell of a lot more of. She must have recognized it too because her features softened. And then, just like in the movies, they were on each other.

His lips found hers, hers found his, and his tongue demanded entrance to her mouth. She tasted like cinnamon and smelled even better. Her arms wrapped around his neck, and she tugged him down to her as he wrapped his hands around her back and held her against him. Her luscious breasts in the thin, white, cap-sleeve T-shirt pressed against his chest, and he could tell her nipples were beginning to bead.

With his eyes shut, he had to go by feel, but at the moment, he was feeling fucking incredible. Her hot little tongue tangled with and tasted his as he backed her up toward her desk. The iron bar in his shorts knocked her thigh when she hit the front of her desk, and he lifted her up to plunk her butt down. Not once did their lips unlock. Her hands unraveled from behind him and trailed down his shoulders, her nails scraping and sending shivers coursing through him. She went to work on the buttons.

Holy fuck, she wanted this.

She wanted him.

And Jesus fuck, did he ever want her.

With one hand fisting her ponytail, he yanked her head back by her hair and sank his teeth into the side of her neck almost hard enough to draw blood.

The sharp inhale next to his ear, followed by a low, cat-like purr, said she didn't mind a nice bite. He nipped her again, only this time gentler, then laved across the bite marks with his tongue at the same time his free hand pushed up the hem of her shirt. Trailing his fingers along her silky-soft skin and feeling her shiver beneath his touch, he found the underside of her breast. The material of her bra was thin, and when he cupped her, her nipple pebbled beneath his fingers.

She'd finished with the buttons of his shirt, and ignoring his growl of protest, broke their kiss, peppering her lips and swirling her tongue down over his clavicle toward his chest.

Was she wet? He needed to know. Now plucking her tight nipple through the material of her bra with one hand, his other hand slid over her thigh, gathering the fabric of her skirt and pushing it upward. His fingers skimmed along her calf, behind her knee. He chuckled when she shivered against him. He hoped to do more than just make her shiver. His fingers continued up her leg to her thigh, the heat between her legs drawing them, and pushing aside her panties, he dipped two fingers in.

She wasn't just fucking wet, she was saturated. His thumb strummed her clit, and her head lurched back, her eyes flared open, only to slam shut a moment later. Her lips fell back to his neck, her kisses more eager and fervent as her body quivered against his. He pushed his fingers inside her slick, swollen entrance, and the exploration of her lips on his chest stopped. She let them rest on his shoulder, her breath hot puffs of air against his skin.

He opened his eyes and started down at her. Even though he couldn't see her face, she was a sight to behold. Flushed skin, long, curly blonde hair, little whimpers and gentle shudders each time he raked his thumbnail over the hood of her sensitive nub.

He continued to tease her, torment her, loving the way she bucked against his hand, rode his fingers and gasped when he tugged just a little harder on her nipple. He swore it was as hard as his dick was at that moment. Was she going to come? He thought she'd been close for some time now.

He was about to add a third finger when the growl from the woman riding his fingers like a mechanical bull caused him to pause. She lifted her head from his chest, grabbed his face in her hands and practically yelled, "Are you going to fuck me or what?"

Where the fuck had this little tiger come from?

Hell, fucking yes, he was going to fuck her.

He slipped his fingers from her cleft and finished ruffling up her skirt, then slid her panties down her thighs and over her legs. She helped him by lifting her butt off the desk. Her fingers raked down his bare chest, the tiger claws coming out. She reached for him. "Fuck me, Atlas."

She didn't have to tell him twice.

His shorts were down to his ankles in a flash, and he was cupping her ass. She reached between them, grabbed his length and angled it toward her. He intended to go slow, but she wouldn't allow it and bucked forward, taking him inside her nearly to the hilt. With a grunt and thrust from both of them, he was seated inside her.

Thank fucking God.

She cupped his face again and crashed her mouth to his, prying his lips apart with her tongue and wrapping the slippery muscle around his, sucking on it, sparring with it. The woman could fucking kiss.

It was like the floodgates had finally opened, and when she squeezed her muscles around him, the light switch not only flicked on, it was damn near blinding. He began to move, one hand cupping her ass, the other back up her shirt and toying with her nipple. It wasn't the best position for great sexual leverage and momentum, but it would have to do.

Papers shuffled and crinkled beneath her, and he was pretty sure he heard a jar of pens or something crash to the floor, but none of that fucking mattered. What mattered was the woman wrapped around his dick like cellophane, and the way her tongue licked and sucked on his was like he was fucking citrus cooler ice cream and she couldn't waste a drop.

Her fingers pushed the sleeves of his shirt over his arms, and she squeezed his biceps, groaning when he flexed them, which made them both laugh, still never breaking their intense kiss.

Her heat around him began to grow slicker and her cadence waned. He swallowed her whimper, morphing it into a groan of his own as her nails dug into his arm. That's when he noticed the tattoo on the inside of her wrist. Words in very distinct—handwritten—printing. But he pushed the thoughts of her tattoo aside and focused on the woman around him, the woman consuming him. Every noise, every move she made said she was close. Or at least he fucking hoped she was, because he was ready to goddamn blow.

She broke her lips away and scraped her teeth against his neck. "Oh God."

He pumped harder. She squeezed tighter.

She stilled. Her mouth opened on a silent plea and ... she exploded around him, cursing him, calling on a deity and making animal noises that he couldn't get enough of. The intensity of her orgasm pushed him to his own. Every squeeze of her hot, slick channel pulsing around him drew out his own release.

His mouth found her neck.

He drove deep one more time, grunted against her skin, bit down harder on that delicate spot where her neck met her shoulder and his balls emptied. It'd been a long fucking time since he'd had such an intense release, his cock pulsing like it had its own heart as he filled her.

Even though she'd just had her orgasm, she helped his along by tightening her walls around him, drawing him in deeper, milking the head of his cock for every drop. And he would give her all he had.

11

TESSA LOCATED her panties and discreetly tugged them back on, careful not to meet Atlas's gaze from where he stood, buttoning up his shirt. She didn't have to see his face to know he was staring at her though. The heat from that intense gray probe made her whole body turn to molten lava.

She blew out a breath and tucked a few loose strands of hair behind her ears.

Holy crap. What the heck had she just done?

What the heck had *they* just done?

Had some world-rocking, life-changing, soul-shattering sex on your desk, that's what.

She walked around behind her desk to pick up the steel pencil holder that they had knocked over, and a gush of liquid fled from between her legs, filling her panties.

Oh God.

"We didn't use a condom!" she blurted out, fleeing from behind the desk and coming to stand directly in front of him.

He lifted his head, his eyes the size of dinner plates. "Oh my God. We didn't. You're right."

"It's been so long since I've used them, I forgot. I just got out of a long-term relationship. I mean, I'm on the pill. But ... "

He raked his fingers through his hair and then scrubbed that same hand down his face. "Me too. Haven't used condoms in ... " His head shook. "Ten years? Maybe more? Was in a long-term relationship—obviously. She was on the pill. Then we were trying and then ... "

"I—I don't know if I'm clean. Oh my God. He was unfaithful, and it all just happened recently. I haven't had a chance to get myself checked. I am so sorry."

"I'm clean," he said, his tone so understanding, she wasn't sure this was the same guy who had come barreling into her studio not too long ago. "We'll both go get checked, make sure. I'm sure it's fine though. Unless your ex was out whoring around?"

Her shrug was stiff. "He could have been. I mean he's with one woman now, apparently been cheating with her for a while, but who knows. I'm really sorry, Atlas."

"It'll be okay."

But he knew as well as she did that he couldn't promise that.

"At least I can't get pregnant." The laugh that followed was forced and choppy. Her face fell into her hands, and she spun away from him, wandering aimlessly through the studio. "Never in a million years did I think that *this* was going to happen. What the hell?"

"You're not ... regretting it, are you?" His voice behind her made her jump, but the big, warm hands that fell to her shoulders were a surprising comfort. A firm squeeze encouraged her to turn around. "I mean, it was consensual, right?"

She nodded. "It was. I wanted it too. And, no ... I'm not regretting it. It's just ... I mean, did you think that *this*, that *that*"—she pointed at her desk—"was going to happen when you came here tonight looking to tear a strip off me for wrecking your child with my hippie-dippie ways?"

His lips twitching at one corner was all she got from him. "No. I did not. But you hit the nail on the head with all of it, with what you said. I'm blaming you for my parenting failures because it's easier to blame someone else than yourself. Particularly since I'm doing the very best I can at the moment and that's still not enough."

She cupped his cheek, and strangely it felt like the most natural thing to do so. "I know you are. But it's okay to ask for help. Who is with the girls now?"

"A babysitter."

"See, you asked for help. That's a good thing."

He snorted and averted his gaze. "I asked someone to watch my kids so I could come and ream you out. Class-A asshole right there."

"Well, I *did* call you an asshole."

He dipped his forehead to hers. "You did." His eyes closed. "I'm sorry for the things I said. I didn't mean any of them. If we're going to dig even deeper into my fucked-up head, I guess I'm also angry at myself for being attracted to you."

Her sudden inhale caused him to open his eyes.

"Because I am. I have been since the first day I brought Aria in."

Her lips twisted before she spoke. "So a week ago?"

Those stormy gray eyes rolled. "Yes, fine. A week ago. But still ... I didn't think I'd ever be attracted to another woman, and now here I am—"

"Attracted to another woman who is *not* your wife," she finished that sentence for him on a shaky breath.

"Yeah," he exhaled. "And it's just a lot to take in. And of course, because I'm a man—"

"It couldn't possibly be your fault that you're attracted to me, so you came to get mad at the source. Lumping all your life frustrations into one big ball of fury and launching it at the only person you could think of to blame."

His bottom lip relaxed, and his eyes widened. "Yeah. Pretty much."

"I get it."

"You do?"

"I'm a hippie-dippie therapist, remember? What you might not know about my oil-diffusing, crystal-wearing, moon-worshipping kind is that we're very understanding and forgiving."

His chuckle was quiet, but it shook his chest and shoulders. "Is it weird I feel like I've known you longer and better than just a week and three sessions?"

"No, because for some weird reason I feel the same."

His fingers linked with hers at the same time their mouths met. She breathed him in, tasting his swollen lips from their earlier kisses and feeling his warm velvet tongue slide across hers. His name was like a mantra in her head. *Atlas.* Strong and powerful and oh-so-masculine. He really was carrying the whole world on his shoulders.

He was the first to break the kiss, his lips falling to her neck, nose nuzzling beneath her ear. "What are we doing, Tessa?" he murmured, his mouth tracing a path along her jaw, teeth nipping.

A groan bubbled up from deep in her chest. "I don't know. All I know is that this feels really good, and I don't want to stop." Her fingers pushed into his hair, and she tugged his head back up, taking his mouth once again.

He met her groan with one of his own, deepening the kiss and bending her back, his hand moving from hers to the small of her back, keeping her safe ... but not from falling.

HE THOUGHT his head would have been a dense fog after leaving Tessa's studio, but for some fucked-up reason, he felt clearer than he had in ages.

Was that all it took to clear the mind? A good fuck?

You know she's more than that. Stop kidding yourself.

After double-checking that Tessa was indeed okay after their impromptu ... fuck? Tryst? Meeting of the minds and genitals? He said goodbye to her, hopped back into his Land Cruiser and headed home. As he knew they would be, both girls were sound asleep, and Kimmy was watching a movie while texting on her phone.

"How'd the night go?" he asked, setting his wallet and phone down on the coffee table before sitting down in his recliner.

Kimmy shrugged, finished whatever the hell she was doing on her phone and then stood up. "Pretty easy, Mr. Stark. I wasn't able to get *all* the marker off Aria, but I got a fair bit. I didn't want to hurt her by rubbing too much. Google says to just give it time and the rest will wash off eventually."

He breathed out a full exhale. "Thanks, Kimmy. Can I e-transfer you the money? I don't have any cash right now."

She smiled. "Sure thing, Mr. Stark. I'm going to head home now. My dad is walking to meet me."

He stood again and walked her to the door. Her father was already in view down the street. Even though it was still light out and a totally safe neighborhood, he and Kimmy's dad had set up this plan in the wintertime when it got dark early, and it just sort of stuck.

She waved goodbye to him again and took off toward her dad. Atlas waved at Hank before shutting the door, his back hitting it and his eyes shutting. Sure, his head was clear, but his heart was doing all kinds of fucked-up things now.

Four big feelings were duking it out, and he could hardly make heads or tails of any of them. On one hand, he felt like his feelings for Tessa were a betrayal to Samantha. But he also felt like they were a bit of a betrayal to Marie, too. Because even though they'd never met, he'd had more "conversations" with her than he had Tessa. He knew more about Marie (kind of) than he did Tessa.

Did he have feelings for Marie?

Yeah, he kind of did.

Did he have feelings for Tessa?

Yeah, he definitely did.

And then there was the whole Aria thing. He felt like the shittiest father of the year the majority of the time he was with her and even more so when he wasn't. He could only imagine how he was probably fucking up life for Cecily. Probably not as much as it would have been, but he was no prize of a parent either.

And now that he'd gone and had sex with Aria's therapist, could he continue to take her to Tessa? Was it now a conflict of interest because he was interested in his daughter's therapist?

He released a slow breath at the same time he whispered, "Fuck."

What was he going to do?

His phone pinging and vibrating on the glass coffee table had his eyes opening and his feet on the stairs. He snatched it off the table and began scrolling through the messages as he made his way into the kitchen to pour himself a bourbon. There was a new message from Marie.

Thanks for the chat last night. That really helped. Called a lawyer this morning, and they have time to meet with me on Friday. They think I have a case.

She'd called him last night after her confrontation with Carlyle and Blaire, he'd been tempted to go over there, punch the shit out of Carlyle and steal the dog back himself. The cops were already on Marie's side, and Atlas knew some of the best defense attorneys in the city. He didn't need to worry. But he hadn't because, well, it wasn't his battle to fight, and as much as he was in Marie's corner and would help her out where he could, he had two children he had to worry about and a job he wanted to go back to.

He texted her back as he sipped his drink and headed back to the living room. *What lawyer did you end up going with?*

Richelle LaRue. You said she's good, right?

A slow smile spread across his mouth. Oh, she was good all right. Good in the courtroom, and Liam could attest to her talents elsewhere as well. Not that Liam ever spoke about his elusive Wednesday-night fuck buddy.

She's a great attorney. Good choice.

Why did he feel like he'd cheated on Marie with Tessa? He and Marie were nothing but ... friends? If you could even call them that, and yet he felt as though he'd somehow betrayed her. Should he tell her he slept with someone? They didn't even know each other's first names, and he didn't know what she did for a living. This whole thing was absurd. But absurd or not, those fucked-up feelings were there.

I'm thinking of getting another tattoo to remember Forest. Just in case I don't get him back.

She had a tattoo? Of what? Where?

Now he was thinking about Tessa's tattoo. It was small and subtle on the inside of her wrist and down the back of her forearm. Maybe three inches long, two lines. He hadn't been able to make out the words, but by the way it was scrawled, he was guessing they were the words of someone important.

You'll get him back, he replied. Though he actually hated to give false hope, because there was a chance that she might actually not get him back or she'd have to settle for shared custody. Shared custody of pets did happen—he'd facilitated the agreements himself.

You have other tattoos? Would she show him her other tattoos? Take a picture of just that patch of skin?

I do.

Oh, she was playing coy now. Did he have to offer her up something in return to see what kind of ink she was sporting?

I'll show you mine if you show me yours.

He didn't have any tattoos, but his daughter's earlier foible with the Sharpies gave him an idea. Setting his drink and phone down, he got up and grabbed a black marker from the counter and drew a small, long-necked dinosaur on the top of his thigh right over his knee. He was a terrible artist. Even stick men looked more like just sticks, but he had mastered the long-necked dinosaur. Too bad Aria preferred the Triceratops. Because of course she did.

He snapped a picture of his dinosaur and sent it to her, chuckling at himself as he sipped his bourbon.

Cute "tattoo." Did you just get that? she messaged back.

Yeah, ink's still fresh. Hurt like a bitch.

She sent him a crying-laughing emoji followed by an image of her tattoo.

I Love you, kiddo

~Dad

It's for my dad. It was the message he wrote to me in the last birthday card I received from him before he died.

Atlas's glass fell from his hand, the rest of the bourbon spilling onto his lap and the chair. But he didn't care. He stared unblinking at the tattoo on the screen.

He'd seen that tattoo before.

Earlier that night, in fact.

That tattoo belonged to Tessa.

12

SHOULD SHE CALL HIM?

Was he ghosting her?

She'd sent him a picture of her tattoo, followed by a few other text messages asking him if everything was all right and where did he go, but she'd only received silence in return.

And that was yesterday.

She was going nuts wondering what the hell happened to David. Was he anti-tattoo?

No, that couldn't be it. He didn't seem anti-tattoo, particularly because he joked about having his own and was so interested in seeing hers.

Was she overthinking things and he'd simply fallen asleep or had an emergency with his kids?

Yeah, that had to be it. They'd taken their "relationship" from texting to a few phone conversations now, and although she wouldn't call herself the *best* judge of character, given her choice of fiancés, she could tell he wasn't the kind of guy who would ghost her.

She hoped.

She hadn't resorted to calling him yet though. That just

seemed desperate. She kept herself busy heading into work early to clean the tables, toys and art supplies. Her first client had called in sick, so she didn't have anybody coming in until ten, and that was absolutely fine by her.

Singing along with the radio, she barely heard her phone ping and vibrate on her desk. Her skirts swished around her ankles as she went to retrieve it, the sight of her desk bringing back pleasant and tingly memories from last night. Normally, she never wore a skirt when she rode her bike to work, but yesterday she decided to pack her skirt and change at work. And she was now very glad she did. If they'd had time to stop and remove her pants, maybe they would have stopped altogether—or at least hesitated and looked for a condom.

She shook her head and mumbled "stupid, stupid" as she brought up her messages. She was thirty-five freaking years old. She should know better than to have sex without a condom. Should know, at the very least, to check with her partner for his ... history.

Though it wasn't Atlas's history they had to worry about. It was hers. Or more importantly, Carlyle's and Blaire's.

Her heart thumped hard in her chest when she realized the message was from David. *Hey, sorry about last night. Emergency with the kids. What are you up to today?*

She knew he wasn't a ghosting ass. Just a busy single father with two kids to tend to. Her mouth split into a smile as she texted him back. *First client of the day canceled, so I'm just at work cleaning. Hope the emergency with the kids wasn't too serious.*

She waited for his reply, but it didn't come.

Exhaling through her nose, she went back to her cleaning, but she was only on her hands and knees for a moment before her phone on her desk began to ring.

Sandals slapping against the tile, she moguled around the small table and chairs. The caller ID said it was a private number—Carlyle? Blaire? Bracing herself for a showdown she held her breath and answered it on the fifth ring. "Hello?" she said, releasing her breath in a long, loud woosh.

"Tessa?"

David?

"David?"

"It's Atlas. Do you have any time today for Aria? We had a rough night and I ... I think she needs somebody besides me to talk to."

Scratching her head, she blinked away her confusion at how similar Atlas's voice was to David's—must just be a coincidence. Two deep, gravelly voiced men who could make her toes curl by just saying her name, what were the odds? She turned to face the windows and the street below. "Oh, uh ... sorry. You sound an awful lot like another friend of mine. As a matter of fact, I had a cancellation for nine o'clock if you guys can get here in half an hour?"

"We will leave right now. Thank you." He sounded chipper-*ish*, but there was also some weird undertone to his voice as well. One she couldn't put her finger on and that unnerved her in a most unsettling way. Was he having second thoughts about last night? Was he upset that he now had to go and get tested to see if Carlyle or Blaire had given them both chlamydia or something?

"Okay," she said, trying not to read too much into their short conversation. "See you shortly."

"Yes. And Tessa?"

She swallowed. "Yeah?"

"I don't regret last night." Then he hung up, and the butterflies in her belly all burst out of their cocoons at once and began to flutter around in a cosmic frenzy.

She didn't regret last night either.

UP THE STAIRS Atlas and Aria climbed, the nerves inside of him doubling the closer to the door they got. He hated the thought of deceiving Tessa the way he was, but he couldn't tell her on the phone that he knew who she really was. In person was the only way for any of this to work.

But what were the fucking chances?

The woman who had randomly texted him just over a week ago, ranting and raving at her ex who had cheated on her and stole her dog, was the same woman who he hadn't been able to get out of his head since the moment he saw her. In fact, he hadn't been able to get either woman out of his head. Turns out they were the same woman.

It explained so much though. She mentioned last night that her ex had just broken up with her, and the fizzy testiness with which she challenged him just screamed "sick of men and their bullshit." Understandably so.

But now, it was all different. Tessa was Marie and Marie was Tessa. Tessa Marie Copeland. And he was having a hard time getting her out from under his skin, no matter how much he knew he had no time for her to be there. He'd blocked his number when he called her that morning, because the woman was no fool, so she'd probably be able to put two and two together that his number and David's number were one of the same. Up until now though, he'd been communicating via email with Tessa with anything regarding Aria, including booking her appointments and receiving her status updates so the fact that she hadn't recognized his number as David's number before now also made sense.

"We're here, Daddy," Aria said, releasing his hand and opening the door. "Tessa!"

"Aria?" Tessa's head poked out from around the corner where the bathroom was located. "Just doing some cleaning. Almost done."

The sink ran, then the light flicked off, and there she emerged, all flaxen-haired, blue-eyed and with another one of those sexy, flowy skirts down to her ankles. He'd never been a fan of those hippie skirts until he saw Tessa wearing them. Now he thought they were pretty damn hot. Particularly with how low it rode along her hips, revealing the smallest sliver of skin at her belly when she walked.

Her eyes lasered in on his, but her smile was for Aria. "Are you ready to do some more art?"

Aria nodded. "Can we do a puppet show today? Maybe make the puppets?"

"That sounds like a spectacular plan. You know where all the supplies are. Go get what you need, and I'll come join you in a moment."

Aria nodded again, then skipped off toward the drawers and bins of labeled supplies, calling out a half-assed, "Bye, Daddy," without bothering to turn around.

He took a step toward Tessa, inhaling that delicious, unique scent of hers. He wanted to touch her, run his knuckle down her cheek, kiss her neck, but he wouldn't. Not with Aria right there.

"How are you?" he asked, keeping his voice just above a whisper.

Her serene smile made his insides twist. "I'm well, thank you."

You have to tell her the truth NOW!

He swallowed down the lump in his throat. "I have to show you something. And before you say anything, please know that I only found out last night. I haven't been keeping this from you, I swear."

Her brows furrowed and her lips twisted. "Okay ... "

He'd worn shorts on purpose, but even still, they were long enough to hide the Sharpie on his thigh. With a deep breath, he lifted his leg and planted his foot on a child-size chair. "Notice anything?" he asked, pulling his shorts up enough to show off the dinosaur above his knee.

She squinted for a moment, but then her eyes shot wide open, and her jaw went slack. Her hand clasped her mouth, smothering the gasp. "Oh my God."

Eyes as blue as the sky outside flitted back and forth between his face and his knee, the look of shock still very apparent. "You're ... you're ... "

"Atlas *David* Stark, yes. And you're Tessa *Marie* Copeland?"

She nodded. "We've been ... "

"Yes."

"And then last night we ... "

"Yes."

"And all this time we've been the same ... "

"Yes."

"You had no idea?" Her expression turned skeptical.

He lifted a brow. "Did you?"

She hung her head. "No. Oh my God."

He shrugged and put his foot back down on the floor. "At least I can stop feeling guilty about developing feelings for two women at the same time." The weight of the last twelve hours made the corners of his mouth tough to lift, but he tried his best.

Her laugh was breathy. "Would you believe I was having the exact same feeling?"

This time he didn't have to work at making his mouth form a smile. It happened naturally.

"Tessa, come on!" Aria pleaded from the green triangle table. Kimmy had managed to get most of the permanent marker off his daughter, but even from a distance, he could still see streaks up her arms and a few on her neck. She looked like some sort of zebra-human scientific experiment abomination.

"I'll be there in one minute," Tessa said, taking a step back from him.

"No, *ten* minutes," Aria said impatiently.

"She has no concept of time," he murmured with a chuckle. "Makes bedtime easy."

Tessa's laugh was soft, but her smile made his insides quake with the need to touch her. Making sure Aria's head was down as she worked on her puppet, he reached for her hand. "I want to help you get Forest back. Now that I know it's you, I want to help. Cecily is with the nanny. I'm going to head over to my firm now and speak with another lawyer over there."

"B-but what about Richelle? I don't want to dismiss her after she agreed to take my case. That doesn't seem right."

"We'll work with her too."

She shook her head and pulled her hand from his. "I can't afford one lawyer, let alone three. Thank you for the offer, but I'll see what Richelle can do for me." She went to head to Aria, but he reached for her hand again and pulled her back toward him. Even that small gulf of space between them was too much for him now. She'd cast a spell on him, and now that he knew Tessa and Marie were one and the same, he was drawn to her more than ever.

"Richelle and Liam both owe me favors. We're going to get you your dog back, I promise." He knew better than to make those kinds of promises, so why was he making them now?

She batted long, dark lashes at him, her chin tilted up almost in defiance. "And what favor do I owe you?" The sparkle in her eye made him want to crush his mouth to hers and have an encore of last night. The child in the corner of the room had him refraining from his carnal inclinations and instead laying on the charm. He bent his head at the same time his thumb brushed over the back of her hand. "Come by the house tonight."

Her eyes flared.

Shit. Was he laying it on too thick? Did she think he actually expected her to pay him for his legal services with sex? He squeezed his eyes shut and let out a heavy exhale. "That's not what I meant. I don't expect you to pay me for legal counsel with ... " The fingers of his free hand raked through his blond hair, and he scratched the back of his neck. "You know what I mean, right? I mean I want to start something with you ... you got that, right?"

Those lips he was dying to kiss smiled demurely. "Yes, I got that."

"I'm really crappy at this, you know. It's been a long fucking time since I dated anybody, since I courted or wooed or whatever the fuck you want to call it. I don't even know if it's done the same way now, what with all the fucking apps and shit."

She squeezed his hand. "You're doing just fine. I'll come by tonight when *David* texts me the all clear. Sound good?"

"Tessa!" Aria called impatiently.

He released her hand.

"Coming," she said, giving him one last smile that made the room seem just a bit brighter before she showed him her back and went off to sit with his daughter.

ATLAS KNOCKED on Liam's office door.

"Come in," Liam barked from inside.

Even though Atlas knew he could have just waltzed right in, not even bothering with a knock, he preferred to show his boss just a touch of respect, especially considering what he was about to ask of him.

"Can't stay away from me, can you?" Liam said with a chuckle as he set his phone down.

Atlas rolled his eyes and took a seat across from his boss and friend. "Something like that."

"Where's Cecily?"

"With Jenny. Aria's with Tessa."

Liam nodded. "So to what do I owe the visit? You're supposed to be on sabbatical right now. You didn't come to take me to breakfast, did you? Because I already ate, but I could eat again." He rubbed his belly and flashed that famous Dixon smile.

"I've come to call in a favor."

"But you just called in one. What the hell do you need another one for? You're not even supposed to be working." His friend's casual demeanor shifted like that of a lion catching the scent of a wounded gnu on the savannah.

"Which is why I am calling in my favor now. You owe me, remember?"

"For what? I gave you my McGregor favor. Those things are worth fucking gold."

"You gave me the McGregor favor so I didn't lose my shit after you and the other name partners forced me to take a mandatory one-month stress leave. You gave me the McGregor favor as a sign of goodwill, friendship and apology. Now, I'm calling in a favor from *you*. You owe me one after I helped you cut that deal with one of your ex-wives' best friends, remember? She wanted your jugular and was willing to do whatever it took to get it, and I stepped in and defused the situation. I got all the clients the best deal possible. And you said you owed me."

Liam scratched at the close-shaved beard on his chin, shaking his head. "Jesus, I can't remember the last time I heard you string this many words together in one sitting. What's gotten into you?"

Atlas sat back in his chair, laced his fingers together and cradled the back of his head in them. "I slept with Aria's therapist."

"You WHAT?" Liam, ever the drama queen, actually pushed to his feet and stood up in surprise. "When?"

"Last night."

"WHAT?"

Atlas rolled his eyes. "Sit down. You look ridiculous. Listen, it's even more fucking complicated than that."

"How? I mean, Mark got lucky when he fucked his kid's therapist. Everything turned out all hunky-dory for him, but even he nearly fucked it up with his temper. And your temper is worse than his. Tori's a fucking angel for taking Mark back after the things he said to her."

"We all know she is. But that's beside the point here. Listen."

"Oh, I'm fucking all ears."

"I know you are. Been meaning to ask why you don't grow your hair out to cover those things. Surprised nobody calls you Dumbo."

Liam chucked a stress ball at his head, but he caught it midair.

"I'm serious. I need your help. Richelle's too."

Liam's smirk dropped, and he leaned forward in his chair. "What can I do?"

"THAT'S QUITE THE STORY," Richelle's raspy voice said over the speakerphone in Liam's office.

"You're telling me," Liam said, shaking his head. "Second time I've heard it now, and I'm still fucking gobsmacked. How did you not recognize her voice?"

Atlas frowned. "I can't tell the difference between my mom and sister on the phone. The phone distorts voices."

His friend made a frown of his own and nodded. "Fair enough. My mom can't tell the difference between me and Scott on the phone either."

"Gentlemen ... " Richelle said, her tone only slightly irritated. The woman was fair and kind, but she was also all business, and he could tell she was growing weary of his and Liam's banter.

"Right, sorry," he said, shooting Liam an annoyed expression for once again getting them off topic. "So I figure if the three of us work together, we can not only get Tessa her dog back but get her a reasonable deal in their split. He's got a comic book and record collection that are apparently worth decent coin. Tessa wants to offer a trade, but I say we go for the dog *and* the collections. Compensation for emotional anguish and the stress this prick has caused."

"I say we take his fucking car, his mother's car, his father's boat and strip him of everything he's got. Then tar and feather the bastard and make him walk through the street with a nun following him around yelling 'shame,'" Richelle replied.

Liam chuckled. "Shame. Shame."

Atlas lifted a brow.

"I still can't believe you guys had no idea what *Game of Thrones* was when you named your kid," Liam said. "And apparently you still have no clue."

Atlas grunted. "Prefer reality, not fantasy."

"Yeah, because those serial-killer documentaries are *really* fucking healthy on the psyche."

Richelle cleared her throat. "Gentlemen, can we get back to business, please. Time is money."

"As much as I'd love to chain him, hang him, gut him and burn him," Atlas said, earning a bewildered look from Liam,

"I think we need to be pragmatic here and just go for what we can. I think Carlyle has money, so even though he's only going on what *Blaire* the first-year law student has told him, he could hire somebody who knows their shit."

"Yeah, but we're *three* people who know their shit. I'm the best fucking divorce attorney in the city," Liam said. "Some might say the state."

Richelle snorted on the phone. "Be sure to leave your ego at the office tonight."

Liam's dark brown eyes glittered. "You don't want to have a threesome with me and my ego?"

Her deadpanned response of "No" made Atlas chuckle.

"So we agree then? Liam and I will either come to your Friday meeting with Tessa or at the very least conference-call in on it?" Atlas asked, wanting to get back to the task at hand. He had to go and get Aria pretty quick but wanted to make sure everything had been set in motion before he did.

"Sounds good to me," Richelle said. "When I heard her case, my heart just broke. I didn't tell her this, but after her gasp of surprise when I told her my fees, I decided to waive a few things in order to take her case. The woman works with children who have experienced trauma, for Christ's sake, and now she's lost her dog. Fuck, I'd do it pro bono if I had to. Need to string this fucker up by his grapes."

Atlas's eye widened, but Liam simply smiled and mouthed, "Her divorce was ugly."

Ah, fair enough.

"Okay, I'll be in touch Friday morning to confirm everything," Atlas said. "Thanks, Richelle. I appreciate this."

"Anything for you, Atlas," she sang.

"What about me?" Liam asked, incredulous.

"What about you?"

He took the phone off speaker and put it back to his ear, spinning around in his seat so Atlas could no longer hear his murmurs or see his lips moving. Despite how his friend's own divorce had left him jaded and hating love, Liam had true feelings for Richelle. That was obvious. He just refused to acknowledge them as any more than two friends scratching itches. Or maybe, now that he knew Richelle's divorce had been ugly, it was Richelle who kept their relationship in neutral rather than drive. She didn't want to risk her heart again, didn't want to put herself or her daughter out there to get hurt.

Hmm ...

"Okay, see you tonight." Liam spun around and set his phone back down on his desk.

"You love her," Atlas said before he could stop himself. Jesus fuck, what had come over him lately? He'd never been this chatty or positive in ages. Not since ... Samantha.

Liam's perma-smile drooped. "Nope, I don't. Though I do love the noises she makes when I'm ... "

Atlas held up his hand to stop his friend. "Forget I said anything."

Liam's grin was back.

Atlas stood up, and his friend stood with him, following him to the door. "Thanks for doing this," Atlas said, his hand on the doorjamb of the open door. "I'll owe you one."

"Damn straight you will," Liam said, slapping Atlas on the back. "But maybe we can call it even, because I've honestly never seen you this ... content. At least not in a really long time. Even though I know the kids are stressing you out, I think this sabbatical is going to be a good thing, and I can already tell this Tessa ... or Marie or whatever has been good for you. The cloud over your head isn't nearly as dark as it has been." His mouth tilted up at one corner. "You know we're all here if you need us."

And he did know that. He knew that so well that it made his chest hurt with how much love he had for his fellow single dads. And even though in his year of belonging to their group, he'd been pretty moody and quiet, none of them had judged him or stopped inviting him places. They accepted him for who he was and what he was dealing with and just continued to always be there if he needed them.

Atlas smiled at his friend—his *best* friend. "Thanks, man." Then he left to go grab his daughter and let the woman who had suddenly come to mean a great deal to him know that he and his team were going to help her get her dog—and her life —back.

He only hoped that after they won her case, she'd still be interested in letting him be a part of that life.

13

"But Daddy, I don't want to go to bed. I'm not sleepy," Aria protested as he sat on the edge of her bed, leaned over and pecked her on the forehead. "I want to stay with you."

Atlas pursed his lips together. "It's bedtime, sweetheart. You know the rules."

Her blonde brows furrowed and her mouth dipped into a frown at the same time she crossed her arms over her chest. "Not fair."

"It is fair. Daddy has some work to do, and it's too hard to do when you and Cecily are awake." Tessa coming over to "visit" wasn't exactly "work," but it was an easier explanation to a three-year-old than the truth.

Aria's frown lifted. "Daddy, I'm sorry for hitting Cecily with the train."

Holy shit.

He had to keep himself from falling off the bed. She'd certainly surprised the fuck out of him.

"I want to like her."

Another huge fucking surprise. Was this because of Tessa?

"You have time for her but not me. Makes me sad. And mad."

He cupped his daughter's soft cheek, leaned back down and pressed his forehead to hers. "I know you're sorry, sweetie. And I'm sorry that I haven't made our relationship and our time together enough of a priority. I promise that's going to change, okay. I'm going to make more time for just us."

Her eyes lit up. "Can we have that time now?"

He smiled down at his precocious, opportunistic daughter. "Not tonight."

She pouted.

"I want you to like Cecily, too, sweetie. I want you to love her. She's our family. Always has been, only now she's an even bigger part."

"Where's her mommy? Same place as my mommy?"

Pain funneled into his heart the way it always did when Aria brought up her mother. Then there was this cold, dizzy feeling that lasted for no more than a second, and he fought to climb his way out of a sudden, desolate impenetrable blackness. Her warm hand, soft on his arm brought him back to the moment, and he smiled down at her as best he could. Aria didn't ask about Samantha very often anymore, but when she did, it made his entire body ache with a sense of loss he knew he'd never fully recover from. Aria should not be growing up without her mother.

She. Should. Not.

Swallowing, he shook his head. "No, sweetie. Cecily's mommy is in the hospital. Remember? She's really hurt, and the doctors are doing everything they can to make her better."

Her bottom lip jutted out, and those big hazel eyes blinked. "I'm sad for Cecily and her sick mommy. My mommy was sick too and then she died. I hope Cecily's mommy doesn't die."

His throat tightened, and he gripped her hand with his. "Me too, sweetie. Me too."

His little girl with the kind heart, stubborn streak and zest for independence yawned. "Love you, Daddy."

"I love you too, sweetie." He pecked her on the nose, then stood up. Her eyes were already closed by the time he reached her door.

Bringing out his phone as he closed Aria's door two-thirds of the way, he texted Tessa. *Coast is clear. 1324 Applecross Avenue. Park in the driveway. Please don't knock or ring the bell. Door is unlocked.*

Then he went to his master bathroom and had a shower. It'd been ages since he'd been on a "date" with anyone, and he was nervous as fuck about "dating" Tessa. He wasn't even sure he was ready to start dating, and he certainly didn't have the time to add another woman to his life. But none of that mattered when he thought about her, about Marie and how much both women—the same woman—had made him smile over the last week. That had to mean something, right?

AFTER WORK, Tessa ran to the clinic to get a blood test, then, after being drained of her precious O negative, she ran home, changed into her exercise clothes and went for a much-needed, stress-relieving jog. She needed to clear her head after the fuzziness caused by seeing Atlas and learning that he and David were the same person.

What were the odds?

After her run, she had a long, hot shower where she shaved, buffed, tweezed and scrubbed her body until she was as fresh as she could be. Then she slipped into a light and airy, soft, light blue denim T-shirt dress with a wide black belt at the waist and a pair of cork wedges—not too high—but high enough to make her calves pop. She let her hair do its natural curly thing down her back—after copious amounts of product, of course—and kept her makeup minimal. She spent an awful lot of time getting ready for a man she hoped didn't care what she looked, smelled or dressed like. Crap, she hated dating.

Once she got his text, she checked her lip gloss in the mirror, looked longingly at Forest's empty bed and then headed to her car. She would have loved to have tossed on some jeans and rode her Ducati, but the beauty made too much noise, and they were trying to keep their *whatever it was* on the DL and not let the kids know just yet.

She parked in the driveway behind his Land Cruiser and turned off the ignition. He lived in a nice neighborhood on the edge of Rainier Vista, and the house was well maintained and the yard nicely kept. It wasn't a mansion, but she could tell that he did well as a lawyer.

Stowing her nerves in her back pocket as if they were a pack of gum, she fluffed her hair, smacked her lips and headed up the small stone path to the front door. His text said the door would be unlocked, but that just felt weird going into a house she'd never been in before. She reached for her phone and went to text him when the door in front of her swung open.

"Saw your headlights," he said, stepping out of the way so she could enter.

She glanced down at her chest to see if her nipples were out.

"Not *those* headlights." He reached for her coat, and she let him take it.

"Keep your shoes on. We'll head down to my office slash the rec room." He reached for her hand and led her down a half flight of stairs and into a cool, dark hallway. His fingers tightened around hers when they reached a closed door. "I'm really glad you came." He pushed the door open to reveal a cozy room with high windows, a desk, computer and office cabinets in one corner and a small home gym in the other. A couch took up one wall, faced toward a big flat-screen television, and there were a few bins of toys in the same IKEA storage shelf she had at the studio. A gas fireplace below the TV was on, but she could tell there was no heat coming from it. They didn't need it.

He led her over to the couch, a bottle of wine and two glasses sitting on the coffee table in front of them.

"Wine?" he asked.

"Please."

Nothing but the gurgle and blub of the cab sav filling the glass could be heard in the room—unless he could hear her pulse thundering in her ears. She certainly hoped he couldn't. He handed her the first glass, and she put it to her nose.

"This is weird, isn't it?" he said, setting the bottle down and turning to face her, their knees knocking.

She sipped her wine, eyeing him over the rim of her glass. "It is and it isn't."

"Yeah, that's how I feel. Like, I've had some pretty in-depth conversations with *Marie*, though at the same time, we kept it superficial. I never asked about her—I mean *you*—about her ... *your* job or family life. But I wanted to."

She held the wine on her tongue for a moment, processing his words and coming up with her own. She allowed the liquid to slide down her throat. "We hadn't laid down any rules, and yet they made themselves up. There were things I wanted to ask you, too, but was nervous I was going to overstep and then I'd never hear from you again. You're the only person who knows what Carlyle did to me, the only person I could talk to about it, confide in. If you hadn't recommended the Rage Room, I probably would have strangled them both when I went to their apartment."

His delicious lips twitched into a small smile. "Tell me now. Tell me all the things I was too stupid not to ask before. Your parents, family, siblings, school. I don't know what's going on here, Tessa, but I know that when I'm with you, talking to you, touching you, I feel more normal than I have in too fucking long."

The hair on her arms tingled, and her heart began to beat wildly. No man had ever said such moving, thoughtful, beautiful words to her. And even though she didn't know Atlas/David very long, she knew he was a widower, and she knew that he loved his late wife immensely. So to say that with her he felt normal—that was one hell of a compliment.

Setting her wineglass down, she reached for his hand, cupping it in both of hers. "Knowing you're in my corner means a lot, and even though I just got out of a long-term relationship, heck, an engagement, this is no rebound. I have some really deep feelings for you too. Feelings that"—she shook her head and laughed choppily—"feelings that both excite and terrify me."

"We'll take it slow, then." He set his wineglass down as well and let his other hand join hers. "I come with some baggage, and ... " His throat bobbed on a swallow. "And I—"

"You love your wife. I got that right away when you told me how long she's been gone for. I'm not looking to fill anybody's shoes."

He nodded, a pained expression flitting across his face. "We were high school sweethearts. Went to college and law school together. She was my"—he glanced up at her, his eyes beseeching, almost worried—"my first and only."

Her mouth opened. "You mean ... "

"Last night was a *huge* deal for me, and the fact that we

went at it like angry animals surprised and scared the fuck out of me."

"Pile on the whole no condom thing." She released his hand and shoved her fingers in her hair. "I went and got a blood test today, just so you know. Again, I am *so* sorry. I have condoms in my purse."

"You brought condoms?"

Oh, crap.

"Was that not what tonight was about?" She stood up, stepped away from him and began pacing in front of the fireplace. "Oh my God. Did I assume? Did I overstep? Was this a date with no ... Do you not want to, you know ... with kids in the house? Oh my God. Oh my God. I am *so* sorry. I should just go." She made to leave, but he was up off the couch and had his hands on her waist before she had even reached the door.

"Tessa, come sit down." He led her back to the couch, handed her her wine and took a sip of his own. The glint of humor in the dark gray of his eyes and the crook at the corner of his sinfully sexy mouth said he found her little fluster hilarious.

"Don't laugh at me," she scolded, drinking more wine.

"I'm not laughing at you. I happen to think you're adorable and sexy and wonderful."

She sat back against the couch. "Say more things like that."

His grin stole every molecule of oxygen clear from her lungs. "You're beautiful, Tessa. Smart, sweet, kind. And the fact that you like to ride a crotch rocket while also wearing healing crystals ... " He reached out and gently picked up the crystal pendant that fell between her breasts. "It just makes you all the more unique and multifaceted."

She raked her top teeth over her bottom lip. Her body was an inferno, her nipples had grown tight, and her pussy was pulsing. His thumb caressed it and an ache formed deep in her belly, spreading lower and growing into a throbbing warmth.

"I like you, Tessa. I want to get to know you. And if sex is where tonight goes, then great. But I'm okay if that is not where we end up. The girls are upstairs in bed. I have their monitors linked to my phone." He tilted his head toward his iPhone. "We can watch a movie down here. I can pop some popcorn. Or we can just talk and get to know each other. I *need* to take this slow, and by slow, I mean I need to learn how to be with a woman who is *not* my wife. And not just in bed; in every way. She was my first girlfriend—my only girlfriend ... *ever.*"

"You're a unicorn," she whispered.

He snorted. "I suppose you could say that."

"I'm okay taking it slow," she said. "I was just dumped, and he stole my dog. I'm not looking to rush into anything either. Plus, I have my PhD defense coming up in a month, and my mom ... "

Like a curious puppy, he tilted his head. "What about your mom?"

Right, her mom.

"She's in a home, and it just takes a lot of time and energy out of my day to go and see her is all." She wasn't ready to reveal the big *A* that hung over her head like a scarlet letter.

"And from what you said about your tattoo, your father passed away?" he probed.

"Yeah. He was a helicopter pilot and went to go and find some lost hikers up on the mountain. They say he got caught in a blizzard and the crash of the helicopter against the side of the mountain caused an avalanche."

"Oh my God."

"About two years ago now, I guess. Feels like longer, but at the same time it feels like just yesterday he and I were tinkering on my bike in his garage."

"I feel the exact same way about Samantha."

She blinked up at him and reached for his hands again. "I'm okay if you want to tell me about your wife, if it will help, or even if after speaking about her you realize you aren't ready to be with me. Don't think you can't ever talk about her to me."

His small, placid smile spoke of appreciation and acceptance. "Maybe over time. But not yet, at least not much." He placed one hand on her knee. "But thank you for that."

She untangled their hands, and they both reached for their wine.

"So should I go pop us some popcorn?" he asked, reaching for the wine bottle and topping them both up.

She grimaced inwardly.

Now came the whole conversation about *all* the things she didn't eat in the hopes it gave her a brain a few extra years before it turned to mush.

His expression turned quizzical. "You don't like popcorn?"

"I like popcorn. I just don't *eat* popcorn. But you don't have to feed me. I ate before I came over. It's okay. I have some dietary *restrictions* or preferences or whatever, and they can be a bit much to take on." Damn it, she should have just brought herself a container of raw veggies like she did most places. Kept her from going hungry and deviating from her healthy-brain meal plan.

"Like allergies?" He seemed genuinely concerned. "You're not deathly allergic to anything, are you?"

She shook her head. "No. Not anything like that. It's just there's a family history of some illnesses I'd rather not get into right now, and I'm just being proactive and preventative by keeping on a strict, healthy diet."

He seemed to understand and nodded. "What about

some raw veggies cut up? Nuts? Are nuts out of the question?"

Damn, he really was a unicorn. Carlyle had never been so accommodating to her, even when they first started dating.

His gaze turned more intense and probing. "Can you eat that stuff?"

Smiling, she sipped her wine. "I can, thank you."

"I'll be right back." He turned on the television, brought up Netflix and then handed her the remote. "Find something for us to watch." Then her unicorn headed out of the room, leaving her alone with her thoughts, Netflix and the wine bottle.

ATLAS PILED ALL the sliced celery, peppers, cucumbers and baby carrots on a plate, then grabbed the jar of mixed nuts from the pantry. He was just about to head back downstairs when Cecily's cry from down the hall gave him pause.

Shit.

He waited a moment. Sometimes she simply cried out in her sleep but wasn't actually awake and he didn't need to go to her. Other times, she managed to settle herself back down without his intervention. Compared with Aria at this age, Cecily was a breeze.

She cried again, but it wasn't urgent-sounding. With light footsteps on the wood floor, he headed down the hallway. That's when he heard the quiet but distinct sound of Aria in Cecily's room.

What the ... ?

"Shhhhh, baby. It's okay. Aria's here."

Careful not to let either of them see or hear him, he adopted stealth ninja mode and hunkered down onto his knees before peering around the doorjamb into Cecily's room.

What played out before him was damn near unbelievable.

Aria was on the floor of Cecily's room on the plush carpet next to the crib, with a blanket from her own bed and her own pillow, and she was holding Cecily's hand through the bars. Cecily was smiling and cooing now.

"I'm sorry, baby," Aria whispered. "I won't hit you again."

Cecily giggled.

"Sleep, baby," Aria whispered.

Cecily said something in baby-speak, then giggled again.

"Go to sleep, little baby. Go to sleep, little one. When you wake in the morning, you'll be greeted by the sun," Aria sang, butchering the song and mispronouncing her *th*, but nonetheless making Atlas's heart melt on the spot. Samantha used to sing that song to her when she was still pregnant and Aria was restless, and then when Aria was a baby and colicky. He hadn't sung that to her once since Samantha passed—it was just too hard—but it amazed him she still remembered it.

"The birds will sing a song for you. The flowers will smell extra sweet. Sleep now, my child, rest your head, for on the morrow, our hearts will meet." Aria lifted up and pressed a kiss to Cecily's hand. "Love you, baby." Then she settled down on the carpet, beneath her blankets, and Cecily seemed to quiet down too, their hands still clasped.

It was like night and day. His child was ... his child again. And in only three sessions with Tessa. Was she really the miracle worker Zak claimed her to be?

She's managed to bring you out of your miserable funk. Why wouldn't she also help Aria?

Leaving his girls to sleep as they were, he left the food on the counter and raced down the stairs. This woman, this magician, this sorceress, she'd put a spell on all of them, and they were all the better for it. He'd left the door to his office open and found her sitting quietly on the couch, sipping wine and flicking through the movie list on Netflix. Without a word and in three strides he was with her, pulling the remote from her hands and crushing his lips to hers.

She was startled at first, but the moan that bubbled up from the back of her throat and the way she melted against him said it was a surprise she liked. Her arms wrapped around the back of his neck, and she pulled him down to her. He spread her out on the couch and covered her body with his, careful not to rest his full weight on her. Their tongues tangled and teased, teeth nipped and lips sucked. He'd been dying to kiss her again since last night and couldn't believe how much he missed the taste of her already.

After a moment, she pulled her lips from his and tucked her face into the crook of his neck. "Not that I'm complaining, but what was that for?" Her chest heaved against his, and her words came out as a bit of a pant.

"Aria has finally accepted Cecily—at least for now. She's upstairs in Cecily's room, sleeping on her floor, and they're holding hands. That *never* would have happened before. I would have had to worry about her smothering Cecily with a pillow rather than comforting her. Whatever you're doing with her ... " He lifted his head and gazed down at the woman who had bewitched them all. "I'm a convert. Keep doing what you're doing. I feel like I finally have my daughter back."

She smiled up at him and blinked those beautiful blue eyes of hers. "I'm just giving her an outlet. Giving her a chance to express her feelings in a constructive and positive way, and when she discusses those feelings with me, I help her sort them out. She realized today that Cecily is not to blame for things and that as a baby, she can't be Aria's target. It took a bit of convincing, but by the time you came to get her, she'd pretty much figured it out. She's incredibly bright, and her language is quite advanced for three and a half. You're doing a great job with her."

Pressing his elbow into the couch, he swept the hair off her face and cupped the side of her head. "You're the miracle worker." His lips fell to hers again.

She chuckled against his mouth. "Aria isn't that bad off. Cut yourself—and her—some slack. She has a stable home environment, a father that loves her and she's well socialized with kids at pre-school and other children. She's just hit a rough patch, but she's going to be just fine. It also helps that you're home more for her. That is really helping."

"So I'm not raising a future serial killer because she hit her cousin with a toy train and then screamed in her face?"

Her laugh made both their bodies shake. "Not at all."

"She apologized to me for doing that earlier this evening and then apologized to Cecily just now." The knuckles of his free hand traced the delicate line of her collarbone.

"She's an emotional child but also very sensitive and empathic. You'll have your hands full as she gets older and sorts out those emotions, but as long as you provide her with a constructive outlet and let her know that her feelings are okay and that you're there for her, she's going to be just fine." Her fingers toying with the hair at the nape of his neck felt really good, and he tilted his head a bit for her to get a new spot, his eyelids growing heavy at the same time. "You're a great dad, Atlas."

He blinked wide at her, studying the gentle contours of her face, the pink in her cheeks and flecks of white in her eyes. "Say more things like that."

Her smile was magnetic. "You are a great dad," she repeated. "And damn sexy. A bit moody, but we'll work on that."

He lifted an eyebrow at her, but she lifted one back at him in challenge.

"You're raising great kids," she continued. "Don't beat yourself up over Aria's reaction to Cecily's arrival and you working. Life has its challenges, and she's coming to learn that the world *doesn't* revolve around her. A hard concept— one that some adults never learn—but one that will make her a better person in the long run. I don't have kids, but I know that nobody is perfect, and as long as your children know they're loved, they're going to be all right." Her fingers tightened their hold in his hair. "Did you forget the nuts?"

Huh?

He wanted to kiss that smile clean off her face. "The nuts and veggies. Did you forget them when you were overcome by lust and raced down here?"

He rolled his eyes and levered up to a sitting position. "More gratefulness than lust, but there was certainly some of that in there too. And no, I'll run up and grab them." He stood up and headed toward the door, unable to keep his eyes from her and how goddamn gorgeous she looked all flush-faced and easily ravishable on his couch.

Sitting up, she smiled coyly as she took a sip of her wine. "My purse is on your coat hook on the landing. Maybe grab it for me, please?"

"Okay?"

She lifted her brows.

Oh, right! The condoms.

He nodded, then raced upstairs to grab the veggies and nuts, snatching her purse on his way back down.

He still wasn't sure how things were going to go or whether he was ready to move on, but he knew that not taking a chance on Tessa and the connection they had would be something he'd regret for the rest of his life.

14

"You've got to be fucking kidding me," Atlas ground into the phone the following Wednesday night as he and Tessa once again sat on the couch in his office and watched a movie.

"Believe me, we're all equally pissed off," Richelle replied. She and Liam were at Liam's house and on speakerphone with Tessa and Atlas. "So the meeting with them has been pushed back for three weeks until they return from their vacation. How fucking convenient."

"Is that even legal?" Tessa asked, tears welling up in her eyes. "Who has Forest while they're off on their European vacation? Why didn't they just give him to me?"

"It is legal," Atlas said grimly, wrapping an arm around her shoulder and pulling her into his body. He wanted to punch and maim this Carlyle fucker, but he needed to rein in his anger and focus on the woman beside him who needed softness and comfort. "And he didn't give you Forest because he's a fucking douchebag who is making a power play."

"If he's like a couch—property, of which I own half, can I not just go to the boarding kennel or dog-sitter and take him?

It's not like I'm stealing my own dog." She leaned into him and wiped beneath her eye with the hem of her T-shirt.

"I'm afraid not," Richelle said with reluctance. "At this point, even though your name is on the registration, until the courts decide on who owns Forest, it would appear as theft. I know this sucks, Tessa, and if it were legal, I would be right there with you picking up that dog and helping you bring him home, waving the court order in the face of anybody that protested. But for now, we just need to sit tight and wait."

She sniffled and shuddered against his body. "But he's my dog ... This doesn't make any sense. Why would Carlyle do this to me?"

Atlas rubbed his hand down Tessa's arm. "I'll see if McGregor can find out where they took Forest. If it's a boarding kennel, we might be able to get you visitation. If it's just a random friend or dog-sitter, I'm not sure what we can swing. Particularly if Carlyle and his little first-year Jezebel had the forethought to forbid the dog-sitter from letting you see him."

"I wouldn't put it past Blaire," Richelle replied. "She's a first-year law student, don't you know? Means she knows *everything* about the justice system."

"Thank you for calling," Tessa whispered, her entire body having seemed to collapse in on itself. She seemed so small in his arms now, so defeated.

"I'll be in touch," Liam said, remorse in his tone.

Atlas turned off the speaker and put the phone back to his ear. "Has Rickson hired counsel yet?"

"Not that we're aware of," Liam said. "But that doesn't mean he hasn't, just that he and his lawyer haven't filed anything yet. Do we know what he does for work?"

Atlas turned to Tessa. "What does fuckface do for work?"

"He's got a bachelor's degree in biology. Was working for some environmental agency for a while, but he applied at the college not too long ago for an opening they had in one of the labs."

"You hear that?" Atlas said to Liam.

"Sure did. I wonder if Adam knows anything about him? He was, after all, just made dean of the biology department."

Atlas grunted. "It would be worth following up on. I can take care of that, call him tomorrow."

"And I'll get McGregor to do some hunting, too."

"Thanks, I owe you one."

"You certainly do. And hey, Emmett's throwing Zara a surprise birthday party Sunday at Paige's bistro if you want to bring the girls. And maybe ... "

"Where did this sudden interest in seeing other people happy come from?"

"You've gone from Eeyore to Tigger in the course of two weeks, man. Tessa is either a witch and cast a serious spell on you, or she just makes you happy. I can't ridicule that."

"Look at you going all soft," Richelle teased.

"Will *you* come to the party?" Liam asked her.

"No, and you knew my answer before you even asked."

"I'll think about it. Thanks, guys," Atlas said, rolling his eyes at their weird relationship. "Let me know what McGregor says. Wait, why are you inviting me and not Emmett?"

"He planned to message you when he got home from work tonight, but I said I'd relay the invitation when I spoke with you today."

"'K, talk soon." He hung up and turned to the sad woman beside him. The look on her face shredded his heart and made him want to go find Forest himself just to see her smile again. "We'll get him back," he said, tucking a knuckle under her chin.

"I'm beginning to think it might be hopeless. Forest must be so confused. He was a rescue, you know. Found malnourished and neglected with matted fur and a large, infected wound around his neck from being chained up. He's going to think I've abandoned him just like everybody else." Hot, plump tears dripped from her glassy eyes, and she turned her face into his shoulder. Soft sobs caused her slight frame to tremble. "I don't know what I'll do without him."

"Shh," he murmured. "We'll figure it out." Her warm tears fell with abandon on his shirt, soaking through to his skin. "You've got three lawyers, and he's got a first-year law student. If we don't kick his ass, get your dog back and take him to the fucking cleaners, then I'll disbar myself."

Of course, he was exaggerating. This was a small claims case over a single piece of property. Lawyers weren't even really needed. But that didn't mean he and his friends couldn't lend her a hand and help her get her best friend back. He just wanted to reassure her that he, Richelle and Liam were going to do everything they could to help her.

Her laugh was breathy and forced, but when she lifted her head to look at him, her gaze tired and beseeching, he saw just the smallest glimmer of hope still hiding behind all the pain. "Thank you. I don't know if I would have had the strength to go this alone."

He wrapped both arms around her and tugged her into his lap. "You're not alone." He kissed her on the forehead and held her tight. She kissed his neck. He kissed her temple, then her cheek. Her lips, damp from her tears, fell to his jaw, her teeth scraping along the scruff of his beard.

"I feel safe when I'm with you," she whispered. "With my mom in the home and my dad gone, I have no one ... besides you." She arched her back and pulled her head away from him, her sapphire eyes glittering from the tears but with more hope and less agony swirling inside them than before. "You take away some of the hurt." Then she wrapped her arms around his neck, and their mouths collided.

From gentle kisses and soft touches, their movements and passion went from a flickering cinder to white-hot dancing flames. The movie on the screen was forgotten as they peeled away layers of clothing, kissing and biting each new bit of exposed flesh. She had an incredible body, soft and feminine with just the right amount of curves. But she was also fit. He knew she took care of herself, ate well and went to the gym. The woman was disciplined. And the way she responded to his touch was enough to get any man's engine going.

Every caress, every kiss she would moan or shiver, buck into his hand or grip his hair and demand more. As fragile as she seemed at times, particularly just now, he knew her to be fierce and to go after what she wanted. She had, after all, texted him quite the scathing messages when she thought he was someone else. The woman had fire, the woman had passion, and he saw that more than ever when the clothes were off and it was just them.

Relieving her of her tank top and bra, he scraped his teeth over her tight nipple, loving the way the skin around it and her areola prickled with gooseflesh. Her eyelids hung at half mast, and her top teeth dug into her bottom lip, creating little white marks beneath. She was easy to torment too, which was so much fun. Swirling his tongue around the taut bud, he slid his fingers down over the swell of her hips and between her legs. The hair there was sparse and nicely trimmed. Past her mound, he dipped his middle finger between her lips and pressed on her clit. Her hips instantly shot off his lap.

"You're evil," she murmured, churning her pelvis in such a way his finger slid down through her folds into her wet heat.

"Evil?" He chuckled. "Would an evil man do this?" He was on his knees with her feet on his shoulders and her pussy against his mouth before she could utter a word of protest, just a squeal of delight from his rough movements and demands.

"Oh God." She sank into the couch, her fingers finding her nipples and tugging. He loved to watch her touch herself, enhance her own pleasure. They'd only had sex three times so far, but he was already coming to know her likes and to read her body language.

Reading a person was how he'd become so successful in the courtroom too.

She loved to have her tits played with, her nipples tugged and bit, past the point of pain, it seemed. And when he sucked on her clit, she was like her motorcycle, purring when he hit the throttle just right.

Sliding two fingers into her slick channel, he pumped as her ridges tightened around him, squeezing and drawing him deeper. His lips enclosed around her clit and he sucked hard, feeling it swell and harden when she drew closer to climax.

He released her clit, enjoying the whimper of protest but relishing the moan of delight when he raked his chin over the hypersensitive nerve bundle.

"Oh God." Her groan fueled him.

He hit her with his scruff again, and her hips jerked beneath him. Around and around her clit he whirled his tongue, until that warm gush of sweetness flowed over his fingers and the woman surrounding him came hard against his mouth. Her body went stiff, her clit even harder, even more swollen as her fingers pulled at her nipples and her upper body shot off the couch.

She was a sight to behold when she came, whether from his mouth and fingers or his cock inside her. Last Wednesday, he hadn't gone down on her, as they didn't have the all-clear from the lab about her blood tests, but those results had come Friday, and he had her over again on Sunday so that they could celebrate properly.

"Atlas," she crooned, having reached her peak and then gently slid down the backside of her climax. She released her nipples and reached for him. "Inside me, now."

Grinning, he wiped the back of his hand over his mouth and crawled up her body. Now that they knew they were both clean and she was on the pill, they didn't even have to think twice about stopping to locate condoms. He simply slid home, right where he fit perfectly, right where he felt like he belonged.

ATLAS inside her was the absolute best feeling in the entire world. Never in her years of being with men had she ever felt so utterly satisfied, so completely consumed, so ... whole. He completed her, and the fact that they'd only known each other for a few weeks and *how* they came to know each other made it all the more scary and exciting.

"I want you on top," he murmured, dipping his head to scrape his teeth along her shoulder, sucking when he reached that sensitive spot that joined her neck.

"Hmmm," she hummed. "I want that too."

She felt the loss of him from her body the moment he pulled out, her pussy clenching and pulsating around nothing and growing more desperate by the second to yet again be filled. He sat up on the couch, and she scrambled into his lap, straddling him, lifting up and aligning their bodies so that she could drop her hips and once again take him inside her.

Their sighs of contentment were simultaneous when he hit the end of her, his cock twitching, her pussy squeezing in response. They'd only been together a few times, but it already felt so natural, so right. With other men it'd taken time for them to learn what made her *tick*, but Atlas seemed to figure it out right away, and that was saying something for a man who could count his sexual partners on one elbow.

Wet from her earlier climax, their bodies made some interesting noises, but neither of them seemed to care. Besides, those slapping and squelching sounds were drowned out by Atlas's grunts of pleasure and her whimpers of delight as his lower belly hit her clit just right each time she dipped down.

She arched her back and shoved her breast in his face, rubbing her nipple over his mouth until his lips parted and he drew the needy bud inside, sucking hard for a moment and then tugging even harder with his teeth.

Yes. Just the way she liked it. He was a fast learner. She liked that too.

Her hands on his shoulders weren't enough for decent leverage, so she placed them on the back of the couch behind him and really started to move, up and down with a bit of a back and forth motion as well, feeling every hard inch of him inside her, coasting along her walls until just the tip remained inside. Then she'd sink back down, slowly, squeezing her muscles as she went, reveling in his quick, shallow breaths and the way he groaned against her breast.

"Tessa." His words were hot against her skin, his fingers tight on her hips.

"Hold on," she whispered. "Almost there."

She picked up speed a bit, dropping and lifting faster, taking him deeper, grinding her clit over his belly. Reaching behind her, she found his balls and cupped them in her palm, squeezing gently, then a little harder until he drew in a sharp inhale and growled, "Careful."

Smiling, she dropped her mouth to his ear. "What's the fun in that?"

He growled again, lifted his head from her breast, making sure to take her nipple with him for a bit, and then claimed her mouth with his. His fingers forced their way into her hair, and he angled her head just the way he wanted it, letting her know that he was in control now. Her pleasure, her kisses were all his.

Her grip on the back of the couch tightened. She dropped her hips one more time, deepened the kiss and let the orgasm crash through her. Around and around, the spirals in her mind swirled as the pleasure shot outward from her core to her fingers and toes, causing them to curl and stiffen. Then the moment of pure bliss arrived, that euphoric drift of weakness and semiconsciousness, what the French called *la petite mort*. The little death. Because when she was with Atlas and she climaxed, it was like dying and going to heaven for just a blip in time. As the sensations faded, her senses reappeared and her synapses stopped firing all at once. She was reborn. Awakened with a new sense of hope and vitality—if not a little exhausted.

When he knew she'd come, he broke their kiss, squished her breasts together, buried his face between them and came. He didn't have to be loud to be passionate. She was learning that about the man too. Just a quiet grunt followed by a strained sound at the back of his throat, then a garbled, "Oh God." A few long, slow exhales and he was done, his tongue laving at her nipples and a content, almost goofy smile on his face.

They sat there in post-coital silence for a moment, letting their heart rates return to rest and their breathing even out. Even though it had been a hot day, fading into a warm evening, his basement was cool, and goosebumps broke out on her sweat-kissed skin as he trailed his fingers gently along her spine.

"Feel better?" he asked, his face once again between her breasts.

"A bit," she said, threading her fingers through his hair. "I miss Forest, and as the days turn into weeks and I still don't have him with me, my hope begins to dwindle."

He lifted his face from her chest. "I know. We're going to do everything we possibly can to get him back."

She made to climb off him. "I know you will." The downstairs bathroom was located across the hall from his office, and even though the kids were upstairs in bed, she still threw her skirt and tank top on before she made her way out the door to go clean up.

She hadn't even touched the bathroom door handle when a cry of "Daddy!" from upstairs made her freeze.

"Shit!" Atlas murmured from inside his office. She heard him grumbling and swearing, and seconds later he emerged wearing just his jeans, his sexy torso and chest with the sprinkling of hair making her engine rev once again. He rolled his eyes at her as he passed. "Be right back." Then he took off up the stairs, his footsteps heavy.

Tessa entered the bathroom and got herself cleaned up and properly dressed. She didn't like this sneaking around thing, but they both knew it was for the best at the moment. Things with Aria were going tremendously well both in therapy and at home. The last thing any of them wanted was to rock the boat of progress or cause some regression by confusing the poor child with who Tessa was to her and her father.

Besides, she and Atlas were still trying to figure things out, and if *they* couldn't put a label on what they were, there was no sense trying to explain things to an inquisitive, bright child like Aria. The questions would undoubtably be endless.

Protests and cries from upstairs filtered down through the vents and flooring. Now it sounded like both girls were up. Oh man, he really had his hands full. No wonder his work had suggested he take some time off to get things sorted. She only hoped that the two of them getting together wasn't adding to his stress pile and instead, in some little way, her presence helped him sort through his stress and maybe even reduce it a bit. But that wasn't likely, not at least with the Carlyle/Forest/Blaire debacle currently weighing them down.

Like the unicorn in shining armor that he was, he'd gone and made her problem his problem, and no matter what she did to try to convince him that she could fight her own battles, he insisted on helping her.

He still hadn't said how his wife had died. Did he have a bit of a failed hero syndrome? Did he think that because he couldn't save his wife from ... whatever she'd passed from, he was determined to save Tessa—from her narcissistic ex?

She'd have to stew on that a bit more. It did make sense though. The same reason why he'd taken in Cecily after the baby's father died and her mother was in the hospital, nearly burned to death. He had the savior complex. He was determined to save those he could because he hadn't been able to save the one who mattered most.

This was what she needed her own therapist for, to work through some of these complex issues. Her supervisor for her PhD was a bit like that. The two had known each other for years, and Tessa could talk to Carey about anything. In some ways, she was a surrogate mother for Tessa, but Carey was also very professional, and although they were friends, and mentor and mentee, Carey made sure not to let the lines blur. She had her own family: husband, children and grandchildren. As much as she liked Tessa and the two had a great relationship, she'd made it clear that if Tessa needed therapy, Carey—a trained psychiatrist—was not going to be the one to give it to her. That didn't mean Carey's calming presence and words of wisdom weren't treasured when Tessa was fortunate enough to receive them.

Perhaps she should go back to therapy, work through

some of the crap going on in her head with her mother and Carlyle.

Oh yes, that reminded her, she'd gone to see her mother again.

Like a terrible daughter, she'd avoided going back to see her mother after Lily had lost it on Tessa when she was there the last time. She knew her mother wouldn't remember the incident, but Tessa would never be able to forget it, and that was why she came up with every excuse and jumped on any distraction to delay seeing her again. At least until the wounds from her mother's verbal slashing were no longer fresh. She gave the nursing home a wide berth for a full seven days, the longest she'd ever gone without seeing her mother since moving her there. But she just needed the space.

She also knew, though, that she needed to go see her mom. If something happened to Lily and Tessa hadn't made a point of seeing her, she'd never forgive herself. So after work and before heading to Atlas's, she'd stopped by to check in on her mother.

"Hey Mom," Tessa said, knocking on her mother's bedroom door. "Can I come in?"

"Tessa!" Her mother's eyes lit up when she pivoted her gaze from the canvas to Tessa in the doorway.

Was her mother lucid? Did she recognize Tessa? Holy crap.

Stepping inside, she rushed to her mother's side. "Yes, it's me. Hi, Mom." She hugged her mom and melted when her mother hugged her back. "How are you?" Tears stung her eyes. She'd caught her mother at a rare lucid moment, which was more priceless than gold these days.

"I'm busy," her mother said with a tired sigh, though her tone wasn't the least bit testy. "Have you seen your father, or is he out in the garage tinkering on that bike of yours?"

Damn it. She wasn't lucid. She was just trapped in the past. Nineteen-some-odd years in the past.

She knew to just play along with whatever time period her mother was currently caught in. It made the outbursts and upsets less frequent and kept the conversation pleasant —even if it did make Tessa's heart feel as heavy as a bag of rocks. "I think he is, Mom. The engine was making a funny sound when I rode home from school, so he said he'd take a look at it after dinner. But you know him, he couldn't wait until after dinner and he's out there now."

Her mother smiled. "Nothing means more to him than your safety." She dipped her paintbrush into some white paint and then dark green paint, swirling the colors together on her paint palette until they formed a light, celery-like color. "How was school? Did you enter your piece in the art fair like I suggested?"

Smiling at the memory of a very similar conversation they'd had eons ago, Tessa nodded. "I did. My art teacher thinks I might take first prize."

Her mother's eyes were focused on the canvas, but they filled with joy. "Excellent, dear. I'd say you got your artistic talents from me but ... " She wrinkled her nose and squinted at her painting.

"But what, Mom? I *did* get my love of painting and artistic talents from you. I was practically born with a paintbrush in my hand. Dad says that all the time."

Her mother's eyes turned harsh, almost angry, then they flicked toward Tessa. "You didn't get it from me, and your father needs to stop saying things like that. He knows damn well you weren't born with a paintbrush in your hand. He knows damn well."

Her shoulders dropped with a sigh. "Okay, Mom." The last thing she wanted to do was rile up her mother again, so she just dropped it.

"Dinner is on the stove. I can't stop what I'm doing right now. Go eat without me. I need to finish this." She flicked her hand in a dismissive motion, invariably telling Tessa to *git*. "Tell your father that he needs to eat something," her mother said absently, no longer really giving Tessa the time of day. "He's getting thin."

Tessa leaned in toward her mother and pecked her on her cool cheek. "I will, Mom. I'll go get him from the garage now."

Her mother did nothing but grunt a response.

Tessa glanced at the piece her mother was painting, and just like all the rest stacked against the wall, it was a mother holding a baby. Both mom and child had their eyes closed, but small smiles tilted their lips. Were they simply sleeping? She hoped so.

Her parents never mentioned losing any children and always changed the subject when she asked why she didn't have a sibling. She'd written Santa for years, asking for a brother or sister. But any time she brought it up with her parents, they said there wasn't anything sturdier than a stool with three legs, then they'd hand her a cookie or put on the television. Eventually, she just stopped asking.

By the time she left her mother, she was more confused than ever but with less of a heavy heart than their previous visit. At least this time her mother recognized her—kind of. She thought Tessa was a sixteen-year-old version of herself, but at this stage of the game, she needed to take her wins where she could get them. She promised to return on the weekend with more blank canvases. Her mother had also asked for gold leaf, which of course Tessa agreed to.

Thank God for her father's life insurance policy and the nice price tag the Realtor had listed her parents' house for. Otherwise, she didn't know how she would be able to afford her mother's care at the nursing home. It was one of the best in the city, and its monthly fees, which were more than some people made in a month, reflected that.

She washed her hands in the downstairs bathroom sink of Atlas's house and stared at her complexion in the mirror. How long before she no longer recognized the people around her? How long before she stopped recognizing herself? She was getting her PhD in a month, but was it even worth it? All that education, only to wind up with mashed potatoes for brains in a few years. Perhaps she should be abandoning all that she'd worked so hard for, and going off to travel the world during the few years of lucidity she had left.

As much as she loved her mother with all her heart, it was like picking a scab and reopening a wound every time she went to visit her. The constant reminder was right in front of her face that just like Lily, she would most likely end up with Alzheimer's. She knew she should tell Atlas about it, about her mother and the fact that she probably carried the gene as well, but she just wasn't ready to take that plunge.

Because once you knew, you couldn't unknow. Once he knew, he couldn't unknow, and that would forever change how he treated her, what he thought of her. And at the moment, she was enjoying the blissful ignorance of Atlas's affections for her, and she was going to take her wins where she could get them.

15

"YOU'RE LEAVING?" Atlas asked, thundering back down the stairs after dealing with the girls. "I wasn't gone *that* long, was I?"

After cleaning herself up in the bathroom and getting dressed, Tessa sat alone with her thoughts on the downstairs couch for several minutes, and the longer she sat there, the more she knew she needed to go.

"Aria wanted water, and because my child has no volume control, she woke up Cecily, even though they were in separate rooms. That prompted Cecily to stand up and start yelling at me for *her* water bottle. She also crapped herself. So it took a while to get her back down. I'm sorry if I made you wait. I didn't think I was going to be that long."

Shaking her head, she forced a fake smile at him and slid into her sandals near the front door. "It's okay. It's getting late, anyway. I should probably go. I still have some reading to do before bed. I'm trying to read at least one journal article a night in preparation for my defense."

He sat down on a step near the landing, his chest still

bare, along with his big, sexy man feet. She wasn't sure she'd seen anything sexier in all her life than Atlas with his mussed-up sex hair, wearing jeans, no shirt and no socks. "How is the studying going?"

She shrugged. "Okay. I mean, I'll undoubtedly be a bundle of nerves when I defend. I was when I got my master's degree, too, it's just who I am. But I got the notes and feedback on my dissertation from my supervisor and the other two people I submitted it to for critique, and they all said it looks good. A few tweaks here and there on wording, but otherwise, I don't have much to change."

His smile was magnetic. "Fuck, you're smart." The gray in his eyes turned almost silver. He stood up and approached her, his body feeling extra big and tall as he invaded her space and pinned her up against the door. His warm breath beat rapidly against her lips. His jaw was working and his eyes so intense, they seared her.

Her eyes shot up the stairs toward the hallway. Aria could come out at any time and see them there. Then what?

"I ... I should go," she said, but her body said differently, and she turned to pudding against him. Her knees buckled, and she would have fallen into a heap on the floor if he hadn't pressed his hips against hers to hold her up. She could feel his need for her against her thigh.

"You should go," he whispered against her jaw, his breath kissing her in a way that made prickles race along her skin.

"I should go."

"You should go."

"I should go." Her purse landed on the floor with a thud, her arms wrapped around his neck at the same time his hands gripped her butt cheeks, and he hoisted her onto his hips. Her lips parted for him as his tongue swept inside, claiming her, tasting her, devouring her. Still carrying her, he headed back down the stairs toward his office, but they didn't make it there before he stopped in the hallway, her body still perched on his. He pressed her back hard against the wall. She whimpered when he bit her bottom lip, her chin, her jaw. His teeth scraped; so did his beard.

Almost as if they hadn't just had sex half an hour ago, the man was practically frantic, the way his hands roamed her body, caressing and kneading. His fingers traced along her arms, lifting them above her head, where he pinned them up with one hand. His other hand made surprisingly quick work of his jeans. She had to hand it to the man, holding her up against the wall with his legs, keeping her arms up with one hand and unfastening his jeans with another—he continued to surprise her with his prowess and talents.

She had underwear on, but he'd just have to pull them aside to—*rip*. Oh, well, then never mind. He'd torn them clean off.

With a bit of an adjustment and pushing her skirts out of the way, he was back inside her in seconds, hammering her hard up against the wall, grunting with each heavy thrust.

She couldn't even hold on to his shoulders. He had her hands in a vice grip, had complete control over her body and how he wanted it. How he wanted her to take him. Every plunge and every draw of his cock inside her had brighter stars flashing behind her closed eyelids. His teeth raked a track over her collarbone, and she inhaled sharply from the snap of delightful pain. All the while, he just kept driving into her, never letting up on his rhythm. His ferocity was coming at her in full force with each hard, measured thrust.

She was close. Her clit pulsed, and her pussy tightened around him as he drove up and into her. The first time they'd had sex had been fueled by an attraction they'd tried hard to resist, an attraction they knew was wrong but finally succumbed to. She'd also been kind of pissed off at him, and for some reason the angry sex was really hot. But tonight, his passion came from somewhere else. It was no less wild, no less hot, it was just a place she didn't recognize, a place she didn't understand.

"Fuck, Tess," he grunted into her neck, the fingers of his one hand digging painfully into her butt cheek.

"Atlas."

"Fuck, Tess," he said again.

She wasn't going to be able to hold on much longer, not with the way he was giving it to her, not with the way Atlas managed to make everything feel so damn good.

She broke with a sharp cry, her lips parting and her head tilting skyward as the orgasm hit her with full force. Every muscle tightened, desperate to hold on to the pleasure that tore through each fiber of her body. Squeezing every drop out of the blissful moment that was her and Atlas together. She gripped him firmly inside her, squeezed her hips around his and held on for dear life as the waves continued to wrack her. It wasn't until a charley horse emerged in her leg that she finally relaxed her muscles.

But Atlas kept pumping. With every deep thrust, he grunted. His rhythm began to falter, and in seconds he was burying his face in her neck, laving at her sweat-misted skin and coming inside her for the second time that night.

ATLAS SWIPED the tip of his tongue over Tessa's collarbone, enjoying the way she shivered in his arms, her legs wrapped like a vine around his hips, his cock still nestled safely inside her heat.

He wasn't entirely sure what had come over him on the

steps there, when she said she was going to leave. He just knew he couldn't let her. Not yet anyway. It'd been a long time since he found someone he connected with on such a level, not only intimately but also personally, and even though he was tired and he knew she had to get home to study, he selfishly wasn't ready to say goodbye.

So he'd charmed the pants—or, in this case, skirt—right off her, seducing her until she gave in. Though he didn't really think the woman would have required that much convincing. She seemed pretty accepting of his insistence she stay for round two.

Did he have a round three left in him?

He dug down deep and attempted to twitch his cock. At the moment, he did not, but maybe if she stuck around for another hour he could try.

She needs to get home, asshole.

Her sigh of contentment, followed by a hum, made him reluctantly lift his face from the safety and comfort of her neck and look her in her soul-piercing eyes. Blue sparkled back at him like a sea full of diamonds. "I really do need to get going home. As much fun as this is, I still have to study."

Nodding, he slid out of her at the same time he helped her off his hips. Without a word, she ducked into the bathroom, and he zipped up his jeans.

If he was being honest with himself, he not only didn't want to see her go yet, but he was also trying to distract her. She was going home to an empty house. There would be no Forest waiting for her, and the thought of Tessa going another few weeks without her dog caused a sharp pain in his chest that he wasn't at all prepared for.

The toilet on the other side of the bathroom door flushed, and then the sink ran. Seconds later she was out, looking freshly fucked and fucking beautiful.

He reached for her hand and pressed a hard kiss to her lips before he led her back up the stairs to the landing. "Aria has preschool tomorrow followed by dance lessons with my friend Adam's wife, and then an appointment with you Friday afternoon. I think I'll take Cecily to story time at the library while Aria is with you."

Her cheeks turned rosy, and her smile grew brighter. "Look at you being super dad. You guys are busy, busy."

He snorted and rolled his eyes. "Keeps them from destroying my house."

"So I will see you Friday then?" Her free hand was already on the door handle.

"Unless you want to come by tomorrow night?"

Say yes. Say yes.

She shook her head. "I'm afraid I can't. I'm meeting with my supervisor to go over the data from a study we've been working on."

Damn it.

"Friday?" he asked, regretting his needy tone.

"Maybe. What about Saturday?"

"Poker night with the guys."

"Sunday?" Well, now he felt a bit better that she was also throwing out days and it wasn't just him. He wasn't beginning to feel weird about how insistent he was being about seeing her so soon again. "Let's touch base Friday," she said quickly. "I was going to wait and go see my mom on Saturday, but I'm thinking that day might be better dedicated to studying, so I might go Friday night after work."

"Is she just elderly and in a home?"

A pain and something else he couldn't put his finger on flashed behind her eyes. "Something like that, yeah. Anyway, I've got to run." She disentangled their fingers, pressed that same hand to his chest and leaned in for a kiss. He deepened it, cupping her cheek in his palm and angling her jaw to grant him better access to her mouth.

His heart ached for Tessa. It must be hard only having one parent alive, no longer independent enough to live alone. He was fortunate his parents were still doing relatively well health-wise. His father had suffered a stroke last year, and his mother was dealing with some pretty debilitating arthritis, but other than that, they still lived on their own in Atlas's childhood home back in Portland. They'd offered to take Cecily when things with Tamsin went down, but he knew it would be a struggle for them to take care of a new baby. So even though his life was a bit of a shitshow, he took her in knowing he could be more hands-on and available than his parents.

Breathless and starry-eyed, she broke the kiss moments later. "I really have to go." She opened the door but turned back to him. "Thank you for the wonderful distraction tonight. You, this, all of it is *exactly* what I need to soothe the ache in my heart from not having Forest with me."

His lip twitched.

Her grin turned vibrant, and she leaned in for one more kiss. "I'm glad you're not such an asshole anymore."

Growling, he kissed her once more, then reached around and pinched her butt. "Go before I cart you back downstairs and distract you some more."

She squealed and jumped away from him, bouncing down the steps toward his driveway. He watched her get into her car and drive away. It wasn't until she was down the road that he finally closed the door, the same moment his phone began to vibrate and ping in his pocket.

At first, he thought it might be Tessa, calling to say that she already missed him, but then he saw that it was his father's cell phone.

"Hey, Dad." He climbed the stairs, then went to the kitchen to pour himself a bourbon.

"Son, I'm afraid I have some terrible news."

Oh no.

A lead weight dropped with a heavy thud in his gut.

Here he'd just been grateful that his parents were both healthy and lived in their own home. What had he done? Jinxed them all?

"Tamsin took her own life today. She's gone, son."

He finished pouring his bourbon, then made his way into the living room, numb as his father went on to explain what happened and how his cousin got ahold of a syringe and injected an air bubble into her own vein. She'd been moved from the ICU burn ward to just a regular hospital room, and apparently the nurses were on strike so there was a severe staff shortage, and she managed to snag a syringe off a nearby cart. She coded, but there wasn't anything they could do to save her.

Tamsin—sweet, confused, troubled little Tamsin, who had been more like a little sister to him than anything—was gone.

Agony and anger swirled inside him until the two created such a vortex, he wasn't sure he'd ever be able to break free of its grasp. He shoved his free hand into his hair and pulled on the ends until a shooting pain began to throb in his skull. A welcomed distraction from the agony in his heart. Scraping his fingers down his face, he pulled on his chin, his throat tight and eyes burning.

"She didn't want a funeral," his father went on, though he was sure his dad had been speaking for some time now. Atlas just hadn't heard him over the white noise of his own thoughts. "Your mother went to see her a little while ago, and although your mom didn't want to talk about it, Tamsin did. She laid out a plan for Cecily in case she died, then laid out a plan and expectations for herself. Makes you wonder how far back she started planning this."

If he knew Tamsin, probably from the moment she looked at her face in the mirror for the first time. She was a beautiful young woman, and after the explosion, she was unrecognizable as her old self. The doctors made no promises they could get her back to looking like she did before the explosion. The burns were too severe, and she was missing part of her nose and cheek.

"She wanted you to adopt Cecily as yours. She signed over everything in the event she passed. She said because she didn't have any money and we all spent a large chunk of her life bailing her out, she didn't want us spending a dime on her in the afterlife."

Atlas sipped his drink to coat his tight, dry throat.

"She said she'd haunt us if we went against her wishes." His dad laughed, but it was forced and died out fast. "All the possessions she had were destroyed in the explosion, except for a locket she wore around her neck. It's to go to Cecily."

His nostrils flared and his jaw pulsed as he fought to reign in the flood of dueling emotions inside him. "Nobody from his family is going to challenge me for custody, are they?"

"You mean Ty's family? I don't think so. He wasn't close with his parents. I'm not even sure who or where they are. Don't even know if they know Cecily exists."

Atlas grunted.

"Besides, you're a big fancy lawyer. You'd win custody regardless."

Atlas grunted again. "You need me to come down there?"

"Naw, son. You're busy with the little ones up there. You guys have your life and your routine. It's a sad thing for sure, but I think your cousin was in a lot of pain. She had a lot of regrets and had sunk into a pretty severe depression. I hate to say this, but at least she's at peace now."

Unsure what to say next, he simply grunted again.

"I know it's going to take a while to sink in," his father said, remorse thick in his voice. "Your mother hasn't been able to stop crying since we found out a few hours ago."

As much as he loved his dad, at the moment, he didn't want to talk to a soul. He just wanted to sit in silence with his grief, with his anger, with his pain—the same way he'd dealt with Samantha's passing. But as if she knew on some deep-down freaky-spiritual level that something was wrong, Cecily down the hall began to cry.

"That CeCe?" his dad asked.

"Mhmm." He drained his drink, then stood up.

"Okay then, son. I'll leave you to it. Kiss the girls for your mother and me, and we'll call again in a few days, okay?"

"'K, Dad." He went to hang up but then thought better of it. "Dad?"

"Yes, son?"

"I love you. Mom too."

His dad was quiet for a moment, but the ragged breathing on the other end said that Rhys Stark was having a hard time keeping it together. "We love you too, Atlas. So much."

"Bye, Dad."

"Goodbye, son."

He disconnected the call and headed down toward Cecily's room, craning his neck into Aria's room first to check to see if she was still asleep. Thankfully, she was.

Cecily was standing up in her crib, her face dripping with tears by the time he got there, her fine, blonde hair all messed up from sleep. She threw her arms in the air and reached for him, the words *up, up,* mixing with her frantic cries. He scooped her up and snuggled her into his chest. Immediately she stopped crying and nestled into the crook of his neck, her whimpers and squeaks soft and content.

Ordinarily, he wouldn't have picked her up but would

simply pat her back to help her get back down. But just like the night Samantha died, when Aria woke, he'd held her for as long as she needed him to. Let her sleep on him, take comfort in his heartbeat and the knowledge that he was there for her, for as long as she needed him, forever and for always. And tonight, Cecily needed the same thing. Tonight, she got whatever she wanted, whatever she needed, because tonight, she'd just lost her mother.

16

FRIDAY AFTERNOON SEEMED to get there in no time, and even though he was still incredibly sad about losing his cousin, Atlas tossed on a brave face for the girls. They needed him to be strong and present, not wallowing in his grief, shutting them and the rest of the world out.

So, as planned, he dropped Aria off with Tessa, then he—with Cecily in the carrier—walked to the library for story time.

She loved it, like Jenny said she always did, and she even tried to take a few steps away from him, only to land with a gentle thud on her bottom when a toy distracted her and caused her to try to turn.

She was snoozing on his back by the time he went to gather Aria, who also appeared tired but in good spirits.

"See, Daddy," his daughter said, coming up to him with a piece of paper dripping in white glue, "I made the beach. Like the one we go to tomorrow."

He promised the girls that he would take them to the beach on Sunday if they behaved for Kimmy Saturday night while he was at poker. Only Aria had no concept of days or time and thought tomorrow was Sunday.

"You mean Sunday," he corrected.

"Yeah, tomorrow."

He rolled his eyes. "Two more sleeps and then the beach."

"Yeah, tomorrow."

"Just give up," Tessa said, chuckling after she finished cleaning up the craft supplies and joined them. "Her development isn't there yet to understand time and dates. It's best to do what you're doing and just use sleeps as a countdown." She winked at him. He'd told her last night about Tamsin, and she'd somehow managed to say all the right things, which, incidentally, was very little. Because he didn't want to talk or listen to someone go on and on about her being in a better place. He just wanted to sit on the phone with someone in the quiet, and that's exactly what she'd let him do.

She studied, he did dishes and tidied the house, but they had their phones on. They were together. She was there for him if he needed her. Present.

And it had been perfect.

Aria's eyes lit up and she gasped like she'd just discovered a new element for the periodic table or someone had asked her to do a voiceover for Frozen III. "I know." She lifted her finger up like a true scientist. "I think Tessa should come to the beach with us." She turned to Atlas. "Please, Daddy, can she come?"

"I don't know if that's such a good idea, Aria," Tessa said, resting her hand on Aria's shoulder.

Aria shrugged. "It's a beach. You need to come."

Kid logic was so cut and dried.

"We will make sand castles and dig for stuff like clams and crabs and whales."

"Whales?" Tessa's eyebrow lifted, and she covered her mouth inconspicuously to hide her growing smile.

"Yeah, but like you have to dig down *really* deep, because whales live in a lot of water." She turned back to Atlas. "Please, Daddy. Say Tessa can come with us." She went to pull on his shorts pocket, but he held her off at the same time he lifted his glance to Tessa. "Beach? Then some friends are having a get-together, and they said you should come." He knew he was taking a huge leap inviting her, particularly to both places, but he also knew he hated being away from this woman.

"Y-you've told people about us?"

He shrugged. "A few. Haven't you?"

"I don't really have very many people to tell." Her face fell. "Despite being a Seattle native, I don't have too many friends. They've all either moved away or had children and have no time for me."

All the more reason she should go with him. "Well, there will be *loads* of women at this party, and I guarantee you by the time you leave, you'll be friends with them. It's just what happens."

The look she gave him was skeptical. "*Loads?* You mean to tell me each one of your male friends has an entire harem?"

"No. Not a harem each." He bugged out his eyes. "Can you imagine? I could not even begin to think how I'd please that many women." Her soft snicker made his heart tighten. "Just one woman each. But they're all single dads too and over the last little while have found a woman who just fits."

"Who just fits," she repeated. "Is that what I am? A woman who just fits?"

He'd been so focused on Tessa, he hadn't noticed Aria's curious eyes swiveling back and forth like she was watching a championship match at Wimbledon. "What you guys talking about?" she asked.

He ran his hand down the back of her head. "Nothing, sweetie. Just grown-up talk."

"You saying how Tessa fits her pants? Because she wouldn't fit into your pants. They too big. And you couldn't fit into her pants. They would break."

Oh Jesus. Out of the mouths of precocious babes.

He'd managed to get into Tessa's pants no problem the other night.

He twisted his lips to keep the smile from stretching too far across his face. "Not quite, sweetie. Why don't you go put your unfinished art away in your bin and then we'll go?"

Aria rolled her eyes, then took off toward her bin, her feet scuffing along the floor like she was walking through snow.

"Come on Sunday," he said, hitting Tessa with his gaze again. "To the beach and the party. It'll take your mind off everything that's going on. And by Sunday, I'm sure you'll need the break if you're just going to study all weekend. Besides, Aria thinks you coming to the beach was her idea. We can keep our hands to ourselves if you want to."

He didn't want to, but he also wasn't sure how much affection he could show Tessa in front of his daughter. He'd never done anything like this before, and he didn't want to confuse the kid, particularly when things were going so well for her at the moment.

Tessa's bottom lip rolled inward, and she snagged it with her top teeth. "I'll think about it, okay? It will depend on how productive my studying is on Saturday."

Aria was back and tugging on Atlas's arm, whining to go.

He shot Tessa a smile and a look he hoped conveyed exactly how he felt about her and how much she meant to him. "Fine. But just know that if you're *not* at the beach on Sunday, you'll be expected to come by that night. I don't want to go the entire weekend without seeing you." He lifted his eyebrow, waited for her reaction, which was exactly what he wanted: dilated pupils, flared nostrils, flushed cheeks. Then he took his daughter by the hand and led them out the door. But not before calling back, "See you Sunday, Tessa."

It was Sunday afternoon, and Tessa was elbow-deep in the depths of her walk-in closet, on the hunt for her big floppy sun hat. She knew it was in there somewhere. She'd only just worn it that past summer, so where was it now?

"Oh, for crying out loud," she hollered to no one in particular as she heaved another one of Carlyle's big boxes of comic books out of the way. She spied her hat, and of course, it was crushed beneath another box of comics.

Son of a bitch.

"I freaking hate you!"

If her sun hat was ruined, she was going to add that to the list of things he owed her, besides her dog and the last five years of her life.

The thought of Forest brought melancholy into her heart, and as fast as the fury came, it fled, replaced by nothing but sadness. Forest loved the beach. He loved chasing the waves, digging in the sand, chasing a stick. He loved everything because he'd lived in hell, and now that he was out of it, he was just appreciative and grateful for every day.

Was whoever Carlyle had left him with taking him for walks? Was he being treated well? She'd never forgive herself or Carlyle if Forest was facing any kind of neglect while he was with Carlyle's friend. A friend she'd never even heard of.

A hot tear slipped down her cheek as she sat back on her heels and brought one of Forest's beloved stuffed toys to her chest. He'd loved this squirrel, torn the stuffing clean out of it more than once. And she just couldn't bring herself to throw it away, he loved it so much, so each time he disemboweled the creature, she'd collect all the stuffing from around the apartment, then perform abdominal surgery on poor Sassy the Squirrel.

"I miss you, buddy," she whispered once again to nobody. Because she had nobody. Had Forest been home, he would have been right in the closet with her, then when she hollered out in frustration, his head would have cocked side to side like a puppy as he tried to understand her.

She should torch the whole comic book collection just to spite Carlyle. Then drop each one of his precious records from the Ballard Bridge. He could freaking swim to collect them.

But then the little voice in her head reminded her of their worth. Not only were they worth a lot of money, but they could also be used as a bargaining chip for her to get Forest back.

Shoving the other big box out of the way, she grabbed her floppy tan sun hat. It was flat and had a weird fold on one side, but it would still work to keep the sun off her face. She went to plop it on her head, but before she could, an envelope fell out into her lap. It was in her father's handwriting, but all it said was *Kiddo*.

Where did this come from? Why had she never seen this before? Had Carlyle hidden it?

Turning the envelope over in her hand, she slid her fingers over the seal. It hadn't been opened or compromised in any way, so why would he hide it?

Unless he hadn't and it had simply fallen out of one of the many boxes she'd brought over from her parents' house once it sold and then stuffed in her closet because she had no time to go through it all.

Grabbing the corner of the envelope, she went to tear it open when her phone in the pocket of her flannel pajama pants began to vibrate and ring.

"Hello?" Standing up, she took the letter into her room with her and set it down on her dresser.

"Hey, we're just leaving the house now. Can you be ready in ten minutes if we come get you?" It was Atlas, and he sounded unusually chipper. She knew he was still grieving the loss of his cousin, and when he called her the last few nights—even last night after his poker game—he'd been sad, and they simply sat together in silence on the phone. She read her journal articles, and he read the news on his phone or cleaned the house, but they were together, and that was what he'd needed.

But today, he sounded upbeat, almost happy.

"I thought we were just meeting at the beach," she said, pulling her pajama pants off only to slide into denim shorts with a rolled hem that hit her just above the knee.

"Yeah, but why take two cars when we can just take one? Then we'll go home, hose the kids off, and then head to the party."

"Should I be dressing fancy?"

"You mean pack one of those hippie skirts? Sure. I mean, I'll be in a tuxedo, but I'm sure you won't be turned away looking like a flower child ready for Woodstock."

"Neither of us are old enough to bring up Woodstock. And was that a joke? Did Atlas Stark just tell a joke?" He really was in a good mood if he was cracking one-liners.

"It's casual. You'd look beautiful in a potato sack."

Heat filled her cheeks. She set her phone down, hit the speaker option, pulled off her pajama top and then went on the hunt for her bra.

"We're on the way," he said.

"That's right, Tessa. We're on the way," Aria cheered from the background.

"Waaaay," Cecily echoed.

Giggles floated across the line.

"Get your bikini and your SPF on and meet us out front in ten, okay?"

She located her bra and put it on, followed by a sleeveless black-and-white checked button-up shirt. Her sigh was more for dramatic effect than anything, because the smile on her face hurt her cheeks. "Fine. I'll be out in ten."

"Yay!" they all cheered in the car. Then the line went dead.

Tessa glanced at herself in the mirror and was taken aback by just how big her smile was. Despite not having Forest right now, she was happy. Atlas, Aria and Cecily, they made her happy—maybe she did fit?

"Look, Daddy!" Aria announced, lying back in the sand and flailing her limbs all about. "I'm making sand angels. See?"

Tessa turned to hide her face as she snickered. The child was covered head to toe in sand, and now it was going to be caked on her scalp, under her nails and probably in her bathing suit.

"Sweetie," Atlas said gently, standing up from the beach blanket with a slight groan. "You are covered in sand, absolutely covered."

Aria didn't move from her prone position in the wet sand. "I don't mind. I like how it feels between my toes."

Cecily was currently sitting on the blanket between Tessa's legs, happily playing with sand.

"Blech ... ahhhh," the baby began to protest.

Tessa craned her neck around to find a giant wad of sand tumbling out of Cecily's mouth, the baby looking most put out by her current choice of food.

"Oh dear Lord." She chuckled, reaching for Cecily's water bottle. "Have a sip, little one. Here." She held the bottle for her and Cecily guzzled greedily, her chubby little legs bouncing and toes digging deeper into the sand. With water from the water bottle on a corner of a towel, Tessa wiped her up as best she could. Cecily had already moved on from her perturbed state and was back to attempting to dig with one of the sand shovels.

Aria and Atlas wandered back toward them, hand in hand. "I think we might need to give a five-minute warning," he said, kneeling down on the blanket next to Tessa and briskly wiping the sand from his daughter's limbs, though the effort seemed somewhat futile.

"I don't want to gooooooo," Aria protested, stomping her foot and adopting the biggest pout on the planet. "I love the beach, and I *loooooove* that Tessa is here with us."

"Yeah, but we're going to go home, get all cleaned up and then go to a party," Atlas offered. Tessa's belly did a flip-flop at the mention of this party. The only person besides Atlas that she would know there would be Zak Eastwood and his son Aiden. Because Aiden had been a client. Otherwise, she would be the interloper. The intruder that everyone knew about, but she knew nothing about them. She was going in with a serious disadvantage.

"A party?" Aria asked. "For who? Can I wear a party dress?"

Atlas grimaced when he went to rub the towel over her head and sand began to fly everywhere. "We might have to strap her to the roof," he murmured.

Tessa giggled.

"Can I wear my rose dress, Daddy?" Aria asked. "That is my most beautifulest dress. I look like a princess in it."

"You can wear your rose dress," he replied. "And you're right, you do look like a princess."

Beaming, Aria allowed him to continue toweling the sand off her without protest.

Within ten minutes, they were all packed up, re-dressed —sort of—and heading back to Atlas's Land Cruiser. Like he often did, he was wearing Cecily in the carrier, only this time she was forward-facing. Did he know how sexy he looked? Probably not.

With all their gear in one hand and Aria's hand in his other, Tessa was left to carry nothing but the blanket. He had it all under control. As much as he said he was overwhelmed and didn't feel like he could hack the single dad of two girls thing, to her, he was knocking it out of the park.

Aria pivoted her head around. "Come on, Tessa! We don't want to be late for the party."

She hadn't even realized she'd stopped to watch the three of them.

Atlas paused, his sexy feet still bare and covered in sand. He turned around too. "You coming?"

With her heart feeling lighter than it had in ages, she grinned as she jogged to catch up. Aria reached for her hand and she was about to take it when a bark she would recognize in a field full of dogs made her heart lurch inside her chest.

Forest.

There it was again. She would recognize it anywhere. Like a mother penguin locating its chick in a rookery of other chicks, she would recognize his call anywhere.

The beach was dotted with people and dogs enjoying the hot late May day, and with something almost akin to panic in her chest, she spun around searching for that bark.

And then she saw him.

With tongue lolling out, a smile on his face and fur in the breeze, he ran toward her, barking. When he saw that she had spotted him, his canter quickened, and before she knew it, she was on her knees in the sand and Forest was licking her face and going crazy in her arms.

"Oh, Forest." She wrapped her arms around his neck and

hugged him tight, burying her face in the soft fur of his neck. He smelled clean but also salty like the sea. He looked good, felt healthy.

"Sorry about that," a man's voice said, drawing nearer. "I'm dog-sitting for a friend, and although Forest has great recall, sometimes he gets a bit excited."

Swallowing down the razor blades in her throat, she reluctantly stood up. "I'm Forest's owner. I'm Carlyle's ex."

The man was young, like maybe twenty-five if that, and the look on his face was pure terror. He attempted to reach for Forest's collar, but Tessa had it first and backed a step away. "I'm not supposed to let you near him," the guy said. "He says you were cruel to Forest. That you neglected and beat him."

Well, now she thought she might be sick.

Tears welled up in her eyes, and she struggled to stay standing. Forest leaned against her leg for support. "I would never lay a hurtful hand on this dog. Everything Carlyle told you about me was a lie. He is *my* dog, and I love him like I would a child."

Unease drifted into the young man's brown eyes.

"Do you think he would greet me this way if I hurt him?"

She felt Atlas behind her.

"Daddy, whose dog is that?" Aria asked.

"He's Tessa's dog, sweetie," he whispered.

"Oh, I like him. He's pretty."

"I'm sorry, miss," the young man said. "Mr. Rickson left me very clear instructions. I can see that Forest loves you, but I—I can't let you take him." He approached her and Forest as if either one of them might lunge out and bite off his hand. Forest didn't growl, but he did try to hide behind Tessa, ducking his head and backing up around her legs. The young man grew more confident though, and he slid his fingers around Forest's collar. Reluctantly, she released her own grip and stepped away.

Forest went to pull away from the man and return to her. He began to whimper, his feet slipping in the wet sand as he struggled to throw on the brakes and gain some traction. Instead, he just stirred up sand.

A harsh sob caught in her throat, and she wiped away the tears that fell. "Please be kind to him. He's so confused."

The man nodded. "I love dogs. This is what I do for a living. I walk them during the week and then pet-sit on the weekends and during the week. Forest is being well cared for. I promise you."

Well, at least Carlyle had done something right.

Her bottom lip jiggled, and she turned away as the young man led a protesting Forest back down the beach.

"Tessa crying, Daddy," Aria said, sliding her smooth, cool fingers into Tessa's hand. "It's okay, Tessa. Don't cry."

Well, that just made her cry even more.

"Why can't she bring her dog, Daddy?" Aria asked as she took her father's hand again and they began heading back up the beach toward the parking lot.

"It's a bit complicated, sweetie," he said softly.

"What does *comp-i-cate-ed* mean?" Aria asked.

"It means a grown-up problem," he replied. "But Daddy and Uncle Liam are working very hard to get Tessa her doggy back. Don't you worry."

They reached the parking lot, and he somehow managed to hit the fob to unlock his Land Cruiser, all without letting go of the beach stuff or Aria's hand.

"Tessa, when you get your dog back, can you bring him over to play in our backyard?" Aria asked, when Atlas stood her up in the hatch and attempted to rid her of more sand.

Tessa was barely able to stay standing, but she held on to

the side of the vehicle and swallowed hard. "I'd love that, Aria."

Aria bopped a warbling Cecily on the nose, making the baby giggle and smile. "We hope you get him back soon. It'd be nice to add a dog to the family, too."

17

ATLAS FELT HELPLESS. There wasn't a damn thing he could do on that beach to help Tessa, and they both knew it. If they'd tried to take the dog away from the pet-sitter, it would undoubtably seal Tessa's fate of never getting her dog back. Especially since Carlyle had gone and lied through his fucking teeth about Tessa abusing and mistreating the dog. Who's to say he wasn't going to continue to lie? They had to go into their meeting prepared with an arsenal of leverage, otherwise, he was going to be even more underhanded and dirty than he already was and take Tessa's dog away from her for good.

If he ever got his hands on that motherfucker ...

She quietly wept on the drive to his house, and although she was helpful unloading all the beach gear and getting the girls ready, she seemed a million miles away as she did it all.

At least he was seeing Liam tonight, and Liam and Tessa could meet face-to-face. They could talk the whole situation over with his friend and come up with a game plan or, at the very least, reassure Tessa that they were doing everything in their power to get her Forest back.

"See how pretty I am in my dress," Aria said, bouncing out of her bedroom wearing a big, poufy party dress with that netting shit underneath and a ribbon or something around the waist. It was overkill for the party they were headed to, but kids could get away with that kind of thing. Hell, if she wanted to dress up as Cinderella or Dracula, she could, and nobody would bat an eye.

"Very pretty," Tessa said, sipping water from a glass and bouncing an equally gussied-up Cecily on her lap. Aria had insisted that Cecily wear one of her old dresses from when she was a baby. Both girls looked ready for a wedding or christening or something, but who the fuck cared?

Aria beamed at Tessa and took Cecily's hand. "We're so pretty, baby. You're a pretty baby." Cecily kicked and jiggled her chubby body, smiling at all the attention she was getting.

Atlas was just finishing putting all the dishes from the beach picnic in the dishwasher and smiled at the total one-eighty Aria had done with Cecily. She was treating her kindly. She was treating her like family.

"Maybe you should just drop me off at home," Tessa said, her tone so far away and forlorn, at first, he didn't even recognize her voice. "I'm going to be a terrible party guest."

"You have to come," Aria insisted, taking Tessa's hand and then jumping up and down. "You get to meet all my friends. I will tell you who they all are." She began to list them on her fingers. "Gabe and Mira and Jayda and Tia and Aiden and Nolan and Josie and Kellen and Lucas and Freddie and Jordie and ... " Her brows scrunched in thought. "Oh, and the babies: Willow, Brielle and Sophie. I mean they're babies so they don't do much. But they're still my friends." She shrugged. "You have to come so you can meet them."

"She's right," Atlas said, drying his hand on a dish towel and approaching them at the table. "You have to come. It'll take your mind off everything. It will be good to be around other *kind* people. You need more than just work and serial killer documentaries in your life. Plus, Liam will be there, and we can talk about your case if you want to."

Her eyes lit up a bit, but that smile that had blinded him on the first day they met remained hidden. Aria still seemed oblivious to anything more than a friendship between him and Tessa, so relying on her ignorance, he crouched down in front of Tessa and took one of her hands.

Slowly, she lifted her gaze to his. Sadness swirled in the intense blue, and at that moment, all he wanted to do was scoop her up in his arms and take away the pain by any means necessary. He squeezed her fingers, and thankfully, she squeezed his back. "Please come. It would mean a lot to all of us."

A stuttering breath fled from trembling lips, but she nodded. "Okay, I'll come."

"Yay!" Aria cheered, still holding on to Tessa's other hand and swinging it wildly as she jumped up and down.

Cecily reached out and shoved her finger up Atlas's nose, which, as annoying and uncomfortable as it was, seemed to be exactly what they all needed, as it caused everyone including Tessa to laugh—finally that smile broke free.

SOMETHING similar to a sticky wad of peanut butter hung at the back of Tessa's throat while nerves as unmanageable as a bag of cats made her belly turn to the point of nausea. Why on earth had she agreed to go to this party? She didn't know anybody. She was sad, and as much as she loved seeing Forest, it nearly killed her (for the second time in a week) to see him and then let him go. The universe was a cruel bitch to be putting her through this. Made her wonder what kind of karmic malevolence she'd done in a past life to deserve losing her father, having a mother who was but a shell of who she once was, all things Carlyle, Forest stolen from her, and of course, she couldn't forget that big *A* eating away at her brain. Who had she wronged?

"I want a churro and one of Aunt Lowenna's chocolates," Aria said, allowing Tessa to help her out of her car seat. "You should have one of Aunt Paige's churros. They are so yummy in my tummy. They can be yummy in your tummy too." She reached for Tessa's hand and met Atlas and Cecily on the sidewalk of the strip mall in front of all the businesses. The Lilac and Lavender Bistro was situated next to a photography studio, which was a few doors down from a dance studio. According to Atlas, all three businesses were owned by his friends. The parking lot was quite full, despite most of the businesses being closed on Sunday, and through the window into the bistro she could see several bodies moving around. The door was open too, letting Top 40 hits at a respectable decibel flow out. Kids laughing and adults chatting didn't have to compete with the music.

Atlas grinned at her and propped Cecily up on his hip before he reached for Aria's other hand. "Shall we go in?"

Aria nodded, the tiara that she'd chosen to wear last minute glittering in the late afternoon sun.

Tessa took a deep, fortifying breath, nodded and allowed them to lead her inside.

The bistro smelled amazing. Like fresh pastries and bread with that delicious hint of vanilla and chocolate swirling up to the rafters. Although still nauseous, her belly betrayed her and grumbled at the delicious smells bombarding her senses. The moment they walked in, the entire place went dead quiet.

They all stood inside just beyond the door, stock-still, as dozens of sets of eyes took them all in.

Oblivious to everything going on around her, Aria

released both their hands and took off toward the children in the back corner, who were all playing happily or drawing at one of the tables.

Atlas cleared his throat, shaking everyone from their collective trance. Murmurs and conversations slowly filled the space again, but it seemed that everyone was still keeping one eye on Atlas and Tessa. Was it her they were all looking at, or was it Atlas? She couldn't tell.

"Hello!" A gorgeous brunette with big blue eyes and a stunning smile bounced up to Tessa, her ponytail swinging behind her. "I'm Tori. You must be Tessa."

"I am. It's nice to meet you."

A woman who could have nearly been Tori's twin came up behind her. "I'm Isobel, Tori's sister. We're all really happy you could make it."

Atlas made a noise in his throat beside her.

"Yeah, we're glad you could come too, Atlas," Isobel said with an eye roll. She reached for Tessa's hand. "Come on, we want you to meet the rest of us."

She didn't have a choice but to go with them, as each woman took a hand and led her through the crowd and back into the enormous commercial kitchen, where platters of food sat on the center stainless steel table. Tessa's mouth watered at the sight of it all.

Tori and Isobel released her hands, and before she could even blink, a flute of champagne was pushed into her hand by another gorgeous woman with gentle brown eyes and dark blonde hair. "Can't meet a bunch of new people without liquid courage. I'm Aurora, Zak's girlfriend." She rested her hand on Tessa's shoulder. "So nice to finally meet you. Aiden and Zak have nothing but wonderful things to say about you. Zak says you're a miracle worker."

Tessa laughed awkwardly. "I don't know if *miracle worker*

is the right word, but I enjoy what I do, and I think—I *hope*—that comes through in my work."

"That's exactly how I feel," Tori said. "I'm getting my behavioral consultant certification. I work with children on the Autism Spectrum. That's how I met Gabe and Mark."

Oh, thank goodness, a kindred spirit. Someone who understood what she did and why she went into the field she did.

"And Gabe is ... " She was having a hard time remembering everyone's names.

Tori grinned. "Gabe is Mark's son, and he's on the spectrum. I'm dating Mark."

"And I'm with Aaron," Isobel chimed in, "who is holding baby Sophie out there. You see the big hunky redhead who looks like he could break your neck with just a look?"

Tessa poked her head around the corner to peer back into the restaurant portion, where lo and behold there was a big, redheaded man with tattooed arms holding a baby. He had no smile, and his blue eyes were fierce. He really did look like he could snap your neck with just a look.

A woman wearing a baby in one of those stretchy wrap things blocked her view of the intimidating Aaron. "Who you gawking at?" Her green eyes held humor, and her hand a flute of champagne. "Is this where the women are congregating while we wait for Emmett and Zara to arrive?"

"We are," another woman, this one a beautiful brunette with gray eyes, said. She slid a box of what looked to be chocolates across the table, and the woman with the baby beelined it straight for them.

"I'm Violet, and I'm nursing and I'm starving," the woman with the baby said, cramming a decadent-looking pink bonbon into her mouth. "And this chocolate goddess is Lowenna." She wrapped an arm around Lowenna and planted a kiss to her temple. "God, you're wonderful, and these chocolates ... What is this flavor?" She rolled her eyes back and made a blissful face.

"Raspberry mascarpone with white chocolate and vanilla bean," Lowenna said with a triumphant smile. "We've started making our own vanilla in the chocolate shop, and I really think it makes all the difference to scrape the beans fresh into the filling."

Hands shot out, and soon the box was empty except for one. Lowenna pushed the box toward Tessa. "You're one of us now. Grab yours."

"But the birthday girl," Tessa said softly, overwhelmed by all the people but also the openness from these women.

"I brought her an entire box of her own, don't worry," Lowenna said. "This one is yours." She nudged the box closer.

Tessa reached forward and took the shiny little morsel, popping it into her mouth. Her reaction was similar to that of Violet's. Her eyes rolled back before closing completely, and a moan of delight bubbled up from the depths of her chest.

"Now she's really one of us," another woman said. She was wearing an apron and had dark curly hair in a ponytail behind her. "I'm Paige, by the way. This is my restaurant."

"Thank you so much for having me ... for having *us*," Tessa said, reluctantly swallowing down the remainder of the chocolate.

Paige smiled. "My pleasure. Now, eat up. I didn't make this food for it to all go to waste. Emmett just texted me to say that they are five minutes out."

"So you met Atlas through his daughter's art therapy?" a redheaded woman asked, sidling up next to Tessa and picking up a giant prawn off a platter and popping it into her mouth. "I'm Eva, newest member of the Bitchin' Chicks in Business sisterhood."

"Is that what we're calling it now?" Aurora asked.

"I think so," Lowenna said. "Aren't most of us entrepreneurs?"

"I'm not," Aurora said. "But I am in the business of the law. I like the name. Let's keep it."

All the women nodded.

Tori lifted her champagne flute. "The Bitchin' Chicks in Business."

They all clinked glasses—Tessa included. "The Bitchin' Chicks in Business," they all echoed.

"So tell us how you and Atlas got together. Was it love at first sight?" Aurora asked. "Because I'd been in love with Zak for six months before he even noticed me. I kind of maybe stalked him just a little bit. But not in a 'collect his hair and make a doll out of it' kind of way."

Tessa nodded. "We did *meet* through Aria coming to see me. But we didn't get along at first. I thought he was a grumpy ass."

Isobel snorted. "Because he can be."

Tessa fluttered her lashes and smiled more to herself than anyone else. He wasn't so bad. She did wonder how many people he allowed to see his softer side though. "Though"— she twisted her mouth—"we kind of met before that, in a rather unorthodox way."

Eyes lifted and pinned on her.

"Oh do tell," Eva said, popping a canape into her mouth. "I'm sure it's better than Scott's and my one-night stand, where we met at a bar and I invited him up to my hotel room, only to find out weeks later that I was his new neighbor."

Tessa's eyes widened. "That is pretty interesting, but no. Not quite like that."

All attention settled on her, and with a sip of liquid courage from her champagne flute, she proceeded to regale them all with her misdialed text-rant and how she and *David* developed a friendship, while she and Atlas butted heads but secretly lusted after each other. You know, normal everyday romance stuff.

Once she finished her story, the kitchen was dead silent, all eyes remained on her, and a number of jaws were slack.

"He just *took* your dog?" Violet asked, swaying back and forth and patting her baby's butt. "I think I'd have ripped out the man's jugular if he'd taken my sweet Tulip from me."

"I wanted to," Tessa said with a pained sigh. "Still do, but my legal counsel says to just hang tight. That Forest is like a couch and the division of property, if not handled amicably outside of court, has to be handed legally and properly *inside* the court or boardroom or whatever."

"Liam and Atlas representing you?" Paige asked.

"Yes, and Richelle LaRue. I somehow managed to get a three-lawyer team."

Several women gasped. Jaws went even more slack, and they all closed in around her.

"Did you say *Richelle* LaRue?" Tori asked slowly.

Tessa's brows furrowed. "Yeah, why?"

"Well, for starters, she was *my* divorce lawyer," Eva started. "She's fabulous and will win you all the money, custody, and if you want one of his kidneys, she might be able to get you that too."

"But more importantly, she is Liam's secret girlfriend or fuck-buddy or whatever," Isobel whispered. "She's elusive, and nobody besides Atlas, Eva and Liam have ever met her."

Tori nodded, growing closer to Tessa. "We're all *so* curious about her. She and Liam meet every Wednesday to have sex, but other than that, he says there's nothing going on between them. But you can't have sex with someone once a week for years without developing something for them. Particularly because I don't think he sees anybody else in between."

"He says they're not monogamous, but Liam was burned hard by his ex and is *the* most loyal guy on the planet. If he's sleeping with one woman, no strings or not, he's only sleeping with that woman," Violet said. "Have you met her in person yet?"

Tessa shook her head. "No, just spoken with her over the phone and on a conference call with her, Liam and Atlas. She was at Liam's while I was at Atlas's."

Eyes turned even more eager.

Violet popped another chocolate from a different box into her mouth. "And what vibe did you get from them?"

"A none-of-your-business vibe." Liam's voice behind them caused every single woman to jump, some of them sloshing their champagne, others clutching their chests as if they'd just had a heart attack. "Seriously, ladies. I love you all, but your obsession with Richelle and me has to stop."

One by one, each woman adopted a face of angelic innocence, averting their gazes from Liam's scolding brown one.

"We just want to see you happy, Liam," Paige said, lifting her head, walking toward him and lifting a tray of food. "Scallop crostini with spring onions and miso?"

The corner of Liam's mouth crooked up. "You know my weakness is your food. You're a wily wench, you know that?" He grabbed a napkin from the table and proceeded to pile six of the appetizers onto it. He bit into one. "And for the record, I am happy. Richelle and I are on exactly the same page. We want exactly the same things."

"Which is?" Lowenna asked, lifting a brow.

Liam shrugged and pushed his food into his cheek. "Sex. We fuck. That's it. Every Wednesday night, she shows up after hitting the gym, showers at my place, we eat Thai takeout, then we bone until my nuts have nothing left. She stays over, we bone again in the morning before we both leave for work. Wash, rinse, repeat on every hump day. It's the perfect setup. No emotions, no expectations. Just sex and Thai food."

All the women, Tessa included, made faces of mild disgust.

"Sometimes we get a little crazy though and order Mexican." His smile was so cocky, Tessa wondered how he and his ego both fit through a doorway. "*Nothing like good tacos and even better dick*, Richelle likes to say."

"Well, that just killed the moment," Aurora said blandly, sipping her beverage.

Liam didn't seem the least bit offended by her comment. He shrugged again, then turned to go, but not before throwing over his shoulder a final warning. "Leave my love life alone, ladies, otherwise I'll cancel poker night and then you won't have *your* Saturday nights man-free anymore." He didn't bother looking back at them because he knew his words had struck a chord.

Tori scoffed. "Methinks the lady doth protest too much."

"Mhmm," Paige agreed.

Isobel's hand rested on Tessa's arm. "Your mission, if you choose to accept it, is to learn as much about Richelle as you can and then report back to us. Liam is so obviously in love with her, he's just gun-shy. We need to make them see that they're meant for more than just *hump day*." She shuddered.

"This message will self-destruct in ten seconds," Paige said, glancing up from her phone. "Because that's how long we have until the birthday girl arrives."

Isobel squeezed Tessa's arm again. "What do you say, fellow bitchin' chick? Fellow *sister*? Are you willing to help us help the last single dad of Seattle find love?"

Sister.

Was it really that easy? Had she been inducted into their club just like that? She already felt so comfortable with these women, and she'd only been standing there with them for all of five, maybe ten, minutes.

"Guys, she's here," a male voice called from restaurant side. "Everybody get ready."

"Do you accept?" Isobel asked again, still clutching Tessa's arm and leading her out to the restaurant side.

Tessa smiled at the same time a beautiful woman she recognized as the florist at Flowers on 5th walked past the bistro window.

She looked behind her at all the people who could so easily become her new family. She knew she was falling in love with Atlas, Aria and Cecily, and if all these people came as a package deal, all the better.

She rested her hand on Isobel's arm. "I accept the mission."

18

THE WARM STRENGTH of a man's arm wrapped around Tessa's waist as she stood next to the pastry case at the front of the bistro, chatting with Zara, the birthday girl. Turned out they had a lot in common, and Zara said she would text Tessa so the two could hit the gym together soon. With great appreciation for helping Aiden after his parents' divorce, Zak had given Tessa one heck of a discount at Club Z Fitness. Turned out they all went to that gym, so when she was introduced to all the men and got to talk more with the women, she started recognizing their faces—which were normally red and sweaty—from the gym.

"How are we doing?" Atlas asked, pulling her into his embrace and pecking her on the side of the head. She leaned into him, their act of affection for each other already seeming so natural. It also caused Zara's blue eyes to glitter.

"Doing well, thank you," she said, wrapping her hand around his waist. "Zara here was just filling me in on Lowenna's sister's wedding back in February and the fiasco that was."

His brows lifted, and he nodded. "Oh, it was something

all right. Still have to see that fucker at work, but at least Lowenna and Mason are together and happy."

Tessa reared her head back. "Wait, you *work* with this Brody guy?"

"Yeah, he's a junior partner at the firm. Major tool."

"Atlas, I think this is the most I've ever seen you smile or heard you speak," Zara said, her smile growing into an almost coy and knowing grin. "It's wonderful to see you so happy. You really deserve it." She rested her hand on his arm. "I am also very sorry to hear about your cousin. So tragic. It's a blessing that Cecily has you in her life."

Tessa practically heard him swallow next to her. She certainly noticed his giant Adam's apple bob heavily in his throat before he cleared it. "Thanks, Zara. It's been hard, but we're getting through it. Cecily is a good baby, and now that Aria has finally accepted her, it's made it a lot easier."

Zara's eyes softened. "Which I believe we have Tessa here to thank for?"

His fingers around her waist squeezed and dug into her hip. "She's been a lifesaver."

Tessa's heart skipped and leapt inside her chest at his kind and candid words.

Tori, who apparently had major baby fever, had snatched up Cecily the first moment she could and was playing with her and the other children off in the toy and art corner.

"How we doing over here, folks?" Liam asked, joining their little tête-à-tête-à-tête.

"I was just about to go and grab some more food before you eat it all," Zara said, placing her cool hand gently on Tessa's bare shoulder as she squeezed past her and Atlas. "Did you leave any of those prawn crostinis for anybody else?" Her tone was more playful than anything, and Liam didn't seem the least bit offended.

"I think I saw Paige bringing another tray of them out of

the walk-in cooler just minutes ago. And I wasn't the one devouring them. That was *your* doctor boyfriend who was two-fisting shellfish like a freaking harbor seal."

Zara snorted and rolled her eyes before she turned the corner and headed into the kitchen.

Liam faced them and opened his palm to reveal a napkin with probably five of the prawn crostinis piled on top of each other. "What I didn't tell her was that when Paige brought them out, I grabbed about a third of them. Hopefully the birthday girl gets there before her man does." He took a bite of one.

Tessa felt Atlas snort beside her, his body jostling gently as he laughed.

"So the meeting with Rickson and his legal representation—whether that's his law student sidepiece or a real lawyer who has taken the fucking bar exam, we don't know—it's set for June eighteenth. So four weeks from now. We tried to push it sooner, but they won't be back. Rickson specifically asked for the eighteenth."

Tessa's gut dropped to her feet.

Of course, he picked the eighteenth. He knew exactly what he was doing when he suggested that date. God, why was he being so deliberately cruel to her? What had she done to hurt him so much that he would plan the hearing for the same day of her defense?

"Is that date a problem?" Liam asked, obviously reading her expression. "I can try to move it."

She swallowed. "That's the day I defend my thesis to get my PhD. He knows that. That's why he suggested it."

"Motherfucker," Atlas and Liam said at the same time. Atlas's grip around her tightened, and she leaned into him for support.

"On the upside," Liam said, finishing off one crostini, "I've decided that when we *do* meet with Fuckface McGee, we're going to bring in an entire battalion. You, me, Richelle, Zak, Aaron and Adam."

Atlas's brows wrinkled. "Why Zak, Aaron and Adam?"

"Zak and Aaron for pure intimidation. They'll pump iron right before, wear tight T-shirts and stand behind us with their arms crossed like muscle for hire, and Adam because he holds the future of Rickson's career in his hands. He has, in fact, applied with the college for a position in their biology department, and even though Adam wasn't on the hiring committee for his position and Rickson was offered the job, which is supposed to start July first—hence his vacation—Adam has the power to cancel the job offer. McGregor also found out that Rickson and *Blaire* have applied for a mortgage and are house-hunting. I've been in touch with all my banking friends and connections in real estate, and with one call from me, it will be fucking impossible for them to get approved for anything, and not one Realtor will take them on as clients."

Tessa liked the idea of having muscle there to scare the crap out of Carlyle. He certainly deserved to shit himself after everything he'd pulled.

"The last person you want to fuck with in this town is Liam Dixon," Atlas said, the pride practically tangible in voice.

Liam's grin grew but then shrank back to a serious flat line across his mouth. "We're going to get you your dog back, Tessa, I promise." His brown gaze turned gentle and brotherly. "And I rarely promise a client anything, but I promise you that we *will* get Forest back."

"Is what you ... what *we're* planning to do to Carlyle legal? I mean, I get the intimidation with the muscled-up guys and everything, but going after his job? His banking and his ability to get a house? That doesn't seem ... *aboveboard*, if you know what I'm saying?" Not that she didn't want to get her dog back, because she wanted nothing more in the world, but she'd also been raised to abide by the law, and what Liam had planned didn't sound all that *legal*.

"It's called leverage," Liam said with a shrug. "We only suggest these possibilities if Rickson doesn't play nice. He needs to be scared enough to give you back your dog, that's all."

"If we had more dirt on him, we'd use that too," Atlas said. "Guy's pretty clean, though, so we have to hit him where it hurts in other ways."

Slowly, she nodded. "Okay, I trust you both."

"And so you should," Liam boasted. "I take care of those I love. And I love Atlas and he *whatevers* you, so therefore, by proxy I *whatever* you too."

Atlas *whatevered* her? Was that Liam being coy and *not* saying the *L* word but actually meaning the *L* word?

Had he told Liam that?

The man in question stiffened next to her, and she felt him retreat inside himself. This was all too soon. Yes, she felt feelings *akin* to love for Atlas, but she would never say those words out loud. Not yet, not right now. Things were still too new, too crazy. He still didn't know about her mother or that in ten or so years, her brains would inevitably be the consistency of soup.

Liam rolled his eyes. "Relax, you two. You both look like you were told the food you ate was full of cyanide. Jesus. What I meant was that Atlas cares about you, so therefore so do I. Let's take that nefarious *L* word out of the equation for fear old Atlas here has a coronary."

She glanced back up at Atlas, and the color seemed to have returned to his cheeks a bit. He grunted, and the muscle in his jaw flexed. "You can be a real dick sometimes," he grumbled.

"Dixon Dickhead, isn't that what you call me?" Liam said,

laughing as he slapped Atlas on the back and wandered back to where the rest of the party guests mingled.

Once they were alone, Atlas released her, only to take her by both hands. "I'm sorry about him. He means well. He just runs his mouth a bit."

Tessa shook her head. "He's helping me get my dog back. The man can say whatever he likes."

His gray eyes turned panicky. "Don't let him hear you say that. He'll take it to heart."

Chuckling, she shook free of his hands and turned them both so they were facing the party. Her hand found his waist and his hers. "Let's go join the party. I really like your friends, and you were right, this was the perfect distraction."

He squeezed her hip. "I'll do my best to get Rickson to change the date of the meeting."

Sighing, she rested her head on his shoulder. "When it rains, it pours, doesn't it? They say things come in threes. Makes me wonder what the third issue is going to be."

He made a deep, rumbling noise in his throat next to her. "Let's hope it's no more devastating than a hangnail."

"From your mouth to the ears of the universe," she said, letting go of him to scoop up a grunting and rapidly crawling Cecily. She plunked the little girl on her hip. "Hello, angel. And how are you?"

Cecily shoved her finger that had just been on the floor up Tessa's nose.

"Well, you're one of us now," Atlas said with a deep chuckle. "She only does that to the ones she loves."

One of us.

She could get used to that. Finger up the nose and all.

19

IT WAS June fifteenth before they knew it. The weeks leading up to Tessa's defense and her meeting with Carlyle went by in a blur as well as slogged along at a snail's pace. It baffled her to think that they could do both, but somehow, they did. Before she knew it, her defense was upon her, but it also felt like forever since she'd seen her beloved Forest.

She, Atlas and the children fell into a quick and lovely routine, where the two of them no longer hid in the depths of the basement when she came over after work, but rather she joined them all for dinner, helped with bath time and stayed until midnight or so.

They still hadn't had sex in Atlas's bed—which she suspected was because that had once been his bed with his wife, and he wasn't quite ready to take that leap—but at least she was no longer sneaking in and out of the house as quiet as a church mouse.

Liam and Atlas had used their pull and powers of persuasion to get Carlyle to move the defense date to the nineteenth, rather than the eighteenth, so at least she didn't have to deal with two stressful things on the same day. Just back-to-back.

With three days to D-Day, or defense day, Tessa had kept her schedule light with only a few clients and lots of time spent reading journal articles, studies and going for long, mind-clearing walks along the beach. Sometimes Atlas was able to join her; other times she went on her own. Twice, Violet, baby Brielle and Isobel with baby Sophie joined her. It was so nice to finally have some friends, and even though these friends also had children, they didn't snub her like her other friends with children had.

It was also nice to have someone to talk to, because when she walked the beach alone, she missed Forest more than anything. He was her beach walking buddy. When he was with her, she was never alone. Dogs frolicked in the waves and chased sticks, but not once in those three weeks—where she visited the beach any time it didn't rain—did she bump into Forest and his pet-sitter again. It was almost as if the pet-sitter was deliberately avoiding that beach now because he figured Tessa would be stalking it in hopes of another run-in with Forest.

Which she kind of was.

Today, thankfully, Isobel, Violet and Lowenna all met her at the beach with their babies in those front carriers. She was tired of feeling left out, so Atlas let her borrow Cecily, his carrier and his Land Cruiser with the car seat. Now she felt like she belonged with all the mommas, even if it was just for a few hours.

"Nice carrier," Violet said to Tessa, adjusting the fabric of her baby wrap. "Is that a Tula?"

"I think it's a Beco," Isobel said, having strapped Sophie to her back. "Or maybe a Lillebaby."

"I think it's just a really nice Ergo." Lowenna had Willow on her front in a carrier with straps similar to the one Tessa was wearing Cecily in. Because she was a noob at all of this, the women suggested she put Cecily on her back, as it would be more comfortable for both her and the baby.

"I have no idea what any of those words are," Tessa joked. "You might as well be speaking Latin for all I understood of that."

The women chuckled as they hit the fobs to lock their vehicles and took off through the beach grass down to the sand.

"You'll understand someday," Violet said. She pursed her lips. "I mean I guess I should ask, *do* you want to understand some day? Do you want children?"

"More than anything," Tessa answered. Though she wasn't sure if children of her own were in the cards any longer. Or if she should tempt fate at all and pass along her messed-up genes.

"Then you'll understand," Isobel replied with a gentle smile.

"So what do you have for us on Richelle?" Lowenna asked, pecking Willow on the top of her head before she placed a big floppy sunhat on her.

Tessa took in a deep breath. "She is unlike any woman I have ever met, I will tell you that. She is this tiny, little, pixie thing, with short, very blonde hair, fine features and the fiercest amber eyes. They're like hawk eyes. She sees everything."

The women stared at her as they walked down the beach, soaking up everything she had to say.

"But even though she may not even be five feet tall, her power, her fierceness, her sheer tenacity are the size of a freaking Amazon woman. She's also crazy fit. I'm pretty sure she could kick all our asses at once. The arms on her alone are enough to make you think she knows her way around a boxing ring."

"Liam did mention she goes to the gym," Violet said thoughtfully.

"Yeah, but obviously not Zak's gym," Isobel said. "Probably on purpose. Or if she does, it's one farther away from the two that most of us frequent."

"Yeah, but Zak says he's never met her," Lowenna added. "He's even done a search for her in his membership list and she doesn't come up. She goes elsewhere on purpose. She does not want to be a part of Liam's life other than for Wednesday night sex."

"There has to be more to it." Violet glanced out at the horizon. "I mean, we all know that Liam is putting on this whole *born-again bachelor* BS. Since Mark and Tori got together to now, he's definitely softened his resolve about how anti-love he is."

They all nodded.

"Maybe this is all coming from Richelle," Isobel offered, her blue eyes sparkling in the glow of the morning sun. "Maybe Liam has asked for more, but she refuses, so he just takes what he can get?"

"That would make sense." Lowenna kicked off her flip-flops and began walking in the sand with her bare feet. "Though Liam is a great guy, so I don't know why she wouldn't want to be with him."

"She's a divorce lawyer too, don't forget," Tessa added, enjoying the fact that she could now contribute to the conversation because she knew everyone they were discussing. "And Atlas made a passing mention of her having been through her own ugly divorce. Maybe she's just really jaded and playing it cautious? Eva wasn't kidding when she said the woman went for the jugular. She's out for blood with Carlyle —that ferociousness can't just come from being a good lawyer. There must be something deep-seated that drives her to take a man's jewels the way she's determined to take Carlyle's."

Violet and Isobel snorted their laughs.

"That would make sense," Lowenna murmured.

"If that's how she's acting, I get it. I've been there, too," Tessa said, more to the seagull in the sand beside her than anyone else.

Lowenna bumped her shoulder. "You and me both, sister."

Sister.

She would never grow tired of hearing that.

She had a family now. She had sisters, and she was going to do everything she possibly could to keep them—and never forget them.

AFTER A WONDERFUL WALK with the women and babies, Tessa texted Atlas to see if she could keep Cecily a bit longer. She wanted to pop in and see her mother and thought perhaps bringing a beautiful baby by might cheer her up. After all, her mother was always painting babies. Maybe a real one would spur some pleasant memories, or perhaps Cecily's presence might help her mother shed some light on *why* she was always painting babies.

This time, she decided to wear Cecily on her front and let the little nugget face forward so she could see the world, rather than have to crane her neck around to see out. She also had no idea how to get the baby on her back without help and didn't want to risk dropping the child on her head in the parking lot to achieve it.

She said hello to the nurses at the front desk of the home and asked if her mother was in her room—she was. She always was. She took most of her meals in her room and rarely, if ever, socialized with anyone. Only once in a while she would go out to the garden and sit under the willow tree by the duck pond, but not very often or for very long. Along with Cecily, she had a bouquet of flowers that Zara specially did up for her mother in the hopes they might brighten her spirits and bring her joy.

With Cecily's little fist wrapped firmly around her index finger and the bouquet in her other hand, she knocked a knuckle against the partially opened door. "Mom?"

"I'm busy," came her mother's distracted voice from the other side.

Tessa pushed inside anyway. "Mom, it's me."

"I'm busy. I told you that."

Continuing to ignore her mother's routine dismissal of her, Tessa wandered farther into the room and toward the window, where her mother stood behind the canvas. Her pace slowed the closer she grew to her mother, because when she finally caught a glimpse of her face, there was nothing but worry painted across it. Her mother wasn't even holding a paintbrush. She was standing in front of a blank, pale blue canvas wringing her hands and spinning her wedding ring around and around on her finger.

"Mom?" She set the bouquet down and reached for her mother's shoulder. "Is everything okay? You look worried."

Her mother continued to wring her hands, muttering words Tessa couldn't hear or make sense of. She couldn't tell if her mother even knew she was there. She hadn't acknowledged her in any way, not even a lip twitch or the tilt of a brow.

"Mom!" She snapped her fingers in front of her mother's face. "Mom! It's me, Tessa. Mom, look at me. Look at me, please."

Lily blinked slowly once, twice, and then swiveled her gaze toward Tessa as if seeing her there for the first time. Her mouth opened, then her gaze dipped to Cecily, and her brows furrowed in a deep V.

"What are you doing here?" She was speaking to Cecily, not Tessa. "Why are you here? Why are you haunting me? Leave me be, Georgia. I love you. I miss you terribly. My heart shattered when you died, but please, child, let me be. I can't be a good mother to Tessa with you always there, always reminding me."

What the heck was she talking about?

"Go!" Her mother screamed into Cecily's face before she pressed her hands to the side of her head and spun on her heel to face the window. "Go! Leave me be! Please!"

Startled by the screaming, Cecily began to cry.

This was not the visit Tessa had anticipated at all. What on earth was her mother talking about? Who was Georgia? Somebody was haunting her? How long had she been seeing *someone*? How long had Georgia been haunting her? Years? Was this the reason for her depression all these years? Was her mother crazy?

She just had so many questions.

Cecily's cries grew louder and more frantic. Tessa was quick to unhook the carrier and pull the baby into her chest, nuzzling her and shushing her until she began to settle. Sniffles and moans along with hot tears blended together as the little girl buried her face deeper into the crook of her neck. She rubbed Cecily's back. "Shh, baby, it's okay. It's okay, sweetheart. I'm right here."

"Go, Georgia, please," her mother begged, still showing Tessa her back, her hands still squeezing the sides of her head. "Leave me be!"

"Okay, Mom. We're going. We're going," Tessa said, tears stinging the backs of her eyes as she returned to the door. "I'm sorry I upset you." Her lips jiggled and her throat grew painfully tight. Her mother still hadn't turned around. She sat on the cushions of the bay window, holding the sides of her head and moaning.

Cecily nuzzled Tessa even more, her fingers bunched in Tessa's tank top as soft whimpers and baby murmurs fled from her plump little lips.

Tessa wiped away the tear from beneath her eye, took one final look at her mother, then left, making haste to get to the doors and the hell out of there as fast as she could.

How could she have been so stupid as to take a baby there? She only set her mother off worse than she'd seen her in a long time. And now, Tessa had a buttload of new questions that she knew would probably never get answered.

And if they did get answered, it was only a matter of time before she forgot them anyway.

20

TESSA REFUSED to talk about it, but when she arrived home after her walk with the women and Cecily, she was a person Atlas barely recognized. Closed-off, quiet, withdrawn. She handed him Cecily, said goodbye and then turned around and headed to her car parked in the driveway.

Worried about the woman he knew he was falling in love with, he called Violet to find out what the hell happened. She seemed oblivious and said Tessa was in high spirits when they all parted ways.

So he called Isobel. She was freakishly astute when it came to people's true feelings and intentions, so she more than anyone else would have probably picked up on Tessa's weird mood.

She hadn't.

"Aside from being distracted by her upcoming defense and the meeting with her ex, she wasn't sending me any weird vibes," Isobel said. "I'm sorry I can't help you more, Atlas."

"It's okay," he murmured distractedly into the phone. "Thanks, Iz."

"She did mention that she was going to take Cecily to see her mother. Figured the baby would bring her mom good cheer."

Her mother.

Tessa barely mentioned her mother, except for the fact that she was in a nursing home and she went to see her once or twice a week. Other than that, she never brought her up, and Atlas never pried.

"Did she say *where* her mother lived?" he asked. "Which nursing home?"

"Sorry, she didn't. But she did say she was going to swing by Zara's shop to grab her mother some flowers. Maybe she told Zara."

This was getting fucking ridiculous. But at the same time, he was so grateful for all these women and how connected and caring they were. They had welcomed Tessa into their fold without a moment's hesitation.

He hung up with Isobel and called Zara. If he hadn't used all his favors, and Liam's with McGregor, he'd put his top PI on this. But the man charged a hefty fee, so if he could do the legwork himself first, he would.

"She said her mother was at the Seascape Manor," Zara said seconds later. "She asked for extra lilies in the bouquet, as her mother's name is Lily."

Damn, he fucking loved these women.

"Thanks, Zara, I appreciate it."

"We all just want to see you happy, Atlas. Let me know if you need an apology bouquet. They're one of my specialities."

He groaned. "Thanks, Zara."

Double-checking that Jenny could stick around and watch the kids until he got back, Atlas leapt into his Land Cruiser and was heading down the I-5 in ten minutes.

"I'm here to see Mrs. Copeland," he said to the nurse at

the front desk less than half an hour later. "I'm a friend of her daughter's, and after the ... uh, *upset* today, Tessa asked me to come by and check on Lily."

He was taking a gamble that the reason Tessa was in fact upset was because she'd seen her mother. For all he knew, Carlyle could have texted her or she could have run into Forest again. Though if either of those had happened, she most likely would have told him about it.

The grandmotherly nurse pursed her lips and nodded. "Yes, Lily was rather distraught after Tessa left. Kept discussing Georgia—we've never heard her mention a Georgia before. Unless that was the name of the baby Tessa brought with her." She shrugged. "She's in a better mood now. Painting in her room if you'd like to go see her. Room number thirty-four."

He thanked the nurse and then headed off down the hallway toward room thirty-four. The nursing home was very nice, albeit warm inside and a bit stuffy. He regretted that he'd worn a long-sleeved jersey shirt and shorts. He'd probably have pit stains by the time he left.

The door to Lily's room was partially open, but he knocked anyway and pushed it open a touch more. "Mrs. Copeland? Lily?"

"Busy," she murmured from inside.

The nurse said she was painting, and the woman was retired and living in a nursing home. How *busy* could she be?

"Mrs. Copeland, I just need to speak with you for a moment," he said, stepping into the room, which was even warmer than the hallway. The sun shone into the room from the open window behind her. It was hotter than hell and she had the window open? What did she have the thermostat set to, one hundred?

She didn't say anything but hummed to herself and continued to paint.

"Mrs. Copeland, I'm Atlas Stark. I'm a friend of Tessa's, and I just came to ask if everything is okay? Tessa seemed really upset earlier today, and she wouldn't tell me why. I care about her, and I hate to see her so upset when she has so many important things coming up, like her defense and the meeting with Carlyle. I'm sure you're aware of it all."

Slowly, her gaze swung to his face, and focus entered her light blue eyes. "Who are you?"

"I'm Atlas Stark, Mrs. Copeland. I'm a friend of Tessa's."

The woman didn't look like she belonged in a nursing home. She was maybe sixty but appeared to be healthy and capable. Why had Tessa put her mother in a home so early?

Lily's brows pinched into a V. "Who's Tessa? I don't know a Tessa." Her hand fell to her abdomen and she rubbed it as if there were a baby inside. "But my husband and I are expecting, and maybe we should add that name to our list. I like it. He likes Georgia, though." She smiled and caressed her belly again. "I'm sorry I can't help you with your friend Tessa."

This didn't make any sense. Was this not Lily Copeland's room?

"Are you Lily Copeland, ma'am?" he asked, scratching the back of his neck as he glanced to his right to check out her painting.

"I am, yes."

"Then you are Tessa Copeland's mother, no?"

The look she gave him said she was losing patience with him. "I told you, mister, I don't know anybody named Tessa. Now could you please leave me alone? My husband will be home shortly, and he's taking me out for our anniversary. I just need to finish this painting and then go find a dress that will fit over this big belly of mine."

What the hell was going on?

Still cradling her belly with one hand, she dipped her

paintbrush into a pot of yellow and swiped it in the sky above the mother and infant's head.

"Your painting is beautiful," he said before he did as she asked and left the sweltering heat of her room.

Back at the desk and desperate to disrobe down to his underwear, or go jump in the bay across from the property, he waited until the same nurse from earlier was off the phone before he spoke. "Uh ... Mrs. Copeland ... is she *okay?*"

The nurse's smile dropped like an anvil. "What do you mean? How do you know Tessa Copeland? What did you say to Lily?"

"I'm seeing Tessa. She's my ... I'm her ... we're together, okay? But I've never met her mother before. Tessa came home today really upset, and she wouldn't tell me why. She has a lot going on right now, so I thought maybe I could talk to her mother and see what happened. But Mrs. Copeland is pretending she's pregnant and that she doesn't even know Tessa."

"She's not pretending," the nurse said slowly, as if he himself were slow. "She has early-onset Alzheimer's that has progressed rapidly. How well do you know Tessa if she hasn't even told you about her mother?" She turned to grab the phone again. "I'm going to call Miss Copeland and ask her to verify who you are. You're giving me weird vibes, buddy."

Shit.

"No, no, please. Don't call her. I am who I say I am, I swear. But I also know that if she finds out I came here, she'll just be even more upset, and Tessa has so much going on right now. I just want to help her. Please don't bother her." Damn it, why couldn't he be a charmer like Zak, Scott or Liam? He'd never been a charmer, never knew how to properly flirt.

Thank God for Tessa. She'd done all the flirting or whatever you called it. He just wandered around like an idiot hoping that the girl he liked liked him back.

She set the phone back down on the base. "I don't want to see you here again without Miss Copeland."

He nodded. "You have my word."

Then before Nurse Tattletale could change her mind, he vacated the premises as fast as his legs could carry him, bursting out into the fresh air and inhaling the cool breeze in gulps.

"I CAN'T RIGHT NOW, ATLAS," Tessa said impatiently, attempting to shut her apartment door. "I have to study. I'm tired. I just can't. I'm sorry."

But he wasn't going to let her shut him out like this. He pushed on the door, forcing her to open it. "Tessa, why didn't you tell me your mother had early-onset Alzheimer's?"

Her hand fell away from the door, and her jaw went slack. "How did you ... " Anger flashed in the deep blue streaks of her eyes. "Did you go see my mother?"

Shit.

She took a step back into her apartment, her chest rose and fell rapidly and an angry red crawled up her neck

"I did," he confirmed with a sharp nod following her into her apartment.

Her ire didn't matter at the moment though. He had something he needed to straighten out first, and she would just have to listen to him. She could pound his chest with her little fists later.

"Atlas, why did you go see my mother?" Her jaw snapped shut tight, and her nostrils flared.

"I wanted to find out what made you slip away the way you did today. I called Isobel and Violet and finally Zara. Zara told me where your mother lived. Why didn't you tell me about the Alzheimer's?"

Her eyes flared, filling with more fury. The blue darkened to the color of twilight, while the red in her chest spread up her neck and into her cheeks. She looked beautiful, despite how much she probably wanted to punch him in the jaw. "Because it's none of your damn business," she snapped. "Have you ever thought maybe there was a reason I haven't brought you to see my mother?"

"And yet you took my baby?"

She rolled her eyes. "Big difference."

"Why didn't you tell me? What were the reasons? Are you ashamed of me that I'm a single father? A widower?" He couldn't wrap his head around her reasoning, and just as her wrath was beginning to build, so was his. He thought they had something. He thought he was falling in love with her and she with him. But you couldn't have love if there was no trust. And she hadn't trusted him enough to tell him about her mom.

Was she who he thought she was?

Did he know her as well as he thought?

Did he know her at all?

"Ever think it was never about you?" Her voice came out as a pissed-off hiss. "That maybe I wasn't ready to show you that part of my family. That I wasn't ready to show you the person who hardly ever remembers who I am, and when she does, she usually ends up yelling at me? Maybe I just wanted to keep that part of my life hidden for a bit longer, before you met her and changed your opinion about me."

So she was ashamed of her mother? She didn't strike him as the type of person who would be like that. She worked in the field of psychology. She of all people had to understand that the Alzheimer's wasn't her mother's fault. It was a horrible disease that was beyond anyone's control.

"Are you *ashamed* of your mother, then? If you're not ashamed of me ... "

His anger began to subside, though hers seemed to continue to grow.

"I'm not *ashamed*," she said, though he could tell she was really struggling to keep her tone in check, to keep her anger from escalating. "I love my mother more than anything. It's just been really hard these last few years, and I typically don't introduce people to her right away. She can be a bit ... " Clenching her jaw, she averted her gaze, her nostrils flaring, the cords in her throat tight. "I just don't introduce her to people right away, okay? It's not that I'm embarrassed ... it's just ... easier."

Well, fuck, now he felt like the king of douches. Scratch that, Carlyle was the *king* of douches. The fucking Emperor of Doucheville, but at the moment Atlas felt like the Town Fool or congressman of Doucheville.

Taking a small step toward her, he dropped his voice to a gentle whisper. "I understand."

Her gaze softened just a touch, but it turned from angry to skeptical. "Do you?"

He nodded. "I'm sorry," he continued to speak softly, not wanting to spook her. "You just scared me when you dropped Cecily off and acted the way you did. I know you have a lot going on right now, and I just wanted to see if I could help. I'm also very protective of her. For not even a year old, she's been through a lot."

He closed the door behind him and approached her, his hands resting on her hips. She glared up at him, but he could see her walls beginning to crumble. She was cute when she was angry. Her hands on her hips, her nostrils flaring, her mouth all pursed-like, eyes flashing blue flames.

They were toe-to-toe now. Her throat worked a couple of times, but she still said nothing.

He invaded her space even more until there wasn't even room for air between them. "Forgive me."

One eyebrow drew up. "I didn't catch the inflection on the end of that."

He resisted the urge to smile. "Because it wasn't a question."

"You breached my trust. You went behind my back. It needs to be a question. You can't just *demand* I forgive you. You still have secrets too, Atlas Stark, and I don't pry. The trust thing goes both ways. Trust me to tell you more about my family when I'm ready."

Fuck, she was right. He'd stepped over the line. Invaded her privacy, broken her trust. He'd been so hell-bent on figuring out what had upset her that he didn't even think he was invading her privacy. He didn't want the nurse telling her he was there because he worried that would just upset her more. He wanted to be the one to tell her. He just never dreamed she'd react the way she did, even though she had every right.

"I'm an ass," he said sheepishly. "I'm sorry I went behind your back. Forgive me?" This time he made sure to add an inflection on the end of that so she knew it was a question.

The eyebrow that had been lifted twitched. "You're an ass."

That made him smile. "I'm an ass, and you love it. You love that I care so much I do asshole things sometimes."

"I do, do I?" The corner of her mouth lifted on one side. More of the fortress she'd built around herself had begun to tumble down. Brick by brick.

Warm puffs of air from her lips hit his, and she blinked up at him with more love in her eyes than the fire and fury that had been there a moment ago. Now the flames that flickered were of passion ... need. A need he felt himself deep down in his bones. A need he hadn't felt so strongly in a very long time.

"Atlas?" Her voice was now a breathy whisper.

"Hmm?" He nuzzled his nose against hers.

"Don't ever do anything like that again."

And that's why this woman had his heart in the palm of her hand. She was so damn strong—and fierce—even when she didn't think she had the power to go on.

"I promise."

She smiled, and her lips brushed his. "Good."

He was tired of the talk. Their bodies could speak for them. He dipped his head low and crushed his mouth to hers, taking her face between his hands, plundering all that she offered him. She opened for him, her arms looping around his neck and fingers threading into his hair, tugging him against her, down to her—almost frantically.

Within moments, their clothes were almost completely off and he was backing her up toward the couch.

"No," she said, in between kisses, "bedroom."

Okay, fine, whatever. He'd taken her on a desk the first time and a couch every time after that. He welcomed the wide expanse of a bed for once.

In nothing but his boxers, and her in no more than her bra and panties, he scooped her up and laid her gently on her bed, taking in every exquisite inch of her.

Her bottom lip rolled inward, and her top teeth caught it as she cocked one leg slightly and slid her fingers over her torso and up her sides. "You going to just stand there and watch?" Her grin was small, her voice sweet. She was still hurting from whatever had gone down with her mother and from what she considered a betrayal from him, but she was also welcoming the distraction.

So was he. Tessa was a distraction from the bedlam in his life. A distraction he never wanted to let go of.

He dipped one knee in the bed and crawled up her body, pinning her beneath him. "Would you let me just watch?" He drew his nose up her neck and nipped at her jaw. "Just stand there and take in you bringing yourself pleasure all the way to climax. Could you do it?"

She hummed as he angled up on one arm and let his fingers tickle along her ribcage, then dip down over her abdomen and beneath the elastic of her white cotton panties.

Her neatly trimmed hair was already damp, and when he explored further, he found her not just damp—the woman was saturated.

"Seems like you could get there on your own quite easily," he said, pushing one finger and then another into her tight channel. She squeezed around him and moaned.

"I could, but I'd much rather you be an active participant." Her breathy voice buzzed past his ear like a zephyr, followed by a sharp inhale when he raked his thumbnail over her clit. She shivered and dug her nails into his biceps, arching her back so his fingers inside her changed their angle.

"Atlas," she whispered.

"Hmm?" His teeth scraped along her jaw again.

"Quit playing games. I don't need foreplay. I need you."

I need you.

He lifted his head and withdrew his fingers from inside her, but not before raking his thumb over her clit once more, causing her to tremble and her hips to jerk off the bed. Without taking his gaze off hers, he kneeled up on the bed and slid her panties down her legs. She made quick work of her bra, and he pushed his boxer briefs down his thighs enough to let his cock spring free. A drop of precum beaded on the tip, and taking his length in his palm, he ran the pad of his thumb over the tip, swirling the drop around until the purple head glistened.

"Why are you torturing me?" She spread her knees and reached for him with outstretched arms, her fingers making a *gimme, gimme* motion.

"Am I torturing you?" Settling in between her creamy thighs, he reached between their bodies and lined them up, teasing her slick heat with his crown. She pushed down so more of him entered her.

"You are torturing me," she whined. "Please, just ... "

He swirled his hips, only teasing that first inch of sensitive nerve bundles inside her. "Just what?"

Her nails scratched his arms until pain shot through to his fingers. "Just fuck me already."

She rarely ever swore, so he knew when she did, she meant business.

"Yes, ma'am." He surged forward, claiming all of her in one hard, solid thrust that pushed an *oof* from her lungs, followed by a contented sigh.

"Finally," she breathed. "About damn time."

Rolling his eyes and smiling down at the woman who fascinated him more each day, he began a slow, lazy rhythm. One he knew would drive her mental. He wanted to take his time with her, draw her orgasm out until it damn near killed her, only for his kisses to resurrect her like Snow White and for them to do it all over again.

In and out he pumped, taking his time to retreat, swirl the head of his cock around her hot, tight opening, only to languidly slide back inside to the base. Her squirms and whimpers of pleasure and impatience galvanized him. He could tell she was getting frustrated that he wasn't going faster, but she was also really fucking enjoying everything he was doing.

Dipping his head, he drew a hard nipple into his mouth and scissored his teeth before sucking it hard between his lips. The groan from deep in her chest caused his balls to draw up tight against his body and his cock to twitch inside her.

Fuck, he also knew that when he went slow, it made him get close too quickly. He was going to blow before either of them was ready if he kept this going much longer.

"Gonna lick your clit now," he murmured, enjoying the pink flush to her cheeks from his dirty talk. He went to pull out and away, but her nails dug even more into his arms, and she locked her ankles around his back.

"No, you're not. You're going to stay right here and fuck me until we come."

Her walls squeezed like a vice around his cock, and she lifted her hips to change the angle and take him deeper.

Ah, fuck. He wasn't going to last very long.

His rhythm picked up, but it was already becoming erratic. He had wanted to savor her, bring her to the brink, then tug her back, only to finally give her one hard push so that instead of falling, she felt like she was flying.

That wasn't going to happen this time.

Fuck, he was like a damn seventeen-year-old with how quick he was going to come.

Fuck.

"Atlas," she moaned in his ear, swiping her tongue around the shell and then nipping the lobe with her teeth. "So good. Too good."

"Fuck, baby. Gonna come."

"Me too."

Her nails dug trenches into his biceps as she broke with a sharp cry, her body bowing on the bed, tits pointed up to the ceiling. He latched onto a nipple again and tugged, knowing that it would heighten her pleasure as well as prolong it.

Her groan of approval made his balls cinch up and his cock throb. Then he was coming. Every quiver of her pussy sent lightning straight through him, zinging left and right into his limbs, only to double back and land hard in his balls.

He released her bud and tucked his head in the crook of her shoulder, riding out the remainder of his release with her sweet scent surrounding him. Her own orgasm ended with a rush of warm air fleeing her lips and hitting his cheek, her body growing lax beneath his.

"Just because I'm a grumpy fuck doesn't mean you can't talk to me," he murmured into her shoulder, laving off a bead of sweat. "I've been told I'm a decent listener ... for a man."

That made her laugh, which was exactly what he was after. Her laugh was fuel for him. Her smile a balm that soothed the chronic ache he felt in his heart. He knew he'd never be completely over the loss of Samantha, but Tessa was someone special, and he knew Samantha would approve.

"Well, *David* certainly seemed to be a good listener. The jury is still out on this *Atlas* fellow."

That earned a chuckle from him at the same time he levered up onto his elbow and untucked his face from the crook of her neck. He glanced down at her. Her eyes held that glassy, content, just-fucked look, and pink still colored her cheeks. "I mean it, Tess. If you want to talk about what went down with your mother, I'm here."

Her smile was sweet but not entirely convinced. She strained up and kissed him on the lips, just a brush, but it nonetheless sent a jolt straight back down to his balls. "Thank you. And when I'm ready, we can talk about it. My mother's diagnosis is really hard for me to talk about. Even though it's not a *new* diagnosis, it's progressing rapidly, and since losing my dad, it's been tough to deal with."

He understood that. It was still really hard to talk about Samantha a lot of the time. Aria only brought her up once in a while. He felt guilty for how blatantly he avoided Samantha's parents back in Portland. She was their only child, and the loss of their daughter had hit the Nelsons incredibly hard. For the first six months after her passing, they had pretty much become recluses. He couldn't, because of Aria, even though he felt as if he'd locked his heart away like a recluse.

Now that the Nelsons had come back out of their grief a bit, they asked to see Aria, and he did the best he could. But Gina Nelson looked a lot like her daughter, and their house had been turned into a bit of a shrine to their daughter, so he found it tough to go.

"You're thinking awfully hard there, Mr. Stark." She clenched her muscles around him. He was growing soft and was going to slip out soon if they didn't adjust their position.

He rolled off her but turned onto his side to face her. "Just thinking about my own losses. I get that you're not ready to talk about it. Even though your mom is still alive, the mother you knew and grew up with is no longer there, so it still feels like a loss. I understand that you're grieving, and I'll let grieve in your own way." He cupped her cheek. "Just know that you're not alone in this if you don't want to be. Just like you did for me after Tamsin died, I can just sit in the quiet with you if you don't want to be alone but also don't want to talk. Sometimes just having someone there is enough."

She blinked suddenly spiked lashes, and a tear slipped down the side of her head as she turned to face him as well, placing her hand over his where it cupped her face. "Thank you. This means more to me than you could ever know. I've felt alone in my grief for a long time. Even with Carlyle, I still felt alone."

"I get that. It's amazing how alone in your grief you can feel even when you're surrounded by people."

She turned her face into his palm and kissed it, then leaned forward and pressed her lips to his shoulder. "I love you, Atlas."

His quick draw of breath made her pull back. Her eyes held a worry that made his own chest grow tight.

"I ... Tess."

She retreated across the bed and swung her legs over the side. "Never mind. I should never have said it. I was caught up in the moment. The orgasm, your kind words ... " She tugged a robe from a chair next to her bed over her body. "Just forget I said anything. "

Shit.

He was up off the bed as fast as his legs could carry him, cutting her off before she made it to the bathroom and could shut him out with the door. "Tess ... " He took her hands in his and bent his knees so they were eye to eye. "I ... I've never loved another woman before. Never. I *do* love you. I just ... I don't want to hurt you. I'm still healing. We both are. Slow is best for us right now, right?"

Her lips pursed into a thin line, and she gave him a curt nod before pulling her hands from his, retreating to the bathroom and closing the door in his face.

He raked his fingers through his hair as he went on the hunt for his pants.

Fuck him. They'd had a great fuck and he seemed to have gotten through to her, and then he had to go and fuck it all up. He knew he loved her. He was just afraid of what saying it out loud would mean. Love was equal parts terrifying as it was beautiful. Because when you let yourself love someone, when you allowed another person to become infinitely important to you, you had to face the fact that you might lose them. And he'd already lost enough people he loved to last a lifetime.

21

It was June eighteenth.

D-Day.

Defense day.

The day Tessa had been working toward for the better part of her adult life.

After years of hard work, thousands of dollars in education and hundreds of families helped, she was finally standing in front of a panel of people even more educated than she was, defending her life's work in the hopes they would grant her a few very valuable letters after her name.

All was going well. She was confident in her research, in her explanations and her findings. So far, she had answered every one of their questions with sureness and concise answers. That doctorate was as good as hers if she could just make it to the end. A quick glance at the clock said she was forty minutes and thirty-eight seconds into her defense. She could make it to the end—she just had to.

Switching to the next slide on the overhead projection screen, she opened her mouth to speak but was caught off guard when bile rose up in her throat. She swayed where she stood, only to be forced to reach out and grip the table beside her before she collapsed to the floor.

"Are you okay?" Dr. Martin asked, standing up and making his way around the table toward her. "Do we need to reschedule? Are you ill?"

Swallowing down the bitter taste in her mouth and closing her eyes for a moment, she attempted to stand straight up but was forced to hunch over again. "I'll be—" She clutched her stomach with her free hand as the nausea grew more intense and began to ascend her throat. "I'll be okay, just ... "

A hand landed on her back. "Tessa, honey, are you sure you're okay? You don't look well at all." Carey was now there too, as was Dr. Phipps and Dr. Alba. They were all standing around her with matching concerned looks on their faces.

What the heck was going on with her? Was it food poisoning? She thought back to what she'd eaten in the last twelve or so hours, but nothing funky stood out. She'd hardly eaten any breakfast at all that morning. Only half a grapefruit and her coffee. She was too nervous to eat. Carey had offered to take her out for a celebratory lunch after her defense, but food was the last thing she wanted to think about.

"Perhaps we should reschedule," Dr. Martin said. "If she's unable to speak, she's unable to defend."

"I can do it," Tessa said, her mouth filling with saliva as the urge to vomit intensified.

"Tessa, honey, don't push yourself," Carey said. "We're all therapists here. We understand anxiety and nerves. But we also understand the need for self-care and taking a step back. If you're not ready or you want to reschedule, we can."

Tessa lifted her head and pinned her gaze on her friend and supervisor. "Just give me five minutes." Then she cupped her hand to her mouth and elbowed her way through her defense panel toward the conference-room doors. She only barely made it to the toilet in time.

As soon as it was all out, her whole body felt better.

The bathroom door creaked open, and Carey's gentle voice could be heard on the other side of the stall door. "You okay, honey?"

"Just give me a minute, Carey, please. I don't want to postpone this. I can do it. I must have food poisoning or something."

She barfed once more, wiped her mouth and flushed the toilet, emerging through the door a minute later. Of course, Carey was still there, a concerned and motherly expression on her face. Her brown eyes narrowed. "I'm going to put on my friend hat right now, Tessa, okay? At this moment I am not your supervisor, not a therapist, and not a member of your panel. I am your friend, okay?"

Tessa nodded as she stared at her pale complexion in the mirror. She cupped her hand beneath the faucet and brought water to her mouth. She'd never tasted anything so damn delicious in her life.

"Could you be pregnant?" Carey asked slowly.

Tessa's eyes went buggy as she washed her hands. Carey handed her some paper towels.

"I only ask this because, well, your breasts look larger, you're nauseous and you look absolutely exhausted. I've also had three children of my own, and two of those are now women who have also had children of their own. I know what a newly pregnant woman looks like."

She began to shake her head like a dog fresh from the bath. "No. No. No. No. No. I can't be. I ... I'm on the pill. We ... we ... "

"The pill is not one hundred percent effective," Carey said gently. "Now, I know you and Carlyle split up and you've started seeing a new fellow. If you are pregnant, do you know whose it might be?"

Well, now she was going to be sick for a whole new reason.

"Carlyle and I ... I'd had my period right before he left me. We didn't have sex at all that week, and ... " She thought hard, back to the weeks leading up to when Carlyle left. They'd had sex maybe once in that time. She'd initiated at least twice, but he'd rebuffed her—which had been a major hit to her ego. Then she got her period, and then he left her. If she was pregnant, and only *just* pregnant, it had to be Atlas's baby.

Oh God, please let it be Atlas's baby.

"If I am," she whispered, "then it's Atlas's."

Carey's eyes softened. "Well, that's good, then, right? At least you're with the father and like him. Unlike that human equivalent of a Band-Aid in a salad, Carlyle."

Tessa laughed as tears sprang from her eyes. Carey had always had a way with words. She somehow managed to perfectly articulate a moment or person, right down to their Band-Aid-in-salad qualities.

"Are you going to be all right?" she asked, resting a hand on Tessa's shoulder. "None of us mind if you want to postpone this. Even until we simply figure out if you're pregnant or not."

Tessa shook her head. "No. I can do this. I *want* to do this. I'll be okay." She managed to straighten up to her full height, and this time she didn't feel the need to puke nearly as much. "Let's do this." She nodded at Carey and pressed onward toward the door, determined to finish her defense, become a doctor, and then once all that was said and done, find out if she was also going to become a mother.

"CONGRATULATIONS, DR. COPELAND," Dr. Alba said with a big grin, shaking Tessa's hand as they all stood in the conference room and toasted with—of course—champagne.

Oy.

Tessa blinked back the tears of joy as she thanked each one of her panel members. "Thank you, Dr. Alba."

Carey had eyed her warily as Dr. Phipps poured the bubbly and handed out the flutes. "If you are, this much bubbly will *not* hurt it. The bubbles will probably help your tummy settle. Just celebrate and worry about the rest later." She wrapped her arm around Tessa and pulled her in for motherly hug. "I'm so proud of you, kiddo. You did great."

A knock on the closed conference-room door had all their murmurs halting.

Dr. Martin opened the door. "Can we help you?"

Not one to wait or be intimidated by a room full of doctors, Atlas politely (kind of) pushed his way into the room. "I'm here to see Tessa."

"You mean *Dr.* Copeland?" Dr. Martin asked with a big grin. "Why, she's right over there, celebrating."

Atlas's eyes glittered, and his smile was nearly as long as his strides.

She thought he was going to congratulate her, but when she suddenly found herself in his arms and up off the ground being turned around, she couldn't stop the tears from running in thick tributaries down her cheeks. Then the laughter came, and she hugged him back just as tight.

His mouth on her neck murmured how proud he was of her before he set her on her feet and took her cheeks in his hand, resting his lips on hers.

"Well, I hope she knows him," Dr. Phipps said with a chuckle.

Unable to keep the smile from making her cheeks hurt,

Tessa wrapped her arm around Atlas's waist and turned to face the panel. "This is my ... "

"Atlas Stark, Tessa's boyfriend," Atlas said, extending his hand to each member of her panel. "I wanted to take Tessa to lunch to celebrate, but we can move it to dinner if she has plans with her fellow PhDs."

Something was different in his voice, even in the way he stood. He seemed more confident, surer of himself and them than he had before. He'd called himself her boyfriend, introduced himself to her colleagues. He was showing her he was in this.

"Carey and I were going to grab lunch," Tessa said, pinning her eyes on her supervisor. She hoped that her intense stare was appropriately understood by her friend and colleague. As much as she appreciated Atlas surprising her—particularly since the last time they saw each other had been when she'd told him she loved him and he'd reluctantly murmured an agreement—she also didn't want to bail on Carey. And she wanted Carey there with her when she went to buy and use the pregnancy test. Carey was like a surrogate mother to her in many ways, and at the moment, Tessa really needed her mother.

Carey nodded. "Yeah, sorry. I made reservations at Lilac and Lavender. Tessa and I have been working together for a long time now. I figure lunch after everything she's gone through to get to today is the least I can do. I'm not going to let you steal my date." She tucked a strand of silver-blonde hair behind her ear and leveled her gaze at Atlas.

All Atlas did was nod in return. "All right then. I will leave you ladies to lunch, and then perhaps we can grab dinner? Or I could bring dinner by your place if you're too tired. Liam and Richelle would like to chat about tomorrow anyway, so we could do a conference call."

Right. Tomorrow.

For a blip in time, she'd actually managed to forget what tomorrow was.

Getting a doctorate and then finding out you might be pregnant will do that.

But the fact was, she was facing off with Carlyle and Blaire tomorrow in the hopes of finally getting her beloved Forest back. And before that, she needed to find out something else.

She slipped her arm from Atlas's and stepped away from him. "I'll call you later and let you know about tonight, okay? I *am* pretty tired. And I want to be mentally on my game for tomorrow. I might just go to bed early."

His face fell, and his eyes turned sad. "Call me later, okay?" He took her hand and squeezed her fingers before pressing a kiss to her cheek. The confidence he'd brought in with him seemed to have evaporated, and he now glanced around at the other therapists like a rooster in a foxhole. "I'm going to get going. Let you *doctors* continue your celebration. Don't need a lawyer cramping your style." His grin was cunning but a bit fake. She could tell now he just wasn't ready to leave her. The sentiment warmed her heart to a comforting temperature, but she had a lot on her mind, and at the moment, Atlas just made all of that feel heavier than ever.

Once she knew if she was pregnant or not, she would tell him. But there was no sense worrying the man who already had his plate heaping. He didn't need to know until there was something to know.

A wave of nausea swam through her.

Was there something to know?

"Ha ha," Carey said with a chuckle, showing Atlas to the door. "This party is for PhDs only, I'm afraid. The law department is in another building."

"I know it well," he murmured, glancing over Carey's shoulder at Tessa. "Call me, Tess."

She nodded, went to take a sip of her champagne, thought better of it and set the flute down. Atlas's eyes followed her every move, and when she set the glass down without taking a sip, his brow lifted.

Oh no.

Before he barged back in and demanded to know if she was pregnant in front of everyone, she took the tiniest of sips from the champagne flute. "Thank you for coming," she said to him as Carey ushered him to the door.

His questioning gaze softened. "Of course."

"All right, Mr. Stark, we'll see you later. Thanks for coming," Carey said before closing the door on him entirely. Her eyes were wide when she spun back around to face Tessa and the other three panelists. "Man is as kind as he is persistent, that's for sure."

Tessa exhaled, and her hand went to her belly just as it did another roll. "That he is."

ATLAS TIPPED BACK his beer and cocked his ankle on his knee. "I think she might be ending this," he said to nobody in particular. He, Mark, Zak, Scott, Adam and Mitch all sat out on Atlas's backyard patio and drank beer while the kids played in the grass and on the play structure he'd gotten at Costco for Aria's second birthday.

"What makes you say that?" Mark asked. His son had wondered up to their table, grunted and pointed at his water bottle. Mark handed it to him.

"I just have a feeling," Atlas said. "She told me she loved me a few days ago, and I ... hesitated."

Groans around the table echoed.

"Not good, bro," Zak said, shaking his shaggy red head.

"You never hesitate," Scott added. "That's a no-brainer."

"But I *did* say it back. I just ... she just caught me off guard. I've never loved anybody else besides Samantha. It felt weird saying it to another woman."

"You do know this is like the most you've ever spoken to any of us, right?" Scott said with a stupid smile. "And Tessa has done that. How can you not love her when she's pretty much given you back yourself? She's also *fixed* Aria, not that she was broken, but you know what I mean."

"I do love her. And I said it back."

"But you hesitated," Mitch finished for him.

Atlas raked his fingers through his hair. "Yeah."

"And then what happened?" Adam asked.

"We went a few days without seeing each other or talking, but I just chalked that up to her preparing for her defense. I went to the college where I knew she was defending, waited until it was over and then knocked on the door to surprise and congratulate her."

"Wow, that's very *un*-Atlas like of you," Scott said.

He narrowed his gaze at the other Dixon Dickhead. "Old me—*pre* ... being a ..." He struggled to get the next word out. "Widower, no. I was actually not this fucking miserable when Samantha ..."

Was still alive.

He cleared his throat. "I was a very different person ... before." He'd been a happy guy who enjoyed planning romantic surprises for the woman he loved. Then Samantha passed, taking his heart and happiness with her. But now, with Tessa, he felt as though a new heart had grown in the gaping hole left by its predecessor. He wanted to make her smile. Her smiles brought on his smiles. He felt more like his old self than he had in years and that not only made him happy, it made his kids happy. His house was a happy place—and so much of that was because of Tessa.

Scott rolled his brown eyes. "Well, we only know the new you, and to us that behavior is very *un*-you."

Atlas grunted. "Anyway, I wanted to take her to lunch and she turned me down, said she had plans with her supervisor."

"That was probably true," Adam cut in. "I often take my PhD or master's students for lunch after their defense. They've worked damn hard."

"Yeah, but then her supervisor essentially picked me up by my collar like a puppy and hauled my ass out of the conference room. And Tessa let her. It was fucking weird."

"Maybe she just wanted to celebrate with other eggheads," Zak offered, his tattooed biceps bunching as he lifted his beer bottle to his lips. "I'd be intimidated as fuck if I were in a room with a bunch of shrinks."

No, that wasn't it. There was something else going on with Tessa. And the way she'd hesitated with the champagne only to then sip it, albeit with palpable reluctance. Was she just overworked, overtired and overrun with thoughts of tomorrow's meeting with Carlyle and Blaire?

He didn't like to say that he had a client's case in the bag, but between him, Liam and Richelle, this was pretty much an easy win.

"So you want us at your office when?" Zak asked, bobbing ruddy brows. "Mason wants to come too. He's tall as fuck and tatted as well. Aaron and Mase will meet me at the gym an hour or so before, then we'll race over, stand there with our arms crossed and glare at the mo-fo like we want to break his fucking neck."

"Because you kind of do," Adam snorted. "You sure you'll need me there? With all that testosterone and the ego on his one"—he hooked his thumb at his younger brother, Zak

me, CeCe." Aria was off playing with Gabe, Jayda and Mira, the three of them thick as thieves somewhere over in the flower garden. Zak's ten-year-old son, Aiden, and Scott's son Freddie were busy squirting water pistols at boats in a kiddie pool to try to sink them. All the kids were happy. So why wasn't he happy?

"Dude, you need to go talk to her. Figure out where her head is," Mitch said, following Jayda and Mira with his gaze. The little girls and Aria were weaving their way down the stepping-stone path through the garden toward them all.

Grumbling, Atlas drew out his phone. It said five o'clock. Why hadn't she texted him about dinner yet?

He hit her number.

It rang. And it rang. And it rang. And then it went to voice mail.

"It's me. Call me back, please. Want me to bring dinner over later? I can have Kimmy watch the girls." He hung up. His gaze slid to the side. "That wasn't needy, was it?"

All the men shook their heads exaggeratedly.

"No, no, not at all. Very manly. Very aloof," Zak said.

"Very aloof," Mark repeated.

"Let her know you're interested, but don't beg," Scott confirmed.

Atlas rolled his eyes for what was probably the millionth time that day. "You're all dicks."

"Said the king of the assholes." Scott chuckled, lifting his beer bottle. Then all the men slammed their hands down on the table at once.

"You go to her," they each said.

22

"Hey Tessa, wait up," Atlas said, jogging up beside her as she approached the door to the big skyscraper that housed the offices of Wallace, Dixon and Travers law firm.

She took a deep breath and released the door handle to face him. He came to a stop right in front of her, leaned down and pecked her on the cheek. "You okay?"

She glanced up at him beneath her lashes. "Would you be?"

"Fair enough." He fell in line beside her and reached for her hand, lacing their fingers together. "I don't want to fuck things up for your meeting with Carlyle, but I'd really like to talk to you about last night. If I upset you by coming over unannounced, I'm sorry. I thought we would have a celebration dinner together, and Liam and Richelle wanted to talk to us." He squeezed her fingers. "You never let me know about dinner, and I wanted to make sure you were okay. You didn't, go and see your mom again, did you?"

No, she hadn't gone to see her mom. She'd gone to the drugstore with Carey, then home because she was too sick to her stomach to even entertain the idea of lunch. Carey had insisted on staying while Tessa took the test, setting the timer on her phone as they both stared at the stick covered in her pee as it sat forebodingly on her bathroom counter.

He opened the door and they walked inside.

"It's fine. I'm sorry I dismissed you the way I did. I wasn't feeling well, and I just wanted to go to bed. I'm just feeling really run-down right now. It's not you, it's me."

She regretted her words the moment they came out of her mouth. And the way his body went rigid beside her said he took her words just as she hadn't intended them.

Crap.

"That's not what I mean," she stammered. "I mean it's not you, you're great. You're perfect. You're wonderful. I'm just feeling really off, and I knew I would be terrible company last night. I know I should have been riding a wave of accomplishment and bliss yesterday after earning my doctorate, but today has weighed heavily on all of that."

He made an animalistic noise in this throat. "As I'm sure Fuckface Rickson had intended it to when he proposed yesterday as our meeting date."

All she did was hum an agreement.

"Hold the elevator!" Liam's hand shot through the closing doors of the elevator, and his flushed face and brown eyes appeared right behind it when the doors began to open.

"Why the hell aren't you in your office preparing for our meeting?" Atlas asked him, his voice stern, accusatory and downright pissed off.

Liam exhaled, hit the button for the nineteenth floor and away they went. "I've been working on another case all morning." He glanced at Atlas. "I *do* have other clients, you know."

"None as important," Atlas grumbled under his breath.

Despite the sinking feeling in her gut, Tessa's heart warmed at his words, and she moved in closer to him.

Liam rolled his eyes. "We've got this in the bag, trust

me. I saw Zak parking his truck down the road. Mason was with him, Aaron and Adam in the back. They'll be here shortly."

"And Richelle?" Tessa asked, not against all the testosterone willing to help her but looking forward to having another woman in the room with her—a powerhouse of a woman, to be exact.

Liam nodded. "She'll be—" He stopped, reached for his phone and put it to his ear. "Hello?"

Atlas and Tessa exchanged curious looks.

"Oh shit. Yeah, okay. I will. Fuck ... Okay ... Okay. Do you want to conference call in if you can? Yep ... Got it. Okay, bye." He turned to them both just as the elevator doors silently slid open. "Richelle's daughter had an emergency at school. She can't come to the meeting."

"Fuck!" Atlas pushed his fingers through his hair.

"We've got this. It's okay," Liam said, adjusting the sleeves of his gray suit jacket. "We're kickass lawyers too, remember?"

"If we have to remind ourselves out loud, then we're not," Atlas murmured. He detangled his fingers with Tessa's and wrapped his arm around her waist, the two of them following Liam down the hallway of Wallace, Dixon and Travers toward the big meeting room they'd reserved.

"In here," Liam said, opening an opaque glass door and allowing them to step inside. One wall of the room was wall-to-wall, floor-to-ceiling windows; the other was more opaque glass. It felt like a weird fishbowl. She didn't like it.

"They're not here yet," Atlas said, leading her around the long, wooden oblong table to sit in front of the windows at the middle of the table.

"I told Rickson ten o'clock. That way we could get here first. Best to present a united front when he first arrives than have our reinforcements trickle in after the meeting has started." Liam set his briefcase down on the table and popped the latches. Like a robot, he began to remove documents, most of which Tessa had already read.

A secretary poked her head in and asked if anybody would like anything to drink. Liam and Atlas both said coffee, black, and Tessa asked for a water, even though the way her guts were turning, she would have much preferred a ginger ale. But that could have been too suspicious.

All three of them took a seat at the same time four men, three the size of Mac trucks and one no slouch, sauntered into the room. Mason, Zak and Aaron all wore tight black T-shirts. Two wore shorts, and Aaron wore jeans.

"Jesus fuck," Liam started. "Did you fucking bench-press a couple of Fiats before you showed up? I swear I see every fucking vein in each of your arms."

Zak grinned broadly. "You said to come jacked. We came jacked." He and the other two musclemen wandered behind Tessa, Atlas and Liam and stood there, arms crossed. Adam took a seat beside Atlas and waved at her.

"What the hell is this?" Carlyle's voice made Tessa's head snap up and her stomach hit her feet. Sweat instantly coated her palms, but that didn't seem to deter Atlas as his fingers tightened in hers. "You think you need *bodyguards* for this?" He wandered in with Blaire beside him. She was at least dressed like a professional with a black pantsuit and red silk blouse. Carlyle was in jeans, a ball cap and a worn royal blue Atlanta Braves T-shirt, as if he were going to a baseball game.

Meanwhile, Tessa had worn a gray pencil skirt and pink cotton blouse, and Atlas, Liam and Adam were in suits. They dressed to impress—or intimidate.

Did he not have a lawyer with him?

"Where is your legal representation, Rickson?" Liam asked, eyeing Blaire and the surprising confidence she had strolled in with.

"She's right here," Carlyle said, tilting his head toward Blaire.

Both Liam and Atlas squinted. "She can't *legally* represent you," Liam said slowly, as if both Carlyle and Blaire were slow themselves. "I'll report her if she does."

Well, that seemed to get Blaire's attention. She snapped her back straight, and fire burned in her eyes as she glared at Liam. "Oh, well, let me just call my dad, then." She turned to the door. "Oh, Daddy?" As if they'd rehearsed it all, a man with a navy pinstripe suit, slicked-back blond hair and expensive brown loafers swung the glass door open.

"Bertram Tomasino," Liam and Atlas both groaned at the same time.

Who the heck was Bertram Tomasino?

Liam's phone rang in his pocket. He answered it and seconds later was setting it down on the table. "Richelle is on speaker," he said.

"Is everyone here?" Richelle's gritty voice asked.

"With one more surprise," Liam said without inflection. "Bertram Tomasino appears to be our opposing counsel."

Richelle didn't even bother to hide her groan of discontent.

"Nice to hear your voice again too, Richelle," Bertram said, taking a seat next to his daughter.

"Why weren't we apprised of Mr. Rickson's legal representation sooner?" she asked, ignoring Bertram's snide comment.

"You know me, Ms. LaRue. I enjoy the element of surprise."

"More like you enjoy jumping out of the shadows after a fiery car wreck. Fucking ambulance-chasing dipshit," Richelle retorted.

"My degree is the same as yours," Bertram replied, appearing completely unfazed.

"Yeah, but I doubt our schools' rankings were," Richelle

muttered. "What league was yours? Because I'd bet my left tit it wasn't ivy."

Bertram clucked his tongue. "You gather far more flies with honey, my dear."

"I'd gather even more with your hollowed-out carcass. It's up to you which way we go," Richelle snapped back.

"I like her," Zak said with a chuckle behind them. "Pity we can't meet the fireball in the flesh."

"Let's get down to brass tacks," Liam said, straightening his tie.

"Yes, let's," Bertram said, opening a shiny black briefcase on the table and pulling out a bunch of forms, which he passed across the table to Liam. "My client is seeking sole custody of the property in question."

Tessa gasped. "He's *my* dog."

Blaire sat back in her chair, grabbed Carlyle's arm and wrapped it around her shoulder with a self-righteous look on her face. "He doesn't even remember you."

"You speak dog now, Miss Tomasino?" Richelle asked.

Blaire rolled her eyes.

"Well, she is a *bitch*," Zak murmured under his breath behind them.

Carlyle's eyes flicked back and forth between Tessa and Atlas, who were sitting closer together than the rest of them.

"Who's he?"

Tessa went to open her mouth, but Atlas dropped her hand and gathered a stack of papers in front of him, tipping them on the end and tapping the lot against the table. "I'm a friend of Miss Copeland's."

"You always sit that close to your *friends?*" Blaire asked snidely.

Richelle cleared her throat over the speaker. "Mr. Rickson, although you and Miss Copeland purchased the property in question together, we are seeking full custody of the canine. Miss Copeland has evidence that the dog by the name of Forest preferred her, was more loyal to her and accompanied her to work every day. We are prepared to settle. Your extensive and expensive comic book and record collection, which is currently in Miss Copeland's possession, as well as a one-time-only payment of two thousand dollars for full custody of the dog. I think we're being more than reasonable here. The dog itself did not cost two thousand dollars, but we understand that Mr. Rickson did put out money toward the care and entertainment of the dog over the years, and we are prepared to compensate him for that." Papers rustled over the phone. "Take this to court, and we'll go for full custody, the records and comics and emotional damages."

Carlyle made a rude noise in his throat, and the look on his face turned downright smug.

Atlas wished Richelle was in the room and her venom could wipe that look clear off the douche's face.

"You're awfully confident, Ms. LaRue," Bertram said, though the bead of sweat on his upper lip said he wasn't nearly as confident as he had been a moment ago. Was the competency and testosterone in the room finally getting to him?

Richelle scoffed. "Come on now, Bertram, you and I both know this is ridiculous. We're prepared to settle. The dog for the comic and record collections, as well as two grand for expenses and compensation. This is our one and only offer."

"I think that is *more* than reasonable," Liam agreed.

"As do I." Atlas nodded.

Carlyle's eyebrow twitched. "She's not getting the dog back. He's just as much mine as he is hers."

"And I've represented countless parents who fought for and won full custody of their children. It happens. And it should happen here." Atlas pulled the top piece of paper from his pile, spun it around and pointed to the highlighted section. "Miss Copeland is the one who did all the inquiry and legwork to obtain Forest the dog. She is also the only person listed as owner at the veterinarian, the pet store, the obedience class he attended. She *is* the more responsible owner. She takes Forest to work with her, takes him for walks, buys his food, takes him to Earth Dog and agility class. For all these reasons—and the overall well-being of the dog—we find Miss Copeland to be the better-fit owner. We're prepared to offer visitation if it comes to that."

"The fact that you're seeking sole custody is preposterous," Richelle added.

"I could say the same thing about you," Blaire replied.

Carlyle's jaw grew slack as his eyes scanned the paper pushed in front of him.

"Furthermore ... " Atlas pulled the next piece of paper off the pile and slid it in Carlyle's direction. The man's hands left sweaty imprints on the table when he reached out to grab it. "It has come to our understanding that you have applied to the University of Washington for a position in the biology department."

Carlyle cleared his throat. "That's right."

"But you haven't signed the employment agreement yet, have you?"

Carlyle swallowed. "No. These things take time."

"Do they?" Adam asked. "Because as *dean* of the biology department, I thought I'd done a pretty good job streamlining the hiring process."

Carlyle's face went the color of pea soup. "The *dean?*"

"*Dr.* Adam Eastwood," Adam said with a wide, superior smile. "Nice to meet you. Consider this the interview that *truly* matters."

"What is the meaning of this?" Bertram asked, his feathers clearly ruffled. "You cart in three meatheads with muscles for brains and my client's future employer to intimidate us?"

"*Potential* future employer," Richelle corrected. "And I'm pretty sure those *meatheads* have more brains *in* their biceps than you, your client and your daughter combined. We're using what we have, and that's support. These people care about my client and want to see her get her dog back. Particularly after the way *your* client treated her, I think she could use all the support she can get. We've done nothing illegal Mr. Tomasino, and you know that."

Bertram huffed and squirmed in his seat.

"So are you saying I won't get the job unless I give her back the dog?" Carlyle asked, his gaze remaining focused on Adam.

Atlas shrugged. "We're not *saying* anything."

Adam turned his palm up and curled his nails forward, examining them with a bored expression. "I'm just here to meet one of the applicants to my department. As dean, I have every right."

"It's also come to my attention that the two of you have applied for a mortgage and are trying to get into the real estate market, is that correct?" Liam glanced back and forth between Blaire and Carlyle.

"How does he know this?" Blaire asked like the buffoon that she was.

"I know a lot of things," Liam said blandly. "I know a lot of people. The *right* people. Like bankers and Realtors, mortgage brokers and home inspectors. I'm from Seattle. Have worked in this city a *long* time. My connections are endless. The favors I owe people, and that people owe me are *endless*." He pinned his gaze on Blaire specifically. "Something you might want to remember, Miss Tomasino when you're applying for associate positions, hmm?"

Blaire's throat bobbed on a hard swallow.

Liam's eyes flicked back to Carlyle. "Seems pretty stupid to me to be applying for a mortgage and trying to buy a house when you're between jobs there, *Carl*, but what do I know?"

"What the fuck does that mean?" Blaire's voice was getting higher with each question.

Carlyle's eyes went buggy, and he turned to face his lawyer. "They can't do this."

Bertram cleared his throat. "I'll handle this." He turned back to Tessa and her legal counsel. "We're prepared to offer joint custody, with Mr. Rickson maintaining the dog eighty percent of the time."

Eighty percent?

He had to be joking.

Richelle made a rude noise. "You're kidding, right?"

"I think that's more than fair," Carlyle said, sitting back in his chair, suddenly seeming content with things again. "Especially given the way things will go soon enough."

What the heck did he mean by that?

"What the fuck do you mean by that?" Atlas practically snarled.

Carlyle turned his head and shook it, pinning his eyes on Atlas. "Has she not told you? Has she kept it a secret from you too?"

"What secret?" Atlas asked, not looking at Tessa but keeping his eyes laser-focused on Carlyle.

Carlyle rolled his eyes. "So she's hidden her mother from you too then. Until you've fallen for her and know it would look bad to leave her after you see the train wreck that is Tessa Copeland's life. That could and *will* be your life, your future if you stay with her."

Tessa's body went ice-cold, and she began to shiver. What on earth had she ever done to Carlyle to make him treat her like this? Yes, she'd waited for their relationship to be solid before she introduced him to her mother, but that was more self-preservation than anything. Had she been wrong? Was she a horrible daughter, a horrible partner, keeping her mother's illness a secret until she knew she and Carlyle were serious? Is the mental state of your parents something you should disclose before you've even gone past second base? She had no idea of the dating rules anymore.

"What the fuck are you talking about?" Atlas stood up, his hands on the table in front of him as he hinged forward toward Carlyle. "I've met her mother. Whatever you're fucking going on about, Rickson, you better fucking spit it out now."

"Or else what?" Bertram asked. "Mr. Stark, did you just threaten my client?"

"Sit down, Atlas," Tessa whispered, tugging on the sleeve of his coat. "It's okay."

He sat down, but heated rage radiated off him like a superconductor.

"Hmm, Mr. Stark, was that you threatening my client just now?" Bertram probed again. The sheen of his greased-up hair glinted as the afternoon sun shone in through the windows. Made the man look extra sleazy, if that were at all possible.

"No threat, *Bert*," Atlas said through gritted teeth.

"I didn't think so," Bertram replied.

"But I would like to know what the fuck your client is talking about. What *secret* he insists my client is keeping."

"I think we'd all like to know," Richelle said. Tessa had almost forgotten the woman was there, she'd been so quiet.

Carlyle rolled his eyes. "Fine. She's losing her fucking mind, and she knows it. Her mother was or is or whatever, manic-depressive. Was for most of Tessa's life. And now her mother is in a home for people with early-onset Alzheimer's. The woman isn't even sixty, and she already needs help going to the bathroom. I think that's something you should disclose on the first, if not the second date with someone, don't you think? Someone you might have a future with, might have *children* with. But Tessa kept that shit a secret from me, kept her mother a secret from me for nearly a year. She was ashamed, embarrassed. Which is all the more unappealing. Someone who is ashamed of their parent because they're ill." His brows lifted. "Wow."

Atlas growled beside her, and his fists bunched until his knuckles shone white.

"I only met her father, and he was told to keep hush about her mother because, and I quote, 'If I introduce men to my mom too soon, they might run for the hills.' From the horse's mouth, your honor."

"There's no judge here, you fucking shit stain," Aaron muttered. "Even I know that."

Zak guffawed, as did Mason.

Liam turned to face Tessa. "Is this true?"

A tear slipped down her cheek, and she hung her head low. "It is."

"Fuck all of this. And fuck you, Rickson. I don't see how any of that has to do with the fact that you stole my client's goddamn dog. Whoever called you a shit stain was accurate as hell," Richelle called out into the room. "Let's get back to the topic at hand here, which is the skid mark dog thief and getting my client some motherfucking justice."

"Were you a sailor in a past life?" Bertram asked, making a disgusted face.

"I was a pirate, you dipshit, and I'll feed you to the crocodile if you don't start talking some sense into your client. Time is money, people, and you're wasting mine."

Tessa glanced up from beneath her lashes. Liam had a shit-eating grin on his face and was trying to contain his laughter. Now was not the time for her to be thinking such things, but it warmed her heart a couple of degrees to know that Liam was in fact madly in love with Richelle. The look on his face right now was pure pride. Pure love.

"It was the last time we went and saw your mother," Carlyle went on, all smug. "When she walked out of her bathroom without a top or bra on, asked me if I was the doctor and if I could inspect the mole between her breasts."

Heat flooded Tessa's cheeks, and her eyes flicked down to where her hands now knitted and twisted in her lap.

"After that day, I did a lot of research on Alzheimer's. You know you're probably a carrier. Which means our kids would most likely get the gene as well."

"Aren't you a biologist? A scientist?" Zak asked with skepticism. "Wouldn't you like proof before you snapped to judgment?"

"Seems awfully *un*scientific to me," Mason added.

"Mhmm," Zak replied. "Awfully unprofessional."

"Fuckin' douchey is what it was." Aaron's deep voice sounded bored.

Carlyle did nothing more than glare at the three men standing behind her. "I already saw the signs with Tessa. As a scientist, I know the fucking signs."

"You're a biologist, not a psychiatrist," Atlas spat out. "Your *diagnosis* would not hold up in court, and it doesn't hold up here. You're grasping at straws, trying to find a reason to be an asshole."

"I'll warn you to keep your temper in check toward my client, Mr. Stark," Bertram said with arrogance, straightening his tie but only making it more crooked in his efforts.

Blaire smiled and glanced at her father with pride.

Carlyle continued to blather on because apparently now that he was ready to tell the world why he left Tessa, he wasn't prepared to stop. "Seeing your mother like that, it was like a horrible preview of how my life would be in ten, fifteen years. That I'd been roped into the caregiver role, the *nurse* role, rather than the husband. Goodbye to family vacations, getting laid, having a *normal* life. Certainly not the life I wanted for myself."

Another set of hot tears slipped down Tessa's cheeks, but she didn't lift her head. Atlas's hand fell to her shoulder, and he squeezed. The tension she felt mounting beneath his palm was fierce, and she worried she was going to snap soon. "Then why didn't you just end it?" Tessa whispered. "Why put me through all of this?"

ATLAS SWUNG his gaze to Carlyle.

Oh, the man had heard her. His face said it all.

"Because he wanted to make sure he found someone else, found somewhere else to live before he ended it with you," Atlas struggled to say through gnashed molars. His fists bunched beneath the table as it took every modicum of self-restraint he had not to lunge across the table and strangle Carlyle.

Carlyle's lip twitched. "Between your mother's manic depression and now the Alzheimer's, I knew you were a ticking time bomb. I just didn't know *how* bad it could get until that day with your mother ... until I did the research myself. Then on the occasion when you'd forget where you put your keys, forget an item on the grocery list or what we had for breakfast on that trip to Lopez Island, even though you asked me what it was like a dozen times. I knew it was only a matter of time before I was changing your soiled diapers and hiding the knobs on the oven so you didn't burn the house down." He shrugged. "I thought that by taking Forest I was doing him a favor. Doing you a favor. One less thing to forget. What's to say one day you don't go all crazy like your mother and try to kill the dog? Or start losing your mind and memory and then forget to feed him?"

Atlas's blood bubbled through his veins. This man was the epitome of a terrible human being. Atlas had met a lot of scum over the years in his line of work but never one as blatantly malicious and out to hurt as Carlyle.

Tessa was sniffling gently beside him, her head hung low, hair covering her face.

Carlyle lifted a brow toward Atlas. "Not sure if you're *just* her lawyer, but like I said, she's a ticking time bomb." He rapped his knuckles on the table twice, then stood up. "I'm done fighting over this. If you want to be selfish and take the dog, then fine. I'll pick him up from the pound when you wander out into the street in your underwear and the neighbors call the cops on you. That is, if you don't starve the poor dog first."

"Why, you mother—" Richelle started, but Carlyle cut her off.

"Miss LaRue, you've won. Give it up." He faced Tessa again. "I'm done with you. Give me my comics, my records and the two grand ... better yet, make it three and we have a deal."

Tessa began to tremble.

"Two grand," Richelle retorted. Atlas could feel the woman's rage emanating over the phone. "Don't get greedy, Mr. Rickson, or I will come after your fucking kidneys."

Carlyle rolled his eyes. "Twenty-five hundred, leave my job alone, and don't get in the way of my house-hunting."

"It just dropped to fifteen hundred, you motherfucker," Atlas ground out.

"Atlas," Tessa whispered, her hand on his arm. "I just want my dog back."

Fuck!

Through clenched teeth and bunched fists, it was like

tearing the words out. "Two grand and not a penny more. You can take your fucking comics and records."

"But I'm afraid I can't hire you," Adam cut in. "I've seen what kind of a person you are, Mr. Rickson, and I hire team players. Kind people. And you are neither. Besides, as a scientist, I would expect more from you. Research, results, proper data to back up your findings. You abandoned Miss Copeland based on a bit of reading and a hunch. That is not the type of person I want in one of my labs. That is not the type of person I want representing the university. Best of luck in your future career opportunities."

Carlyle's mouth opened.

"Take the deal, man," Liam said. "I'll call off the cavalry and you can buy your house. Can't do anything about the job though, that shit's on you and that bad attitude of yours."

"Offer expires in ten seconds, then we take this before a judge," Richelle said. "And that's where I fucking shine."

"Like the goddamn sun," Liam added.

That's what he was fucking talking about.

Who better than to take a simple civil case and turn it into the next *War of the Roses* than Liam Dixon and Richelle LaRue? They didn't even know it, but they were the fucking dream team.

Carlyle's nostrils flared, and his face picked up a shade of red Atlas usually only saw on a constipated child. "You can have the fucking dog. I tried to be kind, give him a better life, but I can see your troops are prepared to leave me with nothing if I don't bend."

"I leave my enemies with nothing," Richelle replied. "I'd leave you with less. Just remember that."

A tick in Carlyle's jaw told Atlas they had him. The man exhaled. "I'll have Forest ready for you to come by and pick him up within the hour." He glanced at Tessa with disappointment in his eyes. She still hadn't even lifted her head.

Clucking his tongue, he headed toward the door. "I have to say though, he's really taken to Blaire. She's going to miss him."

"Shut up," Richelle snapped over the phone.

With a giant smile on his face, Liam stood up and pushed the agreement in front of Carlyle. "Everything is right there in black and white. The dog for the comics, records and a one-time payment of two thousand dollars. After that you will have no legal claim to the property in question ever again."

Sneering, Carlyle scanned the document. Bertram snatched it and read it, as did Blaire, but Atlas doubted the ditz understood half of what she read.

"Looks fine," Bertram muttered.

Carlyle reached for the pen from the table and scrawled his name on the dotted line.

"Don't forget to initial where it's highlighted," Liam reminded him sweetly.

With a glare that coasted across each and every one of their faces, Carlyle initialed atop the yellow highlighter the pushed the document back toward Liam. He set it in front of Tessa and she signed where she had to.

"Looks like we're done here," Liam said with a satisfied exhale, taking the paper back from Tessa. "I'll forward a copy of this to Mr. Tomasino and Miss Copland will be sure to have your property with her when she collects the dog."

Carlyle stood up, shaking his head and glaring at Tessa. "Good luck with the mashed potato brains, Tess. I really was just trying to do best by the dog." Then, shaking his head like he somehow still held all the cards and Atlas was a fool and Tessa a crazy person, he held his hand out for Blaire, and the two of them left the conference room.

"Well, that was a massive waste of time," Bert muttered as he stowed his papers back into his briefcase and left.

"See ya, *Bertie*," Zak called after him.

Bert only glanced back, then hustled down the hallway and out of sight.

"Good job, team," Richelle replied.

"Agreed." Liam nodded.

"We won, right?" Zak asked. "Tessa gets her dog back. Skidmark McFuckface and his ditzy little sidepiece are giving her back the dog?"

"That's correct," Liam said.

"Seems like a big waste of fucking time," Aaron muttered. "We could have just gone to his apartment and strong-armed the dog from him. Next time let's just do that."

"I couldn't agree more," Richelle said blandly

"Can we sue him for wasting our time?" Mason asked. "The lawyer he hired was a fucking joke."

Atlas rested his hand on Tessa's shoulder. "You okay?" She was cradling her stomach now, and the woman looked like she was ready to vomit. She'd had that same look on her face yesterday when he'd surprised her after her defense and then again when he went to her house to make sure she was okay.

Was she okay?

As much as he tried to push them out of his head, Carlyle's words came back at him. Tessa's mother was a manic-depressive and had Alzheimer's. And Tessa had kept that all from him. Did she already know she carried the genes? Did she already see the signs hitting her? Did she only have ten or fifteen good years left?

It took her several moments to reply. Her head bobbed, just barely. "Yeah, I'm fine."

"You're getting Forest back. That's better than fine," Mason said, resting his hand on Tessa's shoulders. "I say we head to Prime to go celebrate. Richelle, you in?"

"Nice try, boys. But I've got other work to do. I'll call you later, Tessa, okay?"

Tessa's voice sounded hollow and distracted as she agreed.

Liam stood, followed by Adam. "Well, that was fucking weird, but I'm glad it's over. A bit anticlimactic if you ask me. I was hoping to go after his assets, maybe his fish tank, his stamp collection. His mother's pearls."

All this was said in jest, of course. They couldn't go after a damn thing now that it was all done. But it was nice to joke about it.

"Fish tank?" Adam asked with a raised brow.

Liam shrugged. "I don't think Richelle is finished with him. She hates having her time wasted." He rested a hand on Tessa's arm. "You want the man's balls? Richelle will castrate him for you, and hand you his wrinkly grapes in a nice little gift bag, trust me."

"I just want Forest back," she whispered, still not really looking at anyone.

Liam gave Atlas a curious look. Atlas shrugged and shook his head. The guys took that as the sign it was intended to be and left, but not before Atlas thanked them all tenfold for their help in the matter.

Once it was just the two of them, he made sure the doors were closed, then he sat back down next to her, pulled her hands into his and waited for her to lift her head.

"I'm pregnant," she finally said, her voice sounding a million miles away even though she was right next to him. "It's yours."

23

"Pregnant ... you ... you're pregnant?"

He blinked and blinked and blinked, but somehow things still seemed blurry. Finally, he had to shut his eyes, rub the heels of his palms into them for thirty seconds or so and then open them again.

She sat there quietly, worry etched deep across her face.

"I just found out yesterday," she whispered. "I needed the night to process before I told you. I wasn't *not* going to tell you. I just ... I just needed a bit of time."

He was going to be a father again. A slew of emotions swamped him, but the most predominant one of them all was joy. As hard as it was having kids, they were what kept him grounded, kept him living. If it hadn't been for Aria, and now Cecily, he could have easily just wasted away to nothing after Samantha died. But he lived for his children. And now, now he had another child to live for. And a new woman to share that life with.

Even though fear and surprise still prickled along his arms and in his belly, he allowed the smile of joy to embrace his face, released her hands and pressed his palm over her belly. "We made a baby."

Something he could only describe as relief washed across her face. "You're not mad?"

He shook his head. "Not at all. Why did you think I would be mad?"

"Because we've only been together for a month or so ... and after everything Carlyle said ... " It didn't seem like she wanted to look at him. Her eyes were darting everywhere but his face. "I don't know if I should keep it."

What? "Why not? I thought you wanted children?"

He was all about a woman's right to choose and body autonomy, but for the love of God, he could not understand why she wouldn't want to keep their child.

"You heard what Carlyle said. I'm a ticking time bomb. How can I knowingly put you and any child I bring into the world through that? I love my mom, but I wouldn't wish what I have with her on my worst enemy. To watch your parent slip away from you, the way she tears out a new piece of my heart each and every time I go see her. It killed my father to watch her deteriorate the way she did. The woman he'd loved since they were kids no longer knew who he was. I couldn't do that to you."

His jaw grew tight. "Do you know for a fact that you have the gene?" She seemed to be basing a hell of a lot of her choices—their choices—on speculation. He wanted fucking facts before they did anything drastic.

She shook her head. "No. I took the test, but I haven't been able to bring myself to open the envelope. It's been sitting in my desk at work for about a week. After the last time I saw my mom—you know, right before you met her—I did the cheek swab and mailed it off—put a rush on it. I had to know. But now with the baby, I'm afraid to know. I've already started to feel my mind going, particularly lately. That has to be a sign I've got it, right?"

That was probably pregnancy brain, but he wasn't going to say that.

As much as he loved this woman, he couldn't deny the frustration that began to grow inside him at her complete lack of zest for the truth. As a lawyer, he was all about the truth, and yet she seemed to be running away from it.

He made to stand up and bring her with him. "Then let's go to your studio right now and open the envelope. Find out once and for all, then we can go from there."

She pulled free of his grasp and stepped back. "I can't do this to you, Atlas. Let you go through it again. I know that you're still struggling with your wife's death. I can't pile even more onto your plate. It wouldn't be fair."

At the mention of his wife, Atlas took his own step back, and he bit down hard on his back teeth. A flash of pain, anger and sadness hit him in the chest like a bolt of lightning, and his eyes slammed shut for a second to allow the emotions to settle before they completely overtook him.

"You don't know anything," he whispered. "I'm dealing with Samantha's death in my own way. It will always be some kind of a struggle—I lost my wife. Aria's mother. But that doesn't mean I can't function. That doesn't mean I can't help you. Be with you. You're making a lot of assumptions right now. And I know you're scared, but you're allowing your ignorance to run your fear."

Her nostrils flared. Yeah, he could bust out the psychobabble too.

Her throat bobbed on a swallow. "I'm sorry."

He relaxed his shoulders, but anger still ran rampant through him. His fingers twitched at his sides, and a muscle in his jaw thumped in time with his rapidly beating pulse.

Her shoulders slumped, and she exhaled in frustration. "I shouldn't have brought up your wife, but everything else I said was still true. I can't do that to you, to an innocent child."

Oh, for fuck's sake. He wanted to fucking scream. "What the fuck do you know? You haven't even opened that fucking envelope. You know nothing."

Her bottom lip wobbled. He knew all of this was coming from a place of fear. From the hormones running rampant through her. From the adrenaline of her defense yesterday, the showdown with Carlyle today and finding out about the baby. She wasn't thinking clearly, and he needed to help her see that together they were better. Alzheimer's or not. Together he could help her weather the storm. He was her bifocals when the world went blurry. She was his gust of wind when he needed to be swept off his feet and not take life so seriously. They balanced each other out. Why couldn't she see that?

"I'm really scared."

Well, now they were fucking getting somewhere.

He pulled her into his body. Like a shock absorber, he took in every one of her shudders and shakes as she sobbed in his arms. He shushed her and stroked her head. Let her get all the emotions of the last several weeks out. And all the new emotions that came along with a pregnancy.

Her sniffles became muted as she pressed her face into his chest, but her breathing eventually returned to normal.

Once he knew she was in a better state, he released her, held her biceps and looked her square in the eye. She needed to understand a few things before they went any further. He wanted her. Couldn't imagine his life without her. But he also knew he couldn't be with someone who preferred ignorance over the truth. Who preferred to live life in the dark rather than take the light, head on and power through the harsh rays.

Her blue eyes held so much fear, he was tempted to just pull her into him again. She blinked thick, spiked lashes at him, waiting.

"Whatever you decide, I will be here. But *only* if you open that envelope."

The quick draw of her breath stirred his protective instincts, but he kept hold of her biceps. He needed her to hear him out. "If the results are not what we hope for, then we will take the next step. If you want to have the baby but then go off and see the world, live the last few lucid years of your life having adventures, I will take the child. You don't have to keep it. You don't have to be in its life. But you *need* to open that envelope." His nostrils flared and his eyes narrowed again at the same time he released her. "Open the envelope, Tessa. Then come find me when you do."

"Come on, buddy, let's go!" Tessa said, helping Forest out of the back of her car. She hadn't seen her dog this happy since she'd picked him up from the rescue society. And just like he'd known that day, today he knew he was finally coming home. Normally, he pulled a bit and sniffed at every shrub and tree on the walkway up to her condo lobby, but today he remained right at her heels, looking up at her as if she were some deity he revered. His tongue lolled out the side of his mouth, his brown eyes sparkled, and his black lips curled up in a big doggy smile.

Despite everything that had gone down in the last twenty-four hours, an odd sense of calm fell over her as she opened the door to her apartment and Forest went bounding inside past her. He began to sniff every reachable surface, to make sure no usurper canine had played with his toys or lain in his favorite spot on the couch. Once he was satisfied that Tessa's heart had not been won over by another dog, he stuck to her like glue as she went about putting on laundry and tidying up the house.

Since she'd been in study mode for the last month, particularly the last week, her apartment was a disaster zone. She hadn't cooked a meal all week, and takeout boxes from the Healthy Hippie a takeout-only vegan restaurant she frequented—filled the recycling bin, receipts covered the top of the dresser in her room, and there was an Everest-size mound of dirty laundry beside her overflowing hamper.

"You're procrastinating," she muttered to herself as she sorted the colors and whites of her laundry on the bed. "I am not," she replied. "Yes, you are. You know you need to go to the studio and open that envelope, but you're putting it off."

Forest was lying on the bed staring at her, and he cocked his head back and forth like a puppy as he tried to figure out who she was talking to.

"I'm just not ready." She slammed the door of the front-loading washing machine and hit the *on* button before stalking back to her room in a huff. "Who the heck is he to tell me what to do?" She growled. "He's the father of your baby, that's who, damn it." She scooped the pile of receipts off the top of her dresser and tossed them on the bed. Most of them were for takeout, but there were a few here she needed to keep for tax and work purposes. Forest was still on the bed but had shifted his body so that his shiny black nose was buried in the pile of receipts and his front paw was resting on a bunch of them. He wasn't prepared to let her out of his sight. She ruffled the top of his head. "The feeling is mutual, buddy."

Forest whimpered and dragged his paw in the pile of receipts over and over again until he pulled something free from the bottom of the pile.

"Hey, buddy, don't do that. I need those." With a huff, she pushed them all away from his big paws. But he still had a piece of paper beneath his paw. And then the other paw fell on top of it before he rested his chin on it as well.

Tessa planted her hands on her hips. "What is the meaning of this, Forest? Give me my receipt." She went to tug it away from him, but he growled. It was the first growl he had ever given her in his life, and it made her snatch her hand back and take a step away. "What on Earth has gotten into you?"

She tried again to retrieve it, but he growled again. She knew he would never hurt her, but the noise was a warning that whatever piece of paper he had in his grasp was entirely off-limits to her. Rolling her eyes, she gathered the rest of her organized receipt piles and headed to the kitchen.

"You're a weirdo, you know that?" She shot him a look as she left the room. She heard him jump off the bed onto the floor, and his nails *clickety-clacked* on the wood behind her. "Oh, so now you want to be with me?" He was once again right on her heels, only this time he had the piece of paper in his mouth.

"I sure hope whatever you've got there isn't going to cost me a nice tax deduction." Her back ached, her stomach turned and her head spun. That's when she realized she still hadn't eaten anything all day. The clock on the microwave said it was nearly four o'clock. Well, no wonder she was light-headed. The achy back and woozy belly were from something else though.

Her hand fell to her stomach as she reached for a banana and wandered over to the couch. "What are we going to do, Forest?" she asked, propping her feet up on the coffee table and peeling her banana halfway down.

She wanted Atlas.

She wanted this baby.

She also wanted to grow old and know her children, her grandchildren and remember all the amazing things she'd accomplished in her life. Ignorance had been bliss, but it had also been torture. She'd changed her diet because she thought she had this disease, focused on school and was always working her brain. Reading and listening to educational podcasts. The only indulgences she allowed herself were wine, the serial killer documentaries and her motorcycle—which she'd have to stop riding now with the baby on the way.

She was one of the healthiest people her doctor had ever met, and yet, she didn't *feel* healthy. She felt like for her whole life she'd been doing nothing but waiting for the other shoe to drop. For the depression to yank the rug out from under her or the Alzheimer's to claim her earlier than it'd claimed her mother. At least *not* knowing for sure had allowed her a small percentage of hope. Hope that her fretting had all been for naught. She knew she was being stupid. Living her life in the dark, wandering around in a fog of ignorance. But the alternative scared her to death. Knowing definitively whether she would develop Alzheimer's terrified her.

But now it wasn't just her life she needed the answers for. It was her baby's life. Her baby's future. Atlas's baby. Atlas's future. Aria and Cecily's little brother or sister.

She couldn't draw them into her bleak and desolate world of witlessness. They deserved to know. Her baby deserved to know. Deserved a mother who met the world head-on, embraced the truth and the ramifications or beauty that came with it rather than burrowing into the sand and ignoring life as it happened.

She stared at the half-eaten banana in her fist. She didn't feel hungry at all anymore. She felt sick. She felt alone.

Forest whimpered at her feet. Okay, well, she wasn't *completely* alone anymore.

"What am I going to do, buddy?" she asked, folding the banana peel over the uneaten portion and tossing it onto the coffee table. "What would you do?"

As if on cue, he leapt up on the couch beside her as quiet as a jungle cat and plopped the paper he'd had in his mouth directly into her lap. Of course, it had a thin coat of dog slime on it, but it still appeared to be intact. "Why the change of heart, hmm?" She picked up the paper and turned it over, expecting to see a receipt for My Kind of Thai or the Healthy Hippy, but it wasn't a receipt at all. It was the envelope from her dad.

She'd totally forgotten about this. Which was so out of character for her. Normally anything having to do with her father was at the forefront of her mind. It just went to show how distracted she'd been by everything lately.

Now it totally made sense why Forest was being so possessive, he adored her father, and her father adored Forest. It always amazed her how intuitive animals could be. The letter probably held some last remaining traces of her father—maybe a bit of grease from his bike, or a thumb print with salt and vinegar chip residue. Something easily detectable that would make Forest immediately think of her father.

A dull ache spread from the center of her chest outward as the memories of her Dad came crashing back. He really had been the most remarkable, wonderful, patient man in the world. He literally had given someone the shirt off his back once, and then he gave the guy twenty bucks for a hot meal and returned the next day with a suitcase full of more clothes and a two-hundred-dollar gift card to the grocery store.

Tessa had only been about ten-years-old at the time, and

on the way home, with her father sitting shirtless behind the wheel of his pickup on a cold November evening, he turned to her and said, "I'm a lucky man. I don't know his story, and that's not my business. But he's cold, he's hungry and he's out there asking for help. The least I can do is keep him warm and his belly full. I've got lots of clothes, and the fridge is stocked. I'm a lucky man."

Pressing her forehead to Forest's she squeezed her eyes shut and focused on her breathing. It didn't matter that her dad had been gone for two years, if she thought too long or hard about him the pain resurfaced. It always took her a moment to regroup, embrace the grief, mourn her loss and then move forward. She'd gone to quite a few grief counseling sessions following her father's abrupt passing, and she'd been taught not to ignore the grief, but to accept it, embrace it and then move forward.

When she opened her eyes again, Forest's deep, chocolate brown orbs pierced her, a whimper vibrated in his throat and his tongue shot out and licked her chin.

Chuckling, she smiled, grateful that her best friend was finally home again, and bringing her the peace she'd been sorely lacking all these weeks. "You always know exactly how to bring me out of my funk, buddy." Running the pad of her thumb over her father's handwriting, she scratched behind Forest's ear with the other hand. "Did you know this was important? Does it smell like Dad?" Shaking her head at the mystery and wonder of dogs, not to mention how therapeutic it was to have him back by her side where he belonged, she opened the envelope. What came next, she would have never expected in a million years.

Dear Kiddo,

I don't know when you'll get this, but I hope it's sooner rather than later. I've wanted to tell you this since you were a teenager, but from the day we brought you home from the hospital, your mother made me promise I wouldn't. Even as her mind started to slip, she made me promise.

But I can't keep this a secret for any longer.

In every way that matters, you are Tessa Marie Copeland. My daughter. But you're not my blood. You're not your mother's blood either. You, my darling child, are adopted.

You're probably wondering why we kept this big secret from you, but it wasn't to hurt you or even protect you. It was because of your mother.

Two days before you were born, your mother was rushed to the hospital. She gave birth to a premature baby girl—Georgia —who unfortunately passed away after a day and a half. Understandably, your mother was very upset. So was I, of course. On the same day her milk came in, so did a young woman, maybe sixteen or so. She was thought to be a runaway. She'd been in a terrible accident, and they were unable to save her. They did, however, save the baby in her belly—you.

As hard as it was for your mother to lose Georgia, she knew what she had to do, and she put you to her breast. For me, it was love at first sight. You were mine before we were even able to ask about adoption. You slept on my chest when you weren't eating. You settled in my arms the moment I held you. You were mine and I was yours, there were no two ways about it. We became inseparable. Eventually, we were able to take you in as foster parents, and after a year or so we adopted you. However, it was around your third birthday, after we tried for another baby and your mother lost that one, that she slipped into a deep depression. Her grief and guilt over losing Georgia and the other child made it hard for her to be a mother to you. I know she felt awful about it, and you have to know that she loved you with all her heart and the best she knew how. She just lost a big piece of her heart when Georgia died, which made her unable to give you her whole heart.

I'm telling you all of this because you deserve to know the truth, and if something happens to me before I'm able to tell you in person, I would never forgive myself. I know your mother is too far gone with her Alzheimer's to tell you, and even if she wasn't, I'm not sure she would tell you. She never wanted you to know the truth. Her reasons were ... complicated.

I have spent several months now trying to track down your biological mother's family but have come up fruitless. The same goes for your biological father. You may have more luck with one of those ancestry websites.

But no matter what those websites say, never forget that no matter what, blood or no blood, you are my daughter, Tessa, in every way that counts. I love you. Your mother loves you, and we are both so proud to call ourselves your parents.

I love you, Kiddo.

~Dad

She read it four times over until the ink was blurry from her tears and her body shook with each wracking sob. Forest's head was now in her lap, and he whimpered and pawed at her, trying to figure out what was wrong.

She was adopted.

Minutes ticked by, and the sound of rush-hour traffic whizzed past outside, but none of that mattered as she allowed the information in her father's letter to slowly sink in. It was dated—because her father was nothing if not organized—and of course, he'd written it a week before his helicopter had gone down. He'd always been crazy intuitive. Maybe he knew in some weird way that he wasn't going to get a chance to tell her in person. Who knows? Either way, all her fears about her mother's disease living inside her screamed at her to be released.

Wiping away the last of her tears, she folded up the letter, tucked it back into its envelope and into her pocket. "Want to go for a drive, buddy?" she asked Forest, standing up from the couch with a shudder in her chest and a lightness in her heart. She knew it was too early, but she couldn't deny the weird fluttery feeling inside her belly or the way it made her insides warm. Her hand once again fell to her stomach, and for the first time since that stick showed two lines, she glanced down at her hand over her stomach and she smiled.

24

ATLAS PACED BACK and forth in Liam's office, his hands twitching and gesticulating as he ran through it all with his friend.

"I just don't know if I can be with someone who prefers to live in the fucking dark," he said, raking his hands through his hair and then aggressively scrubbing them down his face, pulling on his chin. "I mean, knowledge is power. Facts are power. The truth is power. And she refuses to learn the truth about herself." He paused, spun on his heels and tossed his hands in the air. "Who the fuck does that?"

"People who are scared of the truth," Liam offered plainly.

"Yeah, but she's a fucking therapist. Scared of the truth or not, she should know better. It doesn't make any sense."

"First of all, therapists are some of the more messed-up people out there. The only reason they even go into psychology or become therapists is to figure their own shit out. Which usually doesn't work. Same reason I would never represent myself in court. Secondly, can you look at this from her perspective for just a second? That here she's been living her whole life wondering if she was going to turn out like her mom. Manic-depressive and with Alzheimer's. I mean, that's had to weigh heavily on her. I don't know if I'd be *ashamed* to introduce people to my mother if she was like that, but I'd certainly be selective in *who* I introduced to her. People can be fucking judgy fuckers."

"Tessa's not ashamed," Atlas stated.

"Fuckface Skidmark McGee said she was."

"Fuckface Skidmark McGee is also a liar."

Liam shrugged. "So what are you going to do? Could you still be with her if she decided to terminate because she has the Alzheimer's gene?"

Atlas didn't fucking have a clue. Sure, he'd gone and said all the right things because he loved the woman and the idea of having a child with her made him feel happier than he'd been in a long fucking time. But even though Carlyle was the skidmark of skidmarks, he had a bit of a point. If she *did* in fact carry the gene, she could pass that on to their child. And if she did carry it, the likelihood of her winding up a lot like her mother was high. They maybe had ten or fifteen years before she would start to show signs. Possibly sooner.

If the roles were reversed, he certainly wouldn't want to saddle her with the responsibility of playing nursemaid to him as well as raising their children.

Fuck, he just didn't know what to do. He didn't know how he felt about any of it.

He loved her. Loved the way she was with his kids. Loved the idea of having another kid with her, but ... fuck!

"I should just go to her studio, open the letter myself and find out once and for all if she has the gene," he murmured.

"Yeah, because opening someone else's mail *isn't* a federal felony." Liam rolled his eyes. "Sit down and have a drink." Without even getting out of his seat, he spun in his chair. The sound of glasses clinking and liquid being poured competed with the pulse thudding in Atlas's ears. Liam turned his seat back around and handed Atlas a short, stocky tumbler with bourbon in it. Liam drank scotch, but he kept bourbon in his office for when Atlas came by. "Now, you're going to sit your ass down in that seat, shut the fuck up for a second, drink your goddamn drink and listen to me."

Atlas glared at Liam. Liam's smile grew.

"Sit."

He did as he was told, tossing back half his drink as he did. The bourbon was top-shelf and slid down his throat like melted butter.

"Now, listen up," Liam started. "You love her. She loves you. You're far less moody and miserable since you got with her. Your kid is in a better place since you hooked up with her. Hell, we all like her. Even Richelle likes her, and Richelle hardly likes anybody that isn't paying her money or sticking their dick into her." He snorted. "Sometimes I'm not even sure she likes me, she just likes my dick."

Atlas rolled his eyes.

"Fucking go to her, man. Sort this shit out and come to a solution together. You walked away from her today when you should have stayed. She's confused. She's scared. I know you're all that shit too, but you're not the one knocked up and with possible grits for brains."

"When the fuck did you get so *pro*-love, all of a sudden?" Atlas grumbled.

"Since I saw what love has done for the people I love. I'm not saying that shit is for me, but it's made you all a hell of a lot happier. But like I told Scott when he and Eva got together, if you and Tessa go sideways and she hires Richelle again, I can't represent you. We have a pact to never be on opposite sides in the courtroom."

Atlas rolled his eyes again. "You're a dick."

"No, I'm not. I'm your best friend, and I'm also right."

He was. And he was.

Atlas narrowed his eyes. "Fuck you."

Now he wanted to punch his friend in his big cocky smile. "No thanks. But I will take a rain check on a steak dinner as payment for my pro bono services today."

He hadn't told Tessa, but he'd made Liam waive his fees, and Richelle was only charging Tessa twenty percent of what she normally charged. Atlas, of course, was doing it for free. Though now he owed both Liam and Richelle some hefty favors that he knew they would both cash in down the road.

"I also want to suggest you extend your sabbatical until September," Liam said, tipping up his scotch.

"What?" Atlas's drink paused midair. "No."

"Just listen to me. Take the summer with your family. Figure out your shit with Tessa. Take the kids camping. Go see your parents for a week. You have the money to do it, so do it. They're only this little once. Before you know it, they'll be teenagers and want nothing but money from you. We can all cover for you. We'll give the associates your cases, and name partner isn't going anywhere. It'll be here when you get back." He finished his drink. "It *is* yours, Atlas. You've earned it by working your ass off. Now it's time to reward your ass with a little bit of a break. I've already talked it over with Rocky and Jerrika. They totally support it."

"There you go again—"

"Having my friend's back."

"I was going to say making decisions for me ... but yes."

Liam grinned. "I knew you'd see it my way. Now finish your drink and get the fuck out of here. I have work to do, and you have a woman to win back, or whatever." He made a dismissing movement with his hand like Atlas was some school-age delinquent who had just been given demerits by the principal and was now being sent to detention hall.

Rolling his eyes again, Atlas finished his drink and turned to go.

"Oh, and, Atlas?" Liam called from his desk, already with a case file open in front of him.

Atlas grunted.

"Congratulations on the baby."

"THERE'S YOUR OLD BED, buddy. Did you miss it?" Tessa swung open the door to her studio, and Forest bolted for his dog bed in the corner. He sniffed and scratched at it, then proceeded to wander the perimeter of the room and sniff that too.

Her desk sat in one corner, and inside it lay the envelope. Her DNA. A map of her past, her present and most definitely her future.

Just because Lily wasn't her biological mother didn't mean Tessa couldn't still carry the gene. Perhaps her birth parents carried the gene as well, and if her biological mother had lived longer, she would have succumbed to the same disease. But now that she knew Lily and Bruno Copeland had adopted her, she couldn't stop there in finding out the truth of things. Not when she had a little peanut growing inside her. She deserved to find out the answers for the baby. For Atlas. And for herself.

With cautious but determined strides, she made it across the room to her desk, fished her keys out of her purse and opened the drawer.

Even in just the span of a week, the envelope had meandered its way to the bottom of the drawer, so she had to do a bit of digging, but eventually she found it, crumpled but still sealed. Still holding all the answers.

Standing up to her full height, she slid her finger beneath the seal and opened the envelope.

A throat cleared across the room before she could open up the folded papers making her jump. Normally she locked the door behind her if she wasn't expecting clients, but she must have forgot to. Baby brain? With wild heart palpitations, she lifted her head only to find Atlas standing there with pain in his eyes and fear dragging down the lines of his face. He approached her slowly.

"She was diagnosed with invasive ductal carcinoma, a very aggressive form of breast cancer."

Tessa's eyes widened.

"She'd felt a lump in her breast shortly after Aria was born, but when she brought it to the doctor's attention, he said it was a clogged duct and that it would eventually sort itself out. He said this to her three times over the course of six months. We sought a second opinion, but as you know, the medical system in this country is broken, and it took weeks to get in to see another doctor for an assessment. By the time we did get a second opinion, the cancer had spread. She underwent a double mastectomy, but even that wasn't enough. It had spread to her lymph nodes. Her liver. Her pancreas. After a year of chemo and radiation that made her sicker than the cancer ever did, she finally decided enough was enough." His words were coming out tighter and tighter, and his lips trembled as he fought to power through the emotions. She could tell he was clenching his teeth as muscles on either side of his jaw pulsed with each squeeze. He was standing only a foot or so away from her now, and she could see just how hard it was for him to talk about his late wife. But she also knew that he wouldn't do it if he didn't want to, and she needed to let him finish.

So she took his hand in hers and squeezed. He closed his

eyes and shook his head before opening them again, showing an agony so deep that it even hurt her.

"She died a week after Aria turned two. On a cold, rainy October night in my arms. I was angry. So ... angry. At the world, at the doctors, at myself, at Samantha. I hated so much, so hard."

He hated so much and so hard because he'd loved so much and so hard. His heart had been ripped from his chest, and all he had left was pain. That rage was completely understandable, and she probably would have felt the exact same way.

Tessa hiccupped a sob, unable to stop the tears that spilled down her cheeks and along the crease of her nose. "I'm so sorry, Atlas."

His own eyes had finally turned glassy and damp, and with his free hand, he wiped beneath them.

"Did you sue that doctor for malpractice?" she asked. "I mean, had he not dismissed the lump, maybe they would have caught it in time."

"I sued him for everything I could. Had his license revoked. He left town, was forced to sell his practice because I dragged his reputation through the mud. I didn't just go for his jugular, I went after every vein, every artery. I went after everything in his life." His tone was so deadpan, so lacking inflection that it actually scared her a little bit, just how ruthless he could get. But then it also made her love him all the more that he was able to love that hard. Samantha had been his life, his first everything, his whole world, and one man's negligence had cost Atlas his wife, Aria her mother and the Stark family their future. Tessa would have probably gone for the doctor's everything too.

"What did you do with the money? Donate it?"

"Half of it went into a trust for Aria that she can't touch until she's twenty-one. The other half went into an education fund for her. I didn't touch a dime of it. It wasn't about the money, never was. I make more than enough. It was about the fact that he dismissed my wife's concerns and she ultimately paid for it with her life. Aria paid for it—she lost her mother. I paid for it—I lost my wife. He needed to lose things too, know just a fraction of what it felt to lose something you cherished more than anything in the world."

"Did he have a wife and kids?" She didn't know why she was asking him that, but for some reason, she knew that his response would change the way she looked at him.

"No. I wouldn't have gone after so much if he had. Trickle-down effect is not how I do things. *He* fucked up. *He* needed to pay. Not the innocents in his life. He was a rich, selfish bastard who should have fucking retired a long time ago. He was divorced, and he and his ex-wife never had any children. The only person that paid when I went after him was the doctor that killed my wife."

She released the breath she'd been holding and went to him, wrapping her arms around his waist and absorbing just a fraction of his pain. "You're a good man, Atlas Stark. An incredible man."

He shrugged off her praise. "I don't like to talk about my wife because it still hurts. But you deserve to know my truth. You deserve to know what's in my heart, my aches, pains and scars and why I am the way I am. Why I believe that knowledge is power. Had we known sooner that Samantha had breast cancer, had they caught it earlier, she might have survived."

"Thank you," she whispered, knowing that he deserved just as much from her, and yet she'd been dishonest with him —she'd been dishonest with herself.

"I know this is your choice, but *I* can't live my life in the dark. Are you here to finally find out the truth?" he asked, his voice husky and strained.

She nodded and blinked away the remaining tears in her eyes. "In a way, yes. Though I found another envelope at home that revealed even more than this envelope will." She reached into the back pocket of her jeans, pulled out the letter from her father and handed it to him.

With a slight shake to his limbs and a stutter to his breathing for a moment, Atlas broke their embrace, took the letter from her and opened it.

She waited for him to read it before she spoke again.

When he got to the part about her being adopted, his eyes flew up off the page to her. "She's not your birth mother."

Tessa shook her head. "She's not. So her genes aren't my genes."

"Holy shit. So then you don't even have to open this." He flicked the other letter in her hand.

"But I want to," she replied. "I want to know the truth. When I found that letter from my dad and read it, I realized then and there how foolish I've been all these years living in ignorance. I don't want to live in the dark anymore either. Knowledge is power. The truth is power. And if I have the ability to know the truth, then why not find out?"

"Do you want me to leave so you can open it in private?" he asked, handing her back the letter from her father.

She shook her head. She never wanted him to leave again.

"I shouldn't have left you in the first place," he said, moving back into her, his touch sending tingles down her arms and warmth into her belly. "I'm sorry for the things I said. I will support you in whatever decision you make, and whether you keep the baby or not, have the Alzheimer's gene or not, I want to be with you. You're not my *do-over*, you're my fresh start. And even if I only get ten or fifteen years with you, we'll make sure that they are the best ten or fifteen years possible."

Fresh, hot tears burned the backs and corners of her eyes

as she fought back a sob. "I want this baby, Atlas. I want this baby so bad. I also want to know the truth about myself, but I'm scared. What if my birth parents were even more messed up than my adoptive parents?"

He took the folded papers from her and opened them. "Only one way to find out."

"WELL, THAT WAS QUITE THE READ," Atlas said after they made their way through the four pieces of paper that outlined Tessa's genetic makeup. "I will say, I am awfully glad to know that the likelihood of us being related in any way is pretty nil."

Half-laughing, half-crying, she swatted him on the chest with the back of her hand. He'd taken a seat on one of the beanbag chairs over in her therapy corner and pulled her into his lap. He needed her close, to feel her breath against his cheek, her pulse beneath his fingertips.

She nodded. "And no predisposition to Alzheimer's, diabetes or any of the really scary cancers that hit women."

"I'd say you kind of hit the jackpot when it comes to genes."

Her sigh came out as more of a shudder, and she nestled into his chest, still holding the papers in her hand. "Yeah, I mean as much as this test can tell us, I guess I did."

His hand rested on the flat of her stomach. "Which *means* our kid has also hit the genes jackpot. Because I'm going to be honest here: I am one hell of a healthy specimen."

There was the laugh he was after. He kissed the top of her head and held on tighter to her and their baby.

"I'm sorry I was such an idiot earlier," she said, folding up the papers and setting them on the ground beside her. "The emotions of the past few days got the better of me, and I took it out on you. You were right, you know. Knowledge is power."

"And do you feel powerful now?" he asked, even though he already knew the answer, even if she didn't. Tessa Copeland was one of the fiercest, kindest, most powerful women he knew. She'd taken what was left of his cold, shattered heart and warmed him up from the inside out, filling in the crevices with her patience and love until he once again felt something akin to whole.

"I feel better knowing," she said with a shrug. "But maybe I can only say that because what I know isn't bad."

"I think you'd feel better either way," he said, rubbing his hand down her arm. "Because then you'd be able to stop living your life in limbo and start living it fully."

"Perhaps." She yawned and adjusted her position on his lap. "I mean there are still hundreds of unknowns out there about me, more so now than if Lily and Bruno had been my biological parents. Because at least then I could run my mother's DNA and find out more about myself. But I have no clue where to start now. I have no idea who my birth parents were, where they were from. I could still develop Alzheimer's, not all forms are detectable."

He growled, his brows furrowing at how dark she was going again.

Her coy smile had his knitted brows relaxing. "But knowing that what my mother has isn't in my DNA does give me some kind of comfort." She relaxed against him. "I have no idea what tomorrow or the next week or month will bring, but I do know I like my odds of remembering it all."

He chuckled against her, pressing his lips to the side of her head.

"So now what?" she breathed, melting even deeper into his arms—where she belonged.

"Now?" He kissed her again. "Now we celebrate. We won

the case against Rickson, you have your dog back, you have your PhD, you're having my baby, and I was just given two and half more months of sabbatical leave. We can celebrate all summer if we want to."

Her phone buzzed her in pocket, and she reached for it, hitting the answer button and putting it on speaker. "Hello?"

"Hello, Miss Copeland. This is Jolene over at *Frozen Moo Juice*. We have your custom ice cream flavor ready for you to pick up."

Atlas narrowed his gaze on her curiously. "Ice cream flavor?" he mouthed.

"Right, thank you so much," Tessa said, a sly grin now on her flushed and gorgeous face. "I'm just down the street, so I'll swing in shortly and grab it. Thank you."

"See you soon."

They disconnected the call, and she glanced up at him from her phone. "I commissioned a discontinued flavor. Perhaps you've heard of it ... *citrus cooler?*"

As if he couldn't love this woman any more.

"An ice cream celebration it is, then," he said, shaking his head and smiling hard at how fucking happy he finally was. "We'll grab you some pistachio while we're there and the girls some of that godawful Tiger Tiger garbage."

"I want to celebrate everything with you." She hit him hard with those sparkling blue eyes, which told him everything he needed to know about the future. "I want to celebrate everything with you for the rest of my life."

"And that is going to be a very long, very lucid, very happy life." Then he claimed her mouth as his, because it was. Because Tessa was his.

EPILOGUE

Nine months later ...

ATLAS CRACKED his neck side to side and let out a grunt. How long had they been at this? He was sure he was going to have shit in his hands any minute if they didn't get a diaper out soon.

"Just like that, guys, perfect. Now if Mom and Dad can move their hands down just a bit so we can actually *see* baby Magnus's head and not just big grown-up thumbs, that would be awesome. Yeah, perfect. Great." Mitch's camera clicked half a dozen times as he crouched down in front of Tessa and Atlas, who were holding their naked ten-day-old son in front of a black backdrop. "Okay, Tori, your turn."

Tori, who was an amateur photographer and studying under Mitch, had offered to take free newborn photos of Magnus and the family, but she wanted the baby "extra squishy," as she said, which was why they were there not two weeks after Tessa had given birth.

She took up Mitch's post, crouched down on the ground.

She didn't snap a pic, but glared at Atlas. "Smile, you big grump."

He rolled his eyes. "I thought we were supposed to be all serious and in love," he replied, tossing on a half smile.

"That's fine, but you looked like you'd rather be anywhere else but here," Tori said, beginning to snap pictures.

Tessa chuckled, then slid her thumb down farther so as to not block their son's face from the shot.

"Now one with the girls," Tori said. "Everybody sit on the ground like the big happy family that you are and stare at Magnus like he's the most beautiful baby you've ever seen. Call Forest over too. It's not the whole family without that big fur baby."

Tessa whistled for a sleepy-eyed Forest who had curled up next to the heater and he immediately trotted over to her, sitting at her feet obediently and gazing up at her with all the love and patience in the world.

Atlas beckoned to Aria and Cecily, who were sitting on the ground with mouths full of dinosaur-shaped fruit snacks to keep them in line. The girls rose from their spots and joined their parents.

Because they were *their* parents. Tessa had embraced motherhood with Aria and Cecily as if it were second nature to her, and now with Magnus, she was every bit the glowing, capable new mother he expected she would be.

Tessa gently encouraged Forest to spin around and face the camera and the big lug did as he was told, but sat on her feet and gazed up backward at her, his brown eyes soulful and almost worried. She rubbed his head. "It's okay, buddy."

"Forest!" Tori sung, snapping her fingers and then whistling.

Forest dropped his head and his eyes widened at the same time his tongue dropped out the left side of his mouth in a smile.

"Perfect," Tori cooed. "Okay, everyone smile and look at Magnus." Tori's camera clicked, and she shifted about on her knees to get different angles.

"Have the girls kiss his forehead," Mitch instructed.

"Girls, can you give Magnus a kiss on the head?" Tori asked.

"Mag-ass kissy kissy," Cecily cooed, giggling as she bent over and kissed her brother on the top of his head.

"His forehead is wrinkly under my lips," Aria said.

Tori continued to snap pictures.

"Okay, now one of just Mom and Dad," Tori said, catching Atlas's eye and winking over her camera.

He nodded and took the baby from Tessa.

"What? We've already done that. Where are you going with my baby?" Tessa asked, a mix of worry and confusion on her tired-mama face.

Atlas ignored her and passed a now-snoozing and still very naked Magnus off to Mitch. "Diaper him, will ya? Kid's due for a shit any minute."

"I'm snipped because I didn't want to do diapers anymore," Mitch joked, taking Magnus from him and wandering over to the blanket next to the heater. "No swimmers, means no diapers, period."

"What's going on?" Tessa asked again. "My boobs are starting to hurt. I think he might be hungry."

"He's sleeping," Tori said, dismissing Tessa's worry and helping her stand up. "Just roll with it, Tessa. I want to get a few pictures of the happy parents."

"Without the baby?" she squeaked. "What about with me and the girls?"

"We'll do that after," Tori said. "But first I want to get this."

Tessa's eyes were pinned on Mitch as he attempted to diaper Magnus. "Get what?"

That was Atlas's cue. He reached for the ring in his back

pocket, slid down onto one knee and waited for his exhausted woman to finally get a clue and look down.

Tori cleared her throat. "Tessa."

"Yeah?" Tessa still didn't look down. "Mitch, he needs a bit of diaper cream on his butt. It's getting a little red."

"On it," Mitch called, reaching into the diaper bag.

Atlas made a noise in his throat this time. She still didn't look down. He and Tori exchanged amused glances at each other, and he rolled his eyes. His woman loved her son more than anything in this world, and Atlas wasn't sure Magnus and Tessa had been this far apart from each other yet. Even though the baby was just across the photography studio, to Tessa it probably felt like a million miles.

"I can change his diaper if it's too hard," she called to Mitch.

"Changed thousands with my own kid, Tess. I got this," Mitch replied. "Maybe you should look down instead of criticizing how I put zinc cream on a butt crack."

Tessa's brows furrowed, and she finally glanced down.

Atlas's knee was beginning to ache on the concrete floor, but he maintained his position and held up the ring.

Tessa's eyes grew with surprise, and her mouth opened. A gasp followed.

"Finally," he said, reaching for her hand. "Tessa *Marie*, you brought me back from the brink, shed light on and patched up my dark and broken heart, making me whole again. Marry me, please?" He'd never been one to wax poetic, but he'd rehearsed what he figured he should say over and over in his head. Do you think that's what came out when the moment came? Fuck no. But he said what was in his heart, how he felt and what Tessa meant to him. He hoped she knew she meant everything to him, even if he couldn't get all the right words out.

Her eyes welled up with tears, but her smile said it all as

she nodded and held out her hand.

He slid the ring onto her finger, but it didn't quite fit.

"Damn it, I'm still puffy," she whined, more tears spilling down her cheeks.

He shook his head and stood, pulling her into his arms. "We'll get it resized, or you can wait to wear it in a few months. It doesn't matter. I love your fingers just the way they are." He pulled her fingertips to his lips and kissed each one.

All through this, Tori was snapping photos. He'd arranged to propose at this photo shoot, thinking that it would be a nice memento for Tessa as well as their kids down the road.

Tori pulled out from behind the camera, her own blue eyes watery. "Well, that was absolutely beautiful. I can't wait to go through these shots." Mitch was entertaining the girls and a now-diapered Magnus over on the blanket and Forest was back sleeping next to the heater, snoring like a bear. Tori took her cue and gave them some privacy.

Atlas turned to Tessa and laced their fingers together. "I meant what I said. All of it and more. You are my new light. A beacon in the storm that I thought I was destined to live in for the rest of my life. My crotch-rocket-riding, hippie-skirt-wearing, serial-killer-documentary-loving woman. You are my fresh start and my happy ending, and there is no one I'd rather grow old with than you."

A sob caught in her throat, and she collapsed into him. "These are tears of joy," she wailed. "It's the hormones. So many hormones."

He rubbed her back and kissed the top of her head. "And I'll be here to wipe every one of them away, for as long as we both shall live."

She looked at him, teary-eyed and flushed-faced. More beautiful than ever. "I love you, Atlas Stark."

"And I love you, Tessa Soon-to-be-Stark."

FALLING WITH THE SINGLE DAD - SNEAK PEEK

SINGLE DADS OF SEATTLE BOOK 10

Chapter 1

"Ah! Thanks for the fuck." Richelle rolled off Liam, swung her luscious legs over the side of the bed and sauntered her sweet ass to the ensuite bathroom. Moments later she returned, not bothering to climb into bed for snuggling, because that was NOT what this was about.

"Another satisfying hump day—and Thursday morning fuck," Liam said with a laugh. The sigh that followed was accompanied by a mix of emotions. It was both a relief and a disappointment that she wasn't going to stick around longer. A relief that he didn't have to go make a big breakfast, but a disappointment in how business-like their arrangement had become. Hell, he wasn't even expected to see her out or kiss her goodbye. She was not his girlfriend. They were not dating. They were not a couple. This was about sex and only sex.

Good sex.

But just good sex.

"Never had an unsatisfying one yet." Richelle shot him a sassy smile over her sculpted shoulder as she reached for her bra on the floor. "Is that why you proposed Wednesdays be our day to have sex? Because it's hump day?"

He tucked his hands behind his head and shut his eyes, still enjoying the euphoric high that followed a nice long fuck and a killer orgasm. "Might have been. But you know Jordie is with my parents on the Wednesdays I have him." He opened his eyes again.

Richelle nodded as she clasped her bra behind her back. Fuck, she had great tits. The perfect handful, with tight, delicious raspberry-red nipples, dusky areoles that puckered when she became cold or aroused. And the way her breasts squeezed his cock when she titty fucked him, God almighty she was good at that. At the thought of being sandwiched like a Frankfurter between her creamy mounds his dick lurched beneath the sheet. He couldn't get another boner now and take care of it himself. Not after that amazing fuck fest. Could he ask her to stay for one more round?

The clock on his nightstand said it was seven-thirty in the morning. He had to be at work in an hour. He knew his cock could certainly go again, the question was, could Richelle? Would Richelle? Did they have time?

She was still naked besides her bra and he spied her G-string at the foot of the bed. With a slight twinge in his back from the acrobatics they'd engaged in last night, he hinged up and snatched the panties, tucking them into his fist.

"Have you seen my underwear?" she asked, her hawklike amber eyes scanning the bedroom floor. "Hot pink G-string." Her lips spread revealing perfect teeth and a salacious feline smile. "One of your faves, I believe."

"You mean these?" he asked, his teeth now clenched around one of the strings.

She glanced up at him, her socks and shirt in her hand. "Those would be them, yes."

He plucked the G-string from his teeth and held them on one finger. "Come get them."

His eyebrows bobbed in a way that easily conveyed the payment required for retrieving her underwear.

That mouth he knew like the back of his own fucking hand continued to smile. "No time, stud. I have a deposition at nine this morning. Can't be late if I intend to kill it. Then I'm off to Mallory's school for career day." She grumbled. "How fun is that going to be? Going to a school and telling five hundred plus kids how rewarding it is being a *divorce* attorney ..."

She wandered around to the side of the bed and bent down, giving him the ultimate view of her cleavage. He slipped his free hand into one of her cups until he found a nipple and tugged. The moan that rumbled in her chest told him she may not have the time, but she'd certainly make it.

Her lips hovered above his. "I can't."

"Can't? Or won't?" He lunged forward and took her bottom lip between his teeth.

She groaned and her eyes squeezed shut. He could see her resistance crumbling. Feel the heat of her body and the way it radiated off her in a new way, a way he'd come to recognize and respond to primitively. The woman was a sexually charged animal. She also took control in the bedroom most of the time—which Liam had no qualms with—and by the time they parted ways Thursday morning he was exhausted, achy, drained and happy as fuck.

But he also knew how to make his lioness purr. He knew how to make her roll over to her back, show her belly and become a playful kitten.

To look at her, you'd never expect the four-foot-eleven

woman with short blonde hair, hawklike eyes, and the arms of a professional MMA fighter to be as fierce as she was. He reminded her of Tinkerbell—with an axe to grind. Hence, the nickname Tink or Tinkerbell that he'd given her ages ago. He'd even gone so far as to buy her a Tinkerbell costume one time (a sexy one of course) and he wore a generic pirates costume, for a little bit of role-playing.

Somehow, despite his mighty sword and dashing eyepatch, the woman had bewitched him with her pixie dust —or whatever—and he found himself on his hands and knees on the floor of his bedroom sucking her toes as she held his sword to his throat.

That had been one hell of fun night.

He'd called her Tink that night, and the nickname stuck. She didn't seem to mind—as long as he never called her that in public.

He pinched her nipple harder and slid his tongue across her bottom lip. "I promise to have you at your deposition on time."

She hummed against his lips. "You and your promises, Dixon."

"Never broken one in my life, babe. You know that."

"Do I know that? I hardly know you. We eat Thai food, watch movies and fuck, that's it. I really don't know a damn thing about you." Her fingernails scraped down his bare chest and torso to slide beneath the covers, past his neatly trimmed hair to where his cock stood up creating the mother of all tents. She raked her French manicured nails down his shaft until he inhaled against her mouth. She breathed him in and chuckled. "Two can play the game."

"You know I'll play as much and as hard as you want to, baby. You know me better than you think."

"I don't even know your middle name." She wrapped her

fingers around his cock and slid her thumb over the crown, swirling the bead of precum around the tip.

He went to open his mouth to tell her, but she quieted him with her lips—and tongue. "I don't want to know." She murmured, climbing up on to the bed and straddling him. "If I wanted to know, I would have asked." She sat up on her knees over his waist and waited for him to push the covers down, his fingers having to slide out of her bra to do so.

As she waited, she unclasped her bra and tossed it back to the floor.

Once he freed his cock, he reached into his nightstand, grabbed a condom, tore open the wrapper and went to slide it on.

Richelle took it from him. "I'll do it."

"Yeah, baby," he breathed, loving the way she took him so confidently in her delicate fist, and rolled the condom down to the base, pinching the top like a pro.

She sat up on her knees and inched forward until he was perfectly lined up with her sweet pussy. A pussy he had never grown tired of. Would never grow tired of. For three years he and Richelle had fucked nearly every Wednesday, and for three years, he looked forward to it every fucking time. But it wasn't just the tight, wet heat that fit him like a glove that he was incapable of growing bored with, it was also the woman. She challenged him, made him laugh, made him think, and, boy oh boy, did she know how to make him come.

***

The harsh pants of her breath that drifted across his cheek began to settle, and her nails released their death grip on his ass as he lifted his head.

She had that gloriously gorgeous just-fucked look about her. Bright eyes, rosy cheeks, wild spiky hair.

"I wish I could stay inside you all fucking day," he said

nuzzling his nose against hers. "Should we call in hooky? I'm sure one of your associates could run the deposition."

The small placid smile on her face faded and her eyes turned serious. She pushed him away, and he slid out and off her, wandering to the bathroom to dispose of the condom. She wandered into the bathroom as well, and sat down to pee.

Once he'd washed up, he left her to do her thing and headed back into his room to begin making the bed.

"Why do you have to ruin things by trying to make us more than what we are?" she asked, coming out of the bathroom and proceeding to get dressed. She shimmied into her jeans after she'd stepped into her G-string. "What we have works. It's worked for three fucking years. Are you wanting more now because all your single dad friends have found love?" The way she said love was how she always said love. With as much belief in the world as Liam had for the Easter Bunny or Santa Claus.

Liam rolled his eyes. He hadn't bothered to put on underwear or anything. He was going to jump into the shower. After making the bed, he wandered back into the bathroom and began brushing his teeth. Leaning against the doorjamb lazily, he watched her continue to get dressed. "Jesus fuck, woman, relax. I'm not asking you to move in or get my name tattooed on your left tit, I'm just saying, wouldn't it be nice to have more than twelve hours together?"

"More than twelve hours a week turns this into more than what this is," she said, fastening her bra again.

"And this is?"

The look she gave him in the mirror was that of a seriously impatient and pissed off woman. "You know what this is, Liam Dixon. You've known what this is for three fucking years. It's a friends with benefits situation that works for the both of us. We have a weekly fuck fest with no strings, no emotions, no expectations. Just lots of orgasms."

"And you've never thought about turning it into more?" he asked over his toothbrush.

The look Richelle was giving him spoke of surmounting impatience, and the scoff that accompanied that look said she'd reached her threshold. "I don't have time to turn it into more. And neither do you. We're both busy lawyers with children. You have your son, and I'm entering the exciting world of being the mother to a moody, hormonal teenager. Being Mallory's mother is a full-time job. And I already have a full-time fucking job."

Up until recently he hadn't thought about turning it into more either. But after watching each one of his friends fall in love and find their happiness over the past two years, he was beginning to think maybe having a woman who was more than just a fuck buddy wasn't such a bad idea after all.

Maybe.

Particularly Atlas. The last guy to fall and Liam's best friend. He'd been the surliest, angriest widower Liam had ever met. And now the man was fucking smiling—and Tessa and her love had done that. They'd brought Atlas out of the dark and back into the light.

At the last big group barbecue, where all his fellow single dads stood with their arms around their women, with their children off playing together happily, he caught himself more than once thinking how well Richelle would fit in with all the other women in their growing extended family. She already knew Tessa and Eva. And Richelle never spoke of any friends she met with outside of work. Did she have any female friends? Did she have any friends period?

"You're thinking awfully hard for someone so pretty," she said, tossing her purse over her shoulder. She was completely dressed now in a pair of skin tight dark wash jeans, a billowy baby blue tank top and a pair of flip flops that showed off her sexy pedicured toes with the rings on them.

He turned to spit into the sink, rinsed and then faced her again. "If this is all you want, then that's fine. I just want to be with you."

Fear and anger flashed behind her eyes and her nostrils flared. "How do you even know you're the only person I'm sleeping with? We said from the get-go this was not exclusive. Hence why we still use condoms, right?"

Well, that struck his hard him between the ribs like she intended. He also knew when she got defensive it was because she was scared. He knew her better than she thought he did.

"I haven't kissed, fucked or held hands with another woman since the first night you came over for Thai food and tied me to my own bed." He let his lips curl into a small, hopeful smile. One he hoped disarmed her just a little.

No such luck.

"Well, goody for you," she said with a sneer. "I have to go."

He never wanted to ask her if she'd slept with anyone else, because up until recently, he hadn't cared—all that much—they had made an agreement not to be exclusive. Though he couldn't imagine sleeping with anyone else once he started sleeping with Richelle. He was a one-woman man when he committed, always had been. And their arrangement had been a type of commitment, even if it wasn't traditional.

"Can you say the same?" he asked, following her out of his bedroom and through his house toward the front door. The *slap slap* of her flip flops on his concrete floor sent an echo through his large Lake Washington home.

"Can I say the same about what?" she asked with a huff of impatience, spinning on her heel to glare at him.

The way the sun shone in through his enormous dining

room window and fell across her face made her look more angelic than he knew her to be. Her hair was practically white the way it glowed, and the amber in her eyes looked more like spun gold. She really was the most beautiful woman he'd ever seen in his life. Even angry like she was now, she was hot as fuck.

"Can you say that you haven't slept with anyone else since we started seeing each other?" Fear of her answer spun in his gut in a way that unsettled him to the point of nausea. He was also still naked, and the cold concrete floor sent a harsh shiver sprinting up his spine and down again, landing firmly in his balls.

Richelle's lips pinned together as her gaze slid up his body from his feet to his face. Her eyes became laser focused on his. She still hadn't said anything.

All he got was the slight lift of her eyebrow.

And that's when he knew she wouldn't say anything.

She didn't have to.

He sucked in a deep breath and nodded. "All right then. I have my answer."

"You do," she said flatly. "I have to fly to San Diego Tuesday for a meeting next week. I'll be back late Wednesday night, but I'll come by once my flight gets in."

Phew. At least he hadn't scared her away. "Need me to pick you up from the airport?" Oh fuck, now he sounded like a needy bastard. All the happiness, love and bullshit surrounding his friends was starting to fuck with his head.

She hit him with another eyebrow lift, but this time it was accompanied by a lip lift on the opposite side of her face. "I'm going to leave my car at the airport, but thanks for the offer."

Then she did something she'd never done before, with the door open and her car parked in his driveway shining bright red and just waiting for her to drop the soft top, she leaned in and put her hand on his chest. "Thanks, Liam." She pressed her lips to his, chaste-like, but it was still a kiss.

He wanted nothing more than to shove his fingers into her hair and either drag her back to his bedroom, push her head until she was on her knees, or bend her over the hood of her car. But he didn't do any of the above. He simply honked her boob and kissed her back just as lightly.

"Anytime, babe," he said, going for easy and carefree, even though inside, his brains were all suddenly fucked up.

There went that eyebrow of hers again. "Don't overthink things, okay? What we have works. What we have is good. Really good. If it's not broke, don't fix it, right?"

She shot him a wink before she turned to go, sashaying that ass she worked hard at the gym to keep tight over to her car. It chirped and she opened the door.

"Maybe go online and order us some new to try," she called out. "Haven't dressed up in a bit. It's summer, maybe camp counselor and camper?"

"Are you trying to get me to fulfill your Johnny Castle fantasy?" he asked, still naked and leaning against the door-jamb of his front door. His gravel driveway was long and his yard and front door protected from view by an enormous hedge. If he wasn't worried about a sunburn on his family jewels he'd be inclined to mow his lawn in the nude.

"Nobody puts Baby in a corner," she said, turning on her Mustang and revving the engine as the soft top retracted above her. He loved the rumble of sexy V8. And the fact that an even sexier woman sat behind the wheel of that engine made his cock stir and his blood start pumping.

"Nobody could ever put you in the corner, sweetheart. I'd like to seem them try."

A weird look flitted into her eyes, and at first he thought it was just the glint of the sun, but when her smile dropped and her eyes turned hard, he realized there was more to it. What had he said to make the playful Richelle vanish so instantly?

"You okay?" he called out, having to raise his voice over the purr of her beast.

She nodded and smiled back. "Yep. Just peachy." She blew him a kiss, waved, backed out of his driveway, and out of his life for another week, even though the more Liam thought about it, the more he no longer wanted to wait a week to see her anymore. The more he no longer wanted to watch her back out and away. He wasn't sure he was on board with the whole living together and marriage thing like his friends, but he was certainly tired of the emotionless, casual weekly twelve-hour fuck fest Richelle seemed so hell-bent on maintaining. He was forty-one years old. A successful lawyer in the city of Seattle and a devoted father. He had his shit together in a neat little pile. Maybe he was ready to share his shit pile with someone else, and in return share her shit pile with her. Or even consider combining their shit piles into one larger, but still manageable shit pile.

Many hands make light work, right?

Did the same go for shit piles?

He scratched his balls and closed his front door.

First things first though. He needed to have a shower, get dressed and then online shop for some Dirty Dancing role-play costumes. But as he reluctantly scrubbed off the scent of the woman he'd spent the night with from his body, the more he wondered how many other men she role-played with. How many other men she saw during the week and what kinky things they got up to? Kinkier than what she did with Liam?

Or, maybe, was he the only person she was sleeping with and she simply didn't answer his question in order to keep him at arm's length? That or was she legitimately taking their non-exclusivity agreement seriously. He was beginning to get a headache.

"If it's not broke, don't fix it," he muttered, her words echoing over and over in his mind as he got out of the shower and dried himself with a towel.

Some might call him broken.

Could he be fixed?

Was Richelle the woman to heal the hole in his heart left by his exes, or would she just be the woman to not only create another hole in his heart, but break it completely?

IF YOU'VE ENJOYED THIS BOOK

If you've enjoyed this book, please consider leaving a review.
It really does make a difference.
Thank you again.
Xoxo
Whitley Cox

ACKNOWLEDGMENTS

There are so many people to thank who help along the way. Publishing a book is definitely not a solo mission, that's for sure. First and foremost, my friend and editor Chris Kridler, you are a blessing, a gem and an all-around terrific person. Thank you for your honesty and hard work.

Thank you, to my critique groups gals, Danielle and Jillian. I love our meetups where we give honest feedback and just bitch about life. You two are my bitch-sisters and I wouldn't give you up for anything.

Andi Babcock for her beta-read, I always appreciate your attention to detail and comments.

Kathleen Lawless for helping me dig deep with Atlas and take him to that dark place—you know your way around a black moment and a broody alpha.

Author Jeanne St. James, my alpha reader and sister from another mister, what would I do without you?

Megan J. Parker-Squiers from EmCat Designs, your covers are awesome. Thank you.

My street team, Whitley Cox's Curiously Kinky Reviewers, you are all awesome and I feel so blessed to have found such wonderful fans.

The ladies of Vancouver Island Romance Authors, your support and insight have been incredibly helpful, and I'm so honored to be a part of a group of such talented writers.

Author Cora Seton for your help, tweaks and suggestions for my blurbs, as always, they come back from you so sparkly. I also love our walks, talks and heart-to-hearts, they mean so much to me.

Authors Kathleen Lawless, Nancy Warren and Jane Wallace, I love our writing meetups. Wine, good food and friendship always make the words flow.

Author Ember Leigh, my newest author bestie, I love our bitch fests—they keep me sane.

My parents, in-laws and brother, thank you for your unwavering support.

The Small Human and the Tiny Human, you are the beats and beasts of my heart, the reason I breathe and the reason I drink. I love you both to infinity and beyond.

And lastly, of course, the husband. You are my forever. I love you.

ALSO BY WHITLEY COX

Love, Passion and Power: Part 1

The Dark and Damaged Hearts Series Book 1

Love, Passion and Power: Part 2

The Dark and Damaged Hearts Series Book 2

Sex, Heat and Hunger: Part 1

The Dark and Damaged Hearts Book 3

Sex, Heat and Hunger: Part 2

The Dark and Damaged Hearts Book 4

Hot and Filthy: The Honeymoon

The Dark and Damaged Hearts Book 4.5

True, Deep and Forever: Part 1

The Dark and Damaged Hearts Book 5

True, Deep and Forever: Part 2

The Dark and Damaged Hearts Book 6

Hard, Fast and Madly: Part 1

The Dark and Damaged Hearts Series Book 7

Hard, Fast and Madly: Part 2

The Dark and Damaged Hearts Series Book 8

Quick & Dirty

Book 1, A Quick Billionaires Novel

Quick & Easy

Book 2, A Quick Billionaires Novella

Quick & Reckless

Book 3, A Quick Billionaires Novel

Hot Dad

Lust Abroad

Snowed In & Set Up

Quick & Dangerous

Book 4, A Quick Billionaires Novel

Hired by the Single Dad

The Single Dads of Seattle, Book 1

Dancing with the Single Dad

The Single Dads of Seattle, Book 2

Saved by the Single Dad

The Single Dads of Seattle, Book 3

Living with the Single Dad

The Single Dads of Seattle, Book 4

Christmas with the Single Dad

The Single Dads of Seattle, Book 5

ABOUT THE AUTHOR

A Canadian West Coast baby born and raised, Whitley is married to her high school sweetheart, and together they have two beautiful daughters and a fluffy dog. She spends her days making food that gets thrown on the floor, vacuuming Cheerios out from under the couch and making sure that the dog food doesn't end up in the air conditioner. But when nap time comes, and it's not quite wine o'clock, Whitley sits down, avoids the pile of laundry on the couch, and writes.

A lover of all things decadent; wine, cheese, chocolate and spicy erotic romance, Whitley brings the humorous side of sex, the ridiculous side of relationships and the suspense of everyday life into her stories. With single dads, firefighters, Navy SEALs, mommy wars, body issues, threesomes, bondage and role-playing, Whitley's books have all the funny and fabulously filthy words you could hope for.

YOU CAN ALSO FIND ME HERE

Website: WhitleyCox.com
Twitter: @WhitleyCoxBooks
Instagram: @CoxWhitley
Facebook Page: https://www.facebook.com/CoxWhitley/
Blog: https://whitleycox.blogspot.ca/
Multi-Author Blog: https://romancewritersbehavingbadly.blogspot.com
Exclusive Facebook Reader Group: https://www.facebook.com/groups/234716323653592/
Booksprout: https://booksprout.co/author/994/whitley-cox
Bookbub: https://www.bookbub.com/authors/whitley-cox

JOIN MY STREET TEAM

WHITLEY COX'S CURIOUSLY KINKY REVIEWERS
Hear about giveaways, games, ARC opportunities, new releases, teasers, author news, character and plot development and more!

Facebook Street Team
Join NOW!

DON'T FORGET TO SUBSCRIBE TO MY NEWSLETTER

Be the first to hear about pre-orders, new releases, giveaways, 99 cent deals, and freebies!

Click here to Subscribe
http://eepurl.com/ckh5yT

Made in the USA
Las Vegas, NV
02 February 2022